"Plenty of action and romantic drama round out this laugh-out-loud novel. Fans of Evanovich's Stephanie Plum series or Pollero's Finley Tanner series will enjoy the fast-paced antics and fruity cocktails of Tara Holloway."
—*RT Book Reviews*

"IRS special agent Tara Holloway is back in another action-packed, laugh-filled adventure that is sure to keep you entertained from beginning to end."
—*Fallen Angel Reviews*

## DEATH, TAXES, AND EXTRA-HOLD HAIRSPRAY

"As usual, the pace is quick without being frenetic, and the breezy narrative style is perfection—fun and sexy without being over the top."
—*RT Book Reviews*

"This is a rollicking adventure that will have you rooting for the IRS for once—and you won't want to put it down until you find out how Tara will overcome all the obstacles in her way. Keep turning those pages—you'll love every second as you try to find out!"
—*Reader To Reader Reviews*

"If you've never read one of Diane Kelly's Tara Holloway novels, I strongly recommend that you rectify the situation immediately. The series has gotten better with every single installment, and I'd be shocked if you didn't see these characters gracing your television screen before too long (USA and HBO, I'm looking in your direction). Get on board now so you can say you knew Tara Holloway when."
—*The Season for Romance*

"Diane Kelly knows how to rock the romance, and roll the story right into a delightful mix of high drama with great characters."　　　　*—The Reading Reviewer*

## DEATH, TAXES, AND A SKINNY NO-WHIP LATTE

"Readers will find Kelly's protagonist a kindred spirit to Stephanie Plum: feisty and tenacious, with a self-deprecating sense of humor. Tara is flung into some unnerving situations, including encounters with hired thugs, would-be muggers, and head lice. The laughs lighten up the scary bits, and the nonstop action and snappy dialogue keep the standard plot moving along at a good pace."　　　　*—RT Book Reviews*

"Readers should be prepared for a laugh fest. The writer is first class and there is a lot of humor contained in this series. It is a definite keeper."
　　　　*—Night Owl Romance*

"A quirky, fun tale that pulls you in with its witty heroine and outlandish situations . . . You'll laugh at Tara's predicaments, and cheer her on as she nearly single-handedly tackles the case."
　　　　*—Romance Reviews Today*

"It is hard not to notice a sexy CPA with a proclivity for weapons. Kelly's sophomore series title . . . has huge romance crossover appeal."　　　　*—Library Journal*

"An exciting, fun new mystery series with quirky characters and a twist . . . Who would have ever guessed IRS investigators could be so cool!"
　　　　*—Guilty Pleasures Book Reviews*

# Death, Taxes,

## and a Chocolate Cannoli

DIANE KELLY

St. Martin's Paperbacks

DEATH, TAXES, AND A CHOCOLATE CANNOLI

Copyright © 2015 by Diane Kelly.

All rights reserved.

For information address St. Martin's Press, 175 Fifth Avenue, New York, NY 10010.

ISBN: 978-1-250-04833-2

Printed in the United States of America

St. Martin's Paperbacks edition / October 2015

St. Martin's Paperbacks are published by St. Martin's Press, 175 Fifth Avenue, New York, NY 10010.

10  9  8  7  6  5  4  3  2  1

*To my sister Susan, a savvy CPA/CFP and a wonderful sister (even though you fibbed that time about Mom making brownies)*

# $\mathcal{A}$cknowledgments

As always, oodles of gratitude to my editor, Holly Ingraham, for being so wonderful to work with. And thanks to Lizzie Poteet and Eileen Rothschild too, for stepping in to help out on this book. Many thanks also to Sarah Melnyck, Paul Hochman, and the rest of the team at St. Martin's whose hard work gets my books in readers' hands.

Thanks to Danielle Fiorella and Monika Roe for creating such fun book covers.

Thanks to my agent, Helen Breitwieser, for all of your work in furthering my writing career.

Thanks to Liz Bemis-Hittinger and the staff of Bemis Promotions for my great Web site and newsletters.

Thanks to the many fellow members of Romance Writers of America, its volunteers, and the smart and dedicated national office staff. RWA not only launched my career but has given me a place to flourish and grow.

Finally, thanks to my readers. I love connecting with you through the stories, and I hope you'll cheer Tara on as she battles a con artist, a mobster, and a severe cannoli addiction.

# chapter one

## *G*one Guys

At two o'clock in the afternoon on a Monday in early May, I stood on the sidewalk in front of the federal building in downtown Dallas. To a casual observer, I'd look no different from any other female professional in her late twenties. Heck, we were a dime a dozen. But the subtle bulge under the blazer of my navy blue pantsuit set me apart. I didn't just handle business, I *meant* business. And my business was making sure that tax cheats paid for their crimes, both in cash and convictions.

A shiny black sedan with dark tinted windows eased up to the curb in front of me. The passenger window slid down only an inch or two, not enough for me to see the person inside, but enough for me to hear his deep, gravelly voice. "Special Agent Holloway?"

I tried to swallow to clear the tightness in my throat but was unsuccessful. As much as I hated to admit it, bringing tax evaders to justice could sometimes be a little frightening. Instead of speaking, I merely nodded.

The door unlocked with a click. "Get in."

I shifted my briefcase to my left hand and grabbed the

door handle, my heart pumping like an oil jack in my chest. Why was I anxious? Because my boss at the Internal Revenue Service had assigned me my biggest case yet, against mob boss Giustino "Tino" Fabrizio. Fabrizio's acts of violence and extortion were legendary—and the stuff movies starring Robert DeNiro were made of.

Since joining the IRS a little over a year ago, I'd faced down a con artist running a Bernie Madoff–style Ponzi scheme, a killer operating a cross-border crime enterprise, a televangelist who'd fleeced his flock, the president of a secessionist group that was stockpiling weapons, terrorists, a sleazy strip club owner operating a prostitution ring, a country-western superstar who'd thumbed his nose at the IRS, and a violent drug cartel. Guess you could say I'd been busy. You could also say there were as many ways to cheat the government as there were tax evaders. Each had their own unique scheme or scam. But none had gotten past me . . . *so far.*

My earlier successes, as well as my exceptional gun skills, had landed me this mob case. Part of me was proud that my boss had assigned me as the lead agent on the investigation. Another part of me was so scared I feared my sphincters would never release again.

I slid into the car, placed my briefcase on my lap, and snapped the seat belt into place. As FBI Agent Burt Hohenwald pulled away from the curb, I ventured my first glance at him. The veteran agent was a tall, lean fiftyish man with curly pewter-colored hair, a nose like a ski jump, and a gray tweed blazer that made him look professorial. I half expected him to launch into a lecture about the Treaty of Versailles or Plato's theories on the nature of virtue.

Hohenwald cast a glance my way, too, looking me up and down, unabashedly sizing me up. I took no offense.

It was par for the course. After all, the two of us would be working this case together, counting on each other, holding each other's lives in our hands. Unfortunately, in my case, appearances could be deceiving, even to a veteran of law enforcement. My chestnut-brown hair hung in loose curls around my shoulders, my gray-blue eyes were accentuated with liquid liner, and my lips bore a shiny coat of plum-toned lipstick. Along with the basic navy suit, I'd worn my favorite cherry-red steel-toed Doc Martens. Like me, the shoes meant business. The bright color might be a little flashy, but the soles provided good traction should I need to chase a suspect and the reinforced toe protected my little piggies should my foot find itself implanted in a suspect's nards or ass. You'd be surprised how often that happened.

A frown played about Hohenwald's mouth as he returned his focus to the street. "Lu says you're a girl who knows how to get things done."

"I am." Approaching thirty, I was hardly a girl anymore, but I knew my boss Lu "the Lobo" Lobozinski meant no insult when she'd used the term. Besides, at five feet two inches, just over a hundred pounds, and wearing what was essentially a training bra, I appeared more girl than woman. I'd accepted it. Besides, what I lacked in stature, I made up in attitude, which was one hundred percent badass. Okay, ninety-nine percent badass and one percent chickenshit. Seriously, a person would have to be an idiot not to fear a violent mobster, right?

Hohenwald hooked a left on Field Street. "I trust you've read the file I sent over?"

"Thoroughly." I hadn't just read it, I'd highlighted it, cross-referenced it, and made copious notes in the margins, including several *HOLY CRAP!*s a half-dozen *OMG!*s and one very big *YIKES!!!* If Hohenwald wasn't impressed by my physical attributes, maybe he'd be impressed by my reading comprehension and annotation abilities. Not everyone can pull off both a pink and a purple highlighter.

"So you know Tino Fabrizio's history prior to coming to Dallas."

"Up, down, and backward."

According to the file, Guistino Fabrizio had been born and raised in the ritzy Gold Coast neighborhood of Chicago. The youngest cousin of the reigning Chicago mob boss, Tino had worked for his cousin for years as an enforcer. He was suspected in a multitude of beatings and execution-style shooting deaths, the victims including both members of the extended mafia family and unrelated persons. Unfortunately, though he'd been brought in for questioning several times, law enforcement had been unable to pin anything on him. The guy knew how to cover his tracks.

Eventually, Tino realized his job taking people down had no upward potential. As ambitious as Tino was, and as cold as the Windy City's winters were, he decided to head south to Dallas. Though there'd been isolated instances of mob activity in the area, the mafia had enjoyed no real toehold in the Big D since the death in 1970 of local leader Joseph Francis Civello, with whom Jack Ruby, who shot JFK's assassin, was rumored to have ties. These days, organized crime in north Texas existed primarily in the form of drug cartels or gangs that operated in limited circles and with no pretense of legitimacy. Here, Tino could rule the city, put his parka in mothballs, and work on his tan.

"What you don't know," Hohenwald said as he took a second left onto Main, "is what Fabrizio's been up to since he moved to Dallas. The file I sent over to the IRS was heavy enough with just the FBI's background reports. Besides, I figured it would be best to let you get the scoop straight from Detective Booth at Dallas PD."

"Dallas PD?" I repeated. "Local police are involved in the investigation, too?"

"Sure are," Hohenwald replied. "In fact, Detective Booth was the one who put two and two together and realized Fabrizio was connected to a lot of bad stuff."

"Why didn't the police department keep the case?"

"With Fabrizio's history in Chicago, the detective realized his crimes had national implications. She also knew that bringing down his network would take more resources than her department could provide."

"So Booth turned the case over to the FBI?"

"Essentially," he said, "though she's kept a finger in the pie. She wants this guy as bad as we do."

With Dallas PD handing primary responsibility for the matter over to the FBI, and the FBI subsequently punting some of the work to the IRS, it might seem like the buck was being passed. But such was not the case. Rather, law enforcement was hedging its bets. In important yet difficult cases such as this, it was not unusual for several law enforcement agencies to work together and attack a wanted suspect on more than one front. While local police and the FBI could investigate the violent crimes, the IRS could take a different tack and try to nail the suspect for tax evasion or money laundering. Not only did a multipronged approach increase the odds that the suspect would be caught doing something illegal, but it also gave the government additional charges to fall back on should the primary indictment be thrown out. Suspects could be slick, and their defense attorneys could be even slicker. We needed as much ammunition as possible in our arsenal to ensure the bad guys didn't get away with their dirty deeds.

Hohenwald turned south on Lamar and drove several blocks, passing under Interstate 30, before pulling into the parking lot of the Dallas Police Department headquarters. We parked, went inside, and checked in with the uniformed officer working the front desk. He directed us to wait in a seating area crowded with people, none of whom looked happy to be here. Hohenwald snatched a copy of the *Dallas Observer,* the city's alternative newspaper, from a coffee table. Frankly, I was afraid to take my eyes off the group, which likely included a high percentage of felons.

A moment later, a fortyish woman in khaki slacks and a pink button-down stopped in the doorway. She had pointy, pixielike features and honey-blond hair pulled back in a short ponytail. She scanned the seating area, her eyes stopping on Agent Hohenwald.

"Is that Detective Booth?" I asked, gesturing toward the woman.

He looked up from the paper. "Yup. That's her."

He set the paper aside and stood. I followed him over to the woman, who simply lifted her chin in acknowledgment, turned, and led us down the hall and around the corner to a small elevator. Another person was already in the car, so we remained silent. One could never be too careful with confidential information. We rode the car up to the third floor, exited, and trailed the woman to an office at the end of the corridor. The nameplate on the door read DETECTIVE V. BOOTH. I found myself wondering what the *V* stood for. *Valerie? Vivian? Violet?* She stood at the door as we stepped inside, closing it behind us.

Stacks of files stood like a paper skyline at the edge of the detective's desk, flanked by an automatic stapler and an ivy that looked desperate for a drink of water. While the detective rounded her cluttered desk, Agent Hohenwald dropped into one of the two seats facing it and I perched on the other, setting my briefcase down beside me.

Hohenwald made a quick, unceremonious introduction. "Detective Booth, Special Agent Holloway. Agent Holloway, Detective Booth."

Booth and I shook hands over the desktop and offered each other polite smiles.

"What's the *V* stand for?" I asked.

"Veronica," she replied.

That minor mystery had been easily solved. But getting the goods on Tino Fabrizio was sure to be far more challenging.

As we began our powwow, Booth summarized the situation for me. "Giustino Fabrizio is suspected in the deaths or disappearances of at least ten men in the Dallas area over the last five years. Most of the men had worked for him in one capacity or another, some officially, others unofficially."

*Yikes!* And to think I sometimes complained about my job. At least my boss wasn't out to kill me. "So Tino made sure those who knew his secrets didn't live to tell them?"

"Exactly," Booth replied. "Anyone who had dirt on the guy ended up buried in dirt themselves."

The mere thought had me brushing imaginary muck from my arms.

She pulled a thick file from a drawer. "Agent Hohenwald asked me to share my file on Fabrizio with you." She held it out to me. "Take a look, then we can address any questions you might have."

My tax case files contained innocuous things like spreadsheets and bank statements. But police files could be far more gruesome. I took the hefty file from her and inhaled a deep breath to steel myself.

# chapter two

# $\mathcal{O}$dds and Ends

I opened the folder on my lap. The first two items in Booth's file were recent police reports addressing the disappearance of two men on the same night. One of the men who'd gone missing was a professional locksmith. According to his wife's statement, he'd received a late-night call, purportedly from someone who'd locked himself out of his house and needed emergency service. The locksmith failed to return home to his wife and two children.

Booth gestured to the report. "We considered whether he might have simply abandoned his family, but that possibility was quickly ruled out. By all accounts he'd been a dedicated husband and father."

And, as the report noted, he'd taken nothing with him, not even his prized baseball card collection or his beloved Labrador retriever.

The other man, who was unmarried but living with a girlfriend, was a personal trainer who also provided free-lance bodyguard services on a contractor basis. He, too, had received a late-night call, told his girlfriend it was work-related, and left in a hurry, never to come back home. He had also left all of his possessions behind, and had made no contact with anyone, not a family member, neighbor, or friend.

No trace of either man had been found, and according to the reports, both had left their cell phones at home. *Odd.*

As I looked up in thought, my eyes spotted water stains on the ceiling tiles in the detective's office. The building must have suffered a leak at some point, maybe during the last heavy rain. But the leaky roof wasn't the issue of the moment. The current issue was, *Why would the victims have left their cell phones behind?* Most people carried their phones with them at all times. Also, per an inquiry to their carriers, no calls had come in to the men's personal cell phones late that night. More than likely, the men had second, secret phones their loved ones didn't know about.

Pulling my eyes from the damaged ceiling, I returned my attention to the documentation. My specialized role would be to pursue the financial angles, follow the money trails, so naturally information about suspicious income and expenses caught my eye. The statement made by the locksmith's wife indicated that he had taken his family on a trip to Hawaii shortly before he disappeared. She'd reported that her husband's business had been doing especially well in the months preceding his disappearance. The trainer had bought a new Harley-Davidson motorcycle not long before he'd vanished. His girlfriend hadn't asked where the money to buy the Harley had come from. Maybe she didn't want to know. "Looks like these two men came into some unexpected funds."

Booth leaned back in her chair. "Cash payouts from

Fabrizio probably accounted for the sudden uptick in income."

The third item in the file was a police report regarding a mugging that had taken place in the parking lot of a barbecue restaurant late on the same night the men had disappeared. Two masked men had pulled guns on the owner of the restaurant as he went to his car with a zippered bank bag containing the day's cash intake tucked under his arm. The muggers forced him to hand over the cash, his cell phone, and his keys. By the time he walked to a gas station down the road and called 911, the muggers were long gone.

The victim had uploaded a tracking app to his cell phone, and it was located in a storm drain a half mile away, along with his keys. Neither bore any fingerprints. The report noted that, months before, the victim had hired Fabrizio's company, Cyber-Shield Security Systems, to install security cameras and provide monitoring services at his restaurant. A still photo, presumably a screen shot of security camera footage, showed a dark image of two men in ski masks with guns pointed at the victim as he stood next to a car. The terrified expression on the man's face said he was in imminent risk of soiling himself. But who could blame him? The mere photo of the armed thugs had my gut in a clench.

I looked up at Detective Booth. "Given that the mugging victim was a client of Fabrizio's security company and that the mugging happened on the same night the two men disappeared, you're thinking there's a connection?"

"You got it." She plucked a shriveled leaf from the potted ivy on her desk, ground it to mulch between her fingers, and dropped it into the dirt at the base of the plant. "My guess is the two men who disappeared were the ones who mugged the restaurant owner. Fabrizio probably offed them afterward and disposed of their bodies somewhere. He's not the kind of guy who leaves loose ends."

"Did the locksmith or trainer have criminal records?" I asked.

"The trainer had a couple of assaults on his rap sheet. He gave a previous girlfriend a black eye and he'd beat the snot out of someone who'd accidentally backed into his motorcycle in a parking lot. The locksmith had a theft charge. He'd made a duplicate key when installing new locks at a private home. He went back later and attempted to rob the house. The homeowners came home and caught him in the act. He covered his face and ran off, but they'd already recognized him."

It didn't surprise me that the missing men weren't exactly choirboys. Dirty work was done by dirty men.

Booth went on to tell me that it had taken years for Dallas PD to connect the dots and realize Fabrizio had likely played a role in several unsolved crimes. "Too many crime victims have been clients of Fabrizio's security company for it to be mere coincidence."

Most were too afraid to point fingers at Tino Fabrizio, to implicate him in extortion, but the detective surmised the victims suspected that the man who was supposed to protect them and their businesses was, in fact, the one who'd preyed upon them instead.

"Fabrizio's approach is typical," Booth said. "He focuses his extortion efforts on people running mom-and-pop-type businesses. They're easier to intimidate and they control their business's finances."

I supposed it would be more difficult to extort money from a large business client, where the staff member working with Cyber-Shield's salesman probably had no access to the company's coffers and would be more likely to report the extortion attempt to upper management.

"I've spoken with Fabrizio in person," Booth said.

"Strangely enough, the guy didn't give off a single bad vibe. He seemed about as threatening as Barney the dinosaur."

I was familiar with the show, which was filmed locally at the studios in Las Colinas. Fitting, I supposed, since the oil Texas was famous for originated from the bodies of dinosaurs that had roamed the state millions of years ago before keeling over to take a permanent dirt nap. Many claimed a meteor did the big beasts in, but I speculated that perhaps they'd snacked on a few too many lantana, a native wildflower that was pretty but poisonous.

Booth continued. "Of course when I spoke with Tino I didn't let on that I suspected he might be involved in the crimes. I just asked for any evidence his security company might have. He provided me with copies of the camera footage."

I flipped to the next page to find a photograph of a very muscular, but very dead, man lying on a weight bench in a residential garage. A barbell loaded with what looked to be hundreds of pounds of weights rested across his neck. His right arm crooked back under the bar at such an angle it must have snapped under the pressure. My stomach squirmed inside me as I looked up at the detective. "What happened to this guy?"

"Crushed windpipe. By the looks of it he was working out in his home gym without a spotter and got a little overzealous. But I think Fabrizio killed him. This guy had been on Cyber-Shield's payroll for a while, driving one of the security patrol vehicles. He probably knew too much and became a liability."

I turned to the next page in the file and—*gukh!*—suffered an immediate gag reflex. A full-color photograph depicted a man folded over a wrought-iron fence, a pointy post—and approximately six inches of lower intestine—protruding through his lower back. A river of blood had flowed from the fatal wound and down his legs, forming a crimson pond at the base of the fence. The dead man wore blue jeans, a green sweater, and a red Santa hat.

I looked up at Detective Booth. "I'm guessing this wasn't an accident, either?"

"He was stringing Christmas lights on his roof when he '*fell*.'" She made air quotes with her fingers.

"Any witnesses?"

"Conveniently, no."

"But he's linked to Fabrizio?"

"That's a good question. Many of the men Tino Fabrizio hires to do his dirty work have other jobs, like the trainer and locksmith. None of them told anyone they were moonlighting for Fabrizio, but I'm sure he makes it clear they better keep their mouths shut. Santa there," she said, gesturing at the photo, "was an electrician. We think he might have arranged an electrical fire one of Fabrizio's security clients suffered."

I was almost afraid to flip to the next page. But it couldn't get any worse, could it?

*It could.*

My gag reflex went into overdrive. *Gukh-gukh-gukh!*

The next page featured a close-up photo of a man's face with two dozen steel nails protruding from it, the ones in his eye sockets buried up to their heads in his retinas and spongy brain. It looked as if the man had been attacked by an evil acupuncturist. Blood ran from the wounds, nearly coating his face in red rivulets.

Detective Booth didn't wait for my inevitable question. "The man in that photo was a building contractor. He was allegedly trying to repair a malfunctioning nail gun he'd 'forgotten' to unplug." She made air quotes again. "Again, there were no witnesses. We think he might have been in on a theft of a Cyber-Shield client where a bulldozer was used to knock down a wall. The client's safe was scooped up and carried off."

I could go on and detail the rest of the file, but I'd likely lose my lunch. I'd eaten spicy Mexican food that had burned going down, so I definitely didn't want it coming back up. *Moving on, then*.

"With so many victims having a link to Tino," the detective said, "it's clear the man played a role in the crimes. Problem is, Tino knows how to distance himself. If law enforcement is ever going to bring this man to justice, someone's going to have to catch him in the act."

*But what act might it be?* My spinning mind tossed out one gruesome scenario after another until I willed it to stop with a firm shake of my head.

Hohenwald chimed in now. "The FBI has done its best to gather evidence that would directly link Fabrizio to an offense, but stakeout after stakeout had gotten us nowhere. We've followed Tino, of course. We've also tracked his salesmen, installers, and security patrols all the way from Dallas to Timbuktu, hoping they might help us figure out which client Tino might be planning to target next. But we're never in the right place at the right time. We can't seem to pin anything on him. That's why I decided it was time to involve the IRS in the investigation."

And that's where I came in. If Tino Fabrizio couldn't be nailed for extortion or murder, we might at least be able to charge him with tax evasion or money laundering. The strategy had worked on Al Capone and many a mobster since. Might as well go with tried-and-true methods, right?

"If anyone can get this guy," I told the two of them, "it's the Internal Revenue Service." Cocky of me to say so, perhaps, but I knew personally just how good we agents at the IRS were. With any luck, we'd be able to put together a tax case against the man before he could strike again.

The detective chuckled, nonplussed. "All righty, then," she said, holding out her hand for a good-bye shake. "Go get 'im, tiger."

# chapter three

# On the Rocks

After we wrapped things up with Dallas PD, we returned to Hohenwald's car. He headed down the surface streets and merged onto Central Expressway.

Hohenwald changed lanes to bypass a caravan of yellow school buses transporting grade-school kids on a field trip. "That Fabrizio is one coldhearted son of a bitch."

"You can say that again." Tino Fabrizio made the Gambinos look like *bam*binos. "Where are we going now?"

"To speak with Alex Harris. He's the only victim who had the balls to finger Tino."

If Harris were willing to accuse a mobster, he must indeed have large testicles and plenty of them.

Hohenwald exited the freeway at Mockingbird Lane and hooked a left, entering the exclusive Highland Park neighborhood. A minute or so down the road, Hohenwald turned into the Dallas Country Club, parking near the entrance of the Tudor-style clubhouse. We exited the vehicle and went inside, stopping at the desk in the foyer to check in with the receptionist before continuing on to the club's tavern.

A fortyish, sandy-haired bartender looked up as he slid a highball glass across the bar to a man in a blue golf shirt. He lifted his chin in acknowledgment to Agent Hohenwald, then gestured to an empty table in the back corner of the room. "Cover me," Harris called to a second bartender who was refilling the garnish tray with maraschino cherries. "I'll be back in a jiff."

Hohenwald and I took seats in the barrel chairs on the back end of the table, where we could keep an eye on the room and make sure no one could overhear our conversation. Harris dropped into a seat across from us.

Hohenwald introduced the two of us. "Alex Harris, Special Agent Holloway. Agent Holloway, Alex Harris."

Harris and I rose a few inches from our seats and shook hands across the table.

Hohenwald explained my presence to Harris, though his words were a bit cryptic. "We're having some fresh eyes take a look at Giustino Fabrizio, exploring some new angles."

Harris cut a look my way. "I hope you can nail that bastard."

*Nail. Eek.* His words had me thinking of the nail gun. Better not show my fear, though. I looked Harris in the eye. "I'll do my best, sir."

"It can't hurt to have some fresh ears on the case, too," Hohenwald added. "Tell Agent Holloway what happened."

"Gladly." Harris went on to tell me that he and his wife had owned a small neighborhood bar in Plano, a suburb about ten miles to the north. "Not much more than a hole in the wall, really, the kind of quiet, comfortable place a couple might go after a date or business associates might negotiate over a couple of beers. We'd built the place from

the ground up, had a regular clientele, made a respectable profit. Then one day about two years ago, a salesman from Cyber-Shield comes in, offers us a great deal
on security cameras and a combination burglar and fire
alarm system. A pizza place not far from us had been
robbed at closing time only a week before, so we figured
it couldn't hurt, you know?"

"Makes sense," I said, nodding. Cameras could not
only provide evidence to solve crimes, but they could also
serve as a deterrent to would-be thieves.

"So we get the system," Harris said. "Everything's
fine for a month or two, then the salesman comes back
and tries to sell us additional services. First he says we
should install some kind of fancy computer security system. I told him I didn't see the need for it. We only had a
couple of computers at the bar and the only people who
used them were me and my wife. He seemed a little put
off, but not too much yet. Then he tells me it would be
a good idea to hire a security guard to keep an eye on
things. Says it'll run two grand a month and gives me
some kind of bullshit about paying the guard in cash
since technically he'd be an independent contractor."

Harris was right to be suspicious. Cash payments
were a red flag.

"Again," he continued, "I didn't see the need for a
guard. We weren't running the kind of place that attracted
the college kids or young party types who get plastered
and out of control. The bartenders and I could handle the
occasional mean drunk until the cops arrived to deal
with the situation. I told the salesman as much, told him
I couldn't afford to hire a guard, either. You know what
he does? He looks me in the eye and says 'You can't afford not to.'"

"An implied threat," I said.

"Yeah," Harris said. "Only I wasn't going to let the guy

push me around. I told him I'd take my chances." He scoffed. "That's a gamble I lost. A month later my place burns to the ground. When I asked Cyber-Shield for a copy of the security-camera footage from the night of the fire, they gave me footage showing my car pulling up to the back entrance at three A.M., twenty minutes before the smoke alarm went off and alerted the fire department."

I wasn't sure I was following him. "You were at the bar just prior to the fire?"

"Hell, no!" he spat. "I was at 7-Eleven buying a pack of cigarettes. Someone had called our home number a few minutes earlier. When I answered, they asked for a Becky. My wife's name is Rhonda and we're not close to anyone named Becky. I told the caller he had the wrong number. After the call woke me up I had trouble getting back to sleep. My wife had been on my case, trying to get me to quit smoking, but I was having a hell of a time of it. She fell fast asleep right away, so I decided to sneak out and grab some cigarettes. I was at the store when the smoke alarm went off at the bar."

"I assume you have proof that you weren't at the bar?" I said. "Maybe camera footage from the 7-Eleven or a receipt with a time stamp?"

"Better." Harris reached into his breast pocket, pulled out a folded piece of paper, and tossed it onto the table.

I picked up the paper and unfolded it to find a copy of an automated red-light citation. The camera had picked up not only the license plate of Harris's SUV, but also his face as he sat at the wheel, a cigarette clamped between his lips. The citation indicated the offense occurred on a date in April two years prior, at 3:16 A.M.

Harris pointed at the paper. "That camera is fourteen miles from the bar. No way in hell could my car be at the bar and at that intersection within a three-minute span."

As he sat back in his seat, my mind considered the information. "So the security-camera footage was doctored."

"Evidently."

"And the wrong number?"

"Was probably some goon from Cyber-Shield checking to make sure I was at home in bed and not somewhere I'd have a good alibi."

Little did the caller know that the call itself would lead Harris to verifiable proof he hadn't been at his bar when the fire started.

Agent Hohenwald chimed in now. "The fire was intentionally set. No doubt about it. An accelerant was used and the fire department ruled it arson. Problem was, there was no concrete evidence to implicate anyone connected with Cyber-Shield."

Harris shook his head, a thick, purple vein throbbing on his neck. "Since the fire wasn't an accident and the security video showed my car on the scene, my insurance company refused to pay up, even after the red-light citation was provided to them. We're still in litigation trying to work something out. Meanwhile, my creditors have sucked me dry. I personally guaranteed the financing for the bar furniture, fixtures, and equipment. The finance company has taken everything but the shirt off my back. My wife and I had to liquidate our retirement fund and sell our house. But the worst thing is"—he lowered his voice and took a quick look around—"I'm always looking over my shoulder, wondering if some thug is going to fill me with lead. And I'm here, working for someone else, rather than owning my own bar like I always dreamed of."

I felt a pang of pity for the guy. He certainly hadn't deserved any of what happened to him. On the other hand, I also admired his balls—figuratively speaking.

He'd stood his ground. Good for him. He might have lost his bar but he'd retained some of his dignity.

When a large group of golfers came into the bar, Harris said, "I need to get back to work."

We wrapped up the conversation, thanked Harris for his time, and promised him we'd let him know if and when there was any progress on the case.

I followed Hohenwald to his car once again and climbed in. "Did anyone examine the video footage for evidence it had been tampered with?"

"We had some of our guys analyze it," he replied. "The results were inconclusive. The bar's security cameras had a low resolution and frame rate. Poor quality recordings like that are much easier to tamper with than higher quality video."

So much for that avenue. "Where to now?"

He turned the key and the engine roared to life. "The belly of the beast."

# chapter four

# The Belly of the Beast

It was nearly five o'clock and traffic on the roadways had picked up as people headed home from work. Still, we were able to make decent time since most of the traffic was heading north into the suburbs and we were going against traffic. Agent Hohenwald drove south on Central Expressway for a little over two miles before exiting and driving into the Swiss Avenue historic district.

Over a hundred years ago, Robert Munger, a wealthy cotton gin manufacturer and real estate developer, came up with the idea of developing an exclusive neighborhood east of downtown Dallas, envisioning an opulent neighborhood of grand homes. His building restrictions stipulated that all homes on Swiss Avenue must be at least two stories high, and that the exterior be constructed of brick masonry. Each residence had to cost a minimum of $10,000 to build, which was quite a big sum at the time. Swiss Avenue was also the first paved street in Dallas. The older homes had been well maintained, and the area's reputation for upscale living continued. The district had given rise to many notable residents, including former U.S. Senator Kay Bailey Hutchison and Carrie Marcus Neiman, the founder of Neiman Marcus department stores, God bless her.

Agent Hohenwald checked his rearview mirror for the hundredth time, probably making sure we weren't being followed. It never hurt to be vigilant.

"Get out your cell phone," he instructed me, "and turn off the Wi-Fi. It's likely that Cyber-Shield's tech staff keep tabs on who's in their vicinity."

"They can do that through Wi-Fi?" I asked, pulling my cell phone from the pocket of my blazer. "Even if a device isn't connected to a system?"

"So I'm told." Hohenwald shrugged. "I don't understand exactly how it works, either. But our specialists at the FBI gave us strict orders to turn the Wi-Fi off on all devices anytime we get near Fabrizio or any of his security systems. Bluetooth, too."

Funny how cell phones made us both safer and more vulnerable at the same time. I did as he'd directed, thumbing the Wi-Fi and Bluetooth buttons to the right. *Wi-Fi off. Bluetooth off.*

We passed many of the stately homes until Hohenwald took a left turn on North Fitzhugh and slowed as he approached the neighborhood's business district. He pointed through the windshield as we came up on a single-story L-shaped strip center comprised of two one-story brick buildings sitting at a perpendicular angle. The building's roofs were slightly pitched and covered with tan shingles. At the upper end of each building, just under the eaves, was a triangular metal grate that would allow air to circulate in the small space between the ceiling and the roof. As hot as Texas summers were, good ventilation was critical.

"There it is," Hohenwald said. "Cyber-Shield's home base."

The right one-third of the building facing Fitzhugh was painted a neon-green color, while the remaining two-thirds was painted white. Cyber-Shield Security Systems took up the smaller green space. Parked in the angled spaces in front of the business were a small fleet of security patrol cars, each painted the same can't-miss vivid green and equipped with fold-out spotlights on the driver's side and a white light on top that flashed. Also parked in front of Cyber-Shield were a gorgeous Alfa Romeo coupe in a sporty orangey-red color and a blue '65 Ford Mustang Fastback. *Nice.*

"The Alfa Romeo is Tino's," Hohenwald said. "The Mustang belongs to his tech guru, a guy by the name of Eric Echols."

Over the larger white space to the left hung a sign that read BENEDETTA'S BISTRO. Adorning the windows were green, white, and red striped curtains, mimicking the colors in the Italian flag. A neon-green sticker with the Cyber-Shield logo was affixed just above the handle of the wide glass door. A sign in the window read HELP WANTED, while a sandwich board situated on the sidewalk out front declared today's special to be half-price chocolate cannoli with any entrée.

Hohenwald tipped his head toward the building. "See that Italian restaurant?"

"They're offering half-price cannoli." My mouth watered at the thought of the creamy filling, the chocolate garnishes, and the crisp, delectable crust. "How could I miss it?"

"I'm more of a tiramisu man myself," Hohenwald said. "At any rate, Tino's wife runs the bistro. Their three daughters help out. Tino spends a lot of time there."

With the bistro sitting alongside Cyber-Shield, I had to wonder if Fabrizio's wife and daughters were involved somehow in his dubious dealings. Perhaps they'd stood ready with alibis, if needed, or maybe they laundered his extorted funds through the restaurant's accounts. "You think his wife and girls know what he's up to? Maybe play some kind of role?"

"We've had no indication they're involved in any way," the agent said. "Hell, I'd be surprised if they were even aware of his nefarious deeds. By all accounts Tino Fabrizio is a stand-up family man. He's even a Eucharistic minister in one of the Catholic churches here."

Ironic. Or perhaps appropriate. It sounded like Tino was used to dealing with flesh and blood. Still, it wasn't unusual for the families of mobsters to be in the dark, either by design or because they purposely stuck their heads in the sand. It was food for thought. Not delicious food like a chocolate cannoli would be, though.

"Of course, you never know," Hohenwald added, hedging his bets. "Some mob wives cover up for their husbands."

More food for thought . . .

The second building comprised three spaces. A frozen yogurt shop occupied the left space, while a photography studio took up the right. Though a sign for HARD CORE MIXED MARTIAL ARTS still hung over the door, the center space stood vacant, a FOR LEASE banner advertising the availability of the space.

"There's our man now," Hohenwald said, cutting his eyes to a man exiting the Cyber-Shield space.

We were too far away for me to get a really good look at the guy. All I could tell was that he was short, bald, and as round as Humpty Dumpty before his infamous great fall. If we were in the belly of the beast, it was a potbelly. But with free access to all the carbs he could eat, it was no wonder Tino had developed a gut. Even so, I was surprised at how harmless the man appeared to be. Heck, I was even a little disappointed. I'd built him up in my head as someone larger than life, yet he looked no different than most men his age.

He made his way down the sidewalk and disappeared into the bistro, but whether it was to launder money or indulge in a cannoli was anyone's guess.

The local FBI headquarters was in far north Dallas, so rather than go to his office to talk, Hohenwald and I decided to talk strategy in my digs. He pulled into the lot at the federal building, which was rapidly emptying as those with regular eight-to-five jobs headed out. *Oh, to work normal hours. Wouldn't that be nice?* But no. Although I might enjoy a more regular work schedule, I loved my job and wouldn't trade it for anything. Working as an IRS special agent was an unusual job, one that required financial savvy, street smarts, and weapons proficiency. Few people had this unique and varied skill set. Not too many gunslinging, ass-kicking accountants out there. We special agents could not only crunch numbers, but we could also crack skulls. Of course, unlike Tino Fabrizio, we reserved the skull-cracking for those who really deserved it.

I stopped in the doorway of my office and held out an arm to invite Hohenwald to enter. As I did, I glanced through the open doorway across the hall, my gray-blue eyes meeting the bourbon-brown ones of Senior Special Agent Nick Pratt, my tall, muscular, dark-haired co-worker and the person on the other end of my booty calls. But no need to worry. Nick and I didn't let our personal relationship interfere with our jobs. Your tax dollars were well spent as far as we were concerned.

Though Nick's expression remained professionally impassive, he winked an eye to let me know he was glad to see me, that he loved me more than life itself, and that, yes, as a matter of fact, these pants made my ass look like a ripe, delectable peach. It was a very verbose wink.

I closed my door after a return wink that said I was glad to see him, too, and that if he wanted to take a bite of this peach all he had to do was ask.

I plunked down in my rolling chair, retrieved a yellow legal pad from my desk drawer, and plucked a ballpoint pen from a coffee mug on my desk. "Before we get started," I said, booting up my laptop, "I want to take a quick look at the tax files for Benedetta's Bistro."

As they say, numbers don't lie.

## chapter five

# *M*aking the List

I logged into the system and discovered that Benedetta's Bistro was operated as a limited liability company, or LLC, a type of hybrid entity that provided the owners with personal protection from lawsuits while giving them more flexibility and less stringent record-keeping requirements than a corporation. The LLC was wholly owned by Tino's wife. The records also told me that the restaurant had reported consistent and remarkable net earnings, much higher than would be expected for a mid-priced neighborhood eatery. Heck, most small family-owned restaurants were lucky to break even, let alone make a profit.

My nerves buzzed with excited energy as I turned the screen to show the data to Hohenwald. "Either she's an incredible businesswoman or some of this revenue belongs to Tino."

"I trust you'll figure out which."

"Try and stop me."

He chuckled. "There's that determination your boss mentioned."

I wondered what else she'd mentioned. Hopefully not my occasional stubbornness and rule-bending.

Hohenwald and I briefly discussed our relative duties. He'd lead his team in following Tino and his men, and I'd lead my team in attempting to locate and follow the money trails.

I tapped my pen on the pad. "Alex Harris mentioned that it was Tino's salesman who threatened him. I'm guessing Tino also has his staff collect the extorted funds. I can't imagine he'd do it himself and risk being caught red-handed. Have you and your agents seen any money change hands?"

"No," Hohenwald said, "but we've seen Cyber-Shield's patrolmen enter some of the businesses late at night, presumably to do security surveillance. It's possible they pick up cash then, too, though none of my agents have mentioned seeing any of the guards carrying anything out with them."

Of course it would be easy to tuck cash into a pocket where it wouldn't be noticeable. I jotted a note on my pad. "Following the money trail will also mean following Tino's men, so we need to make sure our teams work together and don't get in each other's way."

He nodded in acknowledgment. "I've got agents who can follow Cyber-Shield's patrol vehicles, equipment installers, and salesmen. Whoever you assign to sniff out the cash can coordinate with my guys, maybe work tag team to avoid detection. We'll equip the task force members who are running surveillance with a secure radio communications system so they can stay in touch in the field. We'll also get your team new cell phones that can't be traced to the government."

"Perfect."

Hohenwald leaned forward. "I know the IRS is as overworked as the FBI, but the task force can use as many agents as this office can spare. The only way we'll ever take Tino Fabrizio down is if we're on him and his men every step of the way. I'll pull some of my agents off other cases and we'll make a big push. A surge, if you will."

I knew my fellow agents were busy with their own caseloads, too. I also knew several who, busy or not, would make time to help take down a mobster. Not only would the case be a challenge, but working a high-profile investigation like this couldn't hurt an agent's performance review and might result in a sizable raise. Besides, those involved would get bragging rights when we took Fabrizio and his minions down. Because we *would* take them down. No way would I let a bastard like Tino Fabrizio get away with his crimes and become a black mark on my record.

I wrote the word "team" on my pad and underlined it twice. "I'll ask around the office. See who I can get on board."

Three potential names went on my list. The first was EDDIE. Eddie had been my initial partner, the only one in the office willing to train the runt-sized recruit. He taught me everything I knew. Well, *almost* everything I knew. The rest I'd learned from *Sesame Street,* various schoolteachers, and *Cosmo.*

The next name on my list was WILL. William Dorsey was one of the newer agents in our office, having transferred from the Tucson collections office only a few months prior. But he'd quickly proved himself to be tough, capable, and smart.

The third name on my list was HANA. Hana Kim was built like a fire hydrant and could be just as unmoving and forceful when faced with an unreasonable defense attorney representing a tax evader. She was also a star player on the Tax Maniacs, the IRS's softball team. Her batting abilities could come in handy if one of Fabrizio's henchmen came at her with a nail gun. If nothing else, she added more estrogen to the team. As much as I'd like to rule over an all-male harem, it couldn't hurt to even things out genderwise for appearance's sake. Besides, I'd never worked directly with Hana and wouldn't mind getting to know her better.

"To follow the money," I said, "I'll need close eyes on Cyber-Shield's office. We need to know who's coming and going over there and when. I noticed a space for lease in the other building. I'll see about renting it."

The space would give law enforcement the perfect vantage point from which to spy on Fabrizio's security operations. And if I were going to put eyes on Cyber-Shield, why not make it those bourbon-brown eyes I mentioned? I wrote the name NICK on my pad. He could not only give the FBI agents a heads-up on the movement at Cyber-Shield, but he'd also be able to watch for any cash that might be coming in or out of the office. Plus, as a former high school football player, he was the most physically formidable agent in the office. As much as I hated to put the man I loved so close to danger, he was the most capable of defending himself should things go awry.

"As for myself," I added, "I'll see if I can get an interview at Benedetta's Bistro. If I can get inside, maybe I can figure out whether she's laundering money for Tino."

Getting on the inside would allow me to watch Tino and Benedetta's interactions, and give me access to data that would prove or disprove my theory that Tino was laundering his money through the restaurant.

Back in high school, I'd worked at Big Bob's Bait Bucket, a combination bait shop and convenience store that served anglers heading out to the various lakes in east Texas with the hopes of catching bass, crappie, or trout. Though the creaky old building housing the business had been ancient, the cash register was a computerized model that could track inventory, remember a customer's purchase preferences, and print out total sales figures on a daily, weekly, and monthly basis. I'd seen similar registers in restaurants. More than likely, the bistro utilized this type of register, perhaps more than one. If I could gain access to the bistro's registers, I could print out sales reports and compare them to the figures entered on the bistro's tax return. If the figures were comparable, my theory that Tino could be laundering his funds through the restaurant would be proven wrong. But if the numbers didn't jibe, it could be just the break we needed to finally put Tino behind bars.

The restaurant would also provide a second location from which to spy on Tino's operations. If nothing else, maybe I'd overhear something important or be able to wheedle some valuable information out of Tino's wife or daughters.

"Fabrizio trusts no one," Hohenwald said. "I've tried to get agents on the inside, sent a couple of them to interview for jobs at Cyber-Shield, but they can never seem to land a position. It's like Tino's some kind of bloodhound who can smell a mole. Chances are he'll do some digging to make sure any of the bistro's new employees and any new tenants in the shopping center are legit. My office can provide you and your team with new identities. They can arrange apartments for your team, too. It would be a good idea for you to move into a different place while you're working this case. Fabrizio might send his men to snoop around and you don't want to lead them to your real home."

I'd already had one wacko break into my town house and attack me. I certainly didn't need another. It had cost a pretty penny to have the bullet hole in my bathroom floor repaired.

"Got anyone who can hack computers?" Hohenwald asked. "I've had our best guys on it and nobody seems to be able to get into Fabrizio's system. Hell, North Korea was easier to hack into than Cyber-Shield. If we can get in, we might be able to prove that the videos were doctored."

We'd also need to hack in to access Cyber-Shield's financial records, too, so I could peruse them for evidence of tax evasion. "I've got the perfect guy for the job." I added the name JOSH under Nick's on my notepad. "There's no code Josh Schmidt can't crack."

The former martial arts studio would be the perfect place for Josh to work from, too. I knew diddly squat about technology, but I was smart enough to realize that the close vicinity could make it easier for him to attempt to hack into Cyber-Shield's system. The bistro's, too. If he could get in, he could access their financial data and maybe even the security camera video files.

"Do we need to get a court order before we start?"

Hohenwald assured me that the FBI had secured the necessary search warrants authorizing the team to attempt to infiltrate Tino's computer networks. "We're good to go."

When we finished our discussion, I walked Agent Hohenwald back to the elevators. "I'll be in touch once I get all the details sorted out."

"Great." He stepped into an open, empty car and turned back around to face me. "One more thing, Tara."

"Yes?"

"Tell your team to watch their backs."

# chapter six

# $\mathcal{M}$ale Makeover

The door slid closed with a *shwupp,* leaving Hohenwald's words hanging in the air. *Tell your team to watch their backs.*

I scurried to Josh's office, hoping to catch him before he left. Fortunately, he was still at his desk, three laptop computers in front of him. One was his government-issued computer, while the other two were higher-end MacBook Air models apparently seized from a suspect.

Josh had a beautiful mind that could crack computer encryptions in seconds flat, but with his blond curls, baby-blue eyes, and diminutive stature, he nonetheless looked like a young boy on his way to cotillion. He'd been an unlikable, sniveling weenie until Nick returned to the IRS last year and showed him how to be a man. Now, the rest of us not only tolerated Josh, but he'd become our go-to guy for technical help.

I rapped on his door frame. "Whatcha doing?"

His eyes remained on the screen of the laptop in front of him and his fingers continued to work the keyboard.

"Blasting through firewalls, finding evidence of transfers to offshore accounts."

Like a supercomputing superhero. All he needed were some tights and a cape.

I stepped into his office. "Any chance you'd be willing to help me on a mob case?"

His eyes sought mine and his fingers froze in mid-stroke. "Did you say *mob*?"

"Yep." I told him about Tino Fabrizio and Cyber-Shield Security Systems.

"Hacking into a firm that provides cybersecurity?" Josh virtually drooled at the prospect. "I'm up to the challenge. Count me in."

"Great." I gave him Hohenwald's contact information. "He'll put you in touch with the FBI's tech team."

With Josh and his brilliant brain on board, I now needed to recruit some muscle. I walked back up the hall to Nick's office and found him packing things in for the day. Nick was dressed in his usual style, basic Dockers paired with cowboy boots, a white dress shirt, and a belt with a shiny buckle. Today's buckle featured a howling wolf. Despite the fact that Nick lived in Dallas, he was a country boy at heart.

I perched on the edge of his desk. "Wanna help me bust a violent mobster?"

Nick raised a nonchalant yet strong shoulder. "Sure. Why not?"

I gave him a quick rundown of the day's events and the information I'd learned. "Any thoughts?"

"Yeah." He cut me a pointed look. "Keep a gun in reach at all times."

"You know I will." A shiny firearm was my favorite accessory. If one wasn't in my hand it was on my hip, strapped to my ankle, or in my purse.

He went to the wall and flipped his light off, then took my hand in his to pull me to a stand. "Come on. Let's grab some dinner."

"Can we go somewhere that serves cannoli?" I'd been craving the stuff since seeing the sign at Benedetta's Bistro earlier.

"You name the place," Nick said, "I'll make it happen."

An hour later we were seated at Carmone's, our tummies full of pasta, a cannoli sitting on a plate in front of each of us. I finished mine first, no surprise there, and when Nick stopped to take a sip of his coffee I snatched the last bite of his cannoli from his plate.

"I should've known better than to take my eyes off you," he teased.

I glanced around. Nobody was seated nearby, but I lowered my voice anyway and told him about the space for lease in the center where Cyber-Shield was located. "It would be the perfect space for us to use to keep watch on Tino and his men, see if we can follow the cash. I'm thinking Josh could work from there, too. Maybe it would be close enough for him to hack into their Wi-Fi and get into their computer system. I'd love to take a look at their financial records, see if they've reported all their income."

"Sounds like a good plan." Nick set his fork down. "I've got some available time in the morning. Want me to handle the lease?"

"Would you?" I said, wiping my mouth. "That would be one less thing on my plate." Ironic words for a woman who'd just emptied the plates in front of her. "Hohenwald says he can get you a new identity to use. He can get you an apartment to stay in while we're working the case, too."

"Good," Nick said. "That'll make things easier and safer." He took a sip of his iced tea. "When I talk to the leasing agent, what kind of business should I say I'm planning to operate?"

*Hmm.* I took a sip of my coffee, the sugar and caffeine fueling my thoughts. "What about an art gallery?" I suggested. "You could sell pieces on consignment. A business like that wouldn't take much time or money to get up and running. All you'd need is a sign and a few pieces to offer for sale."

His eyes narrowed skeptically and he cocked his head. "You think I can pass myself off as an art dealer?"

He had a point. He looked much more like a cattle rustler than an art aficionado.

"You'll have to lose the belt buckles," I said.

"Hell!" He huffed. "You might as well take my soul."

"Perfect," I said. "That kind of melodrama sounds just like something an art dealer would say."

His eyes narrowed in skepticism. "I'm not sure about this."

He might not be sure but I, on the other hand, knew Nick could do anything he set his mind to. "In the right clothes and with some blond highlights and a little hair gel you'd pass."

"You'll have to dress me."

"I'd be happy to. As long as I can *un*dress you after."

He slid me a sexy grin. "You'll get no argument from me."

I'd met a couple of avant-garde artists recently when working a case against a shady gallery that served primarily as a tax shelter for the owner. I pulled up their phone numbers in my contacts list and gave them to Nick so he could call them and see if they might have some pieces they'd like to place on consignment.

As he entered the artists' numbers into his phone, the waiter arrived with our bill. Nick paid it and we headed out, driving, of course, to the downtown Neiman Marcus store. There, I outfitted Nick with attire that was classy yet trendy. Slate-blue trousers. A diamond-print dress shirt with a club collar. A pair of burgundy tassel loafers.

He scrunched up his nose in distaste. "Tassels are for strippers."

"Strippers and art dealers." I thrust the box at him. "Trust me." Besides, I was hoping Nick might do a little striptease for me at his town house later.

After adding a second pair of pants and a couple more shirts to the mix, Nick paid for his purchases and we left downtown, heading to the closest Walgreens. We stood in the hair care aisle, looking over the color selections.

"Here's what you need." I grabbed a box with a picture of a seductively smiling blonde on it. "Frost and tip."

"If you get to pick mine, I get to pick yours."

"I suppose that's only fair."

He ran his eyes over the boxes, chose one in a bold and vivid red, and held it out to me.

I pointed to the picture on the box. "That color isn't exactly subtle."

"Maybe not," he said, "but it's sexy." He wagged his brows. "You know what they say about redheads. Red on the head, fire in the—"

I grabbed the box out of his hand. "You should be ashamed of yourself."

"I imagine so." He chuckled. "Besides, you're fiery enough already."

I wasn't sure the bright red was the right color for an undercover mission, but perhaps having such boldly colored hair would throw suspicion off me. Kind of like hiding in plain sight.

Our shopping done, we drove back to my town house in the Uptown area of Dallas, just north of downtown. I'd

bought the place a while back when I'd lost my roommate, my BFF Alicia, who'd decided to move out of the
apartment we shared and move in with her then boyfriend. She'd moved back in with me when the two later
had a temporary split. That boyfriend was now her fiancé. Apparently absence not only makes the heart grow
fonder, it makes it get off its complacent ass and propose. Although Alicia had accepted the proposal, she'd
decided to continue living with me until their wedding,
which was only a few weeks away now. Though I was
happy for Alicia, I had to admit I'd miss her when she left.
It was nice having someone to chat with over my Fruity
Pebbles in the morning.

Nick and I went inside to find my fluffy Maine coon
cat, Henry, sharpening his claws on the sofa.

I shooed him away. "Stop that!"

He pulled his claws from the fabric, leaped up to his
favorite roost atop the armoire that housed my TV, and
gave me a look of absolute feline derision before settling
down to lord comfortably over the room.

Alicia sat at the kitchen table, running a hand over the
back of my other cat, Anne, who lay on Alicia's lap, shed-
ding her creamy fur on my roommate's black yoga pants.
Alicia's platinum head was ducked as she pored over a
seating chart for her wedding dinner. As maid of honor,
I'd sit at the head table along with the best man, the bride
and groom, and their parents. Nick, on the other hand,
would be seated among the general riffraff.

"Hey, Nick!" Alicia called. "Would you rather sit
with Daniel's Uncle Joe who's going to regale you with
tales of his gall bladder surgery, or my snooty cousin
Melody who's going to complain about everything from
the food to the napkins to the champagne?"

"Gall bladder," Nick said. "Definitely the gall bladder."

I waved a hand at Alicia as Nick and I walked into the

kitchen. "Finish that later. I need your help with Nick's hair. You're better at this stuff than me."

As far as style was concerned, Alicia had me totally beat. While my chestnut hair hung to my shoulders in a standard layered look, she wore her hair in a funky, short, asymmetrical cut. Her clothes were always cutting edge, too. Mine tended more toward clearance rack. Not that I couldn't hold my own when I had to. I just tended to balance frugality with fashion.

Alicia picked Anne up from her lap and set her on the kitchen floor. "Sorry, girl. Your mommy needs me."

I grabbed the manual kitchen timer from the counter. As we went upstairs to my bathroom, Anne skittering along ahead of us, I explained the situation to Alicia.

"You two are going after the mafia?" she cried. "You just took down a drug cartel! Can't they assign you some easy cases for a change?"

"That would be a waste of our talents," I said with false bravado.

"Yeah," Nick agreed. "Besides, we'd be bored with easy work."

It was the truth. Call us crazy, but we thrived on the challenges presented by cases like the Fabrizio investigation. The more difficult it was to take someone down, the more determined we were to do it.

Turning back to the immediate matter at hand, I said, "Nick needs a style that says 'Look at me! I'm artsy.'" I splayed my fingers jazz-hands style. Nick sat down on the closed toilet seat, while I placed the boxes of hair color on the counter and pulled out all of my hair products. "Here's what we've got to work with."

Nick glanced over at the assortment. "This goes against everything I believe in. The only thing a man needs is shampoo and a comb."

"Hush," I chastised him. "You sound like an old

fuddy-duddy." The fact that my use of the antiquated term made me sound like one, too, wasn't lost on me.

Anne ventured to the doorway and sat down to watch the goings-on in my bathroom.

Alicia looked at the two boxes of hair color. "Please tell me the red isn't for Nick."

"The red is mine."

"Good," she said. "A ginger might work on him but that shade is way too bright for his skin tone."

I directed Nick to take off his shirt so it wouldn't be stained by the dye. After enjoying a quick glance at his rock-hard pecs, I wrapped an old bath towel around his shoulders.

Alicia opened the frost-and-tip box and pulled out the plastic cap, having to fight to get the thing over Nick's head. "It's a little small." With a final grunt and tug, she managed to yank the cap into place and tied the strings tightly under his chin.

Nick turned his head and looked at himself in the mirror. "I look like a woman about to take a swimming lesson."

"A woman from an Eastern bloc country," Alicia teased.

"With a severe hormone problem," I added.

Nick was an attractive man, but as a woman? Not so much. Perhaps it was the strong jaw or the five-o'clock shadow.

Alicia jabbed the hooked tool through the cap and yanked the first strands of Nick's hair through the plastic.

"Ouch!" Nick frowned. "That hurts."

"Buck up," I told him. "Women go through this every day."

"Masochists."

"Keep complaining," I said, "and we'll wax your eyebrows, too."

Alicia continued to pull Nick's hair through the cap and, despite my threat about his brows, he continued to say "Ouch."

When she was done readying his hair, she began to apply the solution to the exposed strands, squeezing it out of the bottle.

"My Lord!" Nick waved a hand in front of his face. "That stuff stinks."

Alicia applied more solution. "What a whiner."

I set the timer for the prescribed amount of time. Nick was right. The bleaching solution did smell bad. "We'll be back."

Despite Nick's protests, we left him in the bathroom to process and went downstairs to pour ourselves a glass of moscato.

"Bring me a beer if you've got any!" Nick called down to us.

We returned a few minutes later, carrying our stem glasses and bringing Nick a bottle of his favorite beer, which I always kept on hand.

He took the bottle from me. "I think I'm high on these fumes. Much longer and all of my brain cells will be dead."

I grabbed my hand towel from the rack and waved it in front of him to clear the air. "Shut up and drink."

A few minutes later and—*ding!*—his time was up. He bent over and stuck his head in the sink. I shampooed the color solution out of his hair and wiped the splashes from the countertop. He dried his hair the best he could with a towel, and I blow-dried the rest of the moisture from it.

Nick's highlights now complete and his hair dry, it was time to give him a new style. Alicia picked up a comb and carefully looked over the products on the counter before selecting a light mousse. She turned back to Nick, sprayed a golf-ball-sized amount of mousse into her hand, and began to work it through his hair. She took his bangs, which normally lay casually across his forehead, and swept them up and over with the comb, then used her fingers to separate and tease the strands, pulling them to stiff points with hair wax. When she was satisfied, she locked the look in place with a thorough coating of the contraband extra-hold hairspray my boss, who wore her hair in a towering beehive, had given me. The stuff was imported from Shanghai and violated all kinds of safety codes for flammability and chemical content. That said, the spray did its job and then some. Nothing short of a nuclear explosion could move hair coated in the stuff.

Alicia stepped back to admire her handiwork. "What do you think?"

"Nice," I said. Nick didn't look like his usual self at all, but nonetheless the style worked on him.

Anne leaped up to the countertop and stretched her neck out to sniff Nick's hair. *Sniff-sniff.* Her eyes grew wide and she sneezed three times in quick succession—*snit-snit-snit*—before she catapulted herself from the counter and scampered off.

Nick turned, eyed himself in the mirror, and groaned. "I look like every other pretentious asshole in this city."

"You look stylish and trendy," I said. *Just like every other pretentious asshole in the city.*

Nick looked up at Alicia. "I'll never be able to do this on my own."

"Sure you will. I'll teach you." Alicia spent a moment showing Nick what she'd done so he could repeat the process tomorrow. "See? Just pluck at it. Easy peasy."

"If you say so." He turned to me. "Don't blame me if I look like some type of circus clown in the morning."

Armed with my mousse, wax, and hairspray, Nick left, giving me a good-bye kiss at the door.

Once he'd gone, I turned to Alicia. "I'll have to stay

at an apartment for a while to maintain my cover. Would you take care of the cats for me?"

"Of course," she said. "I'd be happy to."

"Thanks, Alicia."

She waved a dismissive hand. "That's what friends are for."

"And don't worry," I told her. "I won't let anything get in the way of your bridal shower this weekend."

We were expecting over a dozen women, including Alicia's mother, her future mother-in-law, friends of Alicia's from her temple, and several of our favorite co-workers from Martin & McGee, the accounting firm where Alicia was employed and where I'd worked, too, before leaving to join the IRS.

"Good," Alicia said. "Because if I don't get some of your mother's pecan pralines very soon I just might go into withdrawal."

My mother was famous for her pralines. And her spicy cornbread. And her blueberry pie. Seriously, there was nothing my mother couldn't make that didn't taste delicious. Unfortunately, I'd inherited none of her talent in the kitchen. That's why she was driving in from my childhood home in east Texas on Friday night to help me with the shower.

Alicia put her hands on my shoulders and looked me in the eye, her forehead creased with worry. "Be extra careful on this case, okay?"

Overcome with emotion, all I could do was bite my quivering lip and nod.

Alicia stepped toward me and gave me a tight hug.

*It's good to have friends.*

# chapter seven

# Taken for a Ride

I entered the federal building Tuesday morning with my new flaming red hair. After Nick had gone home last night, I'd colored my hair, too. I felt a bit conspicuous with my vibrant locks, but figured the new shade must work on me when the usual guards at security gave me a "Damn, girl!" and a "Wow!" If I didn't see these guys every morning, I might've taken their comments as harassment. But given that they'd been nothing but professional in the past, I accepted their assessments as compliments rather than come-ons.

"It's not too much?" I asked them.

Damn, Girl! cocked his head. "It's just the right amount of too much."

I continued on through the lobby to discover three older men near the elevators. One of the men wore gray dress slacks with a white short-sleeved shirt and shiny white buck shoes. He had thick glasses that distorted his eyes, making them appear huge and making me feel like I was looking at a fish in an aquarium. Despite being painfully thin and stooped, he was nonetheless pushing another man, who sat in a wheelchair.

The man in the wheelchair was dressed in baby-blue pajamas, a zebra-print fleece blanket tucked around him. The limp arm on his lap told me he'd suffered a stroke. His mouth hung slightly agape, though the side that wasn't paralyzed was curled up in a smile. The half-smile said that while his mouth might not work quite right anymore, his mind still functioned just fine.

The third man had his hands on the side bars of a metal walker with yellow tennis balls on the bottom of each foot. He wore elastic-waist nylon athletic pants, a matching jacket, and a pair of high-tech hearing aids affixed to the outer shell of his ear like a Bluetooth headset.

Goodness. They were like those "see no evil, hear no evil, speak no evil" monkeys.

As Hear No Evil leaned forward in his walker to take a look at the building directory posted on the wall, I stepped up to them. "Can I help you gentlemen?"

"You sure can," he said. "We need to find the IRS criminal investigations office."

"I'm going there myself." I punched the elevator's up-arrow button. "You can ride up with me. Do you have an appointment with an agent?"

"No," said See No Evil. "Do we need one?"

"Depends on what you're here for," I said.

"We want to meet with that woman who shot the drug dealer," See No said.

That would be me. Although my name hadn't been revealed in the newscasts or papers, the reporters had noted that it was a female special agent who'd shot and killed a member of the drug cartel. Got him right between the eyes from across a dark field. It was something I was both proud of and, admittedly, a little sickened by. I'd saved the lives of several undercover agents that night, including Nick's, but knowing I'd put an end to a life, even if it was a worthless one, still gnawed at me sometimes. Is the fact that I'd shot a person to death what defined me now? I hoped not. I'd like to think that I was a complex person, with all sorts of facets, and that I was more than one act taken on one day.

"Why her?" I asked as the elevator doors slid open and we stepped, and/or rolled, inside. If they wanted me to shoot someone for them, they were out of luck. I was a federal agent, not a mercenary for hire.

" 'Cause we need her to find a con artist who took us for a ride," Hear No told me, "and she obviously doesn't take any crap."

My lips curled up in a smile. Okay, so I was flattered by that particular comment.

The doors slid shut and the car began to ascend.

"You know her?" See No asked.

*Very well.* "I *am* her."

The standing men's mouths gaped along with their sitting friend's.

"No kidding?" See No said.

"No kidding."

He looked me up and down. "But you're just an itty-bitty thing."

"I'm taller than you." I put a flat hand on top of my head and moved it out in a simulated salute to show that he didn't quite reach it. "See?"

"That's only 'cause I can't stand up straight anymore," he said. "I used to be six feet two."

*Yikes.* Better add more calcium-rich kale and broccoli to my diet.

The elevator bell dinged as it stopped on my floor.

"Come with me." I motioned for them to follow me as the doors opened. "We can talk in my office."

We stepped off the elevator and started down the hall, the tennis balls on the feet of the walker giving off a soft thump with each step. As we approached my boss's office, she looked up from her desk. Lu's strawberry-blond beehive was coiffed to perfection today, standing tall and proud atop her head, shellacked with her contraband hairspray. Her thick false eyelashes and bright orange lipstick gave her an almost doll-like appearance, despite the fact that she was over sixty. She wore a lemon-yellow dress that, over her full, round figure, made her look like an oversized Peep.

Hear No Evil stopped mid-thump and let loose with a wolf whistle. "Who is that beauty?"

See No squinted behind his lenses. "Is she pretty? I can't tell."

From his wheelchair, Speak No issued a moan that said he agreed with his hearing-challenged friend. He offered Lu his best half-grin.

It was clear the men meant no harm and Lu looked more pleased than offended, her face blushing as pink as her cotton-candy-colored hair.

"She's my boss," I said. "Luella Lobozinski."

Lu stood from her chair and came out of her office. She smiled at the men and turned to me. "Who do we have here?"

"Um . . ." I realized I had no idea of these men's names.

The man with the hearing aids and walker released the bar and held out his hand. "Jeb Proctor," he said. "Mighty pleased to meet you, young lady."

Lu took his hand and gave him a coy smile. "I'm hardly a young lady. And I'm old enough to know better than to fall for some pickup line."

"You're young to me," he said. "I'll be eighty-nine in two months' time."

I chimed in now. "They told me someone ripped them off. I'm taking them down to my office to get the details."

"I'll come, too," Lu said, "see if I can be of any help." She eyed my flame-colored hair. "Love the new look, by the way."

Of course she would. The crazy color was on par with her own pinkish-orange locks.

"Thanks," I replied. "I'm still getting used to it."

We led the men down the hall to my office. When Nick looked up from his desk and realized I had several people who needed seating, he brought his two wing chairs from his space to mine.

My eyes went to his hair. Though his spiky style today wasn't quite as well coiffed as Alicia had managed to accomplish last night, he'd done a respectable job.

His eyes went to my hair, too, and a sexy grin played about his mouth. "I knew Burning Embers would be a good choice."

"I got two thumbs-up from security," I told him, "and compliments from Lu."

Our new hairstyles addressed, he moved on to more pressing matters. "I'm heading out in a few minutes to meet with the leasing agent."

*Good.* We needed to move the mobster case along as quickly as possible.

"How 'bout I pick up pizzas for lunch?" he offered.

The team of agents who'd be working the Fabrizio case planned to gather at noon in my office to get started. Surely they'd appreciate being fed. "That would be great, Nick. Thanks."

Once Nick had gone and the three men and Lu were seated, I plopped down in my desk chair.

The man with the glasses introduced himself as Harold Brinkley. "This is our buddy Isaiah." He hiked a thumb at their friend who was listing in the wheelchair.

"We're all residents in the Whispering Pines retirement community." He straightened his buddy and went on to tell me and Lu that not long ago, all of the residents had received a postcard mailer advertising charter van trips to various vacation spots. He reached into the pocket on the back of Isaiah's wheelchair, pulled out a postcard, and held it out to me.

I took the postcard from him. It featured a photo image of a slot machine with a red number seven in each of the three windows and silver quarters streaming from the coin dispenser. The text read:

TAKE YOUR NEXT GROUP TRIP WITH
TRIPLE 7 ADVENTURES!
TRAVEL IN LUXURY TO CASINOS IN
OKLAHOMA AND LOUISIANA
CALL (214) 555–5729 FOR DETAILS
www.777Adventures.com

"None of us can drive anymore," Harold said, "and we don't get out much, so we thought it would be fun for a bunch of us to get together and go on a gambling junket. One last hurrah, you know?"

Jeb waved a hand. "Pshaw. We've got lots more hurrahs."

I suspected Jeb was right. Despite his age, he seemed to have a lot of life left in him.

Harold went on. "We called the number on the card and the man who answered said he could come by and show us the van and make arrangements for us to take a trip. He said we'd need to pay him half down in cash to reserve the van, but that he'd provide us with a receipt."

Harold reached into the wheelchair's back pocket again and pulled out three pages folded in half. He handed those to me also. I opened them to find three handwritten receipts on preprinted paper with the same image from the postcard and the Triple 7 Adventures logo. According to the information written on the page, each of the men had paid $250 down for a package that was supposed to include transportation to and from the Choctaw Casino Resort in Durant, Oklahoma, as well as two nights' stay in the resort's Grand Tower, a daily buffet, and the guest's choice of spa service. The receipt was dated two months ago, in early March. The purported travel date was to occur in late April.

"I was looking forward to that massage," Harold said. "I've got a hitch in my giddyup." He put a hand on his hip to show us where the problem lay.

Jeb wagged his eyebrows at Lu. "I was going for the full-body sea salt scrub."

She wagged a finger right back at him. "You're a naughty boy, Jeb."

"When the man came to Whispering Pines," Harold continued, "he brought the van with him, even let us climb inside and see how nice and comfortable it was. It had comfy seats and a DVD player and everything. He said he'd even throw in a bottle of champagne for free."

I jotted a few notes on my pad.

Lu cocked her head, her beehive now leaning precariously to the left. "When did things go south?"

"When he didn't show up on the date of the trip," Harold said. "All fifteen of us were standing out front waiting with our luggage but he never showed. We called the phone number but it had been disconnected. Tried the Web site, too, and it was down. We phoned the Choctaw Casino. They said they'd never heard of Triple 7 Adventures and had nothing to do with the man who'd come to Whispering Pines."

Fifteen victims at $250 apiece meant the con artist had pocketed nearly four grand in a matter of minutes. The fact that he'd preyed on elderly victims, who generally tended to be more trusting, was especially egregious.

Jeb banged a fist on the arm of his walker. "We're not going to take this lying down." He glanced over at his friend in the wheelchair. "Sitting down, maybe. But not lying."

Nearly ninety and he hadn't lost his wit. *I hope I could say the same someday.*

"Any chance one of you got the van's license plate number when he came to Whispering Pines?" I asked.

"We didn't think to look," Jeb said.

"How about security?" Lu asked. "Does your community have video cameras?"

Harold's eyes narrowed in thought behind his thick lenses. "I believe there might be one over the front door. Is that right, Jeb?"

Jeb raised a shoulder. "Could be. Can't say for sure."

"What did the man look like?" I asked.

The men exchanged glances. Jeb shrugged.

"All I remember," Harold said, "was that he was wearing a cowboy hat and sunglasses."

I mulled things over for a moment. "I might be able to track the guy down through the phone number or Web site, but there are no guarantees. I'll do my best, though."

"That's all we ask," Harold said.

While Lu chatted with the men in my office, I trotted down the hall to the copy machine and made copies of the receipts and postcards.

When I returned to my digs, I handed the original paperwork back to Harold and obtained contact information for both him and Jeb. Isaiah was asleep so I didn't bother getting his phone number. "Lu and I will walk y'all back to the elevator."

My boss and I escorted the men back to the elevator bank and pushed the down-arrow button for them.

As the car arrived, Jeb reached out and took Lu's hand, raising it to his lips for a kiss. "I'll be looking forward to seeing you again, Miss Luella."

He gave me only a "Good-bye," no hand kiss.

"I'll be in touch as soon as I know something," I told the men.

When the doors slid closed, Lu turned to me and sighed. "Harold's white bucks remind me of Carl."

Carl was a man Lu had met a few months ago via an online dating service. He not only wore outdated leisure suits and shiny white patent leather bucks, but he sported the world's worst comb-over, which lay in an intricate basket-weave pattern across his scalp. But what he lacked in fashion sense he more than made up for in personality. He'd been sweet and doting, catering to Lu's every whim. But when he'd begun to talk marriage, it scared Lu off and she'd broken up with him. Looked like maybe she was regretting her decision to call it quits.

"You miss Carl?" I asked.

"Horribly," she admitted. "But I heard he's dating some young floozy now. She's only fifty-eight. That's practically robbing the cradle!"

"Have you told him how you feel?"

"No. I've got too much pride to go crawling back to him."

"There's no shame in admitting you made a mistake, Lu."

She sighed. "Maybe not. But if he's happier with the floozy and didn't take me back, I . . ." She paused as if collecting both her thoughts and her emotions. "I just don't think I could handle it."

"Come on." I waved a dismissive hand. "You're Lu Lobozinski. The Lobo. You can handle anything." After all, the woman had run herd over a dozen or more federal agents for years now and overseen the collection of hundreds of millions of tax dollars. She'd also battled lung cancer and won. And not just anyone could pull off a pink beehive. A minor setback in the romance department couldn't derail her, could it? I told her as much.

She sighed again. "Tax collection is a cinch compared to matters of the heart." With that, Lu turned and headed back to her office.

As I watched her walk off, I realized I had three missions now. One, take Tino Fabrizio and his violent empire down. Two, do what I could to track down the scammer who'd ripped off the residents of Whispering Pines. And three, reunite Lu and Carl.

# chapter eight

# Team Tara

I spent the rest of the morning snooping on my computer for information about Tino Fabrizio and Cyber-Shield.

According to the IRS records, Cyber-Shield Security Systems, Inc., had brought in a little over two million in gross billings last year. Tino had been paid $200,000 in salary. Respectable, but not excessive given that he owned the business and oversaw its operations. A look at the W-2 filings told me that twenty-two men, presumably salesmen, installers, and security patrolmen, had been paid amounts ranging from forty to seventy grand each. The only woman on his payroll earned a relatively modest $35,000. My assumption was she worked as Tino's administrative assistant. I wondered if she also handled his bookkeeping, and if she did, whether she was involved in laundering money for him. Eric Echols, the tech expert Agent Hohenwald had referenced, had earned a cool $150K.

I spent some time looking further into each of Cyber-Shield's employees, snooping online to determine whether any of them owned unusually expensive cars, boats, or homes relative to the income they'd reported on their individual returns. When people lived beyond their visible means, it often meant they had received unreported cash income. If one of Tino's staff owned assets that were out of line with his reported earnings, it could mean Tino was paying the employee cash under the table to coerce and threaten his clients, or maybe splitting the protection payments the employee collected on Tino's behalf. If I could find such telltale information, it would help us to know which Cyber-Shield employee we should focus our surveillance on.

A preliminary search indicated that one of Tino's installers owned a suspiciously pricey home in the Lake Highlands area. A little further digging revealed that he'd inherited the place from his deceased grandmother, and that he owned only a one-third share, with his two siblings owning equivalent shares. No other immediate red flags caught my eye. Either the men doing Tino's dirty work weren't officially on his payroll, or they weren't spending their dirty money conspicuously. Perhaps they were using the cash to pay for everyday things like groceries and clothing and entertainment, or maybe they were stockpiling it, saving it up for something special.

I turned my attention back to Cyber-Shield's return. After salaries, much of the company's remaining income was paid out for auto maintenance, utilities, supplies, and other standard office expenses, leaving a small net corporate income. Nothing about the return raised any immediate questions in my mind.

I took a second look at the restaurant's tax returns next, willing the numbers to talk to me. Alas, they were silent. Did the return include only the restaurant's earnings? Or was Tino's dirty money being funneled through the bistro? I hoped to figure things out soon so we could quickly nail the guy. *Nail. Ugh.* There was that word again. The thought of that nail-gun incident had me cringing with phantom pain.

I took a look at the Fabrizios' personal tax returns, too. Interestingly, Benedetta and Tino filed separate tax returns. Because spouses filing separate returns were denied a multitude of tax benefits, most married couples filed a joint return. Those who didn't were generally couples who were having marital problems or who'd married later in life and kept their finances separate. On occasion, a taxpayer who suspected his or her spouse of financial shenanigans would file a separate return so as not to be implicated in any tax fraud that might be committed by the spouse.

Did the separate returns in this case mean that Benedetta suspected Tino was up to no good? Or had Tino insisted on separate returns to distance himself from his wife and her bistro so that there'd be one less connection between him and laundered funds?

Of course some couples could benefit from separate returns because splitting their income would allow them to avoid the so-called marriage penalty that applied at the higher income levels. Perhaps their reason for filing separate returns was as simple and benign as that.

I stared at the information on my screen. "If only you numbers could talk."

I looked over both of the personal returns. Other than the fact that the two had filed separately, nothing seemed out of the ordinary or raised any immediate suspicions. Perhaps Tino Fabrizio had properly reported all of his income, even the dirty funds generated through threats and shakedowns. Still, I had my doubts. People who were shady in one area were often shady in another. And if he had reported the extorted funds, he hadn't identified them as such. There was no entry on the "other income" line of his tax return identifying "extortion earnings."

Though my role in this joint investigation was to search for evidence of Tino's financial crimes rather than his violent ones, the two were inextricably linked. I decided to do a little more digging into Eric Echols. If someone had truly doctored the video footage recorded at the bar owned by Alex Harris and his wife, it could have been Echols. While Tino himself might have the tech skills to tamper with the video, I suspected he had someone else do his technical dirty work just as he had someone else do his physical dirty work, at least where his clients were concerned. That way he could maintain plausible deniability if law enforcement came sniffing around.

I logged into the Texas DMV site and pulled up Echols's driver's license. According to the data, Echols was twenty-six years old. Given that four years of W-2s had been filed by Cyber-Shield, reporting wages paid to Echols, Tino must have hired him right out of college. The address on the license told me Echols lived in an apartment a few miles north of Cyber-Shield.

I clicked the mouse to enlarge his photo. Staring back at me from the screen was the king of all nerds. Echols had messy hair in a bland color akin to Parmesan cheese. He could really use a trim. His skin was pale, too, his eyes were bulbous and buggy, and his chin was so weak it appeared as if his mouth were simply part of his neck. He wore a wrinkled shirt, one side of his collar bent at an odd angle.

Though Echols appeared to be a classic computer geek, he did own that nice car. A search of the vehicle registrations confirmed that the '65 Mustang Fastback was listed in his name. Looked like the nerd had an inner bad boy.

A quick peek at his Facebook page told me he had a degree in computer science from the California Institute of Technology, one of the top-rated programs in the country. Some kind of supergeek genius, probably. It also told me he had only three friends, and one of those was his mother. An introvert, apparently. He'd posted nothing new since graduating from college. His posts before then were few and far between, and consisted solely of links to photos or articles featuring new technologies.

The smell of tomato sauce, melted cheese, and garlic preceded Nick when he came to my office a few minutes before noon with three large pizza boxes stacked in his arms. "Good news," he said, setting the pizzas on my desk and pulling a set of keys out of his pocket. "I got the lease."

"Great!" So far so good. Things were going according to plan.

"The previous tenant must have been a Cyber-Shield customer," he said. "There's a Cyber-Shield sticker on the front window and a camera mounted on the back wall."

*Damn.* Tino Fabrizio had eyes everywhere. The fact that Tino could so easily spy on us would make it harder to spy on him, but disconnecting the camera could raise his suspicions. The members of our joint task force would have to be careful not to be spotted.

"Assume the camera is still functional," I said. "Better to play it safe."

"We will. Luckily, the back office looked clean. I didn't see any cameras there. Josh can operate from that space."

"Good."

A minute later, Josh stepped into my office.

I looked up at him. "Did you call the tech guy at the FBI?"

He nodded. "Once everyone gets here I'll fill the team in."

Hana Kim arrived next, bringing her usual anything-boys-can-do-girls-can-do-better attitude. A Korean-American with a stout build, Hana boasted a batting

average that would not only make a minor league baseball player proud, but also made her a star on the IRS
softball team, the Tax Maniacs. She could be brash and
outspoken, like me, but her record of successfully resolved cases showed that she had the smarts and tenac-
ity to get the job done, also like me.

Eddie and Will were the last of the team members to
arrive. Both men were African-American, both were
family men with wives and children, and both were very
intelligent. Eddie was taller and thinner, though, and could
on occasion be a real smartass. Will, on the other hand,
tended to be more polite and professional, which meant
he was a little less fun though every bit as capable.

Nick rolled his desk chair across the hall from his office, while the rest of the group gathered in the chairs
we'd rounded up earlier for the gang from Whispering
Pines. We ate pizza straight from the box, drank sodas
straight from the can, and discussed tactics.

After filling them in on Tino's violent background,
both in Chicago and Dallas, I looked around the group.
"Although it's clear Tino sometimes hires outside help, the
FBI has speculated that the security firm's patrolmen
might have committed some of the crimes against Cyber-
Shield's clients."

I told the group that if the discussion Hohenwald and
I had with Alex Harris was any indication, Tino's typical
tactic was to first send a salesmen to the targeted client
to recommend they sign on for additional services . . .
*or else.*

"If what happed with Harris is Tino's standard MO,
then the salesmen are the ones who make the threats and
demand the protection payments. Since Harris refused to
pay and none of the other victims were willing to rat out
Tino to the police, we can only speculate how much
Tino's bringing in and how the payments are collected.

But my guess is that the salesmen or patrolmen collect the protection money. We need to keep a close eye on Tino, but we'll also need to focus surveillance efforts on both the patrol units and the salesmen. Any of them could be shuttling cash for Fabrizio."

My eyes scanned the group, each of whom nodded or raised a chin to indicate understanding.

"If a salesman visits a business or person who isn't yet a Cyber-Shield client," I pointed out, "chances are the salesman is just trying to get them to sign up for a standard security package. But if the salesman goes to a business or individual who is already a client, he might be trying to extort money from them or collecting protection payments."

Of course it was also possible that the salesman could simply be checking up on things, making a courtesy call to promote goodwill.

I told them about the tax filings for the Fabrizios and Cyber-Shield. "The couple's personal income tax return and security company's earnings didn't seem out of line, so it looks like the extorted funds aren't being reported on either of those returns."

Eddie cocked his head. "So this is an evasion case? Failure to report?"

"Possibly," I said. "But the bistro's tax returns reported at least twice what a successful restaurant its size could be expected to earn. I suspect that Tino might be laundering the extorted funds through the bistro."

Of course Benedetta Fabrizio might have earned her pennies with her penne, but the only way to find out for sure was to get inside.

"I'll apply for the job at Benedetta Fabrizio's restaurant," I continued. "If I don't get it, Hana can try." Hana was in her late twenties, like me, but could likewise pass herself off as an older college student looking for a part-time gig. "Eddie and Will can coordinate with the FBI surveillance team to follow the installers, salesmen, and patrol cars. Depending on whether Hana or I get the job at the bistro, we can help with surveillance, too. Josh and Nick will operate from the gallery space. Nick will keep an eye on Tino and his men, and can let the others on the task force know when they see Cyber-Shield's cars leaving the office."

I gestured to Josh. "Josh's primary job will be to try to hack into Cyber-Shield's system. If he can get in, we can download the company's financial data and look for evidence of tax fraud."

Josh chimed in now. "I've spoken with the FBI tech team who's been working this case. They told me Cyber-Shield has a high-tech surveillance expert on its staff."

"Eric Echols," I said.

"That's him," Josh replied. "We're going to have to be especially careful with our communications or their guy could hack us and figure out that we're after Fabrizio." He went on to tell the team the same thing that Hohenwald had told me. "An expert hacker can get into anything with Wi-Fi access, even if the device isn't actively connected to the Internet. You'll need to make sure the Wi-Fi and Bluetooth are turned off on all of your unsecured devices anytime you're tailing one of Fabrizio's men or within a mile of Cyber-Shield or any of its customers."

"Hold on a minute." Will arched a questioning brow. "Wi-Fi range can go a full mile?"

"Yes," Josh said. "With a chain of routers and extenders, it could theoretically go on forever. But a mile would be a safe bet. The FBI is going to send over a set of secure radios for the team members who will be following Tino and his men, as well as new phones for all of us to use for normal purposes and for contacting each other. We'll need to add each other as contacts in case of an emergency, but be sure not to use anyone's real name or alias in your contacts list just in case Fabrizio somehow gets hold of one of our phones. And don't record an outgoing voice-mail message. Just use the default with the phone number. Be sure to regularly delete any texts and the list of recent calls, too. We can't take any chances."

"Since it'll be difficult and risky to communicate by phone," I said, "let's meet up Sunday afternoon at four o'clock for updates. Does that work for everyone?" I scanned the group again. Everyone nodded or murmured their agreement.

"We can meet at my place," Hana said. She lived in a condo near the Galleria, which would be relatively convenient for everyone.

"That would be great, Hana," I said. "Thanks."

She leaned back in her chair, a hand crooked behind her head. "I think we should come up with a cool name for the case. You know, like the Manhattan Project or Stargate or Fast and Furious."

Eddie snorted. "Fast and Furious was a dismal failure."

"Well, *we* won't be," Hana said.

I wasn't sure we needed a name, but I had to admit the idea got me more excited about the investigation. It would give us a rallying cry, like "Remember the Alamo" or "Tippecanoe and Tyler Too." "How about the Penne Pursuit?" I suggested.

Hana shook her head. "Too cheesy."

Eddie chimed in next. "The Macaroni Mission."

"Uck." Hana cringed. "That's even worse."

Nick's offering of Tortellini Taskforce got a double uck and a full grimace.

Will tossed out another idea. "Operation Italian Takeout?"

Hana pulled her hand from behind her head and pointed a finger at Will. "That's it."

I looked over my team. As the lead on Operation Italian Takeout, I was responsible for my fellow agents whom I'd brought into the case. Their lives would be in my hands. Problem was, my hands were shaking. I knew each of them was going into this case willingly, and that they were highly skilled, but I'd also seen images of the type of horrifying, heinous acts Tino Fabrizio was capable of. If any of my coworkers ended up impaled on a fence post, with a face full of nails, or crushed to death, I'd never forgive myself.

"Any questions?" I asked.

Hana raised a hand. "Can I take the leftover pizza home?"

I looked to Nick. He was the one who'd sprung for lunch, after all.

"Knock yourself out," Nick said.

We wrapped up our meeting, Hana grabbed the pizza box, and we all returned to our offices.

While Nick's new identity had been expedited so that he could secure the lease at the building near Cyber-Shield, I'd had to wait on mine. Late that afternoon, my new identity arrived via courier. The large cardboard box came complete with a driver's license, resume, and the keys to both a car and an apartment. I was now Tori Holland, a twenty-four-year-old part-time student at Dallas Baptist University, majoring in business administration. They'd done a good job of making my alias as close to the real me as possible. The name sounded similar, and the fact that I had actually studied accounting in college would make me able to speak the language should anyone question me. The packet included three used college textbooks and a schedule of my classes at DBU. I'd have to attend, at least until I was sure none of Fabrizio's thugs was following me. According to the schedule, I was signed up for Managerial Cost Accounting, Global Marketing, and Introduction to Linguistics.

*What the heck is linguistics?*

I supposed I'd find out.

According to my transcript, I was merely an average student, my cumulative GPA a 2.8. *Gee, thanks, FBI.* At least they'd given me a new laptop, one that was clean and devoid of any data that would link me to the IRS. The package also included a new cell phone with a bright pink cover. I'd disabled the Wi-Fi and Bluetooth on my government-issued phone to prevent Fabrizio and his men from being able to access it, but I'd leave those functions enabled on my new phone so as not to raise their suspicions. This meant I'd have to be careful with my communications, while at the same time using my phone as a real college student would.

The information included in the box listed the phone numbers for the new cell phones of all members of Operation Italian Takeout, both IRS and FBI. I entered them in my contacts list, giving them nicknames with flip-flopped first and last initials that would identify them to nobody other than myself. Burt Hohenwald became Hayden Beale. Nick Pratt became Pat Nix. Hana Kim became Kimberly Hannigan. Eddie Bardin was now Bart Edwards. William Dorsey became Donald Waltham. And Josh Schmidt morphed into Sam Jacobs.

I wrote DO NOT DISTURB on a Post-it note and slapped it on the outside of my office door, closing it behind me. Using my new pink cell phone, I dialed the number for Benedetta's Bistro.

A woman answered on the third ring. "Benedetta's Bistro," she said. "How can I help you?"

"I saw your ad for help in your window and wanted to see if I could arrange an interview."

"Just a second," the woman said. There was a shuffling sound as she apparently covered the receiver. "Hey, Ma!" I heard her yell. "There's someone on the phone about the job." There was muffled conversation in the background, and the woman came back on the line. "She wants to know if you have any food service experience."

Per my new resume, I'd been a nanny for a family who had three children. Surely that had involved some cooking and kitchen cleanup. "Yes," I told the woman on the phone. "I'm experienced."

"Hold on." There was more muffled conversation, and the woman came back on the line. "Can you come in tomorrow at eleven?"

"That's perfect."

"What's your name?"

"Tori Holland," I replied, pleased at how easily my new name rolled off my tongue.

"Okay. Got you down, Tori."

With the tough job market, there was likely to be some competition for the position. I crossed my fingers that I'd ace the interview and land the job.

# chapter nine

# Who Do You Love?

That evening, Nick and I had dinner together at his place one last time before going undercover. Neither of us could predict how long this investigation might last, and how long we'd be apart. I could only hope the intensive surge we'd planned would lead to quick arrests.

Nick's Australian shepherd mix, Daffodil, shared our meal of barbecue, even indulging in some potato salad and cole slaw. According to the volunteer who'd handled the paperwork when Nick adopted the dog, Daffy had been nearly starved when she'd been brought to the animal shelter. Perhaps that accounted for her willingness to eat virtually anything. The only thing I'd seen her turn down was an olive.

"Daffodil!" I called to get her attention. "Catch." I tore a piece from my dinner roll and tossed it in her direction. She snapped it out of the air with ease, licking her lips when she was done. I loved my cats, but I had to admit that dogs could be fun, too.

"What's your new identity?" Nick asked, taking a sip

from his bottle of Shiner Bock. "Terry Hollandaise? Tamara Hollowpoint?"

Fortunately, the FBI hadn't named me after a creamy sauce or a type of bullet.

"Tori Holland," I told him. "I'm a former nanny and mediocre part-time business student at DBU. I carry a pink cell phone now." I pulled it out and waved it. "What about you?"

Nick showed me his new phone. Unlike my girlie phone, his was a sophisticated silver model. He reached into his wallet, pulled out a business card, and handed it to me. It read GALLERY NICO in a silver script font across the top of the card. The words NICOLAS J. BRANDT, ART DEALER appeared in smaller, blue letters in the bottom right corner, along with the gallery's address on north Fitzhugh and his phone number.

"Fancy schmancy," I said.

"I know." Nick raised his bottle. "I might have to trade in my beer for a cheeky chardonnay."

When we were done eating, Daffodil and I followed Nick up to his room and helped him pack his suitcases. Like me, he'd be moving into a new place, just in case Tino's men decided to delve into the identity of their new business neighbor.

"The FBI got me and Josh a two-bedroom place together," he said. "It'll be less expensive that way, and safer, too."

I tried not to dwell on the fact that I'd be on my own at my new apartment, with no one to watch my back. I was well trained and capable, sure, but Tino and his men were no slouches, either.

Nick laid his two suitcases on the bed and opened them. Daffy hopped up on the bed and settled between them, draping her furry head over the edge of the smaller one. Nick put the new clothes I'd help him select into the larger suitcase, while I rummaged through his closet, pushing hangers aside on the rack, looking through his existing wardrobe for his most unusual items. It wasn't easy. Nick tended to wear western-cut shirts, jeans, and boots during off-hours.

"You know," I said, "you could probably just add a touch of flair to some of your usual clothes to change your look a little. A scarf or an arrowhead necklace or something like that would go a long way. I've probably got some things at my place you could use."

"So I'm cross-dressing now?"

I rolled my eyes. "It's not like you'll be wearing my underwear."

"Thank God. All that lace has got to be itchy."

"It is." Little did he know I only wore the lace panties when I knew we'd be fooling around and they wouldn't be staying on long. The rest of the time I wore comfy cotton granny panties. Comfortable underwear was one of the hidden benefits of working undercover.

Nick added his shaving kit to his smaller suitcase and zipped both bags shut. *Zzzzip. Zzzip.* He set the bags upright on the floor next to the bed, grabbed my hand, and flopped back on the bed, taking me with him. "Come here, you."

We lay side by side, looking into each other's eyes, neither of us speaking for a moment or two. Finally, he reached out and brushed back an errant lock of my newly red hair from my cheek. "Let's bust this guy fast. I don't like being away from you."

I didn't like it, either. But it was the price we paid. Besides, maybe we could find some time to sneak away and get together during the investigation. It couldn't be anywhere public, though, or we'd risk being discovered.

He leaned toward me and pressed his lips to mine, just as he'd done a thousand times before. And just as it had done a thousand times before, my heart shimmied in my chest.

I was crazy about Nick. He wasn't perfect, of course. But I could live with his stubbornness, his occasional snoring, his weekend fishing trips in the spring and summer. Still, I knew that if he and I settled down and started a family someday, one or both of us would have to make some sacrifices, at least where our careers as special agents were concerned. You couldn't take a kid on a late-night stakeout. After all, those baby carriers that strapped to your chest weren't made of Kevlar. One of us would likely have to take a desk job or transfer to the auditing department.

But no sense worrying about that, right? After all, Nick and I weren't even engaged . . . *yet*.

Nick's kisses grew more insistent, and his hands began to roam over my body, touching, caressing, removing clothing. Daffy watched us for a moment or two, a furry canine voyeur, then decided our show wasn't all that interesting. She'd seen it before, knew the script. With a jingle of her tags, she hopped down from the bed and went in search of a chew toy.

Nick and I made love, taking our time, knowing it could be days or weeks before we'd be able to be intimate again. We savored each second, each sensation, the sensual release our interlude gave us.

Afterward, we lay in each other's arms for a long moment, simply enjoying the companionship, until I finally looked at the clock.

"It's after nine," I said. "I need to get packed, too."

He returned the favor, coming down to my place and helping me fill my suitcases. I dug though my jewelry box and found a necklace made of small white rocks that I'd had since my summer camp days back in junior high.

With Nick's western shirts, though, the necklace would be right at home. I also found a basic unisex black scarf.

He took the items from me but scowled. "I thought being a man meant I didn't have to accessorize."

"That's not so true anymore," I said. "Get with the times."

I went through my things, choosing garments that would be appropriate for a nanny-turned-college-student. Blue jeans. Tennis shoes. T-shirts. I also packed some fun items. A pair of stilettos and a shimmery blouse, both in red, my signature color. Black ballet flats, black leggings, and a polka-dot tunic. A sundress in a pale blue and white print.

Stepping to the back of my closet, I unlocked the gun cabinet Nick had bought me for Valentine's Day—*the guy knows me so well*—and retrieved a handgun and some ammunition from my extensive personal collection. My Glock would identify me as law enforcement, but the cherry-red Cobra CA380 I'd picked up secondhand at a pawnshop wouldn't raise any flags if Fabrizio or one of his henchmen happened to notice it. It wasn't unusual for a young woman living alone in a big city like Dallas to own a handgun for protection.

When my suitcases were full, Nick carried them downstairs and put them in my new undercover car, a basic 2007 black Hyundai Elantra, complete with a DBU student parking decal on the back window, a chink in the windshield, and a dent on the back right fender.

He pulled me to him and held me close, resting his chin on top of my head. "I love you, *Tori Holland*."

"Back at you, *Nicolas J. Brandt*."

# chapter ten

# The Interview

It was well after eleven by the time I went to bed and I slept fitfully, worried about my interview in the morning. I had to get this job, get on the inside. The case could depend on it. I also couldn't help but be nervous about getting closer to Tino Fabrizio. The guy was a sick, sadistic bastard, and images of the photographs Detective Booth had shown me kept playing through my mind. I curled up in a ball and pulled the covers up over my head. Some tough federal agent I was, huh?

Wednesday morning came, bringing with it dark circles under my eyes. Fortunately, a thick stroke of concealer sufficiently hid them. I dressed in a pair of slacks and a white blouse accessorized with a necklace of black beads. My feet found their way into my ass-kicking cherry-red Dr. Martens, and a mug of hot coffee found its way into my belly, both serving to bolster my confidence. I'd put dozens of men behind bars and lived to brag about it. Tino Fabrizio might be a brutal killer, but he'd met his match in Tara Holloway.

*Ah, the wonders of caffeine and steel-toed footwear.*

Downstairs, I gave Henry a snuggle, which he tried his best to wriggle out of, and a kiss on the head, which he tried to duck, before returning him to his perch atop the TV cabinet. Anne, on the other hand, welcomed my affections and even rubbed the top of her head across my chin and purred for me.

"I'm going to miss you, baby girl," I told her, doing my best to ignore the tight squeeze in my chest. I laid her down on the couch and glanced up at Henry, who was scowling down at me, still pissed off about that smooch I'd forced on him. "I'm going to miss you, too, Henry. Though I really don't know why."

Alicia was a little misty, too. "I hate it when you go on these dangerous jobs. Each time you leave I wonder if it will be the last time I see you."

Heck, I wondered the same thing.

"You'll see me Saturday," I reassured her—*and myself.* "And after that I'll stay in touch by e-mail."

She gave me a hug. "Stay safe."

"I will. I've got my Cobra. I'll be back here before you know it." Or at least I hoped I would. Given the horrific ways in which Tino Fabrizio had dispatched the men who'd worked for him, I could only imagine the creative killing method he might use on a federal law enforcement officer. *Eeek.* Better not to think about it.

I climbed into my Elantra and headed to the Swiss Avenue Historic District. As I cruised down Fitzhugh, I slowed to take a closer look at Cyber-Shield and the bistro. It was just a quarter past seven, and there were no cars at the restaurant. Understandable given that the place didn't serve breakfast and it was too early for the lunch staff to be on duty yet. At Cyber-Shield, however, I spotted a patrolman climbing out of a neon-green patrol car. Presumably, he'd worked an overnight shift and was winding things up now. Several other patrol cars sat in the lot, their drivers already off duty. Nothing appeared out of the ordinary.

I drove on to my new apartment. It was a small one-bedroom unit on the second floor of an older complex on Bennett Avenue, not far from Cyber-Shield. The place was minimally furnished with a couple of stools at the breakfast bar, a cheap couch and secondhand coffee table in the living room, and only a dresser and a full-sized bed with no headboard in the bedroom. The lack of furnishings would make my stay here less comfortable, but the meager spread did make me look like an authentic college student who had to watch her pennies. At least the place had a decent-sized television, cable, and a DVR. I would definitely miss having my cats for company, but I didn't dare risk their lives by dragging them along on this investigation.

I noticed the apartment had a landline phone in the kitchen. With my new cell phone, a landline seemed redundant and unnecessary, but I supposed it couldn't hurt to have one as a backup. It was an old-fashioned model with a cord, a virtual relic these days. It crossed my mind that the FBI had likely installed this type of phone for a reason. It was probably much harder for someone to tap into a conversation on this type of phone than it would be on a cordless model, which offered a limited number of frequencies.

I unpacked my things, stashed my suitcases in the bedroom closet, and made a quick trip to a nearby grocery store to stock up on essentials. Bread. Peanut butter. Oreos. Toilet paper. *Vogue.* I also bought three spiral notebooks and a backpack.

My menial tasks completed, my mind turned to the job interview scheduled for a mere hour from now, and my anxiety began to build. Could I pull it off? Convince the restaurant staff that I was a college student/ex-nanny? I wasn't so worried about the college student part. My stature made me look younger than I really was and it had only been a few years since I'd graduated from the University of Texas. But the nanny role had me a little pensive. I'd spent some time with my nieces and nephews over the years, but admittedly it was always doing fun things like decorating Christmas cookies, or playing hide-and-seek, or shooting BB guns in the backyard. The instant they began to misbehave I'd turn them over to my brothers and their wives to take care of the discipline.

*What to do . . .*

It couldn't hurt to watch a quick episode of *Nanny 911* on Netflix, right? It might help me better get into character.

I logged into Netflix. Halfway through the show I thought, *Holy hell!* I never knew kids could be such boogers.

I decided the two fictional children I'd helped to raise would be nothing like the kids in the show. Rather, Miles and Tessa were virtual angels, their worst habits being that Miles tended to misplace his shoes and Tessa could be a bit grouchy in the mornings, the silly pumpkin.

I arrived ten minutes early for my eleven o'clock interview. As I pulled into the parking lot, I spotted Josh standing outside the window of what would become Gallery Nico. He was using a stencil and silver paint to etch the name of the gallery on the glass. Through the window, I could see Nick inside. He and a man I didn't recognize appeared to be poring over an assortment of painted canvases. The man was likely an artist wanting to place his work for sale at the gallery. I was glad to see that things were moving along quickly. The sooner the gallery was up and running, the sooner Josh and Nick could devote one hundred percent of their efforts to hacking into the Fabrizios' computer systems, downloading their financial records, and finding and following the

money trails. All, of course, with the aim of putting
Tino Fabrizio behind bars for good.

I parked my Elantra in the center of the shopping center's parking lot. I figured it would appear courteous and
thoughtful if I left the angled spaces directly in front of
Benedetta's Bistro open for potential customers, though
it was unlikely she'd have many this early. She'd obviously
chosen a slow time in which to conduct the interview.

I'd turned off the Wi-Fi and Bluetooth on my IRS cell
phone earlier, but I also turned it to silent now. I locked
it in the glove compartment of my car for safekeeping.
My new pink cell phone peeked out from the side pocket
of the cute cross-body bag I'd chosen for today. It was one
I'd used back in college so I figured it would be perfect
for my new persona, Tori Holland.

As I stepped out of my car, several things caught my
eye. The first things I noticed were Tino's Alfa Romeo
and Eric Echols's Mustang parked directly in front of
Cyber-Shield's offices next door. Heck, my hair was virtually the same color as Tino's car. The second thing I
noticed was the security camera mounted over the entrance to the bistro. Though the camera was white, the
side bore the lime-green Cyber-Shield logo. The third
thing I noticed was another young woman exiting the bistro. She carried no leftovers, only a portfolio notebook,
and was dressed to impress in a black fitted skirt, gray
blouse, and heels. Had she come here for an interview?
Had she gotten the job? I felt a little guilty hoping she'd
bombed the interview, but I obviously needed this job
more than she did. After all, I was both a federal agent
trying to bust a murderous tax cheat and a starving
ex-nanny with tuition bills to pay.

I tucked the manila folder containing my resume under my arm and walked to the door, wondering if someone were watching me through the security camera. I felt

very self-conscious, aware of every movement of my body, every molecule of oxygen flowing in and out of my lungs. It was like being an insecure, pubescent junior-high girl all over again. God, I hoped my steps didn't look as stiff as they seemed to me. I tried to appear relaxed and natural, forcing a light smile to my face.

I pulled open the door and stepped inside, welcomed by the sound of opera music and the mouthwatering scents of garlic, tomato sauce, and freshly baked bread. A glance upward told me there was a second security camera mounted just over the door on the inside, too. Every movement in or around this place seemed to be captured on video.

My eyes scanned the bistro. An empty hostess podium stood just inside the door, a small placard on top asking customers to PLEASE WAIT TO BE SEATED. Three booths ran along the left wall, with another three on the right wall. The center of the room contained eight square, wooden tables in two rows of four, each table surrounded by four chairs. The tables bore green tablecloths and white napkins. A single red rose in a glass vase and a white vo-tive candle sat in the center of each table, along with salt and pepper shakers, shakers of parmesan cheese and dried red peppers, and a small bowl containing packets of sugar and assorted artificial sweeteners.

At the back of the dining room was a refrigerated case featuring the bistro's dessert offerings, including an Italian cream cake, tiramisu, some type of raspberry-filled doughnutlike pastry, and the *pièce de résistance*—or should I say the piece that I could not resist?—a tray of scrumptious-looking chocolate cannolis. My salivary glands instantly activated, and my stomach sat up and took notice, emitting a soft rumble. Each dessert was situated on a white plate and garnished for optimum pre-sentation, the cream cake with a trio of walnut halves, the doughnut with a fresh raspberry, and the cannolis with chocolate chips.

To the right, the case gave way to a well-stocked bar with six padded stools. A computerized cash register sat on the back of the bar, a third security camera mounted directly over it, the lens aimed down at the machine. It reminded me of the ceiling-mounted cameras over the gaming tables in casinos, put there to ensure that the dealers and players didn't try to pull a fast one with the cash or chips. With a virtual eye on them, employees of the bistro would be stupid to try to steal from the register.

A hallway at the back left of the dining room led to the restrooms, while a hallway at the far right appeared to lead to the kitchen. Only one customer was in the bistro, a tall, thin blonde in classy business attire, sipping water as she checked e-mails on her tablet.

A twentyish woman with dark, flowing hair, full lips, and a voluptuous build packed into a tight black dress came out of the swinging door that led to the kitchen. She carried a Caesar salad over to the blonde, setting it in front of her and asking whether she'd like some freshly ground pepper. After a few turns of the pepper mill, the young woman spotted me and made her way over, weaving her way gracefully through the tables. A gold cross on a chain rested between her breasts. "May I help you?" she asked.

"Hi," I said. "I'm Tori Holland. I'm here for an interview."

"Oh, yes," she said, her tone courteous. "My mother is expecting you." She held out a hand to indicate the far booth. "Have a seat there. I'll let her know you've arrived."

While I took a seat, she checked in again with the customer, refilling her water glass from a pitcher she retrieved from behind the bar. I surreptitiously watched the girl as she worked. Presumably she was one of Tino's daughters. I wondered whether she had any idea what her father was up to.

When she finished pouring the water, she disappeared into the kitchen. A moment later, the door swung open again to release a middle-aged version of the young woman. They had the same voluptuous build, the same full lips, the same dark hair. While her daughter's hair flowed halfway down her back, however, Benedetta's locks flowed only to her shoulders. Benedetta, too, wore a cross on a chain, though hers was silver. The religious symbol, nestled as it was between her big bazoombas, was simultaneously reassuring and disturbing.

"Miss Holland?" she asked as she approached me.

I stood from the booth and extended my hand. "That's me." *Or at least who I'm pretending to be.* "Hi."

"Benedetta Fabrizio." Her voice carried a hint of both Italian and Chicago accents, and her big brown eyes seemed warm and friendly. "Please, have a seat."

I sat back down and opened the manila folder I'd laid on the table. I removed my resume and references, and held them out to her. "I thought you might like to see these."

She raised a palm. "Paper won't tell me who you are, *cara.* Let's have a conversation." She glanced at the bar. "Can I get you a glass of wine? Some *vino* always makes conversation more interesting."

"Bored you already, have I?"

She chuckled but eyed me intently. "A sense of humor. Always a good thing in a waitress. Now how about that wine?"

I wasn't sure what to say to that. Was this some type of test? Should I decline in order to maintain my professionalism? Or should I show an interest in the bistro's wine selections?

I decided to go with, "I'd love to sample your favorite selection." That way, it sounded as if I were trying the wine as a way to familiarize myself with her tastes.

"Nice try." Benedetta tilted her head and offered me a playful smile. "My favorite wine is sixty dollars a bottle. You'll get the house red."

I offered her a smile right back. "I'm sure it will be delightful."

Her eyes narrowed now. "Would you tell me if it wasn't?"

Again, I felt as if she were testing me. Did she want a waitress who was always upbeat and positive? Or did she want one who was honest? I went with, "If it wasn't, I'd find a polite way to tell you. But only if you asked for my opinion."

She chuckled again. "Such diplomacy. You should go to work for the United Nations."

She stood, went to the bar, and poured two glasses of wine from the same bottle, returning with them a moment later. She placed one glass in front of me and resumed her seat on the other side of the booth. She held her glass in her left hand, a diamond the size of an olive glittering on her ring finger. I wondered if the oversized gem had been bought with extorted funds.

I took a sip of the wine. "It's lovely." Actually, it was a bit too dry for my taste, which tended more toward fruity and sweet, but I wasn't about to insult her by telling her that. Besides, I still wasn't sure where she fell on the upbeat-versus-honesty thing.

"Isn't it, though?" Benedetta took a sip herself and tossed her head in the direction of the kitchen. "When you called the other day, you told Stella you have experience in restaurants. Tell me about it."

"What I meant is that I have experience in preparing

and serving food. I worked for several years as a nanny for a family with two children."

The woman frowned. "So you made peanut butter and jelly sandwiches. Cookies. Scooped ice cream into bowls."

"Sometimes," I said, "but I also helped out with the family's meals, and I assisted with the cooking and serving when the family threw parties, which was quite often."

She leaned her head one way then the other, as if considering my words. "Why are you no longer working for this family?"

"The father works for an oil company," I told her. "He accepted a position in Dubai. They asked me to move there with them, but I'm not ready to be so far from home."

"You're close to your family?"

"I am," I said. "I'm an only child and it didn't seem right to go off and leave my parents."

"Good girl." She reached across the table and patted my hand before taking another sip of her wine. "Nice girls stay near their mothers. Tell me, Tori, what are your plans for the future? Surely you do not intend to work as a waitress forever."

"No," I said. "I'm a business major at Dallas Baptist University, but—"

"A Baptist?" She motioned to my glass. "Drinking wine?"

I leaned over the table and whispered. "Don't tell anyone, but I sometimes go dancing, too."

She arched a dark brow. "That red hair, too. So wild!" She raised her glass. "To sinners like us."

I clinked my glass against hers. *This seems to be going well.*

"Someday," I continued, "I hope to own my business.

Maybe a restaurant like this. Or a shop of some sort.
Maybe a salon or spa. I'm not sure yet."

"Ah." She swirled the wine in her glass. "You're a girl
with ambitions."

"Definitely."

She smiled knowingly. "I was once like you. A girl
with big dreams and"—she lowered her voice to a whisper and cupped a hand around her mouth—"her grandmother's secret recipes."

We shared a laugh as she took another sip from her
glass. "You're good at business?"

"I like to think so. I've taken several accounting and
finance classes. And I'm taking a marketing class right
now."

Her eyes gleamed. "Prove it." She angled her head to
indicate the thin woman sitting on the other side of the
restaurant. "That woman comes in twice a week and only
orders a salad and water," she said, keeping her voice
low. "We can't make a living on salads and water. Sell
that skinny lady a dessert."

*Uh-oh.* I could take down tax evaders, sure, but I'd
never been much of a salesman. Even when I'd worked
at Big Bob's Bait Bucket in high school he quickly realized I was better at stocking the shelves and manning the
cash register than convincing a fisherman to add a bottle
of off-brand sunscreen to his purchases. "She's never
ordered a dessert before?"

"Not once," Benedetta replied.

## chapter eleven

# $\mathcal{U}$sing My Noodle

*Ugh.* This interview was going south fast, and I didn't appreciate being manipulated. I knew Benedetta's restaurant was making money hand over fist. A customer ordering only a salad wasn't going to bankrupt the place. I felt an urge to tell her as much. Of course I suspected that a hefty portion of the restaurant's reported income was Tino's dirty extortion money, but I couldn't tell her that, either. I had no choice but to play along.

"Anything in particular you want me to push?" I asked, trying to buy myself time to come up with a strategy.

"The cannoli," she said, "or maybe the bomboloni. We've got plenty of those."

"Bomboloni," I said. "Is that the thing that looks like a jelly doughnut?"

"But tastes so much better," Benedetta said. "Yes, that's the bomboloni."

I stood, racking my brain, trying to remember what I'd learned in my marketing classes back in college. Given that I'd been out of school for years now and hadn't used the information, nothing came to mind. *Dammit!* What could I say to convince her? *Hmm . . .* I decided a few choice adjectives couldn't hurt.

I walked over to the woman and offered a pleasant smile. "Did you enjoy your salad?"

"I did," she said. "The dressing was fabulous, as usual."

"Wonderful. How about a dessert to top things off?" I turned my charm up as high as it would go. "We have a delicious Italian cream cake that melts in your mouth, a decadent tiramisu that will make you close your eyes in pure bliss, a scrumptious bomboloni with fresh raspberry filling, and a chocolate cannoli so rich and creamy the pope declared it a mortal sin to eat it." *There. That ought to do it.*

"Hmm. I don't know . . ." The woman's eyes went to the refrigerator case at the back of the room and I would swear she drooled. But still she resisted. How, I had no idea. If I were in her shoes I'd have chocolate and jelly all over my chin by now.

An idea popped into my head. If a picture is worth a thousand words, the real thing would be worth much more, right? It was easy enough to resist a theoretical dessert, but when one was right in front of you it was a different story. That's why wait staff often brought a tray of the desserts to the table, to show people what they'd be missing if they didn't order one for themselves.

I scampered to the case and snatched a bomboloni and a cannoli. If I had to force-feed this woman like a factory-farm turkey she was going to eat a dessert. I returned to the table and held the plates in front of her face where she could see and smell how yummy they were. "Does this help you make up your mind?"

She eyed the desserts and I could see her resolve melting a little.

*Just pick one!* I mentally willed her. *I won't get the*

*waitress job unless you do!* Unfortunately, my attempts at mental telepathy failed and she held strong.

"I can't," she said, pulling her eyes from the desserts. "I'll go over my lunch budget."

*Aha!* She wasn't watching her waistline as much as her wallet. That was something I could work with.

I lowered my voice to a whisper. "I was told you're a regular here. I'm interviewing for a waitress position and the boss said she'll give me the job if I can convince you to buy a dessert. Order one today and your next lunch will be on me."

She smiled. "Well, I can't turn an offer like that down, can I? I'll have the cannoli."

I'd have to pay for the woman's next meal out of my own pocket, but I couldn't risk not getting this job. It would be much easier for me to keep an eye on the cash flowing in and out of the restaurant if I were actually *in* the restaurant.

I turned to find Benedetta standing behind the refrigerator case. I walked over, looked her in the eye, and lied through my teeth. "Told you I was good at marketing. I convinced her to try the chocolate cannoli."

"And you," Benedetta said, a coy smile playing about her lips, "have convinced *me* to hire you."

I'd landed the job. *Thank God*. We arranged for me to start the following day.

When I was done at the bistro, I returned to my apartment, heeding Hohenwald's warning and watching carefully for a tail. *Nope*. Nobody was following me. Good.

I packed the spirals and the textbooks in the backpack, and drove to Dallas Baptist University. Better familiarize myself with the school I purportedly attended, right?

With just over five thousand students, DBU was a

small university by Texas standards, but nonetheless offered a good range of majors. The campus was situated on nearly three hundred acres in southwest Dallas, overlooking Mountain Creek Lake. The beautiful campus, which was made up primarily of traditional red-brick buildings, was lorded over by the enormous, white Pilgrim Chapel, its tall steeple visible from all over the space.

I parked in a designated student spot and consulted the campus map that had been included in the packet sent over by the FBI office. The agent had circled the buildings in which my classes were held so that I could find them easily.

Given that it was early May already, there were only a few classes left before finals. Students streamed into the student center, either heading in for an early lunch or to hook up with study partners. I found my classrooms and turned to head back to my car. A cute guy with black hair and green eyes did a double take and continued to look my way, offering me a flirtatious smile when my eyes met his. I found myself smiling back, a giddy feeling bubbling up in me.

*Jeez, Tara,* I told myself. *Chill. You're here to work, not chase boys. Besides, he's no Nick.* It was true. The kid who'd looked my way was a cute college boy, but Nick was a man. *My* man. And I had no intention of trading him in for a different model. Still, it was nice to know I could hold my own with all of these pretty young women around. Then again, maybe Joe College was simply intrigued by my fiery red hair, wondering if the rumors about redheads were true. *There's fires in hell, boy,* I thought. *And lust is a sin that can take you there.*

I'd done all I could on the Fabrizio case for now, so I decided to do some digging into Triple 7 Adventures. On my way to the IRS office, I drove through a fast-food Chinese takeout and ordered a couple of vegetable egg rolls with sweet and sour sauce. I ate them on the way, situating the plastic sauce container in the cup holder for easy dipping. When I finished the egg rolls, I cracked open the fortune cookie as I sat at a stoplight downtown. I took a quick peek at the fortune.

*A trapped cat becomes a lion.*

Hmm. The fortune cookie was food for thought. Literally. I shoved the cookie into my mouth and chewed. *Crunch-crunch-crunch.*

When I arrived on my floor, Lu looked up from her desk and called me into her office. As I stepped in, she gestured to my chest. "What's that on your shirt?"

I glanced down. An orange blob sat atop my left boob. *Oops.* "Sweet and sour sauce." I swiped it with my finger and, having nowhere to dispose of the blob, licked it off.

Lu made a face but said nothing. I'd once seen her stir a diet shake with a Slim Jim. Who was she to cast aspersions?

She sat back in her seat. "What have you found out about that vacation scam?"

*Sheesh.* What a slave driver. Wasn't it enough that I'd spent all last night packing and had both moved to my new apartment and interviewed for a job this morning to move the mobster case forward?

"Nothing yet. I've been busting my butt getting ready for the Fabrizio investigation." Well, busting *my* butt and cupping Nick's. But hadn't I deserved a final boink before going indefinitely undercover? "But I'm planning to take a look right now."

"Let me know what you find out. I'll call Harold back with your report. Might as well let the taxpayers know the IRS is on their side."

I fought a smile. I lost.

Lu scowled at me. "What are you grinning at?"

"Someone's got a crush," I said in a singsong voice.

She turned and looked away, a sure sign I'd hit the nail on the head. *Eek. Nails.* Why did my mind keep going there?

She turned back to me. "I don't have a crush," she snapped. "It was just nice to get some attention, that's all."

I couldn't fault her, especially when I'd gotten all warm and fuzzy this morning as that green-eyed guy had looked my way.

She flapped her hand, shooing me out of her office. "Get busy."

I grabbed a quick mug of coffee in the office kitchen and took it to my office.

First, I tried the phone number listed for Triple 7 on the postcard and receipt. All my efforts got me was a recorded voice telling me the number was not in service. No surprise there. More digging told me the number had belonged to a prepaid cell phone.

Unfortunately, the provider's service representative would give me no information. She was, however, generous with the attitude. "People buy prepaid phones for a reason, you know. They don't want the government listening in on their phone calls."

I pinched the bridge of my nose. "Fine. How do I get in touch with your legal department?"

She gave me the legal department's phone number and I jotted it on my pad. I didn't bother thanking her. If she was going to dish it out, she'd have to take, it, too. "Later, dude."

Her snotty voice came through the line one last time. "You're wel—"

*Click.*

I phoned the legal department. While the representative there was pleasant, she was just as tight-lipped.

"We'll need a court order before we can release private information."

I'd gone as far as I could with Triple 7's phone number at the moment. Next, I tried the Web site. Still down. My "Who Is" search showed the domain was registered in the name of Tripp Sevin, clearly a play on the business name. The address was also clearly fictional: 333 Anystreet, Somewhere, SD 12345. *Urgh.* This guy wasn't making things easy. He also wasn't fooling me with the alleged South Dakota address. Given that he'd targeted a local retirement home and offered trips to casinos in the neighboring states of Oklahoma and Louisiana, he was likely based somewhere in north Texas. For now, at least. Con artists often hit hard in a particular area, moving on to a new region once they'd milked a location dry or to avoid apprehension by law enforcement.

Though I was fairly sure the name Tripp Sevin was made up, due diligence required me to run a search to be certain. My query for a driver's license in the name of Tripp Sevin came up with only two licenses issued in the United States with that combination. The first belonged to a seventeen-year-old boy in Salem, Oregon. The other belonged to a thirty-six-year-old Asian man in Oakland, California.

Searches of business filings got me nowhere, too. While there were several businesses with the words *Triple Seven* or the combination word/numeric *Triple 7* in their name, none included the word *Adventure* and none listed an owner or director named Tripp Sevin.

I phoned the domain registry and explained the situation to an assistant in the legal department.

She offered me a few pertinent details. "The customer who bought the domain name also purchased a month-to-month do-it-yourself Web site package. Looks like the site was only up for four months."

"How were the fees paid?"

"By credit card."

Finally! Someone was giving me something to move on. "What was the name and number on the card?"

"Sorry," she said. "We can't disclose that information without a court order."

*Gee, that sounds familiar.* "I'll get you one."

As soon as we were off the phone, I dialed Ross O'Donnell, an attorney at the Department of Justice who represented the IRS on a regular basis.

"I'd be happy to help," he said. "But I'll need affidavits from the men to show to Judge Trumbull. You know how she is."

I knew all too well how Judge Alice Trumbull was. She was a rare left-winger in a state that leaned so far right it was a wonder Texas didn't topple over on top of Louisiana and sink into its swamps. Still, I respected the judge. She didn't issue search warrants willy-nilly. She made us government agents prove our cases, do our jobs right. She kept us honest. Not that we needed anyone to keep us honest, but she made sure we never even thought about doing otherwise.

"Thanks, Ross. I'll get the affidavits to you ASAP."

# chapter twelve

# Sign Here

I pulled out the notes I'd taken during yesterday morning's discussion with Harold, Jeb, and Isaiah and typed up an affidavit for each of them. When I finished, I printed them out and headed back down the hall to Lu's office. I held up the documents. "I'm going out to Whispering Pines to get these signed."

She grabbed her purse. "I'll come with you."

Lu pulled up the address to the retirement community on her phone and navigated as I drove. The place sat just south of the Richardson city limits, a mile east of Central Expressway. The grounds were surrounded by a five-foot brick wall sporting an overgrowth of ivy. The entrance was a wide driveway divided by a median of pink and white petunias.

I drove on past, looking for somewhere to pull in across the street. The last thing I needed was to blow my cover on the Fabrizio investigation by showing up with my badge and gun on the security videos of one of their clients. I turned into a pharmacy, hooked a quick right, and drove to the end of the parking lot, pulling into a spot

that faced Whispering Pines. Leaving the engine running, I reached under the seat and pulled out my father's
old high-powered field glasses. I scanned the front of the
building for a sticker or sign featuring the Cyber-Shield
trademark green logo. I saw none. As Harold had noted,
there was a security camera mounted over the front door,
but it was black and bore no security company logo.

*Good.*

We drove across the street to Whispering Pines.
Though the development appeared to have been constructed a few decades earlier and bore a few telltale rust
stains under the outdoor faucets, for the most part it had
been well maintained. The place comprised three separate
five-story wings anchored by a central, one-story section
that, according to the signage, contained the administrative offices, dining facilities, and recreation rooms. A large
fountain greeted visitors from the center of a colorful and
fragrant rose garden. The rest of the grounds were
groomed as well, park benches and picnic tables placed
here and there for residents to enjoy the outdoors.

We parked in a designated visitors' spot and passed
under the security camera as we entered through the automated front door. Though I'd seen nothing to indicate
Cyber-Shield provided security to the home, I averted my
face in an abundance of caution. It never hurt to be too
careful, right?

The foyer floor was tiled in a red and black checker-
board pattern. When Lu and I had made it across the
space to the receptionist, I was tempted to holler *King me!*

"I'm Special Agent Tara Holloway," I told the woman
at the desk, handing her my business card. I held out a
hand to indicate Lu. "This is my boss, Luella Lobozinski. We need to speak with the person who handles your
on-site security."

"That would be Mickey." She retrieved a walkie-talkie from her desk and pushed a button to activate the mic. "Hey, Mickey. There's some people here from the gov'ment want to speak with you."

A male voice came back. "Give me five minutes to finish this sink."

She returned the radio to the desk. "Mickey's in charge of maintenance, too. He's kind of a jack-of-all-trades around here." The woman pointed to a seating area nearby. "Y'all can take a seat if you'd like."

Lu and I sat down on a black vinyl love seat and looked up at the television mounted on the wall. Steve Harvey filled the screen, hosting *Family Feud* in one of his pimp-style suits. A family had been challenged to name five things you might lose on vacation. After getting on the board with *cell phone* and *camera,* they earned their first strike with *virginity.*

A man wearing blue coveralls and carrying a red toolbox stepped up to us. He looked to be in his mid-fifties and had the lean, strong build of someone who makes a living with physical labor. "I'm Mickey. I was told you two were looking for me?"

Lu and I stood. I explained the situation to him. "I'm hoping your camera out front picked up the van's license plate."

"Follow me to my office," he said. "We can review the tape there."

He led us to a clean, sparsely furnished office at the far end of the administrative wing. As Lu and I took seats in the padded chairs that faced his desk, he slid into the standard office chair behind it.

"We don't have many security problems here," Mickey said as he typed his log-in information into his laptop and ran his index finger over the mouse pad to pull up the video camera footage. "The receptionist keeps an eye on who's coming and going during the day. All of the side doors lock automatically once someone goes out so there's no way to sneak inside. At night we've got both a receptionist and a cop on site. We hire off-duty Dallas police officers."

Smart decision. A cop would be a good deterrent to any would-be criminal.

He pulled up the camera for the day in question and dragged his finger slowly across his mouse pad, leaning in to eye the screen, watching for the van. "This must be it."

He turned the computer to face me and Lu, then rolled his chair around the desk so that he could operate the laptop. He right-clicked the mouse to set the video in motion. As we watched, a shiny gray van pulled to a stop at the outer edge of the parking lot. On the side of the front passenger door was a removable white magnetic sign with black lettering that read TRIPLE 7 ADVENTURES. A moment later, a group of Whispering Pines residents flowed out of the lobby, passing under the security camera as they aimed for the van. Harold, Jeb, and Isaiah were among them.

As we watched on the screen, a man exited the driver's side of the van and came around to speak to the residents. He was too far away for us to tell much about him other than that he was a little taller than average. He wore a cowboy hat and sunglasses, not unusual in Texas though I surmised the accessories were more to shield his identity than to shield him from the sun.

After a brief conversation with the group, he opened the van's doors. Several residents, including Harold and Jeb, climbed inside. Not long afterward, they climbed back out. The man retrieved a clipboard from the front passenger seat and began to accept cash payments from the residents, handing them the useless receipts. In groups of twos and threes, the residents filtered back into the building, smiles on their faces as they anticipated their up-coming vacation.

"I'm trying to get the license plate number," I told him. "Can you zoom in?"

"I can," Mickey said, "but we'll lose some clarity."

He zoomed in but the picture became fuzzy. "Let me play with it a minute."

Mickey fooled around on his computer, going back and forth in the footage to find the best angle, zooming in on the front of the van as it drove into the lot. Finally, he was able to narrow in on the plate. It was a bright blue novelty design with three glittery silver sevens.

"Darn it!" My hands involuntarily fisted. "Those plates don't tell us anything."

Mickey pointed out the cross-shaped logo. "The van's a Chevy. Does that help?"

"Definitely." I jotted the information on the small notepad I carried with me. "Can you see if there's an official plate on the back of the van?"

Mickey spent a couple more minutes going through the footage, and zooming in on the van as it drove away. The back bore the same novelty plate as the front. *Poop.* The novelty plates and concealing cowboy hat told me this wasn't the crook's first rodeo.

Lu and I stood and thanked Mickey for his time.

"Happy to help," he said. "The folks around here are like family to me. I don't like to see them taken advantage of."

We shook his hand and returned to the foyer.

"Any idea where Jeb Proctor and Harold Brinkley might be?" I asked the receptionist.

"Water aerobics." She pointed down the hall. "Through the door at the end."

*God help me if these men are wearing Speedos.*

We reached the end of the hall, where a foggy glass

door led to a heated pool area. Lu and I stepped into the warm, humid room, and instantly I felt my hair preparing to frizz. A dozen residents bounced in the pool, moving their arms up and down as directed by an instructor at the front. Isaiah sat in a special seat, doing his best to mimic the instructor's movements. He might not have full control of his muscles, but he certainly had spunk.

I scanned the faces, locating Jeb and Harold not far from their friend. Harold wore his thick glasses, which sported water droplets. Jeb stood near the edge of the pool, one hand on a rail to steady himself. He wasn't wearing his hearing aids. The steam and water probably weren't good for them.

Three women flanked Jeb. He extended his outer leg through the water and played footsie with the one closest to him. She looked his way, her shoulders scrunching as she giggled.

Jeb was quite the flirt. He was also was the first to notice us. He nudged Harold and leaned over to speak into his friend's ear. "That good-lookin' broad from the IRS is here," he bellowed, probably unaware of how loudly he was speaking.

As the woman he'd just been toe-wrangling with scowled, Lu and I each raised a hand in greeting. The two men eased themselves through the water and up the steps, holding carefully to the handrail. Harold helped Jeb to his walker. Thankfully, both men were wearing swimsuits that came down to their knees. Harold's suit was printed with cartoon sharks, while Jeb's featured dark-haired hula dancers. We followed as Harold walked and Jeb thumped over to a bench where they'd placed their towels. Jeb dug in the pocket of his gym bag for his hearing aids and put them on.

"Sorry to interrupt your class," I told them, "but we need your signatures on affidavits for court."

Jeb wagged his brows at Lu. "Pretty ladies like you are welcome anytime."

Harold notified the instructor's assistant, who operated the winch to lift Isaiah out of the water. She helped dry him off, wrapped him in a plush robe, and guided him to his wheelchair.

While I retrieved the paperwork from my briefcase, Harold and Jeb dried themselves off and sat down on the bench. Using my briefcase as an improvised lap desk, they read over the affidavits and signed them. I moved my briefcase to Isaiah's lap, and offered him the pen.

He took it and signed a slow, shaky *X* on his form. When he finished, he gave me his lopsided smile. "Get . . . that . . . Cajun . . . weasel."

Harold squealed. "That's the first words he's said since his stroke!"

With any luck, they'd be the first of many.

I bent down and looked Isaiah in the eye. "Did you say 'Cajun'?"

He moved his head in a barely perceptible nod.

"That's right!" Jeb said. "I'd forgotten, but the man from Triple Seven had a Cajun accent."

"He sure did," Harold added. "Will that help you find him?"

"Maybe." I stood. "Maybe not." Texas had quite a few residents who'd come from Louisiana and vice versa. Not unusual for states that bordered each other.

"We'll be in touch," Lu said. "As soon as Tara solves the case."

"*If* I solve the case." No sense giving these people false hope. Con artists were like cockroaches. There were multitudes of them, and they knew how to hide themselves. They tended to stay out of the open. Besides, the Fabrizio investigation took priority. The crook who'd ripped off the good people of Whispering Pines might have taken their money, but Tino Fabrizio had taken people's lives.

Lu waved a dismissive hand. "You'll figure it out."

I wished I could be as confident as she was.

Jeb and Harold walked us out to the car. Jeb even held out a hand to help Lu in.

As we drove away I said, "Jeb's quite the charmer."

"Yes, he is," Lu said wistfully. "But he's no Carl."

# chapter thirteen

# $\mathcal{M}$y First Shift

Wednesday marked another night of fitful sleep. I felt lonely without Anne curled up by my side, and I wasn't yet used to the new bed and the different sounds at the apartment complex. I hoped my insomnia would soon pass. My mind needed to be sharp for the Fabrizio investigation. A sleep-deprived agent could overlook evidence or make mistakes. This case was too critical. I couldn't risk doing either.

I arrived at the bistro on Thursday morning at ten, ready to begin my new job. Benedetta took me back to her office and had me fill out the requisite employment paperwork. As I completed the forms, I glanced around the room. There was no security camera in the space, at least not a visible one anyway. I knew businesses sometimes used hidden cameras, but wasn't that more for stores where the management hoped to catch employees pocketing merchandise? Perhaps there was no security camera in here because my suspicions were correct and this was where the money laundering took place. No sense in the Fabrizios recording themselves committing a federal crime. They'd risk the footage being seized by law enforcement and used against them in court. Tino had evaded arrest so far. He was obviously too smart to put a nail in his own coffin. *Eek. There's that word again. Nail.*

Benedetta's home screen was pulled up, and I recognized an icon for QuickBooks, a popular bookkeeping software for small businesses. I wondered what clicking on that icon could lead me to. Evidence of tax evasion or money laundering? Or merely the bona fide records of a family-owned Italian bistro?

Could I be sitting within arm's reach of the evidence the government needed to bust Tino Fabrizio?

The question had me nearly squirming in my seat. Things would be much simpler if we could just issue the guy an audit notice. But given that we didn't want to alert him that he was under scrutiny, we had to hold off on that, at least for now. If nothing else panned out, we could audit him as a last resort. But I had a feeling the guy had done as good a job covering his financial tracks as he had covering his murder tracks.

I gestured to the screen. "I see you use QuickBooks. I'm familiar with that program if you ever need help with the bookkeeping."

Okay, so it was a ploy to try to get Benedetta to let me into her accounting records. Sue me. It was my job to try to get into those records.

Benedetta laughed. "I just hired you as a waitress and already you're asking for a promotion."

I returned the laugh and shrugged. "Just trying to be as helpful as I can." *And trying to bust anyone around here engaging in tax fraud.*

When I finished filling out the work forms, Benedetta and I worked out my schedule for the next two weeks. Our tasks complete, she turned me over to her daughters.

Over the next two hours, her daughters taught me everything there was to know about the restaurant.

Stella, the youngest, showed me where to take the dirty dishes and soiled napkins and tablecloths for washing. Luisa, the middle daughter, showed me where the clean silverware, plates, and linens were kept, and how to properly set the tables. Of course I'd learned how to set a proper table at Miss Cecily's Charm School, but that had been years ago and a refresher course couldn't hurt.

Elena, the oldest, explained the shorthand used in their orders. She showed me where to turn in the orders for the cooks and where to pick up the food when it was ready. She even showed me where the three fire extinguishers were located, one behind the bar in the dining area and one mounted on the wall at each end of the kitchen. She explained how to operate them in case of a fire. "Just aim and squeeze."

I gave her a smile. "I think I can handle that." After all, I could aim a gun, squeeze a trigger, and hit a target at fifty yards with no problem. Compared to a firearm, a fire extinguisher would be easy peasy.

Elena took me on a tour of the warm, steamy kitchen and introduced me to the small kitchen staff currently on duty. All wore white chef jackets and all were men.

An attractive twentyish Latino named Juan stood on the other side of the counter, using a small knife to chop a green pepper into tiny pieces. *Chop-chop-chop.* He lifted his chin in greeting, never breaking stride. "Hey."

The pasta and desserts were in the hands of Brian, a white man who looked to be in his middle thirties. He wore thick padded oven mitts as he removed a pan of delicious-smelling garlic knots from the oven. He pulled off his mitt and stuck out his hand for a shake. "Good to know you, Tori."

The last man, Dario, took care of the meat. Dario was a swarthy, beefy guy wearing a blood-spattered apron. He handled the large serrated knife like a pro, slicing through a thick slab of raw meat as if it were butter. He tossed the bone into a bin full of fat and blood and bones. When I became woozy and reached a hand to a counter to steady myself, his lip curled up in what looked more like a sneer than a smile. "This is how the sausage is made, sweetheart. Better get used to it."

At the back of the kitchen sat one of those large, open brick ovens used for baking pizzas. Flames flickered inside the oven. I felt a sudden urge to make s'mores.

Our kitchen tour complete, Elena took me to a door at the back of the room. The door had a peephole drilled into it. "The kitchen staff enters here," she said. "Never let anyone in without checking the peephole first. My dad says robbers sometimes try to sneak in restaurants the back way."

"Your dad?" I feigned ignorance, an act I performed quite easily and believably. Better not to consider the implications. "Does your father work here at the restaurant, too?"

She shook her head. "Did you see all those green cars next door? They belong to his security company."

"He runs, what's it called? Cyber . . . ?"

"Cyber-Shield. He's owned that company since I was little. He started out selling and installing cameras all by himself, and now he's got a whole staff to do all of that."

Pride was evident in her voice. I realized then that even if Benedetta was helping her husband launder his funds, their daughters seemed to be in the dark. Or perhaps they had a blind spot where their father was concerned. It wasn't unusual for parents to idealize their children and vice versa. I wondered how proud Elena would feel about her father if she knew he was an extortionist and a cold-blooded killer.

I realized then that while a successful resolution of this case would take Tino Fabrizio off the streets, it would also take a father and husband away from his family. But I also realized that Tino would be to blame for that, not me. When a criminal was put behind bars, collateral damage was inevitable. Still, I felt a small twinge of guilt. My dad meant the world to me. I couldn't imagine how I'd feel if he were no longer a part of my life.

Elena unlocked the door and pulled it toward herself to open it. We stepped out behind the building. After the carnage in the kitchen, I was thankful for the fresh air. A catering truck was parked out back. The side was embellished with the words BENEDETTA'S BISTRO—EATING WELL IS THE BEST REVENGE.

"Great slogan," I said.

"Our father came up with it," she said.

Huh. At least he'd leave them with a good slogan when he went off to the slammer.

She walked around to the back of the truck and unlocked it with the keys her mother had given her, which hung from a key chain in the bootlike shape of Italy. She showed me where different food items would be stored for safe transport to offsite locations.

"Does the restaurant do a lot of catering?" I asked. The last thing I wanted was to end up at other places off-site when I needed to be here, keeping a close eye on Tino Fabrizio.

"Once or twice a month," Elena said. "Mostly big Italian weddings, but we sometimes do business meetings or family reunions, things like that."

She pointed off to the back of the lot, to a large green Dumpster with black plastic flaps covering the top of the bin. "That's where the garbage goes."

Our outside tour complete, she led me back inside and showed me to the automated time clock on the wall. "When you arrive for your shift and when you leave, you'll punch in the last four digits of your social security number. The machine will keep track of your time automatically. You'll also need to punch in and out when you take a lunch or dinner break."

"Got it." I'd have to remember to use my new fake Social Security number. *Sheesh.* Going undercover required a lot of focus.

Elena's eyes brightened as she looked past me, sending a smile over my shoulder. "Hi, Dad."

*Dad?*

*Gulp.*

# chapter fourteen

# *L*ike a Crime Boss

The already-warm kitchen where I stood suddenly felt hotter, the flames from the pizza oven burning like the fires of hell. Giustino Fabrizio, notorious mob enforcer, extortionist, and killer, stood so close behind me I could see the toes of his white tennis shoes on the floor just to the right of my own feet.

I forced myself to turn and face the guy, praying I wouldn't piddle like a puppy.

*Wait.*

*This was the infamous crime boss?*

He'd looked like Humpty Dumpty when I'd seen him from afar earlier in the week, but I'd expected him to appear far more intimidating up close. I'd been wrong. Before me stood a man who had three inches on me at best, topping out at only five-feet-five inches, a relative peewee. His face was round with a pronounced forehead leading up to his bald head. Up close like this, he resembled a beluga whale, endangered but not at all dangerous. He wasn't dressed like a mobster, either. He wore no gold chain around his neck, no fancy watch, no diamond-studded pinky ring. Instead, he was dressed casually in sneakers, chinos, and a neon-green short-sleeved golf shirt with the Cyber-Shield logo imprinted on the chest. His brown eyes took me in, bearing no hint of malice. His mouth was spread in a wide, almost goofy smile. "Greetings, girlies!"

*Holy ravioli. I'd expected Tony Soprano but instead I got Tony Danza.*

Elena gave her father a hug. "Dad, this is Tori Holland. She's our new waitress."

"Welcome, Tori." Before I knew what he was doing, he'd put a hand on each of my shoulders, performed a European-style double-sided cheek kiss, and stepped back, still smiling. "You'll enjoy working here. We Fabrizios treat our employees like family."

Given that he'd killed a number of the men who worked for him, the sentiment gave me no warm, fuzzy feelings. In fact, the places where he'd kissed my cheeks burned as if seared with a branding iron. Even so, I was finding it hard to believe the unimposing, congenial man in front of me was a coldhearted killer.

Could it be possible that he'd left Chicago to get away from the mob game? That the disappearances of the men here in Dallas had nothing to do with him and were mere coincidences? I knew the FBI wouldn't have put so many resources into going after this guy and wouldn't have pulled the IRS into the investigation, too, unless they were certain. But given that they'd been able to prove nothing, could we be barking up the wrong tree here?

*No.* I forced myself not to be taken in by his looks. Looks, as I knew, could be deceiving. Heck, when it came to deceptive appearances I was exhibit A. I looked like a harmless college girl who'd gone a little crazy with the hair color, when in reality I was a badass federal agent who'd gone a little crazy with the hair color.

"It's nice to meet you, Mr. Fabrizio." *As if.*

"Please," he replied. "Call me Tino."

Benedetta emerged from her office. "Hello, there."

"There's my Bennie!" he sang, spreading his arms as he approached her. "You look like a million bucks."

As he grabbed her in a tight hug, she pretended to fight him off but I could tell she enjoyed every second of it. "Don't you mean only half a million, Tino?"

My lack of comprehension must have been written on my face.

"That's how much he's insured Mom for," Elena told me.

Tino reached out and ruffled Elena's hair. "What's next, Elena? You going to give Tori the secret family recipes?"

Despite the chuckle that followed, Tino's words seemed to be a warning to his daughter to keep her mouth shut. Perhaps I'd been wrong and Elena did know something after all.

I chuckled, too, hoping to give the impression that I'd taken none of the exchange seriously when, in fact, my mind was going a mile a minute, processing the information. Half a million was not an excessive sum by any stretch of the imagination, especially given that the couple had three daughters who were not yet fully independent and relied on their mother's restaurant for their incomes. Besides, it wasn't unusual for businesses to insure their key personnel. Yet something about it gave me pause.

Tino gave his wife a two-cheeked kiss, too, following it up with a direct smooch on the lips. He cupped her chin with his chubby hands. "I could insure you for every penny in the world and it wouldn't match what you're worth."

"Oh, stop." She waved a hand dismissively, but the gesture was belied by her happy grin. "Let me guess. You're here for a chocolate cannoli."

Tino gave her another quick smooch and released her. "Ah, *bella*. You know me so well."

*Does she?* I had to wonder. Could someone be married to a mob boss and truly be in the dark about his evil misdeeds? Or did women like Benedetta choose to stick their heads in the sand?

"You're lucky there's any left." Benedetta gestured my way. "Tori knows how to move desserts. She got a woman the size of a toothpick to order a cannoli at lunch yesterday."

"Did you, now?" Tino turned to look at me. "I take it you're an experienced waitress, then?"

"No. But I worked as a nanny and had to convince two kids to eat their vegetables and to go to bed on time every night. And I'm studying business. My marketing professor says it's a good idea to get some practical experience working in a small business."

"You're a student, huh? Where do you go to school?"

Was it a simple, friendly question, or a way to dig for information on me? "Dallas Baptist University."

Benedetta filled her husband in on my history. "Tori worked for a family that recently moved to the Middle East."

"That's a long haul," Tino said. "What are they doing over there?"

"The father works for an oil company," I said. "He got promoted so they moved the family over there."

"And you didn't want to go with them?" Tino asked.

"I'll miss the kids," I said. "Tessa and—" *Oh, crap!* My

mind had gone blank. What was the boy's name? Nigel? Marcus? Oh, yeah. *Miles!* "Miles were little angels. Well, most of the time anyway. Every kid has their moments."

"Tell me about it!" Benedetta stage-whispered from behind a cupped hand as she hiked a thumb at her girls. The statement earned her a cry of "Ma!" from all three of her daughters, but the soft smiles on their faces told me none of them were serious.

I went on. "I didn't want to leave my own family or friends, and I'm hoping to finish my degree in the next year or two, so it seemed best to stay here."

"You from around here?" Tino asked.

"I live close," I said. "On Bennett Avenue."

"What I meant," Tino clarified, "is did you grow up in Dallas?"

I nodded. "Born and raised here."

Benedetta nudged him in the ribs with her elbow. "Tori's a waitress, not a chicken. Quit grilling her."

Tino raised his palms. "Sorry. Can't blame a guy for wanting to know something about the people who will be working with his wife and daughters."

Benedetta chuckled again. "Look at her, *caro*. The girl wouldn't weigh a hundred pounds soaking wet. She couldn't hurt a fly. You worry too much."

Part of me was glad I didn't look like a threat, but another part of me was insulted. I might not look like much, but I'd shot and killed a man and skewered another with a samurai sword. I might not weigh much, but I wasn't a woman to be taken lightly. On the other hand, the more they thought of me as a little mousy nanny, the better. If they were off their guard, they were more likely to slip up, maybe feed me some information that would nail Tino.

Tino said something to Benedetta in Italian and she replied with a curt response I didn't understand. *Hmm. Too bad I didn't know the language. Maybe I should do something about that.*

"Nice meeting you, Tori," Tino said.

Benedetta and her husband exited through the swinging door and Elena got back to business. "Let me show you how to work the register."

*Now you're talking.*

She led me back to the dining area, circling behind the bar. There was just one register in the place, the one I'd noticed yesterday on my way in. The device was positioned on the back counter of the bar, near the dessert case, where it could be easily accessed by both the wait staff and the bartender. The register was a touch-screen model with a cash drawer below. A magnetic card reader sat to the left, with the miniature receipt printer to the right. And, of course, the device was under constant surveillance by the video camera lording over it from the wall above.

I made a mental note of the make and model number imprinted on the register's cash drawer. *Salespoint 2600.*

"You'll need to create your own unique PIN," Elena said. "It has to be entered before each transaction."

*Damn.* That meant any of my activity on the machine would be linked to me, including any printouts of sales data. I could only hope that nobody would have reason to examine the register entries with close scrutiny or to watch the video feed from the camera aimed at the register.

She pulled up a keyboard on the screen, typed in the name TORI HOLLAND, then gestured to the screen. "Go ahead and pick a four-digit PIN."

I touched the screen, typing in the last four digits of the fake Social Security number that had been assigned to

Tori Holland, and tapped the enter key. The screen popped up with preprogrammed icons for each of the menu items.

"Okay." Elena stepped up closer to me. "To enter an order, all you have to do is tap the items the customer orders." She continued, showing me which buttons to push if a table ordered more than one of the same item, and how to void an incorrect entry. She showed me how to print out a copy of the order to take to the kitchen. "If customers want split checks, you just ring them up separately." She finished by showing me how to make change for cash customers, and how to run a credit card for those who wanted to charge their meal. "Got it?"

"I think so." Seemed easy enough.

"If you have any problems, my sisters and I can help you."

She led me back through the kitchen and into an employee lounge. She opened a cabinet, and pulled out a black apron with three front pockets, handing it to me. "Wear this over your clothes when you come to work. Dress all in black for your shifts."

"Can I at least wear my favorite shoes?" I asked, holding up one of my red Dr. Martens. "They're really comfortable." *And steel-toed in case I need to kick your father's ass.*

She shrugged. "The shoes don't matter so long as the rest of your clothes are black. You might want to buy some new clothes in the next size up."

"Why's that?" I asked as she led me back to the kitchen.

"Nobody stays thin working here." She handed me a white bag filled with takeout containers. "My mother won't let anyone go home without food."

*Yum.* This job would definitely have its benefits.

As I left the restaurant, I raised a hand to Benedetta and Tino, who stood behind the bar, their fingers intertwined and their heads ducked toward each other like young lovebirds. "Thanks for dinner!" I called, holding up my bag. "Have a good evening!"

Tino put his wife's hand to his cheek as she called back, "Ciao, Tori! See you tomorrow morning."

## chapter fifteen

# *W*ill Work for Food

As I walked out to my Hyundai at seven that evening, I spotted Emily Raggio in front of Gallery Nico. Emily was one of the artists I'd spoken with on my recent investigation into the Unic Art Space. Emily, whose husband was a physician, had an unusual medium—medical supplies. Some of her pieces had been made from tongue depressors, expired pills, and hospital dressing gowns.

She probably wouldn't recognize me with the new reddish hair, but better to play it safe. I quickly slipped into my car so she wouldn't spot me. As I watched, Emily opened the back hatch of her SUV and removed a white piece of art the approximate size of a two-drawer filing cabinet. It was shaped like a head and formed from surgical masks she'd turned into papier-mâché. *Intriguing.* I didn't have an artistic bone in my body, though I had been known to use some creative methods when taking down a suspect. A trip-and-shove maneuver. An improvised flamethrower. Tickle torture. Hey, it works on adults just as well as children.

I started my engine and turned out of the lot, heading

to my new apartment rather than my real home. A block
up north Fitzhugh, I noticed a white pickup truck pulled
to a curb on a side street not far from the intersection.
As I drove past, the truck eased away from the curb and
turned onto Fitzhugh behind me.

*Hmm . . .*

It could be coincidence. Or it could be a tail.

Agent Hohenwald had warned me that Tino Fabrizio
trusted no one. Maybe the guy in the truck was one of
his goons checking up on me. At any rate, I had to play
it cool. A college student/waitress would have no reason
to suspect someone of following her. I had to pretend that
I hadn't noticed and do what a college girl would normally do. Still, the badass federal agent in me wanted to
make this guy earn his pay. Besides, it would be fun to
give him the runaround, screw with him a little.

Up ahead sat a nail salon. It had been a while since
I'd had a professional mani-pedi. And given that I'd just
landed a new job, why shouldn't I treat myself?

I turned into the salon's parking lot and went inside,
laughing to myself when I saw that the waiting room had
quite a crowd.

"Do you have an appointment?" asked a technician
giving a leg massage to a woman nearby.

"Nope."

"It'll be forty-five minutes to an hour," she said.
"Would you like to wait or should I make you an appointment for another time?"

"I'll wait." My tail and I had all the time in the world.
*Ha!*

She lifted her chin to indicate a pad of paper on the
countertop at the front of the shop. "Put your name on
the list."

I jotted the name Tori on the pad, dotting the *i* with a

star just for kicks, and informed the woman I'd be right back. I returned to my car outside, forcing my eyes from the pickup at the far end of the lot, and grabbed my backpack. Better use the downtime to study for those upcoming finals, right?

I went back inside and took a seat along the side wall. I knew from experience just how boring it could be to run surveillance on someone, especially when the target was merely going about everyday business. I hoped Tino's goon found every second of watching me to be painfully dull. And so long as I was hoping, why not also wish him a burning case of hemorrhoids and an irritable bowel?

I knew Will and Hana were on duty tonight, working somewhere in the vicinity of Cyber-Shield to follow Tino's patrolmen. I sent the two of them a quick text. *A new friend came with me to the nail salon on Fitzhugh. Want to meet us here for mani-pedis?* My phrasing was intentionally cryptic, but they'd understand. As soon as the text went through, I deleted it.

I opened the accounting textbook I'd been provided as part of my cover, but surreptitiously slipped a copy of *People* magazine inside it. Though I had graduated with honors from the University of Texas down in Austin, my new alter ego Tori Holland had earned only an average GPA and was out of the running for the dean's list. Tori might need to study, but I already knew accounting backward, forward, and upside down, and had no interest in relearning debits and credits and double-entry bookkeeping. While Tori would appear to be hitting the books, Tara would be finding out what Bradley Cooper and Taylor Swift had been up to lately.

An hour later, my celebrity gossip was fully up-to-date and my name was finally called. "Tori?"

"That's me." I returned the magazine to the table, slid my book back into my backpack, and stood.

"Anything special?" the technician asked as I took a seat at her table.

"Any chance you can paint my nails to look like little Italian flags?"

She cocked her head. "What's their flag look like?"

"A green, white, and red vertical stripe," I said. "Like the Mexican flag only without the snake-eating bird on the cactus in the middle."

"I think I can manage that."

She put my fingertips in a bowl to soak before reaching over to her nail polish display and selecting bottles in green, white, and red. We chatted as she took care of my cuticles, then shaped my nails with a file.

"Why Italian flags?" she asked as she applied the first green stripe to my left thumb.

"I got a new job," I told her. "I'll be a waitress at Benedetta's Bistro down the street."

The woman looked at me. "Is that the place with the incredible chocolate cannoli?"

"That's it." So far I'd only seen the cannoli, not tasted it, but if it was even half as good as it looked I'd be in for a treat.

"Tell you what," the woman said. "Next time you need a manicure, bring me a couple of those chocolate cannoli and it'll be on the house."

"Consider it done." Looked like I'd made another bargain involving Italian food. Cannoli had apparently become a type of currency for me.

I emerged from the nail salon a half hour later with adorable Italian flags on my toes and fingertips. The pickup truck still sat at the far end of the lot. If I'd had any doubt the driver was following me before, I had no doubt now. Nobody would sit in a parking lot for that long without a good reason. It was ironic, really. Fabrizio was tailing me, while federal agents were tailing his men. It was a warped game of cat and mouse. Unfortunately, the truck was parked in the shadows cast by the setting sun and I couldn't make out the license plate. With any luck, Will or Hana had been able to swing by and obtain the plate number so that we could identify who the truck belonged to.

As I continued on, my eyes spotted a bookstore. I stopped and went inside, catching them just before they closed for the evening. I picked up an Italian language book that came with a companion CD. Becoming fluent in the language in short order wouldn't be possible, but it couldn't hurt for me to at least become more familiar with it so I could recognize words like *cash* and *money* and *nail gun*.

I slipped back into my little car and headed a half block down the road, pulling into a gas station. The pickup drove past, but as I topped off my tank, being careful not to chip my fresh manicure, it circled the block and came back up Fitzhugh, ready to trail after me again. I dawdled, pretending to be checking e-mails on my phone, forcing the truck to circle the block again. *Neener-neener.* Maybe I should stand there all night until the guy had circled the block so many times he became dizzy and crashed into a tree.

At that point, I decided I'd had enough fun and that it was best to head on to my apartment. After all, a college student would need to get home and continue studying, right? Especially one who wanted to improve her GPA? Seriously, couldn't the FBI have given me an alter ego with a better academic track record?

The pickup followed me, hanging back a little farther now, allowing a couple of cars to sneak in between us. I took a right onto Live Oak, and he took a right ten seconds later. He followed me by a few seconds when I turned left on Bennett. When I turned into my apartment complex, the pickup drove on past. I wasn't sure whether he'd be going on his merry way now or whether he'd circle back to make sure I actually went into my apartment, but I drove on into the lot, parked in a spot near my place, and climbed the stairs to my apartment, my backpack slung over one shoulder, my purse hanging across my body, and my bag of food in my hand. I forced myself to look straight ahead and not check over my shoulder for the truck.

I dug my keys from my purse and went inside, flipping on the lights. Without a roommate or pet, the place seemed empty and quiet and lonely. I picked up the remote and turned on the television. At least the characters from my favorite sitcoms could keep me company.

I set the bag of food on my countertop and took the to-go containers out one by one, peeking inside each of them to see what delectable treats they contained. The one on top contained a chocolate cannoli. *Woo-hoo!* After nearly two hours in my car, the filling had become runny, but a minor matter like that wouldn't stop me from enjoying it. I stuck the dessert in the fridge, hoping the cold air might revive it a little. The next container housed a trio of buttery garlic knots. The final container was filled with ziti marinara. The only thing that would have made the meal more perfect was if a salad had been included. But I supposed I shouldn't look a gift horse in the mouth, huh?

The thought that the food might be poisoned briefly crossed my mind, but I realized I was being paranoid. The chances of Benedetta's daughters or the kitchen staff adding something deadly to the food were slim to none. They'd been nothing but nice to me today, and it was questionable whether Tino's wife and daughters knew of his shady history. Besides, if Tino had figured out I was a federal agent and planned to off me, he wouldn't do it here in this apartment. He'd have me kidnapped and dragged off somewhere, make it look like an accident. Or maybe he'd just make me disappear, like those other missing men. I wondered where they were now. Were their bodies buried in the west Texas desert? At the bottom of Lake Texoma? Had they been chopped up and fed to coyotes?

## chapter sixteen

# $\mathcal{I}$f They Could See Me Now . . .

I washed up, fixed myself a plate of ziti and garlic knots, and plunked my butt down on the sofa. I found myself wondering what Nick was doing now. Was he still at his new gallery, setting things up? Or was he "home" at his new apartment, too, feeling as lonely and isolated as I felt here? At least he'd have Josh to keep him company. This isolation was definitely going to take some getting used to.

When I finished my meal, I rinsed my dishes and stuck them in the dishwasher. I was tempted to peek out the window to see if the white pickup was in the lot, but if anyone caught me looking I might raise their suspicions. I carried my purse into the bedroom and set it in easy reach on top of the dresser next to my bed. Better keep my Cobra in quick reach in case I needed it.

I changed out of my clothes and into my pajamas, and went into the bathroom to wash my face. While I'd been advised not to perform any IRS-related work on my new laptop and knew the FBI was tapped into it, I figured it couldn't hurt for me to play around on it a little. I opened the laptop on my bed and pushed the power button so it could boot up while I went to the kitchen and retrieved the cannoli. I slid it onto a plate, grabbed a fork, and sampled a bite. *Dear Lord, this stuff is delicious!* Elena was right. I should definitely buy bigger pants. I might even need to go two sizes up just in case this investigation ran long.

I moseyed back into the bedroom, turning on the bedside lamp and switching off the overhead light. I plopped down on the bed, setting my plate on the spread and positioning a pillow against the wall behind me so I could sit up to surf the Internet. I climbed into bed, pulled the computer onto my lap, and logged in with my new password. *NannyT1!*

I picked up the plate and shoveled a huge bite of chocolate cannoli into my mouth, moaning with pleasure. After wiping my mouth on my pajama sleeve—I'd forgotten to get a napkin—I logged into a bookstore site, checking for upcoming releases from my favorite authors. A new romance would be out next week, with a mystery the week after that. Good to know. I'd forgo nail-biting thrillers for the time being. With the Fabrizio case, I was involved in my own real thriller. Besides, I didn't want to mess up my cute new manicure.

A notice popped up on my screen, alerting me that an update was available for one of the common programs on my computer. I clicked on the link, allowing it to update.

The underside of my left boob itched where my underwire bra had been rubbing up against it all day. As my computer updated, I gave my boob a two-fingered scratch through my pajamas and took another bite of the cannoli. One of the chocolate chips fell off the fork and dropped to the floor beside the bed. *Ugh!* It was only a tiny morsel, but this stuff was so good it would be a shame to waste even an atom of it. Besides, there was nobody around. No one would know I'd eaten food off the floor. And what about the five-second rule? Didn't germs need at least five seconds to migrate from the floor to something that was dropped on it? I was pretty sure it was a sound scientific principle. Maybe even a physical law. Thus convinced, I leaned over, snatched the chocolate chip from the carpet, and tossed it into my mouth, willing my immune system to kill any germs that might have attached to it.

As long as I was just sitting around with nothing critical to do, I figured I might as well clear my pores and remove the peach fuzz from my upper lip. I laid my computer aside, went to the bathroom, and applied an adhesive pore strip to my nose and a wax strip to my upper lip. While they worked their magic, I returned to my bed, picked my computer back up, and continued to venture around the Internet.

As the heavy Italian meal settled in my stomach, it forced air to the surface. A big gas bubble burbled up and sat painfully at the top of my esophagus, begging to be released. I'd been taught in Miss Cecily's Charm School to stifle my burps behind my fingers or a napkin, but Miss Cecily wasn't here now, was she? No sense fighting it. And no sense adhering to decorum when the only person here to be offended was myself. I released the air with a long and loud *bruuuppp* that would have made a drunk frat boy proud.

Relieved, I turned my attention back to my computer. With Henry and Anne back at my real home, I was suffering a case of miss-my-kitties. But if I couldn't cuddle up with one of my own, I could at least watch videos of funny felines online, right? I took another bite of cannoli and ventured into YouTube to search for new cat clips.

*Brrrring.*

The landline phone in the kitchen rang, the shrill ring

tone nearly yanking me from my skin in my quiet apartment. I set the computer aside, slid out of bed, and went to answer it.

"Hello?" I said.

Agent Hohenwald's voice came over the line. He spoke in a hushed voice. "My tech tells me there's two people logged into your wireless system, you and another user. Someone's hacked into your computer. It's gotta be one of Tino's men. Be careful. They're spying to see what you're doing online. They could even be watching you through your Webcam. That's why I phoned you rather than texting. If someone is watching through your computer's camera, he might have been able to read your cell phone screen through the feed."

My mouth, which had just been watering in anticipation of more chocolate cannoli, went instantly dry. It was one thing to know a spy might be sitting outside in a truck keeping an eye on my place. It was another entirely for someone to be watching me through my computer inside my own apartment. *Oh, God. I'd wiped my mouth on my sleeve, scratched my boob, eaten floor food, performed embarrassing beauty rituals, and belched.* I felt humiliated and violated and terrified that they could get so close without me knowing. Of course anyone watching through my computer camera was probably disgusted by me, so I supposed the score was even.

Through the phone, Hohenwald said, "They might even send you a fake update notice that will plant spyware on your laptop. The spyware will allow them to look back over your browser history without having to be actively online with you."

"Yes," I said.

"They already sent it, didn't they?"

I wasn't sure if whoever was cyberspying on me could only watch through my Webcam or also listen through my laptop's microphone, so I decided it was best to speak cryptically. "Mm-hm."

"And you downloaded it?"

"Right."

"That's okay," he said. "Our tech team added a history to the computer. The fact that you downloaded the fake update is probably good. That's what an unsuspecting college kid would do, and we want you to look like an unsuspecting college kid."

For once my lack of tech skills had actually paid off.

"Now," Hohenwald said, "just in case they can hear through your computer mic, tell me you're happy with your current cable provider and hang up on me."

"I'm not interested," I said into the receiver. "I'm happy with my current cable provider. Good-bye." I hung up the phone.

Knowing I was likely being watched made me horribly self-conscious, but I had to act as normal as possible. After ripping both strips from my face, I returned to my bedroom, fuzzless and with clean pores. I turned my cell phone facedown on the dresser to block any incoming texts from view, even though I knew any of the team members would be smart enough to make any message sound innocuous and cryptic. I climbed back into bed and forced myself not to look at the little round hole at the top of the screen that housed my Webcam.

After watching a couple of cute cat videos, I decided that, like my tail in the pickup, anyone cyberspying on me deserved to suffer a little. Knowing it was most likely a man, I planned to make the next hour a living hell for him. I Googled "natural ways to relieve menstrual cramps," "Ryan Gosling shirtless photos," and spent forty-five minutes on the Neiman Marcus site looking at shoes and purses.

*Take that, mobsters.*

## chapter seventeen

# $\mathcal{A}$ Shift with Shifty

Friday morning, I woke early and downed some leftover ziti for breakfast. Hey, pasta is made of grain just like cereal. Don't judge me.

My tummy full, I showered and dressed in a pair of black slacks, a black blouse with tuxedo-style pleats down the front, and my Dr. Martens. Not the sexiest shoes by any stretch of the imagination, but if I was going to be on my feet all day slinging linguine, at least the shoes would be comfortable. Today, I planned to take my new laptop to work and ask about logging into Benedetta's Wi-Fi system. If I could get the password, it would make it easier for Josh to hack into her system and gain access to her financial records. I knew the task would be a challenge, what with Tino's specialty being cybersecurity and his having a computer expert on his payroll. But Josh was no slouch, either, when it came to technology. Me, though? I was a technological Neanderthal. I could use electronics, but I had no idea how they worked. It was like magic to me.

I was due to appear in court at nine this morning to present the affidavits in the Triple 7 Adventures case. I crossed my fingers as I left my apartment, hoping none of Tino's goons were watching me.

No such luck.

*Damn.*

My tail this morning was no longer a white pickup but a silver sedan. Looked like I'd have to keep up my charade and go to school. I wondered if my follower was as annoyed as I was about this eight o'clock class. Couldn't the FBI have signed me up for a later class and let me sleep in? What's more, I had to commute to school in the middle of bumper-to-bumper rush-hour traffic. *Ugh.* On the bright side, maybe Benedetta would send me home with another chocolate cannoli today.

The driver followed me all the way from my apartment to the DBU campus, staying far enough back that I couldn't make out his license plate number. Fortunately, as I turned into the campus, he continued on, apparently satisfied that nobody who wasn't truly a college student would have put herself through the hassle of waking early and fighting rush-hour traffic to drive all the way out here.

To put some distance between us, I parked on the campus and waited for ten minutes before heading back out. Carefully watching my rearview mirror in case a new tail appeared, I drove a circuitous route to the courthouse to meet up with Assistant U.S. Attorney Ross O'Donnell, praying I'd make it in time for the hearing. I came in just under the wire, rushing into the room and looking for Ross among the assorted suits. *There he is.* I squeezed through the crowd of attorneys and witnesses until I stood beside him.

Ross was a calm, methodical guy in his thirties, with a squat build and dark hair that had begun to recede backward on either side of his forehead. He represented the IRS on a regular basis, prosecuting the tax evaders we special agents arrested. With our exceptional investigation skills, near-obsessive levels of documentation, and expert responses on the witness stand, we liked to think we made his job easy. But with our type-A personalities and constant demands on his time, he might beg to differ.

He read over each of the documents. "Good job here. All the pertinent information is covered." When he got to Isaiah's form, his brows angled in confusion. He held it up and pointed to the signature block. "What's with the *X*?"

"Stroke victim," I explained. "That's the best he could do."

The bailiff ordered us to stand as Judge Alice Trumbull barreled through the door that led from her chambers and ascended to her bench. Trumbull was known as the bulldog, and for good reason. She had the same loose jowls and determined demeanor the dogs were known for.

Wasting none of her precious time, she plopped her oversized butt down into her chair, picked up the file on top of her stack, and called our case. "IRS versus Triple Seven Adventures."

Ross and I were on our feet and in front of her bench in a heartbeat.

"Good morning, Judge Trumbull," he said. "Special Agent Holloway here needs to get some information on a credit card."

"Agent Holloway?" She looked down at me. "I hardly recognize you with that orange hair."

"I'm working undercover."

"As what, a cage dancer?"

Being a cage dancer sounded like much more fun than an ex-nanny-college-student-wannabe-waitress. But I said, "Not exactly." I explained the situation with Triple 7 to her. "The credit card is the only remaining lead we have, and the domain registry won't turn over the information without a court order."

She nodded and skimmed the copies of the postcard and cash receipts, as well as the affidavits. She held up the one signed with an *X*. "Is this signer illiterate?"

"No," I said. "He's had a stroke. But we read the affidavit to him and he seemed to understand. And he was able to communicate to me that the suspect has a Cajun accent." That fact showed that, despite the stroke, Isaiah still had his mental faculties.

"How'd you find out about this con artist?" the judge asked.

"The men who signed the affidavits came to the IRS office looking for me," I said. "They asked me to help them."

She cocked her head. "Heard about you on TV, I'm guessing, hmm?"

I nodded.

She chuckled. "The minute I heard that an IRS agent had shot a drug dealer from long range, the first thing I thought was 'That has to be Special Agent Holloway.'"

I offered her a meager smile. Sure, I was glad that I'd saved the lives of an informant, Nick, and Christina Marquez, a DEA agent who'd become my good friend after we'd worked some cases together. I also knew that I'd had no choice but to make that deadly shot. The man I'd killed had just put a bullet in another man's head, then pointed his gun at Nick, ready to shoot again. Despite my desperate attempts to forget that fateful night, the horrifying image was seared into my memory like a brand. I could still feel the pressure of my finger on the trigger, hear the *blam* of my rifle releasing the deadly bullet. Still, after seeing those horrifying photographs in Tino Fabrizio's file, I realized the mobster and I had something in common. *We were both killers.* The thought made me feel sick to my stomach. I didn't want to be anything like him.

Judge Trumbull signed the order with a flourish and handed it down to me. "Keep up the good work."

All I could do was nod.

As Ross and I left the courtroom, he put a hand on my shoulder and pulled me to a stop. "Are you okay, Tara?"

My lip quivered and my eyes blinked rapidly, attempting to keep tears at bay. I looked down, hoping Ross wouldn't notice. "I'm . . . fine."

He stepped to the side, shielding me from the view of passersby, God bless him. "I don't think you are."

I took a deep breath, held it for a count of ten, and finally got myself under control enough to look back up at him. "It kinda sucks being identified as a killer, you know?"

Ross's face was pensive, thoughtful. "If it's any consolation," he said finally, gesturing down to my red steel-toed footwear, "I've always thought of you as the agent with the really ugly shoes."

A laugh burst from my lips and they ceased to quiver. "Thanks, Ross. That's just what I needed to hear."

I returned to the IRS office and sent the affidavit to the domain registry's legal department via e-mail. I also sent a copy to the cell phone service provider. I knew it would take them a few business days to get back with me, but in the meantime I would keep my fingers crossed. If this con artist had ripped off the folks at Whispering Pines, chances were he'd pulled the same shenanigans on untold numbers of other victims. I'd love to track him down and put his sorry ass behind bars where it belonged. Of course there was a much bigger, sorrier ass I hoped to bust ASAP. *Tino Fabrizio's.*

While I was on the computer, I quickly searched for instructions on how to print out sales data from the computerized cash register system at Benedetta's, the Salespoint 2600. Clicking on the link, I read the instructions over three times, committing them to memory. My work here done, I headed to my second job at the bistro.

It was half past ten—or, as the Italians say, *dieci*—when I parked in the second row of the parking lot at the bistro. A glance at Cyber-Shield told me only that three of the neon-green patrol cars were parked there today. I knew Will had coordinated with the team from the FBI to follow Fabrizio and his salesmen, installers, and security patrols yesterday and last night. I wondered whether they'd had any success figuring out who Tino might be planning to extort money from next.

I exited my car and carried my backpack, which contained my new laptop, to the door of the bistro. Through the glass, I could see Stella, Luisa, and Elena. All wore black heels and fitted black dresses that accentuated their voluptuous figures. The three huddled near the hostess stand, staring out the window.

I turned to see what they were looking at. *Nick.* No wonder they looked so captivated. He was out in front of Gallery Nico with a spray bottle of glass cleaner and a rag, wiping down the windows of his shop. He wore the clothes I'd picked out for him when we went shopping and damn if he didn't look good enough to eat. Not that I was all that picky about what I ate. *Let's forget about that chocolate chip from the floor, shall we?*

While Stella unlocked the door and held it open for me, Elena stepped even closer to the glass, her nose almost touching it. "Look at those arms. He must work out."

"I didn't notice his arms," Luisa said, gazing longingly across the parking lot. "I was too busy staring at his luscious ass."

"I want to get a closer look," Stella said, relocking the door. "Dibs on taking him lunch later."

The heat of jealousy flared up in me. Nick was *mine,*

dammit. No matter how nice these girls had been to me yesterday, I didn't like them ogling my man.

I stepped up next to them and took a look. "I guess he's okay," I said with a shrug. "You know, if you like that type."

Elena shot me a skeptical look. "The *gorgeous* type, you mean?"

"I mean the type who look like they spend a lot of time looking in the mirror." I left it at that and proceeded to the small staff lounge next to Benedetta's office in the kitchen. The door to Benedetta's office was open a few inches, and I could see her seated inside, her back to the door as she placed an order of supplies with one of her vendors.

The lounge was a windowless room that contained two of the same tables as the dining room, pushed together to form one long surface and surrounded by six chairs. Along the right wall was a small television atop a bookcase filled with cookbooks. On the left wall stood a series of narrow floor-to-ceiling lockers. Mine was the one on the end. Elena, who worked as both a server and her mother's right-hand woman, had given me the key yesterday.

I opened my locker, dropped my backpack in the bottom, and hung my purse on the hook. I wrapped my apron around my waist and tied it in a bow in back. Properly attired now, I grabbed a pen and an order pad from the plastic bin in the kitchen and slid them into my apron. The same three men who'd staffed the kitchen yesterday were back at work today, chopping vegetables, boiling noodles, simmering sauces, cutting meat, and squeezing cream from a pastry bag into a dozen cannoli shells.

"Save one of those for me!" I called to Brian.

The pastry chef looked up and gave me a smile.

Stella met me in the laundry room and explained the

standard morning routine. "We cover the tables first, then take care of the glassware and dishes."

"Got it." I pulled green tablecloths from the dryer, and draped them over her arms so they wouldn't wrinkle.

"Oh, my God!" she cried, grabbing my hand. "What a cute manicure."

"I got it on my way home last night." I pulled my foot out of my shoe. "See? Toes, too."

While Stella carried the tablecloths into the dining room, I transferred the white napkins from the washing machine into the dryer and turned it on.

Back in the dining room, I helped Stella spread the cloths on the table. Luisa and Elena followed along behind us, adding the roses, candles, sweetener packets, and shakers to the tables. While we waited for the napkins to finish drying, Stella and I removed the glasses from the dishwasher and wiped them down to remove spots. Luisa and Elena stashed the clean glasses in their proper places on shelves in the kitchen, carrying some into the dining room for the bar. When the dryer's buzzer announced that the napkins were dry, we folded those and set them on the tables in the restaurant along with silverware. We finished up by returning the clean plates, pots, and pans to their proper spots in the kitchen.

We functioned like a well-oiled machine. *Olive*-oiled.

Stella and I were in the kitchen assembling bags of to-go orders that had been called in when Benedetta emerged from her office a few minutes before eleven. "Good morning, Tori," she said.

*"Buongiorno,"* I replied, trying out some of the Italian I'd learned on the drive to work.

She stopped in her tracks, a smile playing about her wine-colored lips. "You're going to be one of those butt-kissers, aren't you?"

"I sure am."

"Good." She gave me a wink.

Stella stepped up. "Take a look at her manicure, Mom."

I held out my fingers for Benedetta to behold.

She took my hand in hers. *"Bellisima."* She reached up and softly pinched my cheek in a sign of affection. "I should make you my honorary Italian daughter."

"I'd like that." *So long as we give Tino the old heave-ho.* Arrivederci, *daddio.*

My arms loaded with bags, I followed Benedetta out into the dining room. While I situated the to-go orders along the bar, she made her way to the front door and unlocked it, welcoming an older couple who'd been waiting patiently on the sidewalk out front.

"Tori will show you to your seats," Benedetta said, her words addressing me as much as the customers.

I scurried over. "Would you prefer a booth or a table?"

"A booth," the woman said.

I led them to a booth along the left side. "How's this?"

"Just fine," the woman said, sliding in. Her husband slid in on the other side.

I handed them each a menu. "Can I start you off with an Italian soda or a flavored tea?" Elena had told me to push the drinks. Like the desserts, they had a better profit margin than the entrées. Besides, a bigger tab meant bigger tips. "We have a delicious raspberry tea today. It's a treat for your tongue."

"That sounds great," the woman said.

"Count me in, too," said her husband.

My first shift was off to a good start.

I headed back to the kitchen to get their drinks. Once there, I found Stella standing at the stove, filling small containers with an assortment of pastas. Fettucine Alfredo. Linguine carbonara. Spinach ravioli.

"You really want to make an impression on that art dealer?" said Dario, the formidable man who handled the meat. "Take him this." He held out a plate bearing two oversized meatballs flanking a huge Italian sausage. A meat penis.

"That's disgusting," Stella said. "I should tell Mom to fire you."

Dario laughed and used a pair of tongs to return the meats to their warming trays. "She can't fire me. I know too much."

# chapter eighteen

# $\mathcal{I}$nto the System

*Hmm* . . .

What, exactly, did the chef know? Was he merely referring to Benedetta's proprietary pasta sauce recipes? Or did he have dirt on the family? Could he somehow be involved in Tino's sinister deeds? I decided to keep a close eye on the guy, see what I could learn. Something about Dario seemed shady, shifty. Then again, maybe he was just an everyday creep. It could be hard to tell the difference.

Stella continued down the row, snagging a freshly prepared cannoli and putting that in a to-go box, too.

I filled two glasses with ice and raspberry tea, and returned to the dining room, setting one glass on each side of the table in front of my customers. "Have y'all decided?"

The wife went for the penne with mushrooms, while the husband opted for the eggplant parmigiana.

"Excellent choices. I'll have those out to you in just a few minutes." I collected their menus and headed back to the kitchen to turn in their order. On my way, I passed

Stella, who was heading out with an enormous bag of food.

"Wish me luck!" she said.

I gave her a smile, but secretly willed her to fall flat on her face in the parking lot. The thought of a pretty twenty-year-old with a great figure hitting on my boyfriend had my blood boiling like the linguini noodles in the kitchen. I tried to force my feelings aside as I turned in the food order and went back to the dining room to seat a party of five who'd just arrived. Luisa helped me push two of the tables together and remove the extra chairs.

The blond salad-eater appeared in the doorway and raised a hand to get my attention. Looked like she was ready to cash in on the deal we'd made during my interview. I scurried over and showed her to a table before one of the other girls could claim her.

Once she was seated, I said, "I assume you'd like your usual Caesar salad and water?"

"Not today." She grinned as she held out a hand for a menu. "I'm thinking about trying one of the seafood dishes. Maybe an appetizer, too."

The seafood items were the most expensive on the menu. This woman drove a hard bargain. She was also likely to drive me into bankruptcy.

I left her to decide just how badly she was going to stick it to me, and rounded up plates for the other tables. A few minutes later, the blonde had decided on the linguini with shrimp, as well as the bruschetta appetizer, a side salad, another chocolate cannoli, and a twelve-dollar glass of white wine. *Gee thanks, lady.*

The front door opened and Stella returned, her face drooping with disappointment.

"How'd it go at the gallery?" I asked her.

"The guy's good-looking," she said, "but he's older than he looked from over here. He's like *thirty.*"

She said the word as if it were a disease. I suppose to a young woman who had yet to reach full adulthood, thirty probably did seem ancient.

"Thirty's not too old for me," Elena said. "I'll take him lunch tomorrow."

*Ugh.*

"You should go over, too, sometime," Stella told me. "The place has all kinds of interesting art."

"I'll do that," I said.

Business picked up, and all of us were hustling for the next two hours. With the large crowd, and most of them ordering the cannoli for dessert, I wondered if I'd been wrong about the bistro's earnings. Maybe all of the reported income had been earned legitimately. Maybe Tino wasn't laundering his money through the restaurant. Of course it was much too soon for me to tell for sure.

While serving minestrone to a couple of diners at a table near the windows, I noticed a man in a green Cyber-Shield uniform walk across the parking lot and enter Gallery Nico. I tensed up for a moment, but realized he was probably going over to try to sell them security services. He hadn't been carrying a nail gun, after all.

During the peak of the lunch rush, I spotted Benedetta heading to the register with a zippered vinyl bank bag in her hand. The bag was blue and bore the Chase logo. She typed her code into the screen, opened the cash drawer, and removed stacks of bills from the till. After zipping them into the bag, she slid the drawer shut and returned to her office.

I continue to hustle and bustle and bus tables. Despite the fact that I'd worn comfortable shoes, my arches began to hurt. I wasn't used to being on my feet for hours at a time. I'd have to soak my feet tonight. Or maybe if I took a cannoli to the nail salon the tech would give me a foot massage.

Around half past one, when things had slowed a bit, I overheard Benedetta on the phone behind the bar, taking an order from her husband.

"Of course I saved you a cannoli, Tino," she said. When I glanced her way, she rolled her eyes in an expression that said *my husband can be such a pain in the neck*. She hung up the phone. "One time in twenty-four years I forget to save the man a cannoli and he won't ever let me forget it."

I offered her a shaking head in commiseration. "I'd be happy to take the food next door," I offered. It would be a chance for me to get my first peek inside Cyber-Shield.

Unfortunately, Benedetta declined my offer. "I can tell your feet hurt. Luisa can get it and you can take your lunch break."

Was Benedetta truly concerned about my welfare, or was she trying to keep me out of her husband's office? I had no way of knowing.

She waved a hand toward the kitchen. "Help yourself."

I wandered into the kitchen and looked over the selections. *Yum*. This job was certainly going to have its benefits.

"What would you like?" Dario said, grabbing a plate and waiting for me to decide.

"Spaghetti marinara," I told him. "And toss some of those fried mushrooms on top."

His nose wrinkled in disgust. "Those mushrooms are an appetizer."

I shrugged. "So?" I'd been known to eat leftover sushi for breakfast. Mixing an appetizer in with my entrée wasn't going to put me off.

He didn't bother to argue further, simply conceding with a return shrug. He ladled red sauce over the noodles and used tongs to add a sprinkling of fried mushrooms. "Let me know how it tastes."

I grabbed a fork and took a bite. *Mmm.* "It tastes delicious."

"Let me try." He grabbed a clean fork and scooped up a huge bite, cupping his free hand under his chin as he put it in his mouth. He let the food sit on his tongue for a moment, then slowly bit into it, his chewing speeding up as he formed his opinion. "It's an interesting combination of crunchy and savory."

"Yep." I snagged myself a chocolate cannoli, too. No lunch here would be complete without it.

I sat in the lounge and ate my fried mushroom spaghetti with my feet propped up on a chair. When I finished, forty minutes of my lunch hour remained. I went to my locker and removed my laptop from my backpack, setting it on the table. A moment later, the system was booted up and I clicked on the icon to search for available Wi-Fi connections. Several appeared. At the top of the list was *BBistro*. Surely that was the link for the restaurant. The second was *CSSecure*. That had to be Cyber-Shield's. The others included *Portraits2Go, YoloYogu,* and *GalleryN,* which were easily identified as belonging to the photography studio, the frozen yogurt shop, and Gallery Nico.

I went to the door of the lounge and waved a hand to catch Brian's attention. "I've got some homework I need to work on. Can you tell me what the Wi-Fi password is?" I mentally crossed my fingers that employees were allowed access to it.

"Cannoli," he called back. "Followed by the number 89 and a dollar sign."

"Thanks."

I returned to my laptop, clicked to connect to the bistro's Wi-Fi, and typed in *cannoli89$* when prompted for a password. One strike of the enter button and I was in.

Keeping up my façade, I retrieved my marketing

textbook from my backpack, opened it on the table next to me, and turned to the second to last chapter. As I came across key terms, I Googled them as if performing an extra bit of research into the core principles taught in the book. Meanwhile, I also took bites of the delectable cannoli, going so far as to lick my fork and the plate clean afterward. If any of Tino's thugs were watching me through the Webcam today, they'd get an eyeful.

The rest of the day went by in a blur. There was a brief respite in the middle of the afternoon, but it gave us just enough time to rewash the linens and prepare the tables for the dinner crowd. I'd thought my job as an IRS special agent was demanding, but waiting tables took a high toll. Not only did my arches ache, but I'd burned my wrists carrying hot plates, bruised my hip when I'd run into the corner of the brick oven in the kitchen, and accidentally shot lemon juice into my eye when positioning a wedge on a tea glass.

I should get hazardous-duty pay for this.

# chapter nineteen

# *I* Gotta Be Me

I left the bistro on Friday evening with collapsed arches, an aching back, and burn blisters on my arms. On the bright side, I also left with a bag full of scrumptious Italian food and a printout of today's sales figures, as well as those for the last week and month. I kept a close eye on my rearview and side mirrors, checking for a tail. There was none. *Good.* I felt smug knowing I'd fooled the alleged "wise guys" of the Dallas mafia. Looked like they weren't so wise, after all.

I drove until I was a couple of miles from Cyber-Shield and pulled into the parking lot of a grocery store. I removed my IRS cell phone from the locked glove compartment and texted Josh. *Bistro's Wi-Fi password is cannoli89$.* I waited a minute or two until his reply came back. *Got it.* With any luck, he'd be able to hack in right away and access the restaurant's financial records.

I deleted the texts, pulled the sales data printouts from my pocket, and looked them over, trying to get a realistic estimate of the restaurant's income. It wasn't easy. Sales seemed to fluctuate significantly day to day, with the weekend figures being nearly ten times that of the weekdays. To be expected, I supposed. More people ate out on the weekends than midweek. They were also more likely to order an expensive cocktail or glass of wine on the weekend rather than a weekday.

Using the calculator feature on my phone, I multiplied today's sales number by 365 to get a ballpark estimate of what the bistro's annual gross revenues would be. I did a similar computation with the weekly sales figure, multiplying it by 52. Finally, I took the figure for the last month and multiplied it by 12. No matter how I estimated the earnings, the numbers fell far short of the amount that had been reported on the restaurant's tax return last year.

Did that prove that Benedetta was laundering money for Tino? Maybe. Then again, maybe not. Other variables could affect the figures. I wasn't sure whether the data was typical, or whether they reflected seasonal fluctuations. I'd heard that people tended to eat out less over the holidays and in the winter months, while they visited restaurants more often during the summer, when they were enjoying vacations. An economic slump or something as simple as road construction could negatively impact a restaurant's income, while an economic rally or successful ad campaign could send earnings through the roof. How much the bistro's catering service brought in was anyone's guess at this point, too. The figures weren't broken out on the bistro's tax return. If Josh could hack into her system, though, we'd have more financial data to analyze and could possibly answer some of these questions.

I listened to the Italian CD on the remaining drive back to my apartment. I'd moved on from numbers, and was now learning the four seasons. *L'inverno. La primavera. L'estate. L'autunno.*

At the apartment, I changed out of my work clothes

and dropped them into the stackable washing machine. I'd picked up a splattering of marinara sauce on my blouse and a smudge of creamy Alfredo on my pants. It was hard to stay clean schlepping Italian food.

Benedetta had given me the weekend off from the restaurant. The weekends were probably the bistro's busiest times, which meant more tips for the servers, and she'd scheduled her daughters to work those prime shifts. Who could blame her? The restaurant was the family's bread and butter—make that *garlic* bread and butter.

A lively Katy Perry tune carried up to my apartment. I turned the mini-blinds in my living room window to see a handful of the complex's twenty-something residents gathered around the pool, beer bottles and wine coolers in hand as they celebrated the end of the workweek. It was the kind of thing Alicia and I had done when we'd worked together at Martin & McGee and shared an apartment.

Though those times had been only a few years ago, it felt like a lifetime had passed since then. I suddenly felt old and excessively burdened, the Fabrizio case weighing on me like that overloaded barbell. For all I knew, the man planned to kill another person this weekend, to do harm to another client who'd refused to give in to his salesmen's unreasonable demands. Other than the kisses Tino had planted on my cheeks yesterday, I'd been unable to get close to the man. I realized I was being much too impatient, that these types of complex investigations can take weeks, months, or even years to complete, but patience had never been one of my virtues. Besides, our plan of attack had been to hit Tino hard, with a large team of agents. Surely that should speed things up, right? One could hope.

I hadn't had the foresight to pack my bathing suit, but I did have a tank top, shorts, and flip-flops. I quickly changed into them, grabbed a towel, and retrieved the still-warm food from the fridge. I grabbed a stack of the cheap plastic plates that were in the cabinet, along with some silverware and napkins. I carried the whole she-bang down to the pool area and set it on an empty table.

"Free food!" I called. The fastest way to a man's heart was through his stomach, but it was also the fastest way to make new friends.

In seconds, a crowd had gathered around and were filling their plates with spaghetti, fettucine, tortellini, and garlic knots. A curly-haired blonde handed me a fuzzy navel-flavored wine cooler. It felt good to relax, to let go of the tension I'd been carrying around all day.

I fixed myself a plate and slid onto a chaise lounge next to my new temporary BFF, who told me her name was Angelique.

"I haven't seen you before," she noted, holding her loaded fork aloft. "Did you just move here?"

"Yeah. A few days ago." I tore a bite from a garlic knot and paused, thinking I should open up in the spirit of making friends like Tori would. "I'm a student at DBU. I had a job as a nanny and lived with the family, but they moved out of the country. It's hot enough here in Texas. No way did I want to move to the Middle East with them. It's like a million degrees over there. What about you?"

"I've lived here for about three years," she said. "I'm a physical therapist at Parkland Hospital."

I gestured to the buildings with my bread. "Which unit is yours?"

Her mouth was now full, so she pointed her fork to indicate an apartment on the first floor, directly under the unit next to mine.

I pointed up to the window from which I'd peeked out at the group. "That's me up there."

She introduced me to several of the other residents. One of the guys even flirted with me a little. I flirted right back, though since I was allegedly a student at a Baptist school, I kept my comments PG-rated. No reason to break character or tempt fate.

The crowd dwindled as residents returned to their apartments. I gathered up the dirty silverware and plates, bade Angelique good-bye, and returned to my apartment, where I stuck the dirty dishes in the machine and started it.

I glanced at my phone. It was nearing eight o'clock now. My mother would be arriving at my town house within the hour.

I figured it would be best to leave the Hyundai at my apartment so that it would look like I was home if any of Tino's men came by to check up on me. Taking my purse with me, I scurried out of my apartment, circled around to the alley, and cut through a strip center to the next block. There, I called for a cab.

I hopped into the cab, gave him my address, and took my compact out of my purse, using the mirror to ensure nobody was following the cab. Again, I was in luck. No tail. A quarter hour later, the taxi driver deposited me at my town house. My mother had already arrived, her car parked in the driveway behind Alicia's Audi.

"Thanks," I said, handing the driver the fee plus a tip.

He thanked me in return and eased away from the curb to go in search of another fare.

I looked up at my place. *God, it feels good to be home!* I'd only been gone two nights, but it seemed like a much longer time. It had been a busy and exhausting couple of days.

I unlocked the door and stepped inside.

# chapter twenty

# Mommy and Me

My mother, who was in my kitchen, clapped her hands and launched herself at me, always glad to see her only daughter. "There's my girl!"

My mother and I had the same small build and the same chestnut hair, though she maintained her color with the help of Miss Clairol. She was dressed in a pair of well-worn jeans and a knit top, comfortable travel/cooking clothes.

"It's great to see you, Mom." I gave her a warm hug, noting that her hair smelled like vanilla and cinnamon and ginger. No doubt she'd spent the entire day back in Nacogdoches preparing fresh-baked treats for Alicia's bridal shower tomorrow. She wasn't just a wonderful mother to me, she was good to my best friend, too.

It crossed my mind that Benedetta Fabrizio and my mother had a lot in common. Both were great cooks. Both were devoted to their children. And both seemed to be generous and caring with those outside their families, too. Still, though my mother adored and doted on my father, I knew she would never tolerate him becoming involved in illegal enterprises or committing acts of violence. I had to wonder, yet again, whether Benedetta had a clue what her husband was up to behind the scenes.

"How's the new case going?" my mother asked.

Alicia's eyes met mine and we exchanged a silent *ugh*. I hadn't exactly lied to my mother about my current investigation, but I'd left out the words *mafia, mobster,* and *extortion*. Also *murder, Christmas lights,* and *nail gun*. My recent involvement in the drug cartel case had been enough to nearly put the poor woman in her grave with worry. I'd left her with the impression that I was simply investigating a family-owned restaurant and that the couple who owned it might not be on the up-and-up.

"It's going okay," I said.

She tilted her head and eyed me. "I don't see why they had to put you in an apartment. They haven't moved you to a new place on your other cases."

I shrugged my left shoulder, faking nonchalance. "Just an abundance of caution."

She crossed her arms over her chest. "Tara Holloway, you're not telling the truth."

"What makes you say that?"

"It took me years to figure it out," she said, "but you've got a tell."

"A tell?" I looked over at Alicia. She raised her palms. Apparently she hadn't noticed anything.

"When you're not being honest," my mom said, "you raise your left shoulder."

Oh. I'd have to make sure not to do that again.

She frowned. "What kind of girl lies to her own mother?"

I sighed. "One who doesn't want her mother to worry."

She tilted her head. "*Should* I be worried?"

"No." My left shoulder lifted of its own accord.

Mom threw up her hands. "You're lying again!"

"Okay, Mom," I said. "You want the truth? I'll tell you. I'm going after a mobster, a mafia boss, like the guys from *The Godfather* and *The Sopranos*. He extorts money from his clients, and when they don't pay up he robs them and destroys their businesses. He's suspected of killing around a dozen men, many of whom have yet to be found."

She was quiet a moment before her eyes brimmed with fearful tears. "I think I'd rather you lied to me."

I stepped forward and hugged her again. "It'll be fine," I said. "I'm working in the restaurant and Nick and Josh are right across the parking lot keeping an eye on things. We've got a whole team working along with a group from the FBI to track the mobster's henchmen. I've got a weapon on me at all times."

That last part was a lie, but only a white lie, so I managed to keep my shoulder down. I kept my Cobra in my purse, but when I was on duty at the restaurant the gun was secured in my locker, not easily at hand.

My mother nodded, then waved her hands in the air as if to clear it of the negative thoughts. "Let's get to cleaning and decorating, shall we?"

I stuck my cats in my bedroom upstairs, where they wouldn't be able to undo all of our work. Although Mom and I told Alicia she shouldn't clean up for her own bridal shower, she insisted on helping.

"This might be one of the last times we three get to spend together," she said.

"Don't remind me." I spritzed Windex in her direction. *Spritz-spritz.*

Alicia and I spent the rest of the evening vacuuming and dusting my living room while my mother washed her crystal punch bowl and glasses. We finally finished around eleven and fell exhausted into our beds. It was great to be back home and sleeping in my own bed, cuddling up with Anne, even if Henry didn't like being confined to my bedroom and kept rattling the closed door with his paw, trying to escape. I wasn't about to let him out so he could cover the living room with his fur again.

The next morning, my alarm woke me much too early. I brewed coffee while Mom made me and Alicia a delicious breakfast of pancakes topped with sliced bananas and pecans. They weren't quite as good a treat as Benedetta's chocolate cannoli, but I wasn't about to tell my mother that.

"Can you just stay here forever, Mom?" I asked between mouthfuls.

"I'd love to, honey," she said, using the spatula to flip another pancake. "But your father couldn't survive without me. He'd try to live on his chili alone."

Dad's chili contained more types of peppers than a person could count and packed deadly heat. Just one swallow would nearly liquefy your insides.

We spent the rest of the morning setting up for the shower. Mom baked a French vanilla cake with strawberry filling, topping it with a heavy glaze and fresh blueberries. She put one of her beautiful white lace tablecloths on my dining room table, and arranged framed photos of Alicia and Daniel, her fiancé, around the pretty centerpiece she'd fashioned herself from silver ribbon encircling a white orchid with a half-dozen blooms. Mom was a Southern Martha Stewart. Though I could certainly appreciate my mother's talents, I'd inherited none of them and knew better than to even try. I could help, though. At her direction, I placed the punch bowl at the far end of the table and lined up the crystal glasses next to it. I placed bowls of those chalky, pastel-hued mints on the coffee table and end tables.

"You've outdone yourself," Alicia told my mother as Mom set out trays of cucumber and cream cheese sandwiches cut into crustless triangles, stuffed cherry tomatoes, and mushrooms in flaky pastry puffs. I counted no less than three dips—one for the fresh veggies, another for the fruit, and a third for the tortilla chips no Southern party could be without. It was a mix of fancy treats and comfort foods, and my mother pulled it off beautifully.

We showered and put on our party dresses. Alicia wore a feminine flowing strapless dress in a pale green pistachio color. Mom dressed in a bright blue shift. I wore a red dress I'd bought last year at an after-Easter sale. I'd originally purchased it with the intent of wearing it to an awards ceremony for my then-boyfriend Brett, who was a landscape architect and had been the recipient of a professional award. Work had gotten in the way and I'd been unable to attend the awards ceremony. My job required quite a few personal sacrifices. Fortunately, my new manicure went with the dress.

*Ding-dong.*

I opened the door to find Christina Marquez on my porch with an oversized gift bag in hand. Christina was a DEA agent who'd become not only my close friend but also a buddy of Alicia's.

"Hey, girl," I said.

"Hey, yourself." She cocked her head. "You're working a tough undercover case, aren't you?"

"How can you tell?"

"The new hair, for one," she replied, gesturing at my reddish-orange locks. "But the tired, raccoon eyes are a big clue, too."

"Do I really look that bad?"

She reached out and gave my shoulder a squeeze. "Only to a trained eye."

We embraced and I stepped back to let her inside. She placed her gift bag on the coffee table and accepted the glass of punch my mother held out to her. She looked over the spread on my dining room table. "This food looks fabulous."

"And it tastes even better," I said, making my mother beam.

Christina was quickly followed by Alicia's mother, one of our fellow CPAs from Martin & McGee, and several others, some of whom had driven over together.

The shower went off without a hitch. We played silly games, stuffed our faces with the delicious food and cake my mother had prepared, and watched as Alicia opened gift after gift after gift. A Le Creuset soup pot. A set of monogrammed towels. A gravy boat. A pair of crystal champagne flutes etched with Alicia's and Daniel's names and the date of their upcoming wedding. That last gift was from me.

Alicia gave me a tight hug. "I love them, Tara."

I smiled, though inside I felt myself vying with mixed feelings. I was truly happy for my best friend. She'd be starting a new phase of her life with the man she loved. But as happy as I was for her, I was bummed for myself. Alicia would be gaining a husband, but I'd be losing a best friend. I had no illusions that our relationship would remain the same once she and Daniel tied the knot. I knew that was how it was supposed to be, that he should become her number one priority, but it still made me feel a little sad.

When the shower was over and the guests had gone, each of them taking home a cello goody bag filled with Mom's homemade divinity and pecan pralines, Daniel swung by to help Alicia move the unwrapped gifts to his loft apartment, where they'd be living together after the big day. He took a look at the huge pile of gifts covering my floor and coffee table and threw a fist in the air. "Score!"

"Daniel!" Alicia scolded. "Behave."

He picked up the soup pot. "Does this mean you're going to learn how to cook?"

"Are you kidding?" Alicia said. Her kitchen skills were as pathetic as mine. "I only plan to use it for warming up soup that comes out of a jar."

I crossed my arms over my chest. "Maybe *you* should learn to cook, Daniel. I hear a lot of husbands do the cooking these days."

He set down the pot and raised his hands in surrender. "Canned soup is fine with me."

My mother looked from Alicia to her fiancé. "This sure was a fun day. Should we go ahead and pencil in a baby shower?"

Daniel looked freaked out, though Alicia only looked thoughtful. "Give us a year or two."

"Or three," Daniel said. "Four maybe?"

"Wuss," I whispered.

The happy couple offered to help us clean up, but we shooed them off after we helped them load the gifts into Daniel's car.

"We've got it," Mom said. "You two go find a place for all this loot."

When they were gone, Mom and I went back inside and picked up the stray bows, wrapping paper, and dishes from the living room.

"Thanks, Mom," I told her. "I don't know what I would've done without you."

"Happy to help, honey. You know I love to cook, and I love to spend time with you even more." She wadded up a ball of torn gift wrap, the paper giving off a *crinkle*, and gave me a knowing look. "I bet it won't be long before Alicia is returning the favor and throwing you a bridal shower."

I tossed a soiled napkin into her bag. "Don't count your chickens before they're hatched."

"You and Nick are nuts about each other," she replied. "Those chicks are already in their eggs, pecking away."

Nick and I seemed to be heading in the direction of the altar. He'd even joked recently that he'd entered a not-so-secret office pool, betting he'd propose to me in September. Still, anything could happen before then. Dario could slice me up with one of his knives and boil me in one of those huge pasta pots. Benedetta could turn out to be her husband's murderous sidekick, force a chocolate cannoli down my throat, and choke me to death with it. Tino Fabrizio could shove me headfirst into the bistro's pizza oven, make it look as if I'd tripped and fallen.

*Sheesh*. Those horrifying photographs and being watched through my Webcam had left me overly apprehensive.

After we'd finished cleaning up, Mom changed back into comfortable clothes for her drive home.

"I hate to have to rush off," she said, "but I promised your brother I'd take Jesse to her horseback riding lesson tomorrow."

Jesse was my favorite niece. I knew I shouldn't have a favorite, but the kid was so much like me it was hard not to feel a special connection.

I went upstairs to spring Henry and Anne from their bedroom prison. That fortune cookie had been right—a trapped cat does become a lion. Anne, who was normally a docile cat, had gone psycho being closed in the room without me. She'd skittered back and forth across my bedspread, leaving it rumpled and askew. She'd clawed at the carpet inside the door and pulled some of the strands loose, the fibers littering the floor, the webbing that held the carpet together exposed in spots. She'd also knocked over my bedside lamp and left claw marks in the wood on my night table. I wanted to be angry at the destruction she'd caused, but the poor thing was upset. What she needed now was love.

I righted the lamp, retrieved Anne from her hiding place under the dresser, and cradled her in my arms. "It's okay, baby. You're free now."

She looked up at me, mewed, and, a moment later, began to purr. Looked like her emotional wounds were healed.

After bidding the cats good-bye again with a kiss on the head and a scratch on the chin, I helped Mom carry her suitcase and the punch bowl out to her car, then climbed in myself. She planned to drop me near my undercover apartment so I wouldn't have to wait for another cab.

When she pulled to a stop two blocks away from my new place, I leaned across the car, put my hands on her shoulders, and kissed her on both cheeks. "That's how the Italians do it."

"And this is how we Southerners do it." She gave me one last, warm hug, so tight one of my vertebrae popped. "Stay safe, Tara. Someday I want to be sending *your* shower guests home with pralines."

# chapter twenty-one

# $\mathcal{H}$oly Fathers and Godfathers

I spent Saturday night at home alone. I'd gone by Angelique's place around seven to see if she wanted to come up and watch a movie, but she was getting ready for a date.

"Some guy came by your apartment earlier today," she said. "I saw him when I was coming back from getting my mail."

*Uh-oh. Had it been one of Fabrizio's men checking up on me?*

"What did he look like?" *Did he have a nail gun? A barbell? A Santa hat?*

She looked up, as if trying to recall a mental picture. "Dark hair. Not tall. A little heavy, maybe."

*Could it have been Dario?* "Did you talk to him?"

"No. By the time I got back to our building he'd come down the stairs and gone."

"Did you see what kind of car he drove?"

"He didn't get into a car," she said. "At least not that I saw, anyway. He just walked off toward the front entrance."

*Hmm . . .*

I thanked her for the information and went back to my apartment. If the man had been one of Tino's thugs checking up on me, what conclusions had they drawn from the fact that I wasn't home? That a friend had picked me up? That I'd gone out for a walk, maybe a swim in the pool? Of course the guy could have simply been looking for someone else and come to the wrong apartment. Or maybe he was a friend of the previous tenant or a solicitor wanting to sell me a magazine subscription.

Regardless, I figured it couldn't hurt to cover my ass and allay suspicions. I went up to my apartment and logged into my laptop, connecting to the Internet to make it as easy as possible for Tino's tech guys to cyberspy on me . . . *if* they were cyberspying on me. I fooled around on my laptop, checked the decoy Gmail account the FBI had set up for me, and, while watching more kitten videos on YouTube, pretended to place a call to a friend on my new phone.

"Hey," I said after I pretended to dial a number. "It's me."

I paused for what I hoped was an appropriate time, having a make-believe conversation with my imaginary friend in my head. *Hi, Tori,* said my imaginary friend. *What's up, bee-yotch?* Yep, my imaginary friend was sassy. Also, a little outdated on her slang. *Bee-yotch* was so two years ago.

"Not much," I said to the phone. "Just got back from a bridal shower." *Did you hear that, Tino's goons? I've been at a bridal shower.* In case they'd noticed my car in the lot all day, I debated mentioning that I'd gotten a ride with someone. But that might make it too obvious that I was trying to cover my tracks, wouldn't it? They could figure that out on their own. "She got so many gifts they wouldn't even fit in her car."

*Marriage,* said my phony friend who, like my alter ego Tori, was only in her mid-twenties. *Ew. Who wants to settle down so soon?*

"I know," I said. "I'm not ready for all of that 'till death do us part' stuff, either. But maybe we'd feel differently if we met the right guy." As long as I was—*hopefully*—punking Tino's tech team, might as well have a little more fun with it, right? "I saw the cutest shoes on the Neiman's Web site the other day."

*You're a student and a waitress,* said my fictitious and now apparently no-fun friend. *You can't afford shoes from Neiman's.*

"Maybe not *now*," I snapped back. "But when I graduate in a couple of years and get a full-time job I could afford to shop there." *Some friend, trying to quash my dreams.* I logged into the Neiman Marcus site again. "Get on their site and search for Sarah Jessica Parker."

*Pause.*

"No, I don't know when she got her own shoe line."

*Another pause.*

"You on the site now? Okay, good. It's the metallic sling-backs near the bottom of the first page."

*Another pause.*

"They do *not* look like stripper shoes."

*Another pause.*

"All right," I said, pretending she'd gotten another incoming call. "Tell him I said hi. Later." I pretended to thumb a button to end the call and tossed the phone onto my bed.

My ass now covered, I spent the evening parked in front of the TV, watching movies on HBO. I might be stuck here, bored and lonely, but at least the apartment came with the premium cable package. Thank heaven for small favors.

When I went to bed, I slept poorly again, wondering

if someone were outside keeping an eye on my apartment or listening to me snore through my laptop's microphone. It was unsettling and scary and I didn't like it one bit. This case better move along fast. I wasn't sure I could endure this type of life on a long-term basis. When Socrates said "the unexamined life is not worth living," he should have qualified his statement. A life should be examined only by the person living it. When someone else was examining your life, especially through a Webcam or by following your car, it actually made your life miserable.

On Sunday morning, I attended an eleven o'clock service at a nearby Baptist church. I went to church for several reasons. One, it was what a Dallas Baptist University student could be expected to do and would maintain my cover if Tino still had me under surveillance. Two, I was a little lonely, a little scared, and wanted to be around people, even if they were total strangers. And three, I figured it couldn't hurt to put in a prayer or two, ask the Big Man to keep our team safe and to help us catch Tino in the act before anyone else got hurt.

*Hallelujah and amen.*

Midway through the service, my cell phone vibrated in my purse. Though I had the ringer turned off, the buzz was nonetheless audible to those sitting nearby, several of whom cast me irritated looks for interrupting their weekly spiritual fix. *Hey, how about some of that forgiveness the minister was preaching?*

I fished the phone out of my purse to find a text from Agent Hohenwald, whom I'd identified as Heidi Brown in my phone. All it said was *Call me*, but I knew he wouldn't have contacted me unless it was something critical, so I read an implied *NOW!* at the end of the text.

I stood, though I kept myself hunched over so as not to block the view of the pastor from everyone behind me. "Excuse me," I said to the woman sitting in the pew next to me. She turned her legs to the side so I could squeeze by. This process continued as I made my way past eight other people, tripping over one man's large feet and nearly falling headfirst into the center aisle. That was the last time I'd sit in the middle of a row.

I hurried to the doors, opening and closing them as quietly as possible. As I bounded down the front steps of the church, I jabbed the button on my phone to dial Agent Hohenwald.

When he answered, he offered no greeting, instead getting right down to business. "We've got a body."

My head went airy and my hand went out, instinctively seeking the railing to steady myself. Grabbing the handrail in a death grip, I lowered myself to a sitting position on the steps. "Whose?"

"The locksmith's."

"Where?"

"A farmer outside Van Alstyne found the locksmith's work truck in his back forty. A hose was run from the exhaust pipe into the window."

Had guilt over the mugging or fear of apprehension led the man to take his own life? "It was a suicide?"

Hohenwald scoffed. "*Assisted* suicide, maybe, if you know what I mean."

I feared I knew exactly what he meant. That the scene had been set up to make it appear as if the locksmith had taken his own life, when in reality his life had been ended by someone else.

*By Tino Fabrizio.*

"The farmer called the sheriff's department, and when the sheriff's department ran the plates on the truck they noted we'd flagged the truck's owner as a person of interest in a pending investigation. They turned the scene over to the FBI. I've got a crew out here now going over the truck. No definitive word yet, but I noted marks and residue on the victim's mouth and wrists that would be consistent with duct tape."

*Yikes.*

"Was there any cash in the van?" I asked. "Maybe a bank deposit slip or something?"

"Nothing."

Part of me was disappointed. Finding a money trail could help my part of the investigation. Another part of me was glad I wouldn't have to go out to the crime scene. Coming face-to-face with a dead man wasn't my idea of fun.

"I'll get back to you when I know more," Hohenwald said. "In the meantime, warn your team to be extra vigilant. If this is how Tino treats guys who've done him a favor, no telling what he might do to a federal agent if he got one alone."

*Gulp.*

# chapter twenty-two

# Progress Reports

At three, I aimed my Elantra for the Galleria mall in north Dallas. I didn't notice anyone following me, but I knew that didn't guarantee I didn't have a tail. There could be more than one car and driver involved. The last thing I wanted was to end up in some farmer's field sucking exhaust, so I had to watch carefully.

On the drive over, my Italian CD taught me the words for common clothing items. *I pantaloni. Il cappotto. La camicia.*

I parked near Nordstrom, which sat at the end farthest from the route to Hana's apartment, and entered the mall. I ducked into several stores as I made my way down the main walkway, but purchased no *pataloni, cappotto,* or *camicia.* Still I noticed no one trailing me, no one who looked suspicious. Though I normally stopped to watch the ice skaters on the rink near Macy's, today I simply hurried into the store. I circled around the perimeter and darted out the doors that led to the parking lot.

Keeping an eye on my surroundings, I power-walked

the mile to Hana's condominium, impressed that I made it in just over fourteen minutes. That Italian food and cannoli hadn't slowed me down yet. I'd just raised my hand to knock when Hana peeked out from the curtain covering the narrow window next to the door. As I lowered my hand, she opened the door.

"Come on in," she said. "There's drinks in the fridge. Help yourself."

After learning about the body Hohenwald had found, I could really go for some alcohol. But I knew that would be a mistake. Alcohol dulls a person's senses and slows down response time. And if ever I needed to be alert and quick it was now, while I was working this difficult, risky case.

I went in to find Eddie and Will already seated on a contemporary mauve and chrome sofa inside. Each of them held a can of soda.

I lifted a hand in greeting. "Hey, guys."

"Hey," they said in unison.

I went to Hana's fridge, admiring her granite countertops and stainless steel appliances. My town house had been built some time ago, and had standard Formica counters and traditional white appliances. Ridiculous of me to have kitchen envy given that the only thing I did in the room was make coffee and feed my cats, but I couldn't help myself. I grabbed a Dr Pepper and returned to her living room, admiring the colorful rug. I took a seat on a modern gray chair. "Nice place, Hana."

She continued to watch out the window for Josh and Nick. "I can't take any credit. My girlfriend did all the decorating."

I'd just opened my soda—*pop!*—when Hana said, "Here they come."

She opened the door and in came Nick and Josh. It was all I could do not to jump to my feet, run over to Nick, and envelop him in a bear hug, but I knew doing so would look unprofessional. I forced myself to stay cool.

He turned his whiskey-colored eyes on me and in an instant they brightened. His upper lip curled in a tight smile. "Hey, you."

"Hey."

Hana directed him and Josh to her fridge, and a moment later we were all seated in a circle around Hana's living room. Nick had chosen the chair closest to me.

"As the team leader," I said, "I guess I'll start. The big news is that they found the locksmith who's suspected in the mugging at the barbecue place."

Eddie sat up. "Is he talking?"

I shook my head. "He's not even *breathing*."

He sat back again. "Oh."

The room was silent for a moment as the news sank in. The horror of it only confirmed that we needed to make fast progress on this case before someone else met a similar fate.

"Tino came into the restaurant the day I interviewed," I told the group. "He was nothing but cordial. One of the chefs seems a little sketchy, but it could be he just has a crappy personality. He did make an odd comment, though. He said that he could never be fired because he 'knew too much.'" My fingers formed air quotes for emphasis.

Nick's eyes narrowed. "What do you think he meant by that?"

"I wish I knew." *Had Dario simply been joking? Or had the reference meant something sinister?*

"We'll follow him, too," Eddie volunteered. "See if he might be up to something."

"Thanks, buddy. The good news," I added, "is that I got Benedetta's Wi-Fi password and passed it on to Josh." I turned to our tech expert. "Were you able to hack into the restaurant's records?"

"Of course," Josh said proudly.

Frankly, despite Josh's superb skills, I was a little surprised he'd gotten in so quickly. With Tino being in the cybersecurity business, I figured the man would have outfitted his wife's bistro with all types of technical bells and whistles to keep hackers out. I wasn't sure whether Josh's easily infiltration was a testament to my coworker's hacking skills or an indication that Tino didn't think the bistro's data needed protection. Perhaps I was barking up the wrong tree and the funds weren't being laundered through the restaurant.

Josh pulled a manila folder from his briefcase and handed each of us a printout that included reports downloaded from the bistro's bookkeeping system. The paperwork also included copies of relevant portions of the restaurant's tax returns. The rest of us flipped through the pages while Josh explained his findings.

"The revenue and expenses reported on the returns coincide with the figures in their internal records," he said.

"Which begs the question," Hana replied, looking up from her copy, "are those numbers accurate or have they been inflated?"

I pulled the cash register sales printouts from my purse. "I snagged some data from the cash register. Let's see if it matches up."

I called out the figures, while Josh compared them to the entries in the bookkeeping system. "They all match."

Eddie raised his palms. "But that doesn't necessarily prove anything, does it? Benedetta or her daughters could be ringing up false sales to inflate the numbers. That would be an easy way to launder funds."

"True," I agreed, "but they'd have to ring up a lot of fake sales for it to amount to anything."

The Cyber-Shield salesman had attempted to extort

two grand a month from Alex Harris, the former bar owner. I had no idea whether the amount was typical, or how many clients might be involved, but it would take a significant number of falsified cash sales transactions to add up to tens of thousands of dollars per month. Besides, the register printout broke down the sales between credit and cash. The percentage of cash sales didn't appear to be unusually high.

Hana took another look at the financials. "Maybe the money's being laundered through the catering account."

I looked at the data. Hana had a point. The catering revenue was substantial, over $300,000 last year.

Will cocked his head. "Wouldn't that be a bad strategy for laundering funds? It would be much easier to verify a few large catering sales than it would smaller cash transactions by anonymous customers. Besides, big catering events would likely be paid for by credit card or check, which would leave a paper trail."

In today's world *paper trail* was a bit of a misnomer. *Electronic trail* would be more appropriate given that most financial transactions were processed electronically. But Will had a point, too. Money was typically laundered via some type of untraceable cash transaction. Cash didn't leave a trail.

Nick posed another possibility. "Tino might be transferring cash to a straw man posing as a catering client, and in return the straw man could pay for bogus catering services via credit card."

"Good point," Josh said. "I'll see if I can find catering invoices on Benedetta's system. If I can figure out who the clients were, I might be able to do some discreet digging and see if things look legit."

"Any luck hacking into Cyber-Shield?" I asked him.

"None." Josh's jaw clenched in frustration. "I've never seen a system as well protected as theirs."

"So Cyber-Shield's system is totally separate from the restaurant's?" I asked.

He nodded. "Different servers. Different routers."

*Darn.* I'd hoped the restaurant's system might somehow be a back door into Cyber-Shield's. I looked down at the floor and thought for a moment. "What about Kira? You think she could help?"

Kira was both Josh's girlfriend and an expert hacker, the only person I knew whose technical skills rivaled Josh's. I'd once seen her remotely open the CD drive on an unsuspecting person's laptop at a coffeehouse. It had been both impressive and creepy at the same time.

Josh shrugged. "Can't hurt to have her take a second look."

I pulled out my cell phone and dialed Lu for authorization to hire Kira, putting our boss on speaker.

Lu had two questions. "Will she work for seventy-five bucks an hour and can she keep her mouth shut?"

After texting Kira to see if she was okay with the rate, Josh responded to both questions in the affirmative.

"All right," Lu said. "But give her information on a need-to-know basis only and cap her at twenty hours. If she can't get in by then, y'all will have to find another way to get the information you need."

I thanked Lu and ended the call.

Josh looked down at his phone, typing again with his thumbs. "I'll see when Kira can start." *Ping.* He read her message and paraphrased it to the group. "She can be at the gallery by ten tomorrow morning."

*Good.* Things needed to keep moving . . . *before someone else stopped breathing.*

# chapter twenty-three

# *T*eam Effort

Forcing the thought from my head, I said, "Someone in a white pickup followed me home from the bistro on Thursday evening." My eyes went from Hana to Will. "Any luck figuring out who it was?"

"We ran the license plates," Hana said, "but they belonged to a Kia Optima. They'd been stolen the week before."

*Damn.*

"Hana and I tag-teamed the truck," Will added. "Stayed on them for an hour before we lost them going through a sobriety checkpoint near the West End."

*Damn, again.* Ironic, too. Detective Booth would love to bust Fabrizio, but officers from her own department had inadvertently gotten in the way of our investigation. It wasn't the first time that different branches of law enforcement had stepped on each other's toes.

I turned the can in my hand. "Agent Hohenwald phoned me not long after I got home that night. His tech support told him that someone else was logged into my apartment's Wi-Fi besides me. He said they could be watching me through my computer's Webcam."

Nick raised a brow. "They see anything good?"

I wasn't about to admit they could've seen me waxing my lip, cleaning my pores, and eating food off the floor, never mind the boob scratch and burp. "No," I lied, "but I spent nearly an hour online window-shopping for stilettos."

"Classic Tara tactic." Nick emitted a combination groan and chuckle. "That'll teach 'em."

I told the group about the silver sedan that followed me to DBU Friday morning. "It never got close enough for me to identify it."

"Josh and I were followed, too," Nick said. "Wednesday evening. We stayed at the gallery late to keep an eye on the comings and goings at Cyber-Shield. The car that followed us was either black or dark blue, a Chrysler maybe. The driver followed us to our new place. The FBI put us in a gated complex, so the driver couldn't follow us inside. But we're pretty sure he circled back by to see that we had actually pulled into a garage. I was able to sneak out later that night and get to a second car we'd parked down the street. I coordinated with Will and we tag-teamed one of Cyber-Shield's patrolmen, but nothing looked unusual."

Will lifted his chin in affirmation. "The guy drove a repeated route between ten Cyber-Shield clients in the Lakewood area. He'd turn on his flashing light, circle their buildings, and shine a spotlight in their bushes and behind their Dumpsters. At a couple of places he got out of his car to make sure fences and doors were locked, but it was all typical security patrol stuff."

"Same goes for me," Eddie said. "I followed a patrol unit last night and he made the rounds of about fifteen clients in the Wilshire Heights and Lower Greenville neighborhoods. Mostly mom-and-pop places. A dough-nut shop. A small veterinary clinic. A pottery store."

Hana set her drink on the coffee table and leaned in. "My experience was different. The patrol guy I followed Friday night didn't stay in one area. He was all over town, different places each night. He went inside at each client's location, too."

"How long was he inside each place?" I asked.

"Not long. A minute or two on the short end and maybe ten minutes on the long end."

"Did he take anything inside or bring anything out with him?"

"Only a flashlight," Hana said. "As far as I could tell, anyway. He wore a Cyber-Shield jacket. It's possible he could have tucked something inside it."

"Like an envelope of cash," Will suggested.

"Since these clients aren't connected by location," Hana said, "maybe the thing they have in common is that they're all paying Tino not to hurt them or damage their businesses. These could be the clients he's shaking down."

I pondered the possibility. "It would make sense that Tino would have only one of his patrolmen picking up the protection money. The fewer people who know what he's up to, the less risky it is for him."

Josh turned to Hana. "Which patrolman were you following?"

"The big white guy with the square head," she said. "The one who drives car number six. I looked up the W-2s for Cyber-Shield, got the names from them, and took a look at the driver's license photos until I identi-fied the guy. His name's Cole Kirchner."

"Let's put more eyes on Kirchner," I said. "Eventually we'll catch them shuttling the money around."

"Or *they'll* catch *us*," Hana said. "It's hard to be incon-spicuous when you're following someone late at night.

Some of these areas are pretty quiet. There's not a lot of traffic."

What a party pooper. Still, she had a point. We couldn't afford to blow our investigation by slipping up and letting one of Tino's men realize the federal government was on to him.

I turned my focus back to Nick. "I saw a man from Cyber-Shield go into the gallery on Friday. What did he want?"

"To sign us up for a security package," Nick said. "He said he'd waive the initial setup fee since there's already a camera in place. I told him my partner and I would need to talk it over. He recommended a software package, but I told him we don't handle a lot of sensitive data, so I thought we'd be safe enough with over-the-counter anti-virus software. He also said that if someone broke into the gallery, the art pieces would be irreplaceable. I mentioned that we had insurance to cover any losses, but he pointed out that the worst part about being robbed isn't necessarily the financial effect but the hassle of dealing with all the details." Nick reached into his pocket and pulled out a Cyber-Shield brochure. "He suggested we get one of these pull-down storefront security gates."

I looked the brochure over. The gates came in a number of styles. Some were essentially open-weave metal screens, like the security gates used on stores inside shopping malls. Others were solid, like garage doors. Some models were designed to be mounted on the interior side of the windows, while others were designed to be mounted outside. The brochure noted that the gates were designed to prevent smash-and-grab-type thefts and acts of vandalism. Some were even hurricane resistant. Not that hurricanes were a problem in Dallas where the closest beach was a five-hour drive away. North Texas did see its share of tornadoes, though. Heck, one had hit Fort Worth recently and overturned a police cruiser. I'd worked a case once with the female cop and K-9 who'd been inside the car. Luckily, neither of them had been injured.

"If we're trying to look legitimate," Nick said, "it would make sense to get one of these gates for the gallery." He pointed at one of the exterior-mounted models. "That's one of the least expensive types. I think we should do it."

While Lu had to approve the hiring of outside consultants, as the team leader I'd been given a budget for equipment and other expenses. I had the authority to approve the gate.

"Good call," I told Nick. "Go ahead and make arrangements." I stood to go, looking around the room. "Next Sunday same time, same place."

With any luck, someone on the team would have some hard evidence against Fabrizio by then. Maybe one of my coworkers would snap a photo of one of the patrolmen walking out of a client's business with a bag of cash. Or maybe Josh could identify a phony catering client or finally hack into Cyber-Shield's bookkeeping system and prove that the numbers didn't add up. Then again, maybe Fabrizio would realize he was under surveillance and shove us all into the pizza oven together, a mass cremation of sorts.

My skin felt hot just thinking about it . . .

# chapter twenty-four

# *M*aking Changes

After the other members of our team had left Hana's condo, Nick and I took a moment to sit down on Hana's front stoop and have a private conversation. We'd had no time together since Tuesday night, and nearly a week without him was taking its toll on me. Add in that I was losing my best friend and my emotions were on the edge.

Nick, of course, picked up on it. The guy could read me like a book—a dog-eared book he could recite word by word, including the copyright page and table of contents.

He reached out and tucked a strand of hair behind my ear. "What's wrong, Red?"

"You know my mom and I threw Alicia's bridal shower yesterday, right?"

He nodded. "Yeah?"

"Well." I looked down, a little embarrassed to be getting so sentimental. "It's just that . . . It feels like . . ." *Oh, quit being a baby and just be honest about your feelings. This is Nick you're talking to. He doesn't judge you.* "I'm losing my best friend."

Nick stared at me a moment, and I was surprised to see a flicker of hurt in his eyes. "Stupid me," he said softly. "I thought *I* was your best friend."

*Great.* Now I'd hurt *his* feelings.

As I stared into his whiskey-colored eyes, wondering what I could say to make things better, I realized that Nick was right. He and I shared a deep, romantic love, but we'd become best friends, too. He might not enjoy romantic comedies or shopping for clothes, and he flat-out refused to accompany me to the salon for a facial, but he'd become my go-to person anytime I suffered an emotional crisis, the person who convinced me of my worth when I got down on myself, the person who listened to me bitch when I'd had a bad day and needed to vent. He was the person I'd want by my side if I could only have one person there. And, obviously, he was the person who knew me better than I knew myself.

"You know what?" I said. "You are. You're my best friend."

"*You* know what?" he said, taking my hand. "I don't think you're upset about losing a friend. I think you and your friends are moving into a new phase of life and it scares you."

Damn if he hadn't hit the nail on the head. It all bubbled to the surface then.

"Everyone's settling down," I said. "Alicia's getting married next month, and Christina and Ajay are engaged. Next thing you know everyone will be having babies, and driving minivans, and joining the PTA."

Nick chuckled. "Nothing wrong with that."

"I know." I sighed. "It's just that I have a hard time visualizing *us* in those roles. Think about it, Nick. If we were married with children, we couldn't be working a case like this. Not both of us, anyway. Someone would need to be home at night to tuck the kids into bed and read them a story." It was one thing for me to leave my cats in the care of my roommate, but children would be an entirely different matter. I wanted to be a top-notch special agent, but I'd want to be a good mother someday, too. I couldn't pawn my kids off on my mother for weeks at a time while I went undercover to catch a mobster. But I wasn't sure I could see myself entirely sacrificing my career, either. I'd worked hard to get where I was, and my job had become a part of me, a critical piece of my identity.

Nick draped an arm over my shoulders and pulled me closer. I rested my head on his shoulder.

"You worry too much," he said. "We'll figure it out when the time comes."

"I suppose you're right."

"I'm *always* right."

"You are not," I said. "Remember when you thought sushi was going to be gross and then you tried it and liked it?"

"Well, I'm not wrong about this. Everything will be okay."

When Nick leaned in and put his lips to mine, I knew it would . . . so long as I had him.

"Tell you what," he said when we came up for air. "When this case is over, we'll spend a whole night watching movies of your choosing. We can even watch something with that guy you're so crazy about. What's his name? Charming Taters?"

"Channing Tatum."

Nick snorted. "Like that's any better."

I was scheduled to work the four P.M. to ten P.M. dinner shift at the bistro on Monday, which would leave my early hours free to check in on my other pending cases. That morning, I got up bright and early and went to my class at DBU. I noted no tail this morning, no one in the hallway peeking into the classroom, no one following me across campus to the parking lot. But just in case I had a tail I wasn't aware of, I performed a series of evasive maneuvers on my drive back into the city. For a mile or two, I drove much slower than the posted limit, which would force any tail to either pass me or slow down and reveal himself. I made a last-minute lane change to take a random exit, and circled back on the overpasses to continue on my way. Nope, no one was following me.

With that same abundance of caution, I parked in a downtown garage across the street from Neiman Marcus, and went into the store, exiting on the opposite side. I hopped onto a city bus that was waiting at the stop, rode it for a couple of blocks, then got off and made my way to the IRS building, cutting through the lobbies of several other buildings on my way.

I grabbed a cup of coffee from the kitchen and made my way back down the hall to my digs. Most of the offices I passed were dark and empty, the special agents who normally occupied them out working the Fabrizio case. What a harsh taskmaster I was, huh?

I plopped down in my rolling chair, took a huge slug of coffee, and noticed the light flashing on my desk phone, indicating someone had left me a voice-mail message. I picked up the receiver and dialed into the system.

A paralegal from the Triple 7 Adventures domain registry had called. I phoned her back right away.

"Got some information for me?" I asked when she came on the line.

"I do," she said. "The credit card number."

She rattled off sixteen digits.

"And the name on the card?" I asked.

"Same as the name on the registry," she said. "Tripp Sevin."

*Ugh*. The made-up name told me the credit card was one of those prepaid types that would work regardless of the name given. I thanked the woman for her time, figured out which bank issued the card, and coerced Ross into accompanying me back to court for another order. Judge Trumbull was in the middle of a hearing, but took a quick break to sign the order for me.

Back at my office, I scanned the order and e-mailed it to the bank's legal department. I hoped it wouldn't take long for them to figure out where the card had been sold. With that information, I might be able to figure out who'd purchased it. Meanwhile, it couldn't hurt to check in with the prepaid phone company and see if they'd made any progress. *The squeaky wheel gets the grease, right?*

An attorney in the company's legal department said, "Oh, hello, Miss Holloway. I was just about to call you."

*Yeah, right.* "What have you found out?" *Squeak-squeak.*

"The phone service was activated in December. It was deactivated last month."

"How were the service fees paid?" I asked.

She hesitated a moment as she looked at the information. "Via credit card." She rattled off the number, which was the same one the paralegal at the domain registry had given me only an hour or two earlier.

"What name were you given for the card?"

"Tripp Sevin," she said.

"Do you know where the phone was purchased?" Maybe I could swing by the store and review their security footage.

"Just a sec." There was a sound of papers ruffling. "Looks like the phone was part of a shipment sent to a Kmart store located in Tulsa, Oklahoma."

Tulsa was a five-hour drive from Dallas. It would be

impossible for me to go to the store in person, but I could at least give them a call.

After wrapping things up with the attorney, I phoned the Kmart store and was transferred to the manager. "Any chance you can determine when the particular phone was purchased so we can pin down the security footage?"

"No can do," he said. "I've been asked the same thing by law enforcement before. Our system can show me when that type of phone was purchased in the store, but there's no way for me to determine the phone number that was assigned to a given phone."

Short of watching the security footage taken at the time of each and every phone purchase, I was out of luck. Chances were that even if I saw the suspect on the screen, I wouldn't be able to identify him, and it was unreasonable to expect the manager to provide me with dozens of video clips.

Frustrated, I thanked the man for his help and hung up again. My only open lead at this point was the pre-paid credit card, and I knew the odds of it leading me to the culprit were about the same as my odds of hitting a triple seven on a slot machine. Slim to none. At least gamblers got free drinks. All I was getting for the efforts I was putting into this case was a headache.

I went down the hall to give Lu an update.

When I rapped on her door, she glanced up from her desk. "Uh-oh. Did somebody die?"

"No," I said. "Why?"

"You're dressed all in black, like you've been to a funeral."

"It's the bistro," I said. "Black is their standard color for the servers." I told her I'd run into walls on Triple 7 Adventure's domain/Web site and prepaid phone.

"Rats. I hoped one of those leads would pan out." She stood from her desk and retrieved her purse from a drawer. "I'll go back out to Whispering Pines. Bad news is best delivered in person."

*As if.* Did Lu think I couldn't see through her? She just wanted to see Jeb again. But I didn't call her on it. She'd let a few things slide where I was concerned. More than a few, really.

I went back to my office and took care of some loose ends on several of my smaller pending cases. Since there was nobody here to go to lunch with, I ordered takeout at a nearby deli and took it back to eat at my desk. As I finished up, Lu returned to my office.

She batted her false eyelashes. "Guess who's got a hot date for Saturday night?"

It certainly wasn't me. Come Saturday night, I'd probably be back on my couch at my apartment, watching television and window-shopping for shoes online. I was happy for Lu, of course, but I didn't want her to put too many eggs in Jeb's basket.

"Jeb's a nice guy and all," I said, "but I suspect he's a bit of a flirt."

Lu waved a hand dismissively. "Flirt, schmirt. Who cares? It's not like we're getting married. Besides, he's taking me to Abacus."

I'd been to the restaurant once. It was the type of place where food was presented like works of art and you were never really sure whether you were supposed to eat some of the things on your plate. "A nice meal like that," I warned her, "he's going to have expectations."

Lu scoffed. "It wouldn't be the first time I traded sex for steak."

"Lu!"

"Want to hear what I once did for a filet mignon?"

I covered my ears with my hands. "No!"

"Just getting your goat, Tara," she said, laughing before she turned a pointed gaze on me. "I'm a big girl, you know. You don't need to worry about me."

"I can't help it," I said. "I think of you like a—"

"Big sister?"

I'd been about to say a second mother or an aunt, but no sense bursting her bubble. "Exactly."

She took a seat in one of my chairs, and we spent a few minutes mulling over where to go from here on the Triple 7 investigation.

"That Cajun accent could be an important clue," Lu suggested. "You could check with authorities in Louisiana, see if they're familiar with someone running a scam like this there."

"Not a bad idea." I looked out my window, watching a pigeon who'd landed on the outer sill. "I suppose I could run a search on fifteen-passenger Chevy vans, too. After all, how many could there be in the Dallas area?"

# chapter twenty-five

# Chasing Cars

One hundred eighty-seven, as it turned out. I discovered this when I ran a search on the DMV's site.

Of those 187 vans, 39 were listed as gray. Of course it was possible this so-called Tripp Sevin had painted the van a different color after he'd registered it, or that the van wasn't even registered in the state of Texas, but I had to start somewhere, didn't I?

I ruled out a dozen that were owned in the name of Winging It, Inc., which operated an airport shuttle service. I'd seen their vans around town. They were all painted with the company's logo, white wings that stretched all the way down the side from the front fender to the back bumper. There was no way the van in the video footage from Whispering Pines could have been one of theirs.

I also ruled out seven vans registered in the name of Kiddie Corral, Ltd., a partnership that ran a chain of day cares with a ranch theme, their buildings painted red to look like barns. Another van was registered in the name of a Methodist church. That left nineteen vans in the names of individual owners or cryptic business names, such as Cargill Brothers Enterprises.

Two of the vans remaining on the list would be on my way to Benedetta's Bistro, including the one owned by Cargill Brothers. I decided to stop by and take a look at them next time I had a spare moment.

Before heading out of the IRS office that afternoon, I ran an Internet search for travel businesses offering overnight charter trips. Four popped up, but when I tried the phone numbers listed, one was answered by a computerized voice that directed my call into an automated messaging system, one was answered by a man with only a slight Southern drawl, and two of them were answered by women, neither of whom had a Cajun accent.

"Sorry," I told the people who'd answered my calls. "I was looking for someone named Becky. I must have misdialed."

Next, I tried the Louisiana Attorney General's office and spoke with their Consumer Protection Division. The investigator to whom I was transferred couldn't tell me much.

"We've had hundreds of complaints against vacation outfits," he said. "Mostly companies that sell time-shares or packages that include flights to foreign locations like Mexico or the Caribbean. 'Course we only go after the big offenders. We don't have the staff or time to pursue them all."

The truth of the matter was that, due to limited government resources, law enforcement couldn't pursue every con artist, and many small-time crooks got away with their crimes. The only upside was that because of the lax enforcement, some experienced con artists became complacent and lazy after a while, and took few, if any, measures to evade identification and apprehension. I could only hope that Tripp Sevin was one of these types and that he'd slip up somehow and give us a way to nab him.

The investigator continued. "I'm not aware of any complaints against charter van companies in particular, but I can ask around and get back with you."

"I'd appreciate that." I gave him both my phone number and e-mail address.

When I'd finished the phone calls, I walked briskly back to the parking garage across the street from Neiman's and retrieved my Hyundai. I drove on to Benedetta's Bistro to start my shift.

Given that it was only four o'clock, there were only two tables occupied in the dining area. Another customer, a man in a business suit, sat at the bar, enjoying a cocktail while he reviewed e-mails on a tablet. Elena stood behind the dessert case, resting her elbows on the top and her head in her hands, a wistful look on her face as she gazed across the parking lot toward Gallery Nico.

"You okay?" I asked, turning my head to follow her gaze out the window.

"Mm-hm," she murmured dreamily. "I met the art dealer on Saturday. His name's Nicolas. He's really hot."

And now so was I. When we'd had our powwow yesterday, Nick hadn't mentioned that he'd interacted with Elena. *Grrr.*

"Did you get to talk much?" I asked.

"Not really," she said, standing up straight. "His business partner interrupted us and they went into the back room. I didn't want to look desperate just hanging around waiting for him so I came back here. I was hoping he'd place an order today, but he hasn't."

Maybe the fact that Nick hadn't mentioned Elena stopping by the gallery meant she hadn't made an impression on him. But, really, how could a beautiful, busty young woman *not* make an impression? Especially on a red-blooded American male like Nick? Even so, just because he might have noticed that she was attractive and interested in him didn't mean he'd act on it. Nick loved me for my special kind of spunk, and few women had it.

"I'm sure you'll get another chance to talk to him," I said. "Be patient."

Elena's tone was mocking. *"Be patient. Be good. Don't let boys see your panties or you'll go straight to hell."* She rolled her big brown eyes. "You sound just like the nuns at our Catholic school." She stepped behind the bar, pulled two wine glasses from a rack overhead, and filled them with a generous amount of pinot grigio. "Here you go." She held out one of the glasses to me. "Mondays are always slow. Wine makes the time go faster."

Like mother, like daughter. The apple doesn't fall far from the tree. And the grape doesn't fall far from the vine, either, apparently.

I gave her a smile and took the wine from her. "I've never worked somewhere where I could drink on the job."

She took a sip from her glass and returned my smile. "Restaurant work is hard on the feet but it does have its benefits."

A twinge of guilt puckered my gut as I turned and walked to the kitchen. Benedetta and her daughters seemed like nice people. They'd probably be devastated by Tino's arrest—assuming, of course, that the joint FBI/IRS team was able to amass enough evidence against him to make an arrest. What would these women think of me when they learned I'd been the one to bust their husband or father?

They'd think I betrayed them, that's what.

I tossed the wine back in one big gulp and forced those guilty thoughts aside. Tino Fabrizio would be to blame for the consequences of his actions, not me. Even if it meant making innocent people suffer, I had a job to do. Which meant I really shouldn't have drunk that wine . . .

Wobbling a little, I went to the staff lounge, dropped my purse and backpack in my locker, and tied my apron around my waist. I emerged only to stop short and gasp when I came face-to-face with Dario wielding a long knife.

He laughed at my reaction. "Take out the trash." He pointed the knife at the overflowing bin next to his prep table. "It's full."

Reminding myself to start breathing again, I stepped over to the bin, grabbed the top of the plastic liner, and pulled. The bag lifted an inch or so inside the bin, but was too heavy for me to pull out.

Dario waved his knife again, offering advice but no assistance. "Turn the bin over and drag the bag out to the Dumpster."

Again I wondered whether Dario was merely a run-of-the-mill A-hole or whether he might have anything to do with the disappearances and so-called accidental deaths surrounding Tino. I supposed I might learn more when my team powwowed again next Sunday.

I maneuvered the bin onto its side on the floor and attempted to yank the bag out of it, having to tug several times to free it from its confines. Finally, it came loose. I tied the top closed and hauled it across the floor to the back door. I turned the knob and pushed the door, banging my nose and forehead into it when momentum carried me forward but it didn't budge. "Ow!"

I rubbed my bruised forehead. Had the door been left unlocked and I'd locked it when I turned the bolt? I turned the bolt and tried the knob again, pushing. Still the door didn't move.

Benedetta emerged from her office dressed in chef's

clothing, and spotted me fighting the door. "Tino had the door replaced this morning. This one's heavier and it opens outward. He said that would make it harder for someone to kick it in."

"Oh."

My embarrassment must have been written on my face because Benedetta patted me on the shoulder and said, "Don't worry, *cara*. We're all getting used to it." She smiled and rolled her eyes jovially. "My husband is always so worried about our safety. Such a sweet man."

*Sweet* would be the last word I'd use to describe Tino. Sweet people didn't send their minions to follow college girls home or spy on them through their Webcams. A sweet person wouldn't impale a man on a fence or crush him with a barbell or gas him to death in his own truck. And a sweet person wouldn't launder money or evade their taxes. Nonetheless, I returned Benedetta's smile.

I opened the door outward and half carried, half dragged the bag past the catering truck to the Dumpster. I wondered if anyone from Cyber-Shield was watching me through the cameras mounted along the back of the building. I also feared the rough asphalt would tear through the bag and cause me to leave a trail of garbage I'd have to clean up. But luck was with me. I made it to the Dumpster with the bag intact. After opening the cover to the bin and being treated to the lovely aroma of festering fettucine, I bent at the knee, grabbed the bag around the middle, and, in one burst of exertion, heaved the bag over the lid and into the huge metal bin. I even managed to do it without giving myself a hernia.

*Hooray for me.*

# chapter twenty-six

## *U*nbreakable

When my feet began to hurt again, I shoved a half-dozen sugar packets in each of my shoes as improvised arch supports. They were surprisingly effective. I only hoped I wouldn't have shoes full of ants in the morning.

As I took orders from a couple seated at a table near the window, I saw Kira exit Gallery Nico across the parking lot and head toward the bistro. Though she owned her own Web site design firm, Kira looked more like a singer in a punk band than a tech specialist. Her white-blond hair was shaved short on one side of her head, while the other side hung in dreadlocklike clumps. She'd encircled her wide blue eyes with her usual black smudges. Her lipstick today was a ghastly black. Kira was as thin as a heroin addict, though I knew that, despite her appearance, she was too smart and too dedicated to her Web site business to touch the life-ruining stuff.

Today she wore a lightweight green cardigan over a white shirt, along with a plaid miniskirt and saddle ox-fords. It was simultaneously cute, like a Catholic schoolgirl uniform, yet slightly disturbing, like a Catholic schoolgirl uniform.

She came into the bistro and our eyes met across the space. I walked over to her, forcing myself to maintain a normal pace when all I wanted to do was rush over and find out how things were going. Had they been able to hack into Cyber-Shield's computer system? Had they found any evidence of tax evasion, maybe a second set of books or some unreported income run through an off-shore account? What about the bistro's catering clients? Anything suspicious there?

Instead, I said, "Hi. Can I help you?"

"I need a chocolate cannoli," she said, "to go." She hiked a thumb over her shoulder to indicate the gallery. "The guys I'm working with over there said it's to die for."

I couldn't imagine Nick or Josh using that term. When Nick liked food he'd merely grunt or moan in appreciation, and the boyish Josh was more of the type to cry *"Yummy!"*

"I'll get you one from the case," I said.

Kira followed me to the refrigerated display case, waiting on the customer side while I made my way around to the back.

I slid open the back door and snatched a cannoli, placing it in a to-go box which I set on top of the case. "How's it going?" I whispered to Kira. "Any luck?"

"Not yet," she said. "I'm tearing my hair out over there."

Or tearing out what hair wasn't shaved anyway.

"Why don't you just shoot the guy," she added under her breath, "and be done with it?"

If only it were that easy. But there was a little thing standing in our way—the U.S. Constitution and its requirement of due process. If the Founding Fathers had met a guy like Tino Fabrizio, surely they would have inserted an exception into the text. Maybe something that read *These rights and privileges do not apply to cruel, coldhearted mobsters.*

My body tensed in frustration. If Josh and Kira couldn't hack into Cyber-Shield's system, nobody could. That left us with nothing else to do but continue to spy on Tino and his men and try not to raise suspicions. Not easy to do. Men trained in security techniques were more likely to realize they were being followed or watched. The longer this case went on, the more likely it was that Tino would be on to us.

Kira handed me a ten-dollar bill and I made change. "Enjoy your cannoli!" I called after her as she left.

At eight-fifteen, as the dinner crowd dispersed and the nine o'clock closing time loomed on the horizon, I ventured back into the kitchen with a handful of dirty dishes. Benedetta stood at the stove, ladling her marinara sauce into a smaller container that would fit inside the refrigerator.

I placed the dishes in the sink and walked over to Benedetta. "I've moved three tiramisu, two cream cakes, two bomboloni, and five chocolate cannoli." Funny, but even though this wasn't a real job for me, I was proud of my performance.

"Good girl." She pointed the ladle at me. "I knew you were the right choice the second you walked through the door."

"How?" I asked, curious.

"Your eyes," she said, watching me intently. "They're smart. They see things."

*Uh-oh.* That wasn't her way of telling me she knew I had my eyes on her husband, was it? Surely not. After all, if she'd figured out I was trying to nail him for extortion and tax fraud, she would've fired me on the spot, right?

Or would she have kept me around, instead? What's that saying about keeping your friends close but your enemies closer? Maybe Benedetta knew exactly what I was up to and gave me the job so that *she* could keep an eye on *me*. Maybe Tino was watching me right now through that video camera mounted in the corner. *Eeek!* Or maybe I was just becoming paranoid. When you spend all day looking over your shoulder, it can happen.

She handled me the ladle. "Put that in the sink, would you?"

"Can I lick it clean first?"

She chuckled. "As long as the health inspector doesn't see you."

I carried the ladle to the sink, then returned for the now-empty pot. "You ever consider bottling your sauces and selling them at grocery stores? I bet you'd make a killing." *Ooh. Bad choice of words, huh?*

Benedetta tilted her head, her expression thoughtful. "You could be on to something, Tori. We've already got a commercial kitchen here, and it's not being used in the early mornings before we have to start getting ready for lunch."

"In business terms," I told her, "that's called 'excess capacity.' "

She put a hand to my cheek. "You're going to be a great businesswoman someday."

*If she only knew.*

"You just need a commercial bottling system and a distributor," I said.

Her head bobbed. "I could hire a driver," she said, thinking out loud. "The driver could use the catering truck to deliver the bottled sauces. It's just sitting out back most of the time, anyway." She picked up a large to-go bag. "I'm going to look into it. For now, you take this food next door to my husband. He's working late."

Excitement bubbled up in me, but I tried not to show it. An IRS agent might get excited about getting closer to a target, but a regular old waitress wouldn't get all worked up over making a delivery.

"Burning the midnight oil, huh?" I said. "Something special going on?" Like maybe Tino planning another robbery or murder?

Benedetta shrugged. "He didn't say."

And apparently she didn't ask, either. Again I had to wonder whether she knew he was up to no good or whether she was deliberately avoiding the subject. Of course I supposed there was a third option, too. Maybe the woman was so busy running her own business that she didn't have time to worry about her husband's.

"You can use my code for the door," Benedetta said. "It's two-three-six-three."

"Two-three-six-three," I repeated. My heart pounded in my chest as I accepted the bag. I was about to get my first glimpse inside Cyber-Shield.

*Better make it count.*

# chapter twenty-seven

# $S$pecial Delivery

I walked back through the dining room and out the front
door, making my way down the sidewalk to Cyber-
Shield. I glanced over at Gallery Nico, and saw Nick
heading toward the front window. He must have spotted
me. He stopped at one of the paintings hanging on the
wall near the front door and pretended to straighten it,
though I knew he was watching me all the while. I felt a
little safer knowing a witness would see me walk into
Cyber-Shield. If I disappeared, at least there would be
probable cause to search the place. I only hoped they
wouldn't find me impaled on a fence post or with nails
driven into my face and brain. Of course Tino was unlikely to use those same methods again. It would be too
coincidental and suspicious, make the alleged accidents
look less like accidents. If he wanted to kill me, he'd
probably fit me with cement shoes and toss me into
Mountain Creek Lake. *Ugh*. I'd much prefer to wear
those Sarah Jessica Parker slingbacks.

As I stepped up to the front door of Cyber-Shield, I
noticed the door contained both a traditional keyed

dead-bolt lock and an automated keypad. I put a hand to the security keypad and typed in Benedetta's code. Two-three-six-three. A click sounded as the door unlocked, and an additional warning alarm buzzed as I stepped inside. *Bzzz.*

The reception area was lit, but the desk sat empty, the administrator having gone home for the day at five o'clock. I glanced around, spotting a security camera mounted in the back corner, aimed at the entrance. I was being recorded at this very moment, maybe even watched on a live feed. Who knew? Behind the desk was a hallway with two doors on each side and one at the end. The first door to the right was open. The other side doors were closed. The door at the far end of the hall was cracked open three or four inches. Mounted over the far door was another security camera that could take in activity in the hall.

"Mr. Fabrizio?" I called. "It's Tori. I've got your dinner."

Tino's voice came from the end of the corridor. "Back here, hon. End of the hall."

I circled the desk and walked down the hall, taking a quick glimpse into the open door on the right. The spacious interior was divided into cubicles. Stacks of Cyber-Shield's sales brochures sat on the modular desks in several of the empty cubicles, along with preprinted triplicate contract forms. A garment rack at the back held neon-green Cyber-Shield uniform shirts and nylon jackets in a variety of sizes. This room appeared to serve as an office for the salesmen, installers, and patrol drivers. Though the lights were on in the room, no one was inside. I supposed that was to be expected, given that most of the work done by these employees was performed off-site at the clients' homes and places of business.

I glanced at the corresponding door on the left. Unlike the standard interior door on the room I'd just peeked into, this door appeared to be made of heavy-duty steel, like the new back door that had been installed at the bistro. A second security keypad was mounted next to this door. Like the front entrance, this door also contained an old-fashioned keyed dead bolt. If my suspicions were correct, this was the room that housed the monitoring equipment and Cyber-Shield's server and Wi-Fi router.

*The control room.*

The next set of opposed doors were marked with the standard male and female signs indicating they were restrooms. The administrative assistant would have hers all to herself. I stepped past them and gently pushed on Tino's door which, like the locked door back down the hallway, was made of reinforced steel. It opened to reveal the man wearing his standard Cyber-Shield shirt and sitting behind a broad desk in a high-back leather chair. Given his short stature, the pinnacle of his head barely cleared the top of the chair. A keyboard, a mouse, and a large flat-screen computer monitor sat on his desk. Behind him was a cabinet topped with bookshelves. Rather than books, each shelf held photographs of his family. Some were professional family or individual portraits, while others were candid snapshots. Again, it struck me as odd that a man who seemed to love his family could have such an evil, violent side. If he loved his family so much, how could he not have empathy for his clients and their families, too?

"Special delivery." I held up the bag and forced a smile to my lips.

"None too soon," he said. "I'm starved."

I set the bag on the edge of his desk and unpacked it for him. The bag held a generous serving of capellini pomodoro, garlic knots, a salad with Italian dressing, and a chocolate cannoli. Benedetta had also included silverware and a cloth napkin.

Tino ran his eyes over the feast. "My Bennie. She sure takes good care of me, doesn't she? I'm a lucky man. I don't know what I'd do without that woman."

"She's a great boss, too," I told him, engaging in idle chitchat to give me time to take a surreptitious look around the office. Oddly, while the rest of Cyber-Shield's space was as secure as a prison, I noticed no security camera in Tino's office. Whatever happened in here, he didn't want it documented, didn't want anyone else to be able to look in. "I like working for her."

He tucked the napkin into the neck of his shirt, like a bib. "She likes you, too. Says you're a hard worker and that you don't complain."

"No reason to," I replied. "Where else would I be treated to a chocolate cannoli at the end of each shift?"

Tino laughed. "Thanks for bringing this over."

Clearly, I was being dismissed. "My pleasure."

I stepped out of Tino's office, pulling his door back to the nearly closed position it had been in when I'd entered. As I headed to the front door, a young man who had to be Eric Echols stepped up to the glass front door of Cyber-Shield. Like the other Cyber-Shield employees I'd seen, he wore the green uniform shirt, although his was not tucked in and was so wrinkled it looked as if he'd slept in it.

He typed in a code on the keypad and came inside, the door giving off the same warning buzz it had when I'd entered minutes before. He was looking down at the cell phone in his hand as he walked in.

"Hello," I said. "Working late tonight?"

He looked up, startled, his buggy eyes even more

buggy. Was it just my imagination, or did his gaze flicker to my upper lip, as if checking for regrowth?

"Yeah." He turned his attention back to his phone, as if avoiding my eyes.

"I'm Tori." I stepped toward him and extended my hand. "I work at Benedetta's."

Still looking down, he muttered, "That's nice," and scurried past me like a mouse running from a cat. He unlocked the dead bolt on the reinforced interior door, typed in a four-digit code on the keypad, and was inside in a flash. I caught only a quick glimpse of multiple, wall-mounted monitors before the door slammed shut behind him.

*Hmm* . . . I couldn't tell whether the guy had bad manners or merely poor social skills. Either way, he could benefit from a few sessions at Miss Cecily's Charm School.

I exited Cyber-Shield's offices to find Echols's Mustang parked at the curb between two of the patrol cars. The guy might be a geek, but he did drive a badass car.

A glance at Gallery Nico told me that Nick still had an eye on me. He stood at a sculpture, lightly brushing it with a feather duster. Even from this distance I could see his shoulders relax as he spotted me exiting the building alive.

Two hours later, after helping Elena and Dario clean up the dining room and kitchen, I wrapped up my shift at the bistro and exited the restaurant with some leftover manicotti and a chocolate cannoli tucked under my arm. I only wished I was leaving with some hard evidence that would implicate Tino Fabrizio.

## chapter twenty-eight

# *A*n Inconvenient Truth

Tuesday morning, I went to class at DBU. A pointless exercise probably, as nobody seemed to have followed me to the campus. After class I went to the library and used one of their computers to e-mail Alicia, as I'd promised I'd do. *I'm fine,* I told her. *But if they don't stop sending me home with chocolate cannoli I'm gonna have to buy bigger pants!*

I was working the late shift at the bistro again today, which would give me a chance to look into those gray Chevy vans this morning.

I swung by the first address. The Cargill Brothers' van was parked in front of the three-story office building that housed several businesses. I went inside the building and consulted the building directory. The Cargill offices were on the second floor. It was a small space, telling me that whatever business the company operated wasn't an extensive one.

When peeking through the glass door told me nothing, I went inside and approached the receptionist. "Hi," I told her. "I recently lost my job in the building and I'm checking around to see if anyone is hiring. Can you tell me what your company does?"

"Sorry," she said. "We don't have any openings."

She hadn't given me the vital bit of information I needed. "What does Cargill Brothers do?"

"Commercial cleaning services," she said. "We provide janitorial services to businesses."

That explained the van. They probably had some large clients who'd need an extensive crew to clean their spaces.

I found the second van parked in the driveway of a two-story house half a block down from an elementary school. The raucous sounds of children playing at recess met my ears as I parked and climbed out of my car.

The back window of the van featured a series of those people-shaped stickers intended to represent a family. This series was particularly long, including a father, a mother, and seven children—four girls and three boys. Per the stickers, the family also had a couple of dogs and a cat. *Holy guacamole!* I didn't like being lonely at my apartment, but it was definitely preferable to living with eight other people under one roof.

I supposed it was possible that the father of the family could be Tripp Sevin, but one peek inside the van told me such was not likely to be the case. The van held no less than three child car seats. The seats and floor mats were hopelessly stained with what appeared to be grape juice spills. Lego bricks and Hot Wheels littered the space. An unwrapped peppermint was stuck to the back of the middle seat, apparently glued there with spit. The residents of Whispering Pines had given me the impression that the van had been clean and spiffy when the Cajun con artist had brought it by. Cleaning up this van to show it to would-be vacationers would take hours and be an exercise in futility. I couldn't imagine anyone putting themselves to that much trouble.

"Can I help you?"

I looked up from the van to find a woman standing in the front doorway of the house, a baby on her hip, a toddler clinging to her leg, and a kid who appeared to be around four years of age standing next to her. The woman was frowning, a leery look in her eyes. Who could blame her? I'd be creeped out if I was home alone with my children and found some strange woman peeking into my family car.

"I thought I heard a noise coming from the van," I told her. "I thought maybe a child had accidentally been left inside. I guess I'm just hearing noises from the school."

"Oh." Her face relaxed. "All of my offspring are present and accounted for. 'Least all the ones that aren't old enough for school."

"Okeydoke," I said, raising a friendly hand in good-bye.

As she went back inside, I headed back to my car. Would we ever find this so-called Tripp Sevin? I wasn't sure. For all I knew the guy was pulling his stunts somewhere else by now. Heck, he could be up in Oklahoma offering some Okies from Muskogee a weekend jaunt to Dallas, plying them with promises of rides on the Ferris wheel at the state fairgrounds or dinner in the revolving restaurant in Reunion Tower.

Having crossed these two possible vans off my list, I drove downtown, parked in a garage a block over from the IRS building, and took the alleyway to my office.

The man I'd spoken with earlier from the Louisiana Consumer Protection Division had left me a voice mail saying that he'd found no cases involving charter van companies. *Darn.*

I'd spent half an hour dealing with items in my in-box when the phone on my desk rang. It was an attorney from the company who'd issued the prepaid credit card Tripp

Sevin had used to purchase his burner phone and to pay for the Triple 7 Adventures domain name and Web site.

"The card was activated last June," the attorney said. "The card was sold at a convenience store in Carrollton."

Carrollton was a smaller city that sat a few miles northwest of Dallas, within easy driving distance. He gave me the date of the sale and the address for the store. I jotted down both pieces of information.

"Thanks," I told him. "This should help."

As soon as we ended our call, I phoned the convenience store and asked to speak to a manager. Luckily, she was agreeable to showing me the footage without a court order.

"As often as we get robbed," she said, "we'd be stupid not to cooperate with law enforcement."

"I'll be right there." I grabbed my purse, tucked a thumb drive into it, and headed back out of the office.

The drive to Carrollton took half an hour. I listened to my Italian CD on the way. Today I learned the names for family members, or *la famiglia*. Daughter was *la figlia*. Wife was *la moglie*. Father was *il padre*. I was looking forward to sending *il padre* to *il slammerino*. Assuming, of course, our task force could get a break in the case.

I pulled into the convenience store and parked out of the way at the far end of the lot. I went inside to find a woman working the cash register and a man stacking cases of beer in the front window.

I stepped up to the counter. "I'm Special Agent Tara Holloway from the IRS. Are you the woman I spoke with on the phone?"

"That's me." She raised a finger to signal the stocker to come take over at the counter before turning back to me. "Those prepaid credit cards you asked about? We

keep those cards behind the counter here." She gestured
to a display behind her. "We used to have them hanging
out front but people kept stealing them. I suppose they
thought they were like stealing cash. Damn fools. Don't
they think we'd know better? A card is worthless until the
cashier activates it."

The man circled around the back of the counter and
the woman motioned for me to follow her. "Let's go
back to the office."

I followed her through a swinging door marked with
a sign that read EMPLOYEES ONLY. She led me past the
back of the refrigerated section to a small, windowless
office. She offered me the only seat in the room, a rolling chair behind the desk.

"We've got two cameras," she said. "One of them is
positioned over the register. The other is over the gas
pumps." Leaning over me, she showed me how to pull
up, rewind, and fast-forward through the video footage,
and how to switch from the inside feed to the outside
feed. "You know what date you're looking for?"

"June nineteenth," I told her.

"All right." She pulled up the footage from the interior camera beginning at 12:01 A.M. on the date in question. "There you go."

I had my doubts that the man I was after would have
come to the store in the wee hours of the night, so I fast-
forwarded the video to six o'clock in the morning and
began watching from there, the speed turned to eight
times real time. As I watched, person after person came
in for coffee. A few grabbed pastries, too, all of them
moving at warp speed. One of the customers caught his
foot on a magazine display rack and spilled his coffee.
One of the store clerks appeared lickety-split and cleaned
it up with a rag mop in three seconds flat. I wished I
could operate as efficiently as someone moving eight

times their normal speed. Just think of all the cases I could handle then!

As the time eased past nine A.M., the customer traffic slowed, most people at this time coming in for a soft drink, candy, cigarettes, or lottery tickets. Around eleven, two young boys entered the store. They ducked down the first aisle and watched from the end until the clerk turned his back to grab a carton of cigarettes for a customer. While the clerk was distracted, the boys darted forward, each grabbing a candy bar and shoving it into their pants pockets before exiting the store. *Twerps.* I made a note of the exact time of their crime in case the manager was interested in pursuing the matter.

At half past noon, a man in sunglasses and a flat-brimmed cowboy hat entered the store. He looked very similar to the man I'd seen on the video at Whispering Pines. Was it the same man? I thought so, but I couldn't be certain.

I slowed the video down to normal pace and leaned in close. He grabbed a beer from the refrigerator and headed up to the counter. Though the footage had no audio track and his words were inaudible, it was clear from the way he gestured at the display behind the counter that he planned to buy one of the prepaid credit cards. He also gestured out the front window. To the van, perhaps? He pulled a sizable stack of bills from his wallet and handed them to the clerk, who put them into the open till of the cash register and ran the purchased card through a skimmer to activate it. The clerk handed the card to the customer, who nodded and left the store.

The man in the hat had to be the crook I knew only as Tripp Sevin. Unfortunately, the hat prevented the camera from getting a good bead on his face. I couldn't tell much about him.

I switched the screen to show the exterior camera

feed and forwarded it to a time ten minutes before the
man had entered the store. As I watched, several cars
came and went at the gas pumps. A minute before the
man had entered the store, a gray Chevy van backed up
to one of the pumps on the screen. Given the angle, the
side of the van was visible, but not the back bumper. I
couldn't get a visual on the back license plate, but I could
see a magnetic sign on the passenger door that read
COAST-N-CRUISE VACATIONS.

*Aha!* As I'd suspected, his scam went beyond Triple 7
Adventures and Whispering Pines.

"Come on," I willed the van on the screen. "Keep
backing up." Just another foot or two and the front bumper would come into view, allowing me to get the license
plate number.

The van rocked as the driver applied the brakes. The
front bumper bore a novelty plate like it had at the retirement home, though this one read LIFE'S A BEACH.

"Dammit," I muttered. The plate wouldn't do me any
good in trying to track the van.

I rewound the video and watched it again, looking for
any clues that might identify the vehicle. The front window of the van bore a Texas registration decal and inspection sticker. At least now I knew for certain that the
van was registered in Texas. That was something. Of
course the van could be registered anywhere in Texas.
The state comprised nearly 269,000 square miles. There
were no guarantees that it was registered to an address
in north Texas, even if it had been driven around the
area in recent months.

I sat back in the chair and thought for a minute. Unlike some states, which require only a single license
plate on a car, Texas law requires vehicles to have both
front and back plates. Novelty plates were not permitted.
If a cop had spotted the van driving around with novelty

plates, there was a chance the driver had been issued a ticket.

I pulled out my cell phone and placed a call to Detective Booth at Dallas PD.

She sounded excited to hear from me. "Please tell me you've got something on Tino Fabrizio."

I hated to burst her bubble, but I had to be honest. "Not yet, but we're still working on it. Any chance I can impose on you for some help in an unrelated matter?"

"Sure."

I explained the situation. "Can you tell me whether any tickets have been issued to the driver of a gray fifteen-passenger Chevy van for failing to have license plates?"

"What time frame are we looking at?"

"Last year or so."

"I'll have one of the administrative staff run a search."

"Thanks. I'm still working undercover at the bistro, so rather than call me with the information it would be better for you to e-mail it to me." I gave her my e-mail address at the IRS.

"Will do."

With that we ended the call. I stuck the thumb drive into the USB port and made a copy of the camera footage. Evidence in hand, I left the store, waving good-bye to the woman behind the counter. "Appreciate your help!"

"Anytime."

# chapter twenty-nine

Having struck out on my search for Tripp Sevin and his van, I continued on to the bistro. On my drive, I learned a few more Italian words. A chair was *la sedia*. A desk was *la scrivania*. *Tavola* meant table.

As I pulled into the parking lot at Benedetta's, my eyes spotted a crew of men in front of the restaurant. They stood on ladders to install pull-down safety doors like those Nick planned to have installed at the gallery. Tino—*il padre*—stood on the sidewalk, supervising the activity.

I walked up. "Hello, Tino. What's going on?" *Killed anyone today? Maybe revved up that nail gun?*

"Just adding some security doors," he said. "Wanna keep everyone safe over here. I worry when Benedetta and my girls are working late. You and the rest of the crew, too. These glass windows? Anyone can see in at night."

Ironic how someone who was such a threat to others worried so much about his family's safety. Perhaps that was precisely why, though. He knew just how dangerous some people—people like *him*—could be.

He hiked a thumb over his shoulder in the direction of Gallery Nico. "The guys at the gallery wanted a set installed to protect their art. Since the installers were already out here at the gallery I figured it was a good time to have them put up a set here, too."

"Makes sense. It's nice to feel safe." As if I'd ever feel safe around that guy. I eased around him. "Enjoy the rest of your day." *Try not to kill anyone.*

It was a relatively slow night at the restaurant. Benedetta was working the kitchen again, along with Juan. Luisa and Stella had the night off. Elena was the only other server working tonight.

I glanced out the window as often as I could, keeping an eye out for Cole Kirchner, the square-headed goon who drove patrol car number six. I knew Nick was watching for him, too. So far there'd been no sign of him.

At half past six, the phone rang behind the bar. Elena was busy carrying salads to customers, so I answered the call. "Good evening, Benedetta's Bistro."

Nick's voice came through the phone. "Hello."

It took everything in me not to react. It was good to hear his voice. It had only been two days since I'd last seen him, but when an agent worked a case like this and was separated not only from her usual, comforting surroundings but also from all of the people she loved, the time slowed to an excruciating crawl.

"This is Nicolas Brandt, from the gallery," Nick said. "I'd like to place a dinner order."

I stepped over to the register to enter his order. "What can we get you?"

He asked for an order each of vegetable lasagna,

linguini formaggio, and spinach ravioli, along with garlic knots.

"No meal is complete without one of Benedetta's signature desserts," I said, smiling at Benedetta, who'd
stepped behind the bar to retrieve a bottle of wine. "How
about a tiramisu or a slice of Italian cream cake?"

"I hear the chocolate cannoli is delicious," Nick said.

Of course he'd heard that from *me*. He added three
cannoli to the order.

I ripped the order from the register's printer. "It'll be
ready in twenty minutes."

"I got it." Benedetta took the order from me and returned to the kitchen.

I hung up the phone and grabbed a pitcher of iced tea,
passing Elena as I walked through the dining room toward one of my tables, where the customers' drinks
were running low.

"Who was that on the phone?" Elena asked.

"The guy from the art gallery. Nicolas."

She looked out the window and across the parking lot
toward Gallery Nico. "I'll deliver the food when it's
ready."

"Fine by me." It was *not* fine by me. Only *I* should be
ogling my boyfriend. I forced my eyes away from a knife
on a nearby table. No sense committing murder over petty
jealousy.

I refilled the customers' tea glasses and offered them
dessert. They declined, requesting only their check.

Not long afterward, Elena emerged from the kitchen,
two bags in her hand. She looked excited yet nervous.
Cold, too. Her nipples were evident through her dress and
she appeared to be shivering. She glanced around the dining room, noting that the only customers in the place
had just been served their entrées and were happily dig-

ging in. "Come with me, Tori. I don't want to look like I'm hitting on him. I can say I brought you over so you could see the art."

"Won't your mother be mad if we both abandon our posts?"

"It'll just be for a minute."

I acquiesced, but not until I'd told the customers that I'd be stepping out for just a moment but would return very shortly.

Elena and I walked briskly across the parking lot. She had her hands full with the food, so I opened the door of the gallery and held it for her.

Nick glanced up from where he sat behind a desk situated along the side wall where he could keep an eye on the comings and goings at Cyber-Shield. Tonight he wore a western shirt with my scarf tied around his neck, along with some type of chunky gold bracelet he'd picked up God knows where. Knowing Nick as well as I did, it was clear to me he was in costume. Fortunately, having never met him before seeing him at the gallery, Elena didn't know any different.

Nick stood, looking from Elena to me and back again. "Hello, ladies."

"Hi, Nicolas," Elena gushed, holding out the bags as she made her way toward him. "We're slow at the restaurant so we decided to bring your food to you and save you the trip."

He took the food from her and set it on his desk. "Well, you've certainly earned your tip tonight, haven't you?"

He reached into his back pocket for his wallet, removed three twenties, and held them out to Elena. "Keep the change."

Elena blushed. "That's very generous. Thanks."

Seeming to remember that she'd dragged me along on this escapade, she wiggled her fingers in my direction. "This is our new waitress. Her name's Tori."

Nick's eyes flicked to my vivid red hair. "Not a Fabrizio, is she?"

Elena laughed. "No. But we consider her an honorary family member."

*Please don't.* The last name was the equivalent of *murderer* to me. Though I had to admit having a mother like Benedetta and three sisters like Stella, Luisa, and Elena wouldn't be bad. They were witty and cheerful, friendly and warm.

I waved my hand in a small arc. "Nice to meet you, Nicolas. Interesting art you've got here."

Nick cocked his head. "We're quite proud of our collection."

I looked around. On a pedestal to my left was the papier-mâché head I'd seen Emily Raggio carrying into the gallery. It was, indeed, made from surgical masks. Next to the piece stood a small tented card that identified the artist and the piece. WE ALL WEAR MASKS—EMILY RAGGIO. Another, smaller card revealed the price of the piece, $3,750.

Mallory Sisko, an emerging artist I'd also met while investigating the Unic Art Space, had a piece for sale, too. It was a large hourglass filled with a variety of small things, including a lift ticket from a ski resort in Santa Fe, a couple of chess pieces, the crumpled cover of a romance novel, a blue square of pool cue chalk, and ticket stubs from movies, theater performances, and music concerts. *Time Well Spent* boasted a price tag of $1,100.

Another artist had made a large heart-shaped picture out of small pieces of raggedly torn red tissue paper. The piece was titled *You Ripped Out My Heart* and was offered at $385.

The gallery boasted numerous other pieces, too, including a series of black-and-white photos of people's bare feet, a charcoal drawing of the Dallas skyline, and an abstract stone sculpture that looked like a sunrise over a craggy mountain from one vantage point and a roaring brontosaurus from another.

A door in the back wall opened and Josh and Kira emerged. It was all I could do not to burst into guffaws. Like Nick, Josh had attempted to dress his part as an art aficionado. I had the distinct feeling Kira had offered her assistance, perhaps even her clothing, too. Josh wore what I could only call a skinny suit—a pair of tight, ankle-length gray pants along with a matching jacket that looked two sizes too small, even for an undersized guy like him. Under the suit he wore a silky white shirt, open at the collar, no tie. His shoes were unusual navy blue loafers with silver zippers up the sides. To top off the look, he'd plunked a gray bowler hat on his head.

Kira was dressed in her usual unusual style, today sporting a pair of polka-dotted leggings, white ankle boots, and a white baby doll top.

"Did we smell dinner?" Josh called.

Nick waved them forward. "It's here. These lovely ladies from the bistro were nice enough to bring it over."

Kira's eyes seemed to darken when she spotted Elena standing at the desk. Like me, she was probably feeling a little threatened by the beautiful Italian woman and her big *bombolonis*.

"Hi." She stepped up between Nick and Josh. "I'm Kiki." She extended a thin hand with a silver ring on each finger, including the thumb.

Elena shook her hand. "You work here, too?"

"Just consulting for a day or two." Kira crossed her arms in front of herself, pointing her opposite index fingers at Nick and Josh. "These two bitches needed a little help curating their collection."

"Oh." Elena's face scrunched in confusion for a moment before she turned to go. "Enjoy your dinner."

I followed her out the door and back through the parking lot.

She cast me a befuddled glance. "What do you think Kiki meant when she called Nicolas a 'bitch'?"

"I hate to burst your bubble," I said, "but I think Nicolas and that other guy are more than just business partners. I think they're *partner* partners."

"Ugh!" Elena threw up her arms, imploring the sky. "Why are all of the good ones married or gay? I can't believe I stood in the freezer for two whole minutes before we went over there."

No wonder she'd been shivering and perky.

"No sense getting hypothermia just to get a man's attention," I told her. "You've got more to offer than your body, Elena."

She turned to me, angst on her face. "Do I, Tori? I feel like I'm in a rut. I don't even know what I'd talk about if a guy asked me out. All I ever do is work at the restaurant. It's all I've ever done and it's what I'll be doing until the day I die."

*Whoa.* I hadn't realized Elena was unhappy. She did a good job of hiding it. "What would you rather do?"

"I don't know." She raised a noncommittal shoulder. "Maybe work in television?"

"If you can spend two minutes in a freezer with no coat, you'd make a great weather reporter."

Her face relaxed and she laughed. "Do you think it would break my mother's heart if I told her I didn't want to run the restaurant with her anymore?"

I knew Benedetta enjoyed having her children around, but she wasn't a control freak and seemed to value her girls' individuality. Besides, I had some experience with this situation myself. As much as I knew my mother wished I'd remained at my safe job at Martin & McGee, she was glad I'd found my purpose in life as a special agent. "Honestly, Elena? I think it would break her heart if you didn't pursue your dreams."

Elena's face brightened. "Really?"

"Really."

We returned to the bistro and immediately checked on our tables. One of mine needed more garlic knots. Apparently, the half dozen I'd brought the two diners had not been enough. Could someone overdose on carbs? Guess I'd find out. "I'll be right back with more."

I grabbed their bread basket, went to the kitchen, and filled it with warm garlic knots, straight from the oven. As I began to leave the kitchen, Benedetta called for me to wait.

She handed me a bag of food. "Take this to Tino and Eric next door. The tortellini is Tino's. The penne is Eric's."

"Your husband's working late again?"

"He tells me they're trying to land a large client," she said. "He's working on a bid."

Maybe. Or maybe he was over there in his office, plotting how to extort money from one of his existing clients.

I dropped the basket of bread at the table and asked Elena to cover for me while I ran the bag of food next door. I entered Benedetta's code in the keypad next to the front door. Two-three-six-three. The door buzzed again as I stepped inside.

The interior lights were turned off in the main foyer tonight. As I rounded the empty reception desk, I noted several things in quick succession. One, there was light under the men's room door, indicating someone occupied it. Two, the door to Eric's room had not been pulled

fully shut. Eric probably intended to take only a quick
potty break and had left the door this way so he wouldn't
have to suffer the nuisance of reentering his number in
the keypad. Third, Tino's door was open only an inch or
so, not wide enough for him to spot me if I took a quick
look-see into Eric's cybercave. Of course, the camera
would catch my movements, but with any luck nobody
was monitoring it at the moment.

As quickly and quietly as I could, I went to the door,
pushed it open, and peeked my head inside. The windowless room contained a built-in modular desk with a wide
work surface. A video camera mounted directly over the
door was aimed at the desk.

Affixed to the wall over the desk were six large
screens, each of which was divided into smaller squares
of varying numbers, probably depending on how many
cameras were at each client's location. Each square
showed a live feed from a video camera. The name and
account number of each client appeared across the bottom of the screen. *Tommy's Tire Town—34762, Wexler's
Furniture—79085, South Dallas Liquor—15393,* and so
on. Two more flat-screen monitors sat on the desk, along
with a half-empty bottle of pink Vitaminwater. On the
flat-screens were static images of what appeared to be the
back door of a business with a man reaching for the knob.
While no name appeared on the door, per information at
the bottom of the screen, the image depicted was of *Looking Good Optical—55629.*

Why weren't these images moving like the others?
Had something gone wrong with the camera feed? Or had
Eric purposely frozen the image for some reason? Was
he doctoring this video like we suspected him of doing
with the others?

Had Operation Italian Takeout caught its first big
break?

*A-hem.*

The sound of someone clearing his throat sent my heart into my esophagus and drew my eyes to Tino's door. *Uh-oh.* The man stood there, staring me down, his normally friendly eyes steely and cold. "What are you doing, Tori?"

Despite the fact that my brain was spinning in terror, I knew I had to play it cool. I raised the bag and forced a smile, hoping it didn't look like the grimace it felt like. "Just delivering Eric's penne and your tortellini. Hope you're hungry. It looks like your wife sent over extra garlic knots and a cannoli, too."

I watched Tino's face. Had I fooled him? Or had the cheer in my voice sounded as false to him as it had to me?

The door to the men's room opened and Eric stepped out. His eyes met mine, but immediately looked away. When he spotted the door to his room standing open, his buggy eyes nearly popped out of his head. His voice sounded squeaky and panicked when he spoke. "Did you go into my office?"

Tino held up a palm, but it seemed more of a warning to Eric than a true attempt to calm him. "She's just brought your dinner."

I circled the bag with my left arm and opened it with my right, retrieving the container marked PENNE. I pulled it out of the bag and held it out to Eric. "Here you go. *Mangia.*"

Eric grabbed the container from my hand and slipped into his office, closing and locking the door behind him.

Tino chuckled, but his laughter didn't make it to his eyes, which were still watching me intently. "Computer geeks. Odd ducks, aren't they? He was probably afraid you'd steal his Iron Man action figures."

I giggled and rolled my eyes. "The only thing I want is your chocolate cannoli."

He reached out for the bag, the friendly twinkle back in his eyes now. "Then I better take it from you right away."

I handed him the bag and turned to go, calling, "Don't work too hard!" back over my shoulder. *Don't work too hard. Don't torch anyone's business. Don't shove anyone off a roof.* Really, shouldn't those things go without saying?

# chapter thirty

# $\mathcal{N}$ow Overhear This

As I left the bistro at the end of my shift a couple of hours later, I noticed Eric's Mustang was no longer in the lot at Cyber-Shield. Neither was Tino's Alfa Romeo. Again I wondered if those two were up to something, plotting another criminal act, fabricating evidence that would implicate someone else and make them appear innocent.

On my drive home from work Tuesday night, I made another stop at a gas station. All this running around town had emptied my tank in short order. As I waited for the gas to finish pumping, I texted Pat Nix, otherwise known as Nick Pratt, from my new phone. *Got look into tech cave. Looking Good Optical on monitors. Next victim?*

Just as soon as I'd sent the text I deleted it as I'd been instructed. No sense keeping evidence of my spying and snitching on me.

The hose stopped pumping and the automated nozzle deactivated with a *clunk*. I returned the nozzle to the pump and climbed back into my car. As I pulled away from the pump, a return text came in from Pat/Nick. *Putting eyes on it.*

Putting eyes on an optician's business. There's some irony for you.

As I continued home through relatively sparse traffic, I took note of headlights a block behind me. Was my tail back? I couldn't tell what type of car it was, but from the fact that the headlights sat up higher than a standard car, I suspected it might be the white pickup again.

Sure enough, as I pulled to a stop at a red light, the white pickup took a right turn into a fast-food restaurant rather than pull up behind or beside me where I could get a better look at the driver and any passengers. Clearly, whoever was behind the wheel of the truck was trying to maintain some distance in an effort to prevent me from realizing I was being followed.

When the light turned green, I continued on. A glance in my rearview mirror told me that the pickup had pulled back onto the street behind me.

Why had Tino put a tail on me again? Was it because he suspected me of intentionally snooping at Cyber-Shield earlier? If that was the case, and Tino was growing wary, it would only make things harder on the federal law enforcement task force. Tino might realize he and his men were under watch and abort any immediate plans to take revenge on a client who'd failed to give in to his extortion. Or he might try to off me. After all, he had a history of dispatching anyone who had the goods on him. The mere thought turned my insides to jelly. I'd become a human bomboloni.

I continued to drive, so rigid with fear and anxiety that the muscles in my back began to ache. With any luck, I could quickly convince those spying on me that I was only a college girl trying to do well in her waitressing job. I made my way back to my apartment complex, parked, and hurried up to my unit. I assumed whoever was in the pickup—possibly Cole Kirchner or Eric Echols— intended only to keep an eye on me, visually and virtually. But there was a chance that whoever was in the pickup intended to do me harm . . . as in impaled-on-a-fence, nail-gun-to-the-face, bench-pressed-into-a-pancake kind of harm.

Inside my place I glanced around, trying to figure out what I could do to make the apartment more secure. I supposed I could contact Eddie or another member of the Operation Italian Takeout team and have them keep watch over my place tonight. But that would mean taking an agent off one of Tino's men to babysit me. If nothing happened, it would look like I was losing my edge, letting the pressure of the case overcome me. Lu might even take me off the case, put another agent in charge. I certainly didn't want that. I'd worked too hard on this case to stop now. I'd suffered fallen arches and burned fingertips from hot plates. I needed to see this through to the end.

So instead I grabbed one of the stools from the breakfast bar and pulled it over to the door. It was too tall for me to lodge it under the knob like I'd seen people do in movies and television shows. *Dang.* I decided to lay the barstool down on its side three feet in from the door. If someone quietly jimmied the lock, they'd trip over the stool on their way in to murder me, waking me and giving me time to get to my gun. I placed the other stool on its side two feet farther into the room. If they somehow managed to avoid the first stool, surely the second one would get them.

In the bedroom, I pulled some lightweight garments from the rack in the closet and hung them from the curtain rod over the window. If someone tried to sneak in that way, they'd have to fight through several layers of cotton and polyester and spandex to get to me. I'd shoot them before they made their way through.

When I finished my preparations, I sat on the bed to think. I was terrified that Tino might now see me as a threat and feel the need to eliminate me. I didn't like feeling scared, and my terror soon morphed into anger at the man who'd made me feel this way. He had no right to do the things he did, to make people fear for their lives. *Bastard.* I logged into my laptop, careful to aim the Webcam away from my reinforced clothes curtains, and bent over next to my bed so that the first thing anyone cyberspying on me would see was my ass.

*Kiss this, Tino Fabrizio.*

Thanks to his wife's chocolate cannoli, I had more kissable ass than I'd had last week.

My buttocks having made their statement, I spent a minute or two checking my fake e-mail account for the benefit of anyone snooping on my computer. I sent responses to my fictional friends and family.

*Studying for finals. Ugh! Hoping for a B in Linguistics.*

*My new job is great! I like my boss. She works us hard but she's nice and gives me free desserts.*

I logged back into the Neiman Marcus Web site and pulled up the Sarah Jessica Parker slingbacks. My hacker could stare at those for a few minutes while I took a quick shower and shampooed the smell of garlic out of my hair. Of course I took my gun with me to the bathroom, placing it in easy reach on the toilet seat while I showered.

I went to bed, sleeping restlessly, waking Wednesday morning alive but still tired. I righted the stools and returned them to the breakfast bar, feeling a little foolish in the light of day. It was only smart to have a healthy fear of Tino Fabrizio, but I couldn't let it overpower me and prevent me from thinking straight. I needed all of my faculties at full capacity to deal with this case.

I attended my morning class at DBU, noting no tail today as I drove to and from the campus. Had I satisfied Tino again that I was simply the young college girl I was pretending to be? Was he thinking himself paranoid for siccing a tail on me when all I'd done was push open a cracked door to look for an employee who was expecting a meal delivery? Really, that wasn't so unusual, was it?

Since I didn't have access to my IRS-issued laptop and didn't want to run a search on Looking Good Optical on the unsecured laptop the FBI had given me, I swung by the DBU library to use one of their shared computers. Before typing the name in the search bar, I quickly scanned my surroundings. All I saw were college students studying, researching, and flirting. Well, one guy was dozing in a chair, but everyone else seemed to be occupied. Nobody seemed to be paying any mind to the redhead at the computer.

I typed the name of the business in the space and hit enter. Up popped a Web site for Looking Good. I clicked on the *About Us* link.

The page featured a photo of the optician with his wife and adorable young son, whose mouth hung wide open in a natural, gleeful smile. The optician was a sandy-haired man who wore wire-rimmed glasses himself. His wife was pretty, with hair the golden-brown color of maple syrup. They looked like a happy young family. The thought that Tino Fabrizio could put a quick end to that happiness made me feel both furious and queasy. The only thing that made me feel better was knowing that multiple sets of eyes were on both the optical business and Tino's men. With a little luck, they'd be able to catch any bad guys in the act before they could cause too much damage to the optician's business or to the optician himself. And, if they were able to connect any would-be criminals to Tino, we'd be able to search Cyber-Shield and Tino's home and get the evidence we needed to nail him for his tax crimes. I still wasn't sure whether he was laundering the extorted funds or completely failing to report them, but it had to be one or the other. Either way, he'd be looking at several years in federal prison on top of whatever the other charges might bring.

Knowing now on whose behalf I was likely working, my resolve was renewed. Nobody would take that cute smile off that little boy's face if I had anything to say about it.

I deleted the browser history and headed out to my car.

I was scheduled for an early ten A.M. to two P.M. lunch shift today at the bistro. On the drive over, my language CD taught me the Italian words for many occupations. Nurse—*infermiera*. Architect—*architetto*. I wondered what the Italian word was for extortionist. *Extortolini,* maybe? The CD continued. Lawyer—*avvocato*. Mmm. That last one put me in the mood for guacamole.

Bendetta stood in front of the bistro, her Italy-shaped key chain in her hand, unlocking the pull-down doors that had been installed the day before. They rattled as she slid them upward, the noise loud enough to penetrate the closed windows of my car. *Waitress—cameriera.*

"*Buon giorno,* Benedetta."

She offered her usual warm smile. "*Buon giorno, cara.*"

I noticed she had the zippered bank bag tucked into the outside pocket of her purse. I knew she went to the bank early each morning to deposit the preceding day's cash intake, but I found myself wondering this morning whether any of the money she'd deposited was the cash

Tino had extorted from his clients. It would be easy enough for Cole Kirchner to bring the funds back to Cyber-Shield, and for Tino to then take them home to Benedetta.

I entered the bistro on Benedetta's heels. Elena was off today, but Luisa was working with me. We prepared the tables, stocked the glasses and plates, and carried desserts to the refrigerated display to entice the takeout customers. I was becoming very efficient at the restaurant routine. Maybe I really could open my own eatery someday. If I did, I'd call it Mom's Southern Cooking and put my mother in charge of the kitchen.

After as the restaurant opened at eleven, Nick called in with an order. "Any chance you can deliver it?" he asked. "We've got a customer in the gallery looking at pieces and we don't want to leave while he's here."

"Of course." I rang up his total on the register. "It'll be thirty-nine sixty-seven."

I went to the kitchen and turned in his order. Dario was back today, sliding a Margherita pizza into the brick oven. I held up the ticket. "Got a to-go order for you."

He nodded in acknowledgment as I placed it in the queue.

As I continued to wait on the tables, I kept an eye on the movement at Cyber-Shield. As usual, there was only minimal activity. I found myself wishing for Superman's X-ray vision so I could see through the wall separating Benedetta's Bistro from Cyber-Shield. By my best guess, Eric's cybercave would sit just on the other side of the wall from the last booth, and would continue down the hallway to the kitchen door. *Hmm.* Was there an air duct that connected the two spaces? Maybe a pipe? An electrical socket even?

I rang up two takeout orders, bidding the customers good-bye with *"Ciao."* Using my newly acquired Italian language skills, I was feeling quite worldly for a person who'd been born, raised, and lived her entire life in the state of Texas.

When Nick's food was ready, I grabbed the bag. As Luisa came into the kitchen with dirty plates, I said, "I'm running this across to the gallery. I'll be right back."

"Wait!" called Benedetta from behind me. "Take this, too." She handed me another container.

"What's that?"

"Tiramisu," she said. "Those boys at the gallery are becoming some of our most loyal customers. Might as well thank them with free dessert, right?" She leaned it to whisper to me. "It's leftover from yesterday. But you won't tell them, will you?"

I pretended to lock my lip and throw away the key. "Your secret's safe with me."

I could only wonder what other secrets Benedetta might be keeping . . .

# chapter thirty-one

## $\mathcal{A}$ Fresh Tactic

I left the restaurant and walked through the lot. A silver Mercedes sat in front of Gallery Nico. Could it belong to the customer Nick had referenced?

I went inside to find Nick speaking with a fortyish man whose dark hair was pulled back into a man bun, a small lock on one side left free, probably on purpose to create an artsy, asymmetrical effect. The man stood bent, his hands on his knees, as he peered into the hourglass Mallory Sisko had filled.

"Such originality," the man said.

Nick pointed me to the door that led to the office. I carried the bag back to the door and knocked. Kira answered and waved me in, and I left the door halfway open behind me.

I unpacked their food, setting it on the desk, and lowered my voice to a whisper. "What have you found out about the catering? Does it look like money's being laundered through the account?"

"See for yourself." Josh grabbed a file folder and handed it to me.

I quickly paged through the paperwork inside. The file included catering invoices dating back three years. The invoices appeared to be primarily for one-time events. Weddings. Family reunions. Office parties. Nothing immediately stood out. One company had been a repeat customer, but given the regularly scheduled dates of the luncheons the catering appeared to be for some kind of quarterly staff meeting. Plus, the amounts that the company spent weren't excessive, adding up to around forty thousand dollars per year. Surely Tino's extortion brought him more than forty grand a year. If not, why bother?

I closed the file. "I don't see any obvious red flags. I assume you checked things out?"

"Of course," Josh said, taking the file from me. "Most of the weddings were announced in the newspaper, and there were photos of the bride and groom all over their Facebook pages. Some of them even included photos of the food." He went on to tell me that he'd called the companies listed on the invoices and posed as a new caterer soliciting business. "I asked them who normally provided their catering services. Some told me it was Benedetta's. A few of them wouldn't give me the information, but I sensed it was because they either didn't know or didn't want to bother looking it up."

Or they figured it was none of his business. "So the catering account is a dead end?"

"Looks that way," he said, "but take a look at this."

He handed me another file. Inside were separate invoices for liquor sales to catering clients. It was not unusual for food and liquor to be invoiced separately. After all, special taxes applied to alcohol sales, so it was important that revenues from liquor be separately accounted for. In addition, the file contained records for events where a cash bar was offered. In these instances, rather than the host being charged for the liquor consumed, the drinks were paid for by the individuals who ordered them. And those individuals paid in cash.

Josh gestured to the paperwork. "There are several weddings and holiday parties where the liquor bill seemed excessive or the cash bar brought in three or four times the amount of the catering bill."

Kira looked up from where she worked at her computer. "You're dealing with Italians, right? They love their *vino*."

She had a point. Of course, Americans loved their wine, too, as did the French. Really, who didn't like wine?

"This could be something," I said, looking over the reports, "then again, it could be nothing."

My mind went back to the April fifteenth parties Martin & McGee threw when I worked at the firm. They'd always treated the staff to a nice buffet of food but, rather than risk bankrupting the firm, they'd provided only a cash bar. After three months of twelve-hour workdays seven days a week, we CPAs tended to tie one on. I could only imagine how much the bar took in on those crazy nights.

"It's definitely something for us to keep an eye on." I handed the file back to him. "Have you had any luck hacking into Cyber-Shield?"

Josh grabbed his blond curls with frustrated fingers. "We're screwed. Kira can't get into their system, either."

Kira huffed a frustrated breath. "I've tried every trick in the book. I'm out of ideas."

"If you two can't do it," I said, "no one can." I racked my brain, trying to figure out what our next step should be. "If we can't get into Cyber-Shield virtually, what if we planted a bug or something?" Maybe we'd overhear something that could help us bust Fabrizio.

Josh sat up straighter and his gaze narrowed as he appeared to be thinking things over. Josh loved gadgets. In earlier cases, he'd supplied me with a GPS tracking device that had helped me keep tabs on an errant minister, as well as a ballpoint pen loaded with a spy camera. Surely he'd have some type of listening device we could plant at Cyber-Shield.

I pulled the napkins and plasticware out of the bag. "Got something I can hide in a cannoli? Maybe a bug that looks like a chocolate chip?" I knew how those chips could get away from a person and fall to the floor. Instead of eating the chocolate bug, though, I'd kick it under Tino's desk where it could transmit his conversations to us.

"I've got all sorts of bugs," Josh said. "Most of which would work on the usual targets. The problem here is that we're dealing with experts in security. Surely they use TSCM technology."

"Speak English, Josh," I spat, "and speak it fast." I'd already been over here long enough to leave the food and collect the payment. I needed to get back to the bistro ASAP before Benedetta began to wonder why I was taking so long.

"Technical surveillance countermeasures," Josh said. "You know, bug sweepers? Virtually all bugs transmit radio waves or a magnetic field or heat that a bug sweeper or thermal camera can detect."

He went on to say that there were some ways to lower the chance of detection, with burst transmissions, for instance. I had no idea what a burst transmission was and was about to ask, when he said, "I think the safest bet here is to place some type of recorder in his office. We won't be able to listen in real time, but we can listen after we retrieve it."

Kira pulled the lid off her takeout container, releasing the enticing scent of pesto. "How will you get the recorder into his office?"

Josh's eyes met mine. It was clear to us how it would have to be done. *I* would have to place it there. I was the only one who had access to Tino's office.

"I'll sneak it in when I make a food delivery," I said, nearly trembling at the thought. If Tino caught me trying to eavesdrop on him, he'd probably drop me from the roof.

"I'll get you a recorder that looks harmless," Josh said. "Don't worry."

"Don't worry?" I let loose a snort. "You just pointed out that Fabrizio's business is security. Won't he be familiar with these types of recorders?"

"Maybe," Josh said, "but commercial security companies don't use these types of devices. Besides, with any luck he won't even spot it, right?"

*Better hide it good, huh?*

"I'll talk to Agent Hohenwald," Josh added. "Before we do this, we need to make sure the warrant allows it."

"It's a plan," I said, switching from federal agent to waitress mode. I held out my hand. "That'll be forty bucks for the food. Plus tip."

# chapter thirty-two

# $\mathcal{S}$afecracker

As I left Benedetta's later that day, I spotted a plain white sedan pulling up in front of Cyber-Shield. The driver's door opened and out came Detective Veronica Booth.

*Holy crap!* Clearly something had gone down that the rest of us didn't know about yet.

She glanced my way, but showed no signs of recognizing me. Either the red hair had thrown her for a loop or she was intentionally pretending not to know me. The safest option was to assume the latter and to pretend not to recognize her, either. I continued on to my car and drove back to my apartment.

Two hours later, a text came in from Hayden Beale, the alter ego in my contacts list for Agent Hohenwald. *Meet me at On the Border on Knox. We can sit in our favorite Booth.*

Given the capitalization of the *b*, I realized the word referred to the detective. *Clever.* I replied with *On my way.* Looked like I might get some guacamole, after all.

I deleted the text, left my apartment, and drove to the

restaurant, taking a roundabout route and using evasive maneuvers in case I was being followed. I was alternately excited and fearful. Had Booth found evidence that would put Tino away once and for all? Or had he struck again, murdering one of his henchmen or a Cyber-Shield client who dared to defy his demands?

I parked and began to make my way to the restaurant's door, when a *"psst"* caught my attention. I turned to see Agent Hohenwald sitting in his unmarked car. Detective Booth, who sat in the passenger seat, lifted her chin in acknowledgment. I scurried to the car and climbed into the back, scooting over on the seat until I was centered. So much for that guacamole. *Waah.*

Booth told me why we were meeting at the restaurant. "After I stopped by Cyber-Shield today, Tino had me followed back to police headquarters. I think he's got eyes on the place, at least for the time being. I was able to sneak out in the trunk of a squad car. I've got two men making sure we're not spotted here."

My eyes scanned the vicinity, spying a Dallas PD cruiser in the parking lot of Restoration Hardware across the street. That must be our lookouts.

Booth leaned in, speaking quietly. "Tino struck again. One of his clients was robbed Monday night."

Hohenwald exhaled a sharp breath. "Which one?"

"The Magic Genie Hookah Lounge."

I'd heard of it. Along with the hookah pipes, it provided its patrons with specialty coffee and tea drinks with an Arab flair. The place was popular with college kids and hipsters.

My throat felt tight, but I somehow managed to squeeze the words out. "Do we have another body on our hands?"

"Thankfully, no," the detective said.

My body relaxed of its own accord, making me realize

just how much tension my muscles had been holding. If this case didn't wrap up soon, I'd need to get a massage or visit a chiropractor.

Booth continued. "When the assistant manager arrived at the lounge Tuesday morning, he discovered that all of the cash had been removed from the safe sometime during the night. The door of the safe was left hanging open. He immediately called the police. Officers reviewed the video footage from the security camera feed and it showed the assistant manager himself, a man named Sadiki, taking the cash out of the safe. Sadiki denied it, of course, but the owner fired the guy on the spot and officers brought Sadiki in. Since the case involved a Cyber-Shield client, it was referred to me. I went out to the lounge and watched the video, made a copy of it."

She held up a thumb drive and inserted it into her computer, which sat on her lap. She turned the device so Hohenwald and I could see the screen. The images showed exactly what she'd described, a young man going to the safe, opening it, and removing the cash, placing it inside a zippered bank bag. But he did so without making any apparent attempt to disable the camera or hide his face.

Booth turned the computer back toward her when the footage ended, carefully closing it and returning it to its bag.

Hohenwald cocked his head. "So I'm guessing the lounge has traditional locks rather than a coded keypad."

"Right," Booth said. "Other than the security camera footage, there's no way to tell when someone enters or leaves the building and who it is. When I spoke to Sadiki at the station, he insisted he was innocent, of course. I showed him the video and he claimed the footage could not have been from the preceding night because he didn't have his tattoo in the video. He has one of those Egyptian ankh symbols on the back of his left hand. He told me he got the tattoo three weeks ago. He even pulled up his bank records on his computer to show me the date of the debit card transaction when he paid for it. I phoned the tattoo parlor and it checked out."

"He could've covered the tattoo with makeup," I pointed out.

"That's possible," Booth agreed, "and that's why I went ahead and processed the guy. Also so Fabrizio would think he'd thrown us off, if he was involved. But I gotta say, I'm pretty sure this Sadiki fellow is telling the truth. He's worked at the lounge for three years. He said the owner had him make deposits two or three times when the owner was away on vacation, but that the owner always changed the combination to the safe when he returned. Sadiki claims he doesn't even know the current combination. The owner confirmed that he hadn't given Sadiki the current combination, but he said that Sadiki is often in the office when the owner removes the money from the safe and possibly could have figured it out if he watched closely."

The hump was becoming uncomfortable. I shifted in the seat. "But you're not buying the owner's version of events, are you?"

She shook her head. "Sadiki's got no record. He's a single guy, lives modestly. Doesn't have much but doesn't seem to want much, either. He's had no unusual financial setbacks or demands that I can see. Why would he suddenly decide to rob his employer? Besides, the security camera is in plain sight. Who would openly rob a safe if they know they're being recorded?"

She was right. It didn't make sense.

"So the video you just showed us was probably doctored," I said. "Someone at Cyber-Shield spliced in old footage of Sadiki when he emptied the safe at the owner's request."

"That's what I'm thinking."

Hohenwald asked, "What happened at Cyber-Shield?"

Booth scoffed. "I met with Fabrizio, told him that, thanks to their cameras, I'd nabbed an employee stealing from his employer's safe. I said we had concerns whether the employee might have stolen smaller amounts that might have gone unnoticed on earlier occasions and asked if Cyber-Shield could provide us with copies of camera footage for the past year. He claimed they only keep the footage for ninety days and then it's automatically deleted unless the client requests otherwise."

"What about the client?" I asked. "Does the client record the footage?" Maybe older footage would be on the lounge's computers.

"No," Booth replied. "Even with the low resolution and frame rate, video files take up a lot of space. Most clients don't want to use up their storage with old video files when most incidents are discovered right away."

Hohenwald let out a long breath. "I'm guessing you asked the owner whether he'd been threatened recently? Whether anyone demanded protection money?"

"Of course," Booth replied, "and of course he denied it."

I chimed in again. "And, of course, you think he's lying about that and that Tino had one of his men try to shake the guy down."

"That's his standard MO," Booth said. "Besides, the owner went all jittery when I asked about threats. He nearly climbed out of his skin. If he'd found the safe first, I doubt he would've reported it."

"The good news," Hohenwald said, "is that nobody got killed and this incident will make it easier to secure the search warrant you'll need to place the recorder in Tino's office."

Looked like Josh hadn't wasted any time getting our ducks in a row. Apparently he'd already contacted Hohenwald to make sure we'd be legally authorized to go ahead with our plan. The last thing we needed was to bust Fabrizio and have the evidence thrown out on a technicality.

"My team has probably already informed your team about this," I said, turning to Hohenwald, "but I got a peek into Eric Echols's lair at Cyber-Shield last night. He had an image up on his screen that I suspect he might have been playing with, manipulating."

"Looking Good Optical?" Hohenwald asked.

"That's it."

"They let us know," he said. "We've got agents keeping tabs on the place."

"I hope you get something," Booth said. "Because we still don't have enough evidence to prosecute Tino."

"Not yet," I said, "but we will."

Hohenwald chuckled mirthlessly and cut his eyes my way. "You young agents. So hopeful and idealistic." He turned his gaze to Detective Booth. "Remember when we were like that?"

"Yeah." She issued a loud sigh. "It was a dozen cold cases ago."

## chapter thirty-three

# $\mathcal{S}$end in the Clowns

"By the way," Detective Booth added, "my staff finished that search you asked us to run for tickets issued to drivers of Chevy vans with novelty plates."

I leaned forward, hopefully. "Any luck?"

"None at all."

*Dang it.* Tripp Sevin, whoever he was, sure was an elusive SOB.

After meeting with Agent Hohenwald and Detective Booth, I went into the restaurant and ordered enchiladas and a large guacamole to go. Though the Italian food from Benedetta's was both free and delicious, my taste buds were begging for a little variety. They'd never tire of her chocolate cannoli, though. Heck, I could easily live on a strict diet of cannoli if I had to.

Thursday morning, I spotted no tail as I headed to DBU, so I played hooky from my class and decided to use my time checking out a couple more gray Chevy vans.

The first van was registered in the name of Blake

Birdwell at a residential address. I pulled up to the house, which sat in an older, low-rent area of homes in desperate need of some TLC. As I climbed out of my car, I heard the sounds of drums, an electric guitar, and a bass coming from the closed garage. I didn't recognize the rock song being played. *Must be an original.* I fought the urge to holler "Freebird!"

I walked up to the porch, knocked twice on the front door and rang the bell, but no one responded. Probably everyone was in the garage and hadn't heard me at the door. I stepped over to the garage door and knocked on that. "Federal law enforcement!" I called. "Open up."

The instruments came to an uneven stop, the bass emitted a final, elongated *bohhhm* before becoming silent. Murmuring came from behind the door. A moment later, the door rolled up with a tinny rattle to reveal three guys in their twenties, all wearing jeans and dark T-shirts. The drummer remained at his set and the bass player was perched on a stool.

"Hi." I flashed my badge. "I'm Special Agent Tara Holloway. I'm looking for Blake Birdwell."

"That's me," said the drummer. He spun his sticks in his hands and set them aside before standing.

His voice bore no Cajun accent, but that didn't necessarily mean he wasn't involved in the Triple 7 scam. He might have faked the accent when he went to Whispering Pines, or he might have lent his van to a friend who'd ripped off Harold, Jeb, Isaiah, and their friends.

"I'd like to see your Chevy van," I said.

His eyes narrowed in skepticism. "Why?"

"A gray Chevy van was used in a financial crime recently and I'm just making the rounds, checking out the vans that fit the description, trying to rule some of them out."

Blake glanced at his friends.

The bass player said, "Don't do it, man. Not without a search warrant."

The electric guitar player, who'd opened the garage door, raised his palms and shrugged. "Don't look at me, man. I'm not a lawyer."

Blake turned his attention back to me. "What department are you from?"

"Internal Revenue Service."

The guitar player launched into his own rendition of the Beatles' classic "Taxman."

"Good one." I offered him a forced smile. "Look," I said, "I'm not trying to hassle you. I'm just trying to figure out if someone used your van in a scam. I could come back with a search warrant, but do you really want me interrupting your rehearsal again?"

Blake frowned but after a few seconds' thought he acquiesced. "It's parked out back. Follow me."

He led me around to the side of the house. I noticed tire marks on the grass leading up to the gate. He opened the gate and pointed to the van, which sat in the grass a few yards away.

Stepping up to the van, I cupped my hands around my eyes to block the sun and took a quick peek inside. The last three rows of seats had been removed. "What's the van for?"

Blake stepped up next to me. "We use it to move our equipment to our gigs."

"Have you let anyone borrow it?"

"Hell, no!" he said. "Last time I lent a car to a friend he wrapped it around a tree. Nobody drives this van but me."

Clearly this was not the van I was looking for.

"Thanks for your time," I told him. "Sorry for the interruption."

He reached into his back pocket, pulled out a folded flyer and handed it to me. "We're playing this weekend at a bar near Fair Park. Tell your friends."

The flyer identified their band as the Rok Godz and noted that they were warming up for another band who called themselves the Bass-tards.

Miss Cecily's Charm School hadn't covered the proper sentiment to express good luck at a music event. Was it break a finger? Break a drumstick? Watch out for groupies with STDs? I settled for "Have a good gig."

This lead having gotten me nowhere, I drove on to investigate another fifteen-passenger Chevy van. As I cruised slowly up the street, looking for the address, I saw the van back out of a driveway a block ahead. It turned to head in the same direction I was going. As it turned right onto a more major road, I sped up and fell in behind it.

The back of the van was packed to the ceiling with what appeared to be a stack of trunks. Unfortunately, the trunks blocked my view into the van. Though I eased across the center stripe of the parkway to try to peer into the van, the tinted windows hampered my vision and oncoming traffic forced me back into my lane.

We continued on for three miles, the van proceeding normally, the driver seemingly unaware that federal law enforcement was in pursuit. I caught a glimpse of the driver's face in the side mirror as we stopped at a traffic light, but all I saw were bright blue sunglasses and bangs in a shade of bright orange that rivaled my own locks.

A minute later, the van pulled into the parking lot of an elementary school and took a spot in the visitors' section. I pulled up to the curb to see who might emerge. As I waited, the words posted on the marquee in front of the school caught my eye. WELCOME RAINY DAZE AND THE SUNSHINE BRIGADE!

The driver's door of the van swung open and out

came a leg clad in baggy purple polka-dot pants that ta-
pered down to wide-toed purple shoes in a size I estimated to be a twenty-three, if there even was such a
thing. The driver hopped down and I got a full view
now. He was a man dressed as a clown, complete with a
bright orange wig, colorful clothes, and the too big
shoes. He pulled a bright orange ruffled parasol out of
the van behind him and opened it. Strings of clear beads
hung down from the inside, as if it were raining under
the umbrella.

The other doors opened now and out hopped four
women, all dressed in bright-colored unitards and colorful
curly wigs, the Sunshine Brigade, for sure. They circled
around to the back of the van and opened it, working together to lower trunks of what I assumed to be props to the
ground.

Looked like this van belonged to Rainy Daze, not
Tripp Sevin. Frustrated, I heaved a sigh. Would I ever find
the man who'd ripped off the nice folks at Whispering
Pines? What were the odds? I was beginning to think
they were as low as the odds of actually spinning a triple
seven.

I continued on to the bistro, my heartrate accelerat-
ing as I pulled into the lot. Given that Tino had had me
followed again recently, I had to wonder whether he suspected me of being someone other than Tori Holland.
And, if he suspected I wasn't the former nanny/college
girl, what did he plan to do about it? *Eek*. Better not to
dwell on it. I wouldn't be able to concentrate on doing
either of my jobs if I let my fears overcome me.

# chapter thirty-four

## Watch Your Steps

Stella was working with me today. We went through our usual ministrations, preparing the tables, stacking the clean plates, and shelving the glassware. As I went to unlock the door at eleven to open the restaurant for business, I spotted Josh exiting the gallery across the street and heading my way.

I held the door open as he approached. "Good morning. Coming in for lunch today?"

"My partner and I are craving pizza," he said.

"We can certainly help with that."

I led Josh over to the register. "What can I get you?"

"A large," he said. "Half black olive and mushroom, half cheese only."

"And for dessert?" I asked, to which Benedetta, who'd wandered into the room wearing her chef's uniform, responded with a sly smile. Over my days at the restaurant, I'd discovered that if I acted as if dessert were a presumptive part of a meal, the diners felt less guilty ordering one. The people enjoyed their treat and their bill increased, as did the restaurant's profits and my tips.

Everyone was happy. I was like Rainy Daze and the Sunshine Brigade, spreading cheer.

Josh ran his gaze over the offerings in the refrigerated display case. "We'll take one chocolate cannoli and one bomboloni."

I rang him up and told him the total. "Nineteen forty-seven."

When Josh handed me a folded twenty-dollar bill, I felt something hard inside it. Lowering my hand behind the counter where the security cameras couldn't pick it up, I separated the device from the bill and took a quick look. It appeared to be a bracelet of some sort. I casually slipped it onto my wrist and counted out Josh's change.

"Here you go," I said. "Fifty-three cents."

Benedetta came around the back of the bar, grabbed a bottle of sherry, and returned to the kitchen.

"It's a recorder," Josh said under his breath once she'd gone. "It's made to look like one of those fitness trackers everybody's wearing these days."

I knew the kind he was talking about. They measured how many steps a person took in a given day. I had no idea how many steps I took every shift at the restaurant, running back and forth incessantly between the dining room and kitchen, but if I had to guess I'd say it was approximately eighty-five million. The last time I'd stopped for groceries I'd had to buy arch supports and gel insoles. If I kept this up much longer I'd probably end up with bunions, too, maybe even hammertoes.

He gave me quick instructions. "Push the button on the right to start the recorder."

"Got it." I hoped I'd have an opportunity to plant the recorder soon. While Tino seemed to get all of his meals from the bistro while he was at work, they weren't all de- livered to his office. Sometimes he walked over to pick the food up himself, and sometimes he ate in the bistro's employee lounge with his wife. Other times one of their daughters ran the food over to Cyber-Shield. I'd have to look for an opportunity to get into his office. "How long does this thing record for?"

Josh whispered his reply. "Up to sixty hours."

That would give us two full workdays of data and then some. Of course we couldn't be sure that Tino would discuss any matters relating to his extortion business during those sixty hours, and we couldn't be sure that if he discussed them that he'd do so in his office where the recorder would be located, but given the lack of cameras in his space it was a safe bet he conducted his dirty business there.

Josh took a seat at a booth to wait for his pizza, while I went to the kitchen to turn in his order. I handed the slip to Benedetta, who was performing chef duties today.

She took the slip, then took my hand, looking down at the tracker before returning her gaze to my face. "What's this on your wrist?"

*Dammit!* I'd been hoping nobody would notice and that I could surreptitiously drop the recorder in Tino's office without anyone realizing it belonged to me. We'd only chosen a disguised device on the off chance that someone would discover it. We didn't intend for it to be conspicuous. I should've pushed the dang thing up under my sleeve.

"It's a fitness tracker," I said, hoping she couldn't hear my pounding heart. "It measures how many steps I take each day. I've eaten so many of your chocolate cannoli my clothes are getting tight. I figured I better make sure I get enough exercise to burn off all those extra calories."

Benedetta released my hand and waved her own dismissively. "You girls, why are you always trying to stay so thin? Men like women with some meat on their bones. Besides, women are supposed to be round and soft."

Rather than linger on the subject of my fitness monitor, which could lead to no good, I switched to a topic I knew no mother could resist—her children. "Has Elena talked to you?"

Benedetta tilted her head, her tone wary. "About what?"

I cringed. "I guess that means she hasn't."

Benedetta pulled a clean ladle from the magnetic rack hanging over the center burners and teasingly brandished it at me. "About *what*?"

"I'm not sure it's my place to say."

She pointed at the brick oven, where flames flickered. "Your place is going to be inside that oven if you don't tell me."

I let out a long, slow breath. "She mentioned that she might like to have a career in television."

"Really?" Benedetta's brows rose. "She'd be wonderful on TV! She has such poise and a smooth voice, too. I wonder why she's never mentioned this to me."

"I think she was afraid you'd be disappointed if you knew she didn't want to help you run the restaurant."

She sighed, offering a small, soft smile as she waved the ladle around. "This place? It's *my* dream. I like to cook, I like to feed people, I like to boss people around. I love running this restaurant, but I want her to love her work, too. The day's too long to do a job you don't enjoy."

I agreed with her totally. I loved my job as a special agent. Well, normally I did. This undercover waitressing gig was growing old. Too many people demanding their dressing and sauce on the side, telling me the exact ratio of ice to liquid they wanted in their glasses, running me ragged with requests for "more of this" and "more of that" then leaving me a pitiful tip. I didn't have the patience or people-pleasing nature to do this kind of work on a regular basis, though I had a newfound appreciation for those who did. Working as a server was a tough job.

I reached out a hand and gave Benedetta's upper arm an affectionate squeeze. "You're a good mother."

"I'll talk to her. Registration for summer classes will be starting soon. Maybe she can sign up at one of the colleges around here."

"You know," I said, "if Elena doesn't have time to help out as much around here, I could take over some of her managerial duties. I could do some of the bookkeeping or scheduling or whatever."

Okay, so it was a ploy to try to get into Benedetta's office and look for physical evidence of money laundering or tax fraud. Maybe I'd spot stacks of unrecorded cash in a safe, or statements from a bank account opened under an alias. I knew these scenarios were unlikely, but if a person was going to hope, they might as well aim high, right?

"That's not a bad idea," she replied. "It couldn't hurt to have someone else on the staff who can handle the books. We'll see how it goes."

I returned to the dining room and seated a group of women in matching blue scrubs who, according to the name embroidered on their breast pockets, worked together at the orthodontist's office down the street. The door opened again and I turned to see Lu's ex Carl and the woman Lu had referred to as his "floozy" coming in the door.

*Crap!*

I'd seen and spoken with Carl on several occasions, and chances were he'd recognize me, too, even with this crazy red hair. I looked around, hoping I could fake a cramp and get Stella to cover for me until Carl left, but she wasn't in the dining room. I'd decided to make a mad dash for the kitchen anyway when from behind me Carl called, "Hey! I know you!"

At the same time, Stella stepped out of the kitchen. She looked over at Carl and back at me. "I think that customer is calling you, Tori."

My heart hammering in my chest, I turned and walked over. Carl wore his usual crisscrossed comb-over hairstyle, a polyester leisure suit, and his shiny white bucks. But, good Lord! Carl's new girlfriend could pass as a Luella Lobozinski impersonator. She had the same full figure, the same false eyelashes, the same outdated attire, though, judging from the high-waist jeans and blouse with shoulder pads, this woman's fashion era appeared to be the 1980s whereas Lu was still stuck in the 1960s. Also, where Lu sported a strawberry-blond beehive, this woman's coppery hair stood up in pointy spikes atop her head. Nonetheless, it was clear Carl had a type.

"Hi," I said. "Good to see you, Carl. Would you like a booth or a table?"

His face showed confusion. He must have been wondering why an IRS special agent was waiting tables at an Italian restaurant.

Before he could say something that would spill the beans, I said, "I work here now." I gave him a prolonged wink with my right eye, which faced away from the security cameras.

"I *see*," he said.

He understood. *Thank God!*

I turned to his date. "I'm Tori."

She looked from me back to Carl. "How do you two know each other?"

Carl appeared flustered, so I answered for him. "We have a mutual friend," I replied. "My former boss."

"Oh, well, nice to meet you," the woman said. "What's good here?"

"Everything," I said with a sincere smile. "But especially the chocolate cannoli."

I showed them to a booth on the opposite side of the restaurant as Josh and took their drink orders.

When I returned to the kitchen, the pizza was ready. I opened a carryout box and Benedetta slid the pizza into it. I carried the box out to Josh and handed it to him. "Enjoy."

"Thanks," he said, adding, in a barely audible whisper, "Good luck and be careful."

I'd be as careful as I could, yet I knew all the care in the world was sometimes not enough. Mobsters had killed members of law enforcement before, judges and jurors, too. The lucky ones were shot execution style, the others . . . Well, let's not go there. No matter how many precautions we agents took, it was impossible to guarantee that an investigation wouldn't lead to injury or death. Then again, targets had tried to kill me before. So far, none had succeeded. *But I suppose that's obvious, huh?* Only time would tell whether my luck would continue—or run out.

I went back to the kitchen to get drinks for Carl and his date, finding him sitting alone when I returned to the booth.

He gestured across the space. "She went to the ladies' room."

"Good," I said. "I'm glad I can speak with you alone."

He looked at me intently. "What about?"

"Our *mutual friend.*"

Carl looked down at the table and rolled his napkin between his fingers. "Lu broke my heart."

"She may have," I said. "But she regrets it. She misses you. We were talking about you the other day and she nearly broke down in tears."

He looked up at me and his eyes lit up like a brick pizza oven. "She did?"

"Yep. But she knows about your new girlfriend. She's too afraid to tell you how she feels because she thinks you might shoot her down."

*Sheesh.* I was spilling everyone's secrets today, wasn't I? All with good intentions, though.

"I'd take her back in a heartbeat if I thought she'd have me," Carl said. "I think this new one's only dating me to make her ex-husband jealous anyway."

I knew Lu had a date with Jeb this weekend, and I didn't think it would be right to spoil their plans, so I suggested Carl give her a call early next week.

"I'll do that," he said, a big smile on his face. "Thanks, Tori."

I gave him another wink.

At half past one, Tino came into the restaurant. Looked like he'd be picking up his lunch himself. I was only scheduled to work until four o'clock, so I wouldn't be here when he placed his dinner order. *Dammit!* So much for planting the device today. Would I ever be able to get this recorder planted in his office?

The longer this case went on, the riskier it became. We couldn't continue to keep such a close eye on Tino and his staff without one of them eventually catching on. We needed a break in this case. And we needed it *now*.

# chapter thirty-five

# Closing In

Friday morning marked my last class at DBU. Finals would be held next week. There'd be a two-week break before summer classes started, but I decided Tori Holland should take the summer off from school so she could go on that vacation with her parents to Disney World in June. In actuality, I'd need the time off for Alicia's wedding. I really hoped I wouldn't still be working the Fabrizio case next month. I'd given up everything to go after this guy. My home. My pets. My boyfriend. The price was starting to feel very high. Maybe even *too* high.

Fridays were the bistro's busiest weekday, with many workers deciding to go out for lunch or to treat themselves to a nice dinner or takeout after the long workweek. All three of the Fabrizio girls were scheduled to work today. While having them all around lightened the workload, it also lessened the chances that I'd be the one to take Tino his lunch or dinner. One of them might grab his bag before I had a chance to snatch it. I needed to get the tracker planted in his office ASAP, before another person could be robbed or killed.

Stella and I spread the tablecloths on the tables, while Luisa and Elena trailed behind with the flower vases, candles, shakers, and silverware. In minutes, we had the dining room ready for business. I returned to the kitchen, where I grabbed plates of desserts to take to the case in the dining room. Benedetta led the way, her arms loaded with the bistro's baked selections.

My curiosity about Benedetta had become nearly unbearable. Did the woman know about her husband's bad deeds? Or was she truly in the dark? I wanted to know. Heck, I *needed* to know. I'd grown quite fond of her. If we busted Tino, there was a possibility she could be arrested, too, if she'd willingly or even unwittingly helped him commit his crimes. Had she deposited any of the protection money in the bank? Maybe laundered it through an account we hadn't found yet? I hoped not. I'd hate to see the Fabrizio girls lose both their father and mother in one fell swoop. They weren't children, of course, but none of them was fully independent yet. They still needed their mother.

As Benedetta positioned the desserts in the case, I casually asked, "I've noticed you have an accent. Where are you from?"

She slid an entire cream cake onto the top shelf, her brows forming a Vee of confusion. "My parents were fresh off the boat from Naples, *cara*. The whole family came over. I spent my childhood immersed in Italian. I can't help but speak with an accent."

"Not the Italian," I clarified. "I get that. But I thought I detected another accent, too. Maybe a New York accent or something? Did you live somewhere else before moving to Dallas?"

"Ah," she said, "it must be my Chicago accent you're hearing."

"Chicago? That sounds like an interesting place to

live. They've got lots of museums and stuff, right? And that big silver jelly bean. You must have liked it there."

She froze, and for a moment I thought I'd blown my cover by asking about her past. But after a few seconds' pause, she retrieved two plates of tiramisu from the top of the case and slid them into place on either side of the cream cake. "Chicago wasn't a good place for us. It's a . . ." She hesitated, as if trying to find the right word. "A *mean* place. I didn't want to raise my daughters there."

So it was her idea to move away, then? Or maybe she'd suggested a move and Tino saw the advantages in it. I hoped I wasn't pushing my luck by asking the next question. "Did you leave family behind? Do you miss them?"

"I miss some of *my* family," she said. "But *Tino's* family? No. I don't miss any of them."

*Be more specific!* my brain screamed at her. "Not warm and fuzzy, huh?"

"No," she said curtly. "Not at all."

She didn't elaborate, and I realized asking any more questions would seem impolite. But her words gave me the first inkling that she might be aware of the shady business Tino was involved in. Or at least that she had an inkling that members of his extended family weren't exactly model citizens.

"Any chance you're free on Saturday evening?" Benedetta asked. "I'm catering a big Italian wedding. Luisa was going to help me but she got asked out on a date. Could you fill in?"

"I'd be happy to." Working an outside event with Benedetta might help me figure out if she was laundering money for her husband through the liquor account.

"Great," she said. "Be here at four."

The rest of morning and the lunch rush passed by in a blur. At one-thirty, Tino called in with his order. I took the call and crossed my fingers I'd be the one to take it over to him.

"Don't forget my cannoli," he said in a singsong voice.

"Never," I replied. *You might kill me if I did.*

I hurriedly served my last lunch table and rushed back to the kitchen, surreptitiously watching as Dario prepared the mushroom ravioli Tino had requested today. I boxed a cannoli and gathered up silverware and a napkin, hoping that by hovering over Tino's bag with the utensils I'd possess some type of squatter's rights that would give me the privilege of delivering his meal. Dario handed me the to-go container of ravioli and I put it in the bag.

As I folded the top of the bag over, I felt both relief and apprehension. It was good that I'd been able to take charge of the delivery, but the fact that I planned to plant a recording device in Tino's office had my insides squirming.

I was halfway through the dining room with the bag when the front door opened and Tino stepped into the bistro. It was all I could do not to hurl his bag of food at him and scream. I didn't need him *here.* I needed him back in his office!

He raised his hand. Three tickets of some sort were splayed in his fingers. "Look what Daddy's got, girls!"

Squealing, Stella, Luisa, and Elena rushed over to him. They jumped up and tried to grab the tickets from his hand, but he playfully held them up, out of reach. Not an easy feat for a short guy like him. Eventually he lowered his hand and Stella snatched the tickets from him.

"Stars on Ice!" she cried. "Woo-hoo!"

"Thanks, Dad," Elena said, leaning in to give her father a kiss on the cheek.

Luisa did the same. "You always know just the thing to make us happy."

Stella looked up from the tickets in her hand. "There's only three tickets. What about Mom?"

Tino waved a hand. "Your mother hated the cold back in Chicago. She'd have no interest in sitting next to a frozen ice rink."

Elena looked my way. "These tickets are for next Thursday night. I know you've got finals next week, Tori, but could you cover for us?"

"Of course," I said. "I should ace my tests. I've been studying a lot." *As if.* I hadn't cracked a book since the night I'd pretended to be studying at the nail salon.

Tino glanced at the bag of food in my hand. "Is that for me?"

"It sure is." I stepped forward to hand it to him, tempted to shove it where the sun doesn't shine and even Rainy Daze and the Sunshine Brigade wouldn't dare to venture. "Enjoy."

*Choke on it, you rat bastard.*

On Saturday morning, I made yet another trip to check out yet another gray Chevy van. This one was registered under the name Adam Stratford. Huh. That name didn't sound Cajun at all.

After having no luck previously, I didn't feel so much as if I was honing in on my target as if I was launched on a wild-goose chase. Maybe the Cajun cowboy lived far out in west Texas. Pecos or El Paso, maybe. Or perhaps he lived in Marfa, famous for its mystical lights of unknown origin. Or maybe he lived down in Houston, the state's largest city. It was an easy four-hour drive up Interstate 45 from Houston to Dallas. Not too far for a con artist to drive if he wanted to rip people off yet reduce his risks of being identified in line at the grocery store. But I wouldn't feel like I'd done my duty if I didn't follow up on all of these leads. On the bright side, surely I'd get a free cannoli for helping Benedetta out with the wedding later.

I pulled up to a house in Garland, a city made semifamous by Jesse Eisenberg in the movie *Zombieland*. To paraphrase, the character he portrayed said the city might appear as if zombies had destroyed it, but that's just the way Garland looks. An overstatement, to be sure. Garland might not be the most exclusive area of Dallas, and it might have some older neighborhoods, but there were no eviscerated corpses lying around. At least not at the moment.

The home on west Avenue D was a wood model, beige with dark green trim, and appeared to have been built in the 1950s. The driveway, if you could call it that, was merely two wide concrete runners, one for each tire, with crabgrass growing between them. The van sat at the far end of the driveway, which proceeded from the street up along the side of the house.

I climbed out of my car and walked up to the van, keeping an eye out for rotting, brain-eating predators, just in case. The van gleamed in the sun, looking as if it had been freshly washed. There was no magnetic sign on the side, no telltale novelty license plates on the vehicle. By all accounts, it looked like this van would be another dead end.

Until I peeked in the passenger side window.

*Bingo.*

On the passenger floorboard lay a magnetic sign. This one read OZARKS EXPRESS. On the seat lay a stack of postcards held together with a rubber band. The postcard pictured beautiful photos of the Arkansas mountain range along with the words *Let Us Take You There!* and a phone number and Web site address. Given that the postcards lay flat on the seat, I couldn't read the backside, but it didn't much matter. It was clear I'd found my Cajun cowboy con artist.

I tried the door of the van but found it locked. I pulled out my cell phone and snapped a picture of the evidence through the window. It was a little on the dark side, but it would have to do.

Now it was time to make an arrest.

After retrieving my Glock, handcuffs, and badge from the locked glove compartment of my car, I went to the door and knocked, my heart bouncing up and down in my chest in anxious anticipation. *Knock-knock-knock.* I waited thirty seconds or so, but nobody came to the door.

I knocked again, louder and longer this time. *Knock-knock-KNOCK-KNOCK-knock.*

The place had no doorbell, so knocking again was my only option. I put some extra muscle into it this time. *KNOCK-KNOCK-KNOCK-KNOCK-KNOCK!*

A voice came from the yard next door. "Adam left earlier in his car," said a fortyish woman who'd wandered out to water her petunias with a garden hose.

"Any idea when he'll be back?"

She shook her head. "Nope."

"Do you know him well?"

"Nope," she repeated. "Met him when he moved in and occasionally he'll come over and ask to borrow a tool from my husband, but that's about it."

Typical neighbor relationship these days, when people valued privacy over idle conversation at the fence.

"I'll check back later," I said.

She didn't ask who I was or why I'd come by. Also fairly typical of people these days. Rather than sticking their noses where they might not be welcome, they minded their own business.

I got back in my car and drove to Whispering Pines to give the residents my good news. I found Harold out front, pushing Isaiah in his wheelchair, making their way toward the rose garden. There was no sign of Jeb. He was probably hitting on women in a knitting class or over cards again.

I pulled my car to a stop at the curb and rolled my window down. "Hi, Harold and Isaiah!" I called, raising a hand. "Got some good news for you!"

I climbed out of my car and walked over to the men. Harold's huge eyes blinked at me from behind his thick glasses, making me feel like I was a specimen under a microscope.

"I found the con artist who ripped y'all off."

Harold's mouth fell open. Isaiah's already hung open so it was hard to tell if he was surprised, too, but the glimmer in his eyes told me he was happy to hear the news.

"I knew it!" Harold cried, clapping his hands. "I knew the girl who killed a drug dealer could find our bad guy, too!"

Back to *that,* were we? *Ugh.*

"Did you arrest him?" Harold asked. "Is he in jail? Can we go visit him and poke him with a stick through the bars?"

"No, no, and I don't think you're allowed to do that."

He frowned. "Well, if he's not in jail, what did you go getting us all excited for?"

*No pleasing some people, huh?* "I know who he is, and I know where he lives," I told them. "Problem was, he wasn't home. I could go back and arrest him, but it would be more fun to beat him at his own game, wouldn't it?"

Harold's eyes flashed with mischief behind his glasses. "You mean con the con artist?"

"That's exactly what I'm talking about."

Isaiah lifted his head. "Count . . . me . . . in."

# chapter thirty-six

# $\mathcal{M}$y Big Fat Italian Wedding

I slipped the fitness tracker around my wrist and pushed it up under the hem of my sleeve. It was doubtful I'd have a chance to plant the thing today, but better to have it with me just in case.

I arrived at the bistro at four as Benedetta had requested. Tino's car wasn't at his office. Looked like he was off today.

Across the parking lot, things were bustling at the gallery. Through the window I could see five or six patrons milling about the space. Looked like Nick might have done too good a job with his cover. Gallery Nico was doing a brisk business. A reporter from the *Dallas Morning News* had even come by earlier in the week to do a piece on the place.

I entered the bistro and stashed my things in my locker. While Elena handled the relatively quiet dining room, Luisa and Stella and I lugged pot after heavy pot of pasta out to the catering truck. It was a wonder none of us suffered a hernia. The garlic knots were much easier to carry, as were the coolers holding the salad. Given that wedding cake would be served at the reception, no desserts had been ordered.

While the girls and I carried the food, Dario stacked cases of wine and assorted liquor onto a dolly and rolled them out to the catering truck, setting them side by side on the floor. He returned to the restaurant two more times, reloaded the dolly, and came back to the truck with yet more cases of liquor. *My gosh!* There was enough liquor here to throw an entire year's worth of frat parties.

When the truck was ready, Benedetta came outside carrying a metal cash box. She handed the cash box to me and climbed into the driver's seat. I sat in the middle with the box on my lap, while Juan sat on the right.

I cast a glance back at the liquor. "Who's going to tend the bar?"

Benedetta said that one of the bistro's bartenders planned to meet us at the event to work the bar. "I'll back him when things get busy."

"You know how to mix drinks?" I asked.

"I know how to do everything, *cara,*" she said with a coy smile.

Tonight's event could be a chance for me to figure out whether cash was being laundered through the liquor account. If I could count the funds in the cash box at the end of the night, I'd be able to compare them to the figure she'd put into her bookkeeping system later.

"I'd be happy to help at the bar," I said. "I don't know how to mix drinks, but I'd love to learn. And I can pour wine or champagne." Merely filling a glass required no bartending skills.

"I'll need you to handle the food tonight," she said. "Besides, you're not certified to sell liquor."

*Ugh!*

"But if you are interested in learning," she added, "I

can schedule you a shift as a bar back so you can get your feet wet."

"Thanks," I said. "I'd like that."

She chuckled and cut a glance my way. "One of these days you are going to take over my restaurant."

I gave her a smile. "I just might." *But probably not in the way you think.*

Benedetta headed onto Central Expressway, exiting on Mockingbird, just as Agent Hohenwald had done only days ago when we went to visit with Alex Harris at Dallas Country Club. Instead of turning left on Mockingbird, however, Benedetta turned right. In minutes we arrived at the beautiful St. Thomas Aquinas church on Kenwood. As we pulled up, I found myself admiring the arched entry and beautiful stained-glass windows. I also found myself wondering whether Tino Fabrizio had ever confessed his sins to a priest. Clergy were bound to confidentiality, but *whoa*. What a burden those secrets would be to bear, huh? And what penance could possibly make up for what Tino had done?

I realized that my idle speculations were ridiculous. Tino had probably never confessed his sins because he probably never felt sorry for the things he'd done. If he had, he wouldn't keep doing them, right?

Benedetta drove around to the parish hall and parked. Juan and I spent the next half hour unloading the catering tables, linens, and food from the truck, while Benedetta supervised and arranged the tables and bar. Finally, we were done setting up. None too soon, either. The doors to the reception hall opened and wedding guests streamed into the room, making a beeline for our Italian buffet.

It was a happy, lively crowd of olive-skinned, dark-haired people. While Juan, with his Latino coloring, fit right in, I stuck out like a sore thumb with my pale skin and bright red hair. I tried to compensate by offering *buon giorno*s to several of the guests, but quickly realized it was a mistake as they'd then begin to address me in Italian.

"Sorry," I told them. "I haven't gotten to verbs yet on my language CD."

I served the salad and bread, while Juan handled the pasta and side dishes. Coffee, tea and antipasti were self-service. Benedetta and the bartender passed glass after glass of wine across the bar, exchanging them for cash. When the guests had finished their dinner, the champagne came out and the usual toasts were made. As the dinner turned to dancing, the crowd switched from wine to hard liquor, keeping Benedetta and the bartender busy nonstop.

Seeing how active the bar was, I wondered if the liquor account was accurate, after all. Perhaps our speculation that it was being used to launder funds was wrong.

"Time to clean up," Juan said finally, handing me a rag to wipe down the buffet table.

The two of us spent the next few minutes cleaning up the area. Our jobs here now done, Juan and I quietly packed up the serving pieces, tables, and tablecloths. When we were ready to go, Benedetta bade the bartender farewell. Fortunately, things had slowed down as the night went on and it looked like he'd be able to manage the bar by himself from here on out.

It was after nine by the time Benedetta pulled the catering van into the parking lot of the restaurant. The pull-down safety doors were already in place at both Gallery Nico and the bistro, enclosing both businesses in an aluminum cocoon. I noted Tino's car in the parking lot at Cyber-Shield, along with three of the patrol cars, including the one marked with the number six. *Hmm.* I wondered if Tino and Cole Kirchner were inside strategizing how to best extort money from Looking Good Optical or punish the optician for refusing to pay their unreasonable demands.

Benedetta circled around to the back of the building, reversing the truck carefully toward the building so that we could more easily unpack the pots, pans, and coolers from the back and take them into the kitchen. She unlocked the back door and swung it outward, using her foot to push the doorstop down to hold it open.

We were halfway through unloading the cargo bay when Tino emerged from the back door of Cyber-Shield. "Would you like some help?"

"Sure," Benedetta said. "Many hands make light work."

Tino grabbed a warming pot with a red streak of dried marinara sauce down the side. After he carried it inside, I noticed him duck into Benedetta's office. He motioned for her to join him. Once she was inside, he closed the door. A minute later, the door opened and the two emerged. I had no idea what had transpired in the office, but I was left to wonder, once again, whether my seemingly sweet boss was aiding and abetting her mobster husband.

No opportunity to slip the recorder into Tino's office presented itself that night. I went home with the device still on my wrist and a bagged cannoli in my hand.

# chapter thirty-seven

## $\mathscr{D}$uty Calls Before Booty Calls

On Sunday afternoon, just like the week before, I parked at one end of the Galleria and slipped through various stores before exiting elsewhere. I'd dressed in workout clothes, and today jogged the distance to Hana's condo. I'd been unable to do my usual workouts while hiding at the new apartment and was out of breath in mere seconds. *No more cannoli for me!*

That was a vow made to be broken, huh?

Nick was watching out the window this time, opening Hana's front door to let me in when he spotted me approaching. The instant I was in the door he grabbed me and pulled me to him, mashing our bodies together so tight it was almost uncomfortable. But I knew exactly why he was doing this and, even though it wasn't exactly the soft, warm welcome either of us would have liked, it reflected exactly how we felt. Desperate to have this case over so that we could be together again. Tired of being worried and scared and wondering if the mobster or his thugs were on to us and meant us harm. Sick of pretending to be someone else and the exhausting mental energy it took to keep up the façade 24/7.

He leaned down and gave me a kiss. Unlike the hug, which was really more of a death grip, his kiss was soft and warm and wonderful. I'd take Nick's kisses over chocolate cannoli any day.

"I miss the hell out of you," he said softly.

"Right back at ya."

"Let's spend some time together after this meeting," he suggested. "Get a hotel room for a few hours."

He wouldn't have to ask me twice. "Perfect."

When everyone had arrived, the Operation Italian Takeout team took seats in Hana's living room to update each other on the progress we'd made since our meeting last Sunday.

Eddie spoke first. "I've followed Dario. Nothing he's done has seemed unusual or suspicious, though it's clear he's looking for a new job."

"Really?" I said. "What makes you say that?"

"I've seen him go into two other restaurants this week. Both times it was before business hours."

And before he'd be due to start work at Benedetta's. *Hmm.* I wondered why Dario wanted to leave. Did he know there was shady business going on and wanted to get out before the ship went down? Or maybe he realized he knew too much and, like me, feared he'd end up in the pizza oven. Then again, maybe he was merely looking to move up to a larger restaurant with more upward potential. As a family-owned restaurant, Benedetta's Bistro didn't offer much room for advancement. Benedetta would always be top chef.

Hana leaned forward in her chair, her arms propped on her knees, one of her legs pumping in excitement. "Kirchner's been doing his same widespread routes, but he also made a couple stops at Looking Good Optical."

"After hours?" I asked. "Or while it was open?"

"Shortly after they closed up shop for the evening," Hana said. "After the employees left but before the owner went home."

"He's talked to the owner, then. Maybe made some threats?"

"Looks that way."

She went on to explain that because Kirchner was suspected to be the one handling the pickup of the protection money, which was the crux of our money-laundering/tax-evasion case, the IRS members of the task force were focusing on him. Meanwhile the FBI members had returned their efforts to Tino and his other patrolmen, who were more likely to be involved in the violent facets of Tino's schemes.

Hana continued. "Kirchner's driven by the optical shop a few times since, both during the day and at night. We spotted him in a parked car across the street yesterday, looking the place over with binoculars."

"But he hasn't gone inside again?" I asked.

"No," Hana replied.

I mulled things over for a moment. "You think the owner might have refused to pay the protection money and Tino's planning some type of punishment?" After all, the clients who paid were presumably left alone. I felt the excitement of a pending bust begin to buzz through me. Clearly, Looking Good was next on Tino's list, but how it would be hit was anyone's guess.

"Looks that way," Hana said again.

"You think they're planning to set it on fire like Alex Harris's bar?" I asked. "Or maybe just rob it like they did the hookah lounge?"

We debated the possibilities. It was doubtful an optical shop would have a lot of cash on hand, so a robbery seemed improbable. More than likely, Tino had ordered his goons to do violence against the man who owned the business. My mind envisioned some type of slow, horrible death involving a lens-grinding machine. Or maybe they'd strap the optician to a chair and drip dilating solution into his eyes until he went blind or his eyeballs exploded. *Could that even happen?*

"He's been casing the owner's house, too," Hana said.

"Oh, Lord." A sick feeling coursed through me as I thought of the optician and his family and I had to bend over to put my head between my knees. What if Tino or Cole decided to target the optician at home rather than attack him at his place of business? The man's wife and child would be there. What if federal agents didn't get to them in time? *Just how far is Tino willing to go?*

I sat back up and swallowed the lump in my throat. "Did anyone else happen to check out the Looking Good Web site?"

Nick's eyes met mine. "You saw the picture?" he asked. "The one with the kid?"

Again he proved just how well he knew me.

"Yeah," I said on a sigh.

"Don't worry," Nick said, reaching out from beside me to give my hand a reassuring squeeze. "We're not going to let the little dude down."

I looked around the group, asking one final, desperate question. "Has anyone seen any concrete evidence that Tino's collecting protection money? Please, one of you say yes." I prayed one of them had seen something solid that would give us grounds to move in before something happened to the optician or his business or his family.

Unfortunately, everyone answered in the negative. All they'd seen was Cole Kirchner going into places of business operated by Cyber-Shield clients and coming back out minutes later. All of the other patrolmen merely made their rounds in their cars, getting out occasionally to check that doors were locked or to shine a flashlight into a dark space between buildings or behind Dumpsters. None of them went inside any of the businesses they visited. The FBI members of the task force reported the same observations.

Josh said, "I was at the gallery early this morning when the patrolmen were coming back from their night shifts. It was around six-thirty or so. I saw Tino go over to the bistro. He rolled up the security doors and went inside. He came back out about twenty minutes later and closed everything up again."

It seemed odd that he'd be at work so early on a Sunday morning. "Was Benedetta at the restaurant?"

"I didn't see her or her car," Josh said. "As far as I could tell, Tino didn't carry anything in or out of the restaurant, but he was wearing a suit. There would have been plenty of pockets to hide money in."

I remembered Hohenwald telling me that Fabrizio served as a Eucharistic minister in his church. Maybe he planned to go to an early mass after dropping by Cyber-Shield. But why had Tino gone into the bistro? Perhaps he was bringing the cash Cole Kirchner had collected from Cyber-Shield's victims so Benedetta could add it to last night's cash-bar receipts and deposit the funds together at the bank tomorrow. Maybe she really was laundering the protection money through the liquor account as we'd speculated. What other reason would he have had to go into her place of business? Even so, I had my doubts. Benedetta seemed like a genuinely nice person. Then again, maybe I'd become too close to her and the girls to stay objective.

We still had no concrete evidence, and we'd need something solid to link Tino to a crime. While Eddie,

Hana, and Will would continue to keep an eye on Cole Kirchner, Josh would continue his attempts to hack Cyber-Shield's system, and Nick would continue his surveillance of the company from the gallery. I'd go ahead with my plan to plant the recorder in Tino's office as soon as I was able. The more evidence we could gather, the better.

We concluded the meeting with mutual expressions of concern.

"Stay safe."

"Watch your back."

"Watch your ass."

It would take a little more effort than usual to watch my ass these days given that it had expanded an inch or two thanks to Benedetta's chocolate cannoli.

Nick rounded up his car from where he'd parked it a few blocks over, and swung back by to pick me up at Hana's. He drove to a nearby hotel, and parked around the back. We really couldn't be too careful. Cyber-Shield's staff lived all over Dallas, and many of them came into the restaurant or crossed paths with me or Nick in the parking lot. We couldn't risk them spotting me here with Nick and mentioning it to Tino.

I stayed in the car, keeping my head low and a keen eye on my surroundings, while Nick went inside and obtained a room. He texted me with the room number: *347*.

I locked his car, took the keys with me, and went into the hotel, bypassing the elevator and instead taking the stairs up to the room. Not only would it burn a few more of the cannoli calories I'd accumulated, it would get me warmed up for what was to come.

And what was to come was warm, indeed . . .

# chapter thirty-eight

# $\mathcal{F}$ree Bug with Every Meal

Monday morning, I had my first final exam for the semester. My Global Marketing final was multiple choice. When the teacher's assistant handed out the bubble forms, I was tempted to darken the circle next to the letter B for each question. With Tori Holland's mediocre GPA and fictional existence, what did it really matter if she failed this test?

But my Tara Holloway work ethic wouldn't let me be so lazy. Besides, what if the Fabrizio case stretched out and Echols decided to hack into DBU's computer system or to access their student records system via the password gleaned from my infected laptop? If Tino learned that I'd failed my finals, it might clue him in that my Tori Holland persona was a fraud. Skipping classes was one thing, but flunking out was another.

Instead, I read through each question carefully, racking my brain to remember what I'd learned in the marketing classes I'd taken years ago at the University of Texas down in Austin. When my memory came up short, I applied common sense or outright guesswork. And when neither approach worked on a particular question, I went with the proven eenie-meanie-meinie-mo method, coming up with C for my answer.

I wasn't due at Benedetta's until two o'clock, so I did my usual Neiman Marcus maneuver, parking in the garage downtown across from the store and pinballing my way to my office at the IRS.

I stepped off the elevator and headed down to Lu's office.

"Good morning," I said to Viola, Lu's administrative assistant.

Viola returned the greeting, assessing me over her bifocals. "Your roots could stand a touch-up."

*Sheesh.* I'm out risking my life going after a mobster and all I get is a rude comment about my hair? But it wasn't worth getting upset over it. I had bigger things to worry about. I might have to stop by the pharmacy for another box of hair color, though. "I've missed you, Viola."

I rapped on Lu's door frame and she looked up from her desk.

"How'd your date with Jeb go?" I asked.

She shrugged. "I suppose I had a good enough time. But he's really not my type after all. I think I just agreed to go out with him because he was so easy. You know, low-hanging fruit."

*Ew.* I really didn't want to think about Jeb's low-hanging fruit.

"Got an update for me?" she asked.

I filled Lu in on the developments in the Fabrizio investigation, and on my plan to plant the fitness tracker/recording device in his office.

"Be careful," she said, "sounds like he's got lots of experience disposing of bodies where they'll never be found."

That's a lovely thought with which to begin the work-week, huh?

The mobster case dealt with, I told Lu about the plans I'd made with Harold and Isaiah to nab Adam Stratford, aka Tripp Sevin.

"I love it!" she said. "Count me in."

I went to my office to set the plan in motion. After closing my door, I ran a search of the tax filings. While I found that Adam Stratford had filed tax returns, the only income he'd reported over the last few years was around thirty-five grand in wages from a warehouse job at a lo-cal big-box store. When he wasn't driving the van, he was driving a forklift. The fact that he hadn't reported any of his earnings from the vacation scam put him on the hook not only for fraud, but also tax evasion.

I used my trusty old IRS-issued cell phone to call the number I'd seen on the Ozarks Express postcards.

A man answered. Sure enough, he had that Cajun ac-cent that Isaiah, Jeb, and Harold had mentioned.

"Hello," I said, adding a warble to my voice in the hopes I'd sound aged. "My name is Melvina . . ." On the spot like that, I couldn't think of a last name. *Ugh!* I should've thought this through better before I'd placed the call. I said the first thing that came to my mind. "Cannoli."

I slapped a palm to my forehead. *Cannoli? Really?* That was the best I could come up with?

"How can I help you, Mrs. Cannoli?" Stratford asked.

"I saw your Web site online," I said, continuing the warble. But rather than making me sound elderly, it made me sound as if I were gargling. I coughed as if to clear my throat and spoke in my regular voice. "Me and a group of my friends would like to plan a trip to the Ozarks. Maybe make a stop in Hot Springs along the way and visit the bath houses. Is that something you could help us with?"

"I sure can," he replied.

"We saw that you offer transportation and hotel packages for two nights?"

"That's right," he said. "Only four hundred dollars for the whole enchilada."

"Oh, I don't like enchiladas," I said, screwing with the guy. "All those spices give me heartburn."

"What I meant," he said after a moment's pause, speaking slowly as if he thought I was an idiot, "was that the fee includes both the van and the two nights' accommodations."

"Oh! Okay. Okeydokey."

"When would you like to depart?" he asked.

I chose a random date in June. "How about June seventeenth?"

"Let me check the bookings to make sure the van's available then."

*Yeah, right.* I had a feeling no matter what date I'd tossed out he'd tell me the van was available.

"You're in luck," he said a few seconds later. "That date is open."

Just as I'd suspected.

"Summer vacations are booking fast, though," he said. "In order for your group to reserve the van, I'll need to collect half of the fee up front from each traveler as a deposit. I can accept payment in cash, or traveler's checks if you prefer."

*Or you can accept it in my orthopedic shoe up your ass, you conniving little whippersnapper!* Eighty-seven years on this earth and the fictional Melvina Cannoli hadn't lost her girlish sass.

"You'll come by to collect the payment, right?"

I asked. "I'm not comfortable putting cash or traveler's checks in the mail and I'm sure my friends will feel the same."

"Certainly. I'll just need an address."

I couldn't give Adam Stratford the address of Whispering Pines or he might realize it was a setup. Instead, I gave him the address for the apartment complex where Alicia and I had lived when we'd first moved to Dallas after college. I'd be sure to be waiting outside when he arrived so that he wouldn't have to knock on the door and bother whoever actually lived in our unit now.

"How's Friday morning?" I asked. I had Friday off from the bistro and wasn't scheduled again to work until the following Monday. "Around ten o'clock?"

"That works fine," he said. "I'll see you then."

*Yes, you will. And you just might be surprised by who else you see.*

At eight that evening, Tino called the bistro. I took the call. He asked for a meal to be delivered to his office.

"What can I get you tonight?" I asked.

"Surprise me."

Oh, I'd surprise him all right. With a disguised recorder. *Hee-hee!* Finally I'd get a chance to plant the darn thing.

"See you soon." *You sorry excuse for a human being.*

I walked back to the kitchen, where Dario stood at the stove, beginning to wind things down for the night. "Tino said to surprise him."

"I can do that." Dario proceeded to fill a container with the remaining mushroom ravioli, covering it with a combination of Alfredo and marinara sauces, improvising a parma rosa, though rather than mixing the two sauces together he applied them in distinctive red and white stripes.

"Creative," I told him.

Benedetta looked up from her desk in her open office. "What did he do?"

"He made stripes with the sauce." I carried the box in to show her. "See?"

"Interesting presentation. I like it." She raised a hand and motioned to her chef. "Dario, come in here, please."

He hung the hooked ladle over the side of the large pot and walked into her office, his expression wary.

"I know you're thinking about taking another job," Benedetta said, giving him a pointed look. "Tino overheard you on your phone out back."

I'd known Dario was job-hunting, too. Of course I hadn't shared that tidbit with Benedetta or she'd have wondered how I'd gotten the information. I couldn't very well tell her that I was an undercover IRS agent and that one of my colleagues had followed the guy.

"I don't fault you for considering your other options," she told Dario. "Sometimes I think you are an ass and that I should send you packing anyway. But the fact of the matter is that you are a talented chef. Other than myself, no one else has been able to make my grandmother's recipes as well as you do. I don't want to lose you." She paused a moment to let her words sink in. "What's it going to take to keep you here? You want more money? More creative freedom? Is that it?"

His expression changed from wary to thoughtful to eager. "I'd love to create some of my own dishes," he said. "Your grandmother's recipes are delicious, but I've been cooking them for years now. I'd like to try something new."

"Come up with some dishes, then," Benedetta said. "We'll make them the daily specials, see which ones are a hit with the customers, and add the best ones to the menu."

Dario grinned. "I've got an eggplant lasagna idea I'd like to try first. And then maybe I'll try Tori's idea and toss fried mushrooms on top of spaghetti marinara."

I raised a finger. "I want credit for that one."

"Of course, *cara*." As she spoke, Benedetta looked up and reached up with one hand, fingers splayed, moving her hand from left to right if reading the words on a theater marquee. "We'll call it Tori's Mushroom Pasta."

*Tori's* Mushroom Pasta? Great. *Tara Holloway* was the one who'd come up with the idea, but my fictional alter ego would get the naming rights. Oh, well. There was nothing I could do about it.

I packed the pasta surprise, a couple slices of toasty garlic bread, and a chocolate cannoli into a bag, along with a napkin and silverware. While my hands were in the bag, I tugged the fitness tracker out from under my sleeve so I'd be able to pull it from my wrist quickly and easily once I was in Tino's office. I pushed the button on the end to activate the recorder. With one last deep breath to steel myself, I headed next door.

As I walked over, I spotted Tino's and Eric's vehicles in the lot. Patrol car number six sat in the lot, too, Cole Kirchner having yet to set out on his rounds for the night. I wondered if tonight would be the night Tino's goons made a move on Looking Good Optical or the optician. Part of me hoped it would be. I missed my apartment and my cats and spending time with Nick. I wanted this case resolved ASAP, assuming, of course, that no one would get hurt.

I punched Benedetta's code into the keypad. *Two-three-six-three*. Though I heard the automated lock release with a click, the door wouldn't budge. Looked like someone had locked the dead bolt.

I rapped on the glass. *Rap-rap-rap*. "Tino?" I called,

hoping he'd be able to hear me through his half-open door down the hall. "It's Tori. I think the dead bolt is locked."

A moment later, he appeared in the door to his office and headed my way. He released the dead bolt and opened the door for me. "Force of habit," he said. "You work in the security business, locking doors is second nature."

Maybe. Or maybe he'd locked the door because he didn't want his wife or daughters or anyone else walking in on him and overhearing something he didn't want them to know.

Lest he simply take the bag from me, I looked down into it and began to rummage around as I headed toward his office. I realized as he rounded his desk that it was the perfect opportunity for me to drop the tracker and kick it under the piece of furniture. Thank goodness his office was carpeted so it wouldn't make much noise. I slid it from my wrist and dropped it to the floor, crinkling the takeout bag to cover any sound. *Crinkle-crinkle.* Just as it hit the carpet, he turned to face me.

*Had he noticed?* I eyed him for a moment. *Nope.* No signs he'd seen me drop the device. *Thank God.*

I simultaneously unpacked the bag and used my toe to push the recorder under the drawers of his desk. The desk sat too low for a vacuum to get under the drawers, but if the custodians used a hose attachment they might suck the tracker out from under the desk. "*Buon appetito!*" *And speak up loud and clear.*

As I left the room, I said a quick and silent prayer that the cleaning crew would do a half-assed job.

# chapter thirty-nine

## $\mathcal{K}$eeping Our Eyes and Ears Open

Tuesday came and went without an opportunity for me to get into Tino's office to retrieve the recorder. I wasn't sure whether that was good or bad. The longer the device was in Tino's office, the more information it could gather for us. But the longer it was in place, the greater the likelihood that we'd miss time-sensitive information, such as plans to do harm to a client.

While I finished removing the soiled tablecloths from the tables in the dining room, Benedetta stepped out the front door of the bistro and used her key to lock it. Standing on the sidewalk, she reached up to pull the security doors down over the windows. The loud rattle as they rolled down their tracks was muffled by the glass but still audible.

Elena glanced over at the covered windows. "I know those doors are supposed to make us safer," she said, "but I don't like them. I feel like I'm trapped in a cage."

I'd had the same feeling each time they'd been lowered before. Despite the spaciousness of the dining room, it gave me a sense of claustrophobia. The outside world was being shut out and we were being shut in.

Separated.

Confined.

*Entombed.*

With the security gates locked in place, the back door was the only way out.

No word came in from anyone on the Operation Italian Takeout team on Tuesday night. It was both good news and bad news at the same time. Good news that nobody had been hurt or robbed or killed. Bad news that there'd been no break in the case and none of us agents had made an arrest.

My accounting exam on Wednesday morning went well. Given that I was the first to finish my test, I daresay I earned the highest score in the class. Then again, maybe I was being overconfident. That was never a good thing. In fact, it was often when tax evaders got overconfident and cocky that they screwed up, giving us special agents the evidence to nab them.

When I arrived at the bistro at eleven, a man I didn't recognize was in the kitchen. He was dressed in navy pants and a blue button-down shirt. He stood in front of one of the two fire extinguishers mounted on the kitchen walls and wriggled it free from the support bracket.

As he headed for the other fire extinguisher, I stepped over to Brian and asked, "Who's that?"

"Safety inspector from the fire department," Brian responded without looking up from the bomboloni he was filling with raspberry goo. "They come by every so often to make sure things are up to code."

That made sense. It wasn't uncommon for restaurants to have grease fires. Without proper safety equipment, flames could spread quickly and endanger the lives of the staff and customers.

The man opened the back door and carried all three of the fire extinguishers outside. I, on the other hand, stepped into the employee lounge and stashed all of my things in my locker. I was tying my apron around my waist when the man came back in a minute or so later.

He poked his head into Benedetta's office, where she sat at her desk. "I tested all of your equipment," he said. "Levels and pressure are good."

Benedetta glanced up. "Good to know. Thank you."

The man scribbled something on the paper tag that hung from each device, probably noting the date of the inspection and his name or initials. As he returned the fire extinguishers to their rightful places and left, I got down to work, performing my usual tasks with both efficiency and a smile, maintaining my grace even when a small child sitting in a booth with his mother managed not only to spill his milk all over the carpet, but also to turn over the salt shaker and cover half the seat with spaghetti. I couldn't much blame the kid. I'd been a tomboy as a young girl and sitting still and behaving properly had never been one of my strong suits.

I tried to be in the right place at the right time to take Tino his lunch, but—*dammit!*—Stella beat me to it. I had better luck with his dinner, which, as always, he took late, after the crowd had subsided. He'd requested another serving of what he called "Dario's striped ravioli" and his standard cannoli. He'd also ordered a small Margherita pizza.

My heart beat so fast it threatened to explode as I carried the food next door. I typed 2-3-6-3 on the keypad. Tonight, the dead bolt was unlocked and I had no trouble getting in. I'd slid a black hairband around my wrist. My plan was to pull it from my wrist to put in my hair, accidentally on purpose drop it to the floor, and feel around under his desk until I found the recorder. I closed my eyes and begged every deity I knew—God, Jesus, Allah, Ra, Vishnu, and the Flying Spaghetti Monster—to please let this go off without a hitch. *If you have to go with the alternative,* I told them, *please let him kill me quickly. And not with a nail gun.*

The door to Eric's cybercave was shut tight tonight, but Tino's door stood wide open. He looked up from his desk as I came in. "Leave the pizza in reception," he said. "Eric can get it when he's ready."

Clearly, Tino didn't want Eric to be interrupted and he didn't want me getting another peek into the room. I could only imagine what Eric was doing in there right now. Probably doctoring another video, preparing to cover up another crime for his boss. I wondered whether Eric was a willing participant in Tino's schemes, or whether Tino had threatened him, too.

I laid the box of pizza on the reception desk and continued down the hall, past Eric's closed door. I went into Tino's office and set the bag on his desk, making small talk as I unloaded it. "Did Benedetta mention that Dario's going to try some recipes of his own at the restaurant?" I stretched my arm across the desk and set the entrée before him. "I can't wait to taste them." Now the cannoli. "I can't imagine they'll be as good as your wife's, though." Napkin and fork.

"She's the best cook on the planet," Tino said. "I'm the luckiest guy in the world."

My hands empty now, and admittedly trembling a little, I pulled the band from my wrist and went to gather my hair behind my head to put it in a ponytail. I opened my fingers just enough to let the band fall. "Oops." I

knelt down, hoping my back would block the view of any
hidden camera Tino might have deployed, and quickly
swept my hand under the desk.

*Where is it?*

*Where Is It?!*

*WHERE IS IT?!?!*

My fingers finally hit something solid and I snatched
up the tracker. *Thank God! And/or Jesus, Allah, Ra,
Vishnu, and the Flying Spaghetti Monster.* I swept my
hand back and grabbed the hair band, too, lifting it to the
back of my head again as I exited his office.

"Good night, Tori," he called after me.

"You, too!" I called cheerily, hoping he wouldn't notice the tightness in my voice.

As I left Cyber-Shield and walked down the sidewalk,
I managed to shift the recorder to my left hand and pull
my hair up with my right. Knowing the cameras out front
might capture my movements, I tucked the recorder into
my pants pocket as surreptitiously as possible. *Nothing to
see here. Just a girl casually putting her hand in her
pocket and trying not to throw up from anxiety.*

Every remaining second of my shift felt like an eter-
nity. Having the recorder in my pocket made me feel
anxious and conspicuous. My worries that it would fall
out at an inopportune time felt so loud in my head I was
sure everyone around me could hear my thoughts. *This
must be what working as a smuggler feels like, knowing
you've got something on you that could get you in a heap
of trouble.*

Finally, the night ended.

Benedetta stepped out front, locked the door, and
pulled down the security gates. Having entombed the
restaurant, she walked around to the back door to reenter.
We cleaned up the dining room and kitchen as usual, put
the dishes in the dishwasher, and gathered up our personal

things to go. The front door covered by the new security gate, we left through the back door, but not before checking out the peephole to make sure there was nobody around outside waiting to bust in and rob the place. The only person outside was Tino, who walked his wife to her car on the nights they both worked late. On the nights he wasn't there, he insisted she have one of the male kitchen staff walk with her.

It was all I could do not to run around the building to my car. I couldn't wait to hear what the recording had picked up. Would it finally give us enough evidence to arrest Tino? I knew that was probably wishful thinking, but I hoped that at the least it would provide information we could use to put the Operation Italian Takeout team in the right place at the right time to bust Tino's sorry ass.

# chapter forty

## $\mathcal{O}$ne-sided Relationships

I aimed for my apartment complex, checking for a tail. The road behind me was virtually deserted. *Good.*

I switched directions, headed out onto the freeway, and drove to the IRS building downtown. After clearing myself with the guy working after-hours security in the lobby, I rode the elevator up to my floor. I found Nick and Josh already in my office. Will, Eddie, and Hana were out following Tino's patrol units, keeping a special eye on unit number six, though we'd fill them in as soon as we knew what the recorder had picked up, if anything.

I reached my right hand into my pocket and panicked when I couldn't find the tracker.

*What the—*

*Oh, yeah. It's in the other pocket.*

*Derp.*

I reached into my left pocket and removed the device, tossing it to Josh. "Echols was still at work when I left," I told him and Nick. "Seems to me that if he's putting in overtime there's something big in the works."

Whatever it was could be merely a security-related

project for a client, but I had my doubts. My instincts told me something big was brewing. But whether it involved Looking Good Optical or another client we couldn't be sure.

Josh quickly disassembled the recorder, inserting the built-in USB into his computer and cueing up the feed. "Okay," he said, staring intently at his screen. "Looks like we've got about forty-eight hours' worth of recording here, beginning Monday evening and ending tonight."

I held up both hands, my index and middle fingers crossed. "Fingers crossed we got something good."

The first thing we heard was the sound of footsteps and a *rap-rap-rap*. I thought back to Monday night. That must have been me knocking on the door to Cyber-Shield.

My voice was audible now, the little device providing surprising volume and clarity given that it looked like a virtual toy. *"Tino? It's Tori. I think the dead bolt is locked."*

Josh stopped the replay. "Is the dead bolt usually locked when you go to Cyber-Shield at night?"

"No," I said. "I normally only have to use the keypad."

Nick chimed in. "Looked like he wanted to make sure no one walked in on him that night."

"I had that same thought," I said.

Tino's voice was the next one we heard. *"Force of habit. You work in the security business, locking doors is second nature."*

There was the sound of paper crinkling and silverware tinkling as I unpacked his bag of food, along with me saying, *"Buon appetito!"*

I cringed. The mix of my Southern drawl and my botched pronunciation of the foreign words sounded ridiculous. Josh and Nick had the good manners not to call me on it.

There was a muffled *thunk* as the recorder hit the carpet, then footsteps sounded, growing softer. I realized they were my own, recorded as I walked out of Tino's office.

*"Nice ass on that one,"* we heard Tino mutter.

*Ew.*

A muscle in Nick's jaw flexed as he ground his teeth. "I'll kill the guy for that."

*Awww. Nick said the sweetest things sometimes.*

The next few minutes were filled with sounds of Tino eating. He smacked his way through his pasta. Slurped his drink. Crunched his way through his chocolate cannoli. When he finished, he let out a loud belch. *Brrrupppp.*

"Well, that's classy," I said. *I know, I know. I'm a total hypocrite.*

For the next quarter hour there was nothing but the sounds of paper shuffling, the clicks of keys being hit on a keyboard, and the sound of a drawer opening and closing.

"Mesmerizing," Nick muttered, shaking his head, obviously frustrated with this experience.

I was frustrated, too, but I knew it was too much to expect Tino to say, right off the bat, *"Hello, Cole Kirchner, who has just entered my office. How about me and you plan to rob and terrorize the optician who runs Looking Good Optical? That will teach him not to give in to our demand that he pay us cash under the table. And you, Eric Echols, got that doctored tape ready? Great. Hey, while I've got you both here, why don't we recite a list of all the crimes we've ever committed and name all the victims and the locations of their corpses?"*

When the clicks continued, I speculated out loud that Tino might have been watching something on his computer screen that he hadn't wanted anyone to see. "Maybe that's why he locked the dead bolt."

Nick let out a long huff. "That may explain things, but since we can't see his screen it doesn't really get us anywhere."

True.

Josh put his hand to his mouse. "Let me see if I can run an analysis on the audio file and search for segments that include significant amounts of sound." He leaned in, the screen giving his face a light glow, his gaze running over the data. "Here." He clicked his mouse. "This is from Tuesday morning around nine o'clock."

For the next three minutes, we listened to Tino engaged in a discussion with his administrative assistant. She evidently showed him a page proof for a Cyber-Shield print ad that was going to run in several community newspapers. Tino didn't like the font. *"It needs to be bigger,"* he said. *"Like it's shouting from the page."*

*"I'll let them know,"* the woman replied.

*"Be sure to have them send a revised proof."*

*"Got it, boss."*

When it became quiet again, Josh forwarded to the next sound segment. I won't describe the next sound we heard, but suffice it to say it was the kind of sound people often try to blame on a chair.

The next significant exchange took place on Tuesday at 6:03 P.M., after Tino's receptionist would have gone home for the day but before the patrolmen would have come in to begin their shifts. Tino addressed someone we assumed was Eric Echols. I'd only heard the guy speak once, when he'd come out of the bathroom and found me standing in front of the open door to his office. His voice had been squeaky when he'd spoken. *Did you go into my office?*

*"How's it coming?"* we heard Tino ask.

Instinctively, we all leaned closer to Josh's computer.

*"I need more time,"* replied Echols. *"The camera shifted slightly. I'm having a hard time making the feed look consistent."*

*"Get it done,"* Tino barked in a voice far more stern than I'd ever heard him use. *"Time's a-wastin'."*

Josh, Nick, and I exchanged glances. Were Eric's words an outright admission that he'd tampered with the videos? That sure seemed to be what he was talking about. Still, the words were probably not sufficient to nail Tino and Echols. Surely they'd lie about what they were discussing, maybe claim they were working on quality control for the videos or something benign like that. A good defense attorney could likely spin the words so they sounded harmless. We needed more. We needed them to discuss specifically what they'd done to doctor the videos, name the clients they'd screwed over with the tampered footage.

And what had Tino meant by "time's a-wastin'"? Were they on a schedule? Up against some kind of deadline?

From the audio feed, Tino answered my questions, almost as if he'd read my mind. *"Everything else is in place. This is going down Thursday night. No delays. No excuses. Not unless you want to be very, very sorry."*

Echols's voice came back, sounding weary and small and, most of all, scared. *"I'll have it ready. Even if I have to work all night."*

Tino's reply was heartless and pointed. *"Yeah, you will."*

"There we go!" Nick wagged his finger at Josh's computer. "Something's going down tomorrow night."

"I'm scheduled to work until closing at the restaurant," I said, "but as soon as I'm done I want to head over to Looking Good." Presumably, that was where this event would go down. No way did I want to miss out on

our team catching Tino's goons red-handed. Once we'd
apprehended them, we'd likely have enough evidence to
implicate Tino and haul him off to the klink, too. I could
hardly wait!

"Josh and I will go with you," Nick said. "But we'll
stay at the gallery until you leave the restaurant so we can
keep an eye on Cyber-Shield."

We listened to the rest of the recording. There were
footsteps and a door closing as Echols left Tino's office,
but nothing else Tuesday night other than the sound of
the custodians cleaning and vacuuming. Thank God
they half-assed as I'd hoped and didn't take a suction
hose to the space under Tino's desk.

The tape continued on to this morning. There was
more silence broken only by the occasional sounds of a
person shifting in their chair, tapping their foot, absent-
mindedly clicking a ballpoint pen. *Click-click-click.*
*Click-click-click. Click-click.*

Nothing of consequence occurred until Stella came in
to bring Tino his lunch. *"Here you go, Dad."*

*"Grazie, Stella bella."*

Tino had brief discussions with his assistant a couple
times in the afternoon, before I arrived with his dinner.
Josh's computer replayed the conversation I'd had with
Tino only a few hours earlier.

*"She's the best cook on the planet. I'm the luckiest guy
in the world."*

*"Oops."*

*"Good night, Tori."*

*"You, too!"*

There was a rustling sound as I shoved the recorder
into my pocket and a *tap* as I deactivated the device.

And then there was nothing but silence.

# chapter forty-one

## *L*ast Supper

It was all I could do not to dance around the restaurant Thursday evening. We'd soon have the goods on Tino and his thugs, and tonight we were finally going to bust them. *Woo-hoo!*

Benedetta cast a look my way as she came back to the kitchen with a load of dirty dishes. Her three girls had gone to the ice-skating show tonight, the one Tino had bought them tickets for, so Benedetta was filling in, pulling waitress duty. "You seem extra happy tonight."

"I am," I said. "My finals have gone really well so far and I have my last one tomorrow morning." Linguistics. Still not sure exactly what that was. Linguini, on the other hand, I was now intimately familiar with.

Benedetta set the plates in the sink and gave me an encouraging pat on the back. "Good for you. You have a lot to be proud of."

I'd be even more proud when I took down her mobster husband later. I was amassing quite of list of impressive professional conquests. Of course I shouldn't have been counting my chickens before they were hatched.

While we assumed that tonight's target was Looking Good Optical, there was always the chance Tino had been referring to another client. We could end up looking like fools, putting all of our resources at one location only to find out that he'd struck elsewhere. After all, he'd pulled off the Hookah Lounge heist right under our noses. Still, we couldn't fault ourselves too much. Even with the surge in agents, we couldn't be everywhere all the time.

Dario, Juan, and Brian were hard at work in the kitchen. Dario had debuted one of his new dishes tonight, one he'd dubbed Tuxedo Temptation. Bowtie pasta tossed in olive oil with lemon pepper and zucchini. We'd offered free samples to the customers in exchange for feedback. All of it had been resoundingly positive, other than an adolescent girl who'd declared it "barfable." Her mother had scolded her but Benedetta had merely laughed. "Honest feedback," she said. "It's what we asked for."

I found myself repeatedly pulling my pink cell phone from the pocket of my apron to check the time.

7:08.

7:33.

7:48.

*Could the time go any slower? My Lord!*

At eight o'clock, Tino phoned. I answered the call. "Dario's whipped up a new pasta dish," I told him. "It's getting rave reviews so far." Well, other than that "barfable" comment.

"I'll try it," he said.

"Great. I'll run some over."

I went to the kitchen and held open a to-go container while Dario filled it with his pasta. After rounding up some garlic bread and a chocolate cannoli, I carried the food over to Cyber-Shield.

*Weird.*

Tino's car, which was usually parked right in front of
the building, had been parked at the far end of the center
row. Maybe he'd left the office for a while earlier and
found the spots in front of Cyber-Shield filled by the cars
of Benedetta's customers when he'd returned, leaving him
with no choice but to park away from the building. Then
again, maybe not. It seemed off, odd, like an omen of
sorts. Things were not as I'd expected them to be. But
perhaps I was overthinking things, feeling a little tense
knowing that major things would be going down later tonight.

There was no sign of Eric's Mustang. No sign of patrol car number six, either. Looked like Cole had already
set out on his rounds. Perhaps he'd started early tonight,
knowing he'd be tied up at Looking Good Optical later.

I typed the code into the keypad and went inside, un-
packing the food on Tino's desk as usual.

He looked up and gave me a smile—a smile I wanted
to slap right off his belugalike face. "You sure are a
hardworking girl."

I gave him my own smile now. "I am," I replied. "I always get the job done."

*And tonight my job is busting you, Tino Fabrizio.*
*Neener-neener.*

I returned to the restaurant, noticing that Nick had
dimmed the lights in the gallery and sat at his desk
across the way, subtly keeping an eye on things here until
it was time for us to meet up with the others.

Just before nine o'clock, Tino came into the restaurant.
I was in the dining room, wiping down the chairs and tables. Benedetta was back in her office and the cooks
were in the kitchen cleaning up.

"Quitting time!" Tino called out in that annoying
singsong tone of his.

"Almost," I said. I'd just checked my phone again. It was 8:57.

Tino disappeared into the kitchen. A minute later, he reappeared with Benedetta's keys in his hand. I recognized the boot-shaped key chain.

He gestured to the cell phone in my apron pocket. "I forgot my phone. Mind if I use yours to make a quick call?"

It was a seemingly innocent request, yet coming from a man bearing as much guilt as Tino Fabrizio it immediately raised a red flag in my mind.

I gestured to the phone behind the bar. "You should probably use the landline. My reception isn't good here."

"That's okay." He stepped over to me and held out his hand. "I'll take it outside. I'm going to lock up for Bennie."

Refusing to give him my phone could let him know I was on to him. Maybe his request was totally benign. The last thing I needed was to raise his suspicions and risk him ordering his goons to abort tonight's plan. Who knew when we'd have such a good tip to move on again?

I plucked my phone from my pocket and handed it to him. Like I'd suggested to Tino, there was always the landline. If I needed to make an emergency call, I could use that.

As Tino headed outside with my cell phone, I noticed Nick, likewise, stepping out of Gallery Nico across the way, ostensibly to close his security gates. But I knew better. Nick was probably wondering what Tino was up to, maybe hoping the guy would inadvertently drop some sort of clue about what would be going down tonight.

There was a *shluck* sound as the dead bolt slid home, followed by the rattle as Tino lowered the security doors. *Yep, Elena was right. This definitely feels like a trap.*

# chapter forty-two

# $\mathcal{I}$f You Can't Stand the Heat, Get Out of the Kitchen

I continued cleaning the dining room. Without any of the girls to help me, it took longer than usual. When I finished twenty minutes later, Tino still hadn't returned with my cell phone. It was possible he was on a long call, but my nerves were feeling as rattled as the security doors.

By the time I went back to the kitchen, Brian and Juan had gone home for the night. Dario and Benedetta sat in her office poring over a proposed menu redesign that included three of Dario's new specialties. Benedetta had laid one of her long metal ladles across the unfolded paper to make it lie flat.

I retrieved my things from my locker and headed back into the kitchen. *Fwump!* My feet slid out from under me and I was on my ass in a heartbeat.

*Whuh?!?*

I looked around. The floor was coated with cooking oil a quarter-inch deep. Cooking oil that was coming from a hose snaked through a two-inch crack in the back door.

I barely had time to scream, "Benedetta! Dario!"

when a flaming matchbook was tossed through the small crack in the door.

*FWOOOSH!*

The kitchen went up in flames, the cooking oil fueling the fire as well as any chemical accelerant. With my pants coated in the oil, I'd soon be going up in flames, too.

The hose was yanked out the back door and the door was slammed shut. Terror seized my mind, but I forced myself to think. There were no windows in the employee lounge, Benedetta's office, or the kitchen. Remembering that the front door was locked and covered with the security gates, I knew the back door provided our only means of escape, even if the person who'd just started the fire was out there. I reached into my purse and quickly readied my Cobra.

I ran over to the door and pushed, smacking my head up against it. While it had opened another inch, it would go no farther. Something blocked it.

"It won't open!" I screamed, panic welling up in me, terror slithering up my spine.

Dario pulled me out of the way. "Let me try!" He threw his substantial body up against the door but had no better luck than I'd had.

The flames continued to snake their way across the floor. Between the electric lights and the fire, the room was so bright it hurt my eyes. But I did see one thing through the flames. A red canister mounted on the wall.

*The fire extinguisher.*

I yanked it from the wall, aimed it at the flames, and squeezed with all my might. *Spuh-spuh-spuh.* All my efforts got me were a few foamy droplets. "Shit!"

Dario grabbed the other fire extinguisher with the same results. Just a sputter and small shower of liquid, as if the device were blowing us a deadly raspberry.

Obviously, that so-called inspector who'd come to check out the equipment had instead sabotaged it.

My mind reeled. *With the fire extinguishers out of commission, what could we do?*

Smother the fire. That's what.

I leaped over a two-foot wall of flame and reached for a stack of tablecloths, grabbing one in each hand and slapping them at the conflagration, trying to snuff it out. All I succeeded in doing was adding fuel to the fire. The tablecloths quickly became engulfed and I was forced to drop them.

Screaming in Italian, Benedetta grabbed a large bag of flour from a countertop and tossed the stuff around, a white cloud forming in the already smoky air. The flour managed to douse some of the flames, but there wasn't enough of it to finish the job.

I darted through the flames to the sink, turned on the sprayer, and directed the stream of water at the fire. That only caused the oil and fire to spread.

*My special agent training did not prepare me for this!!!*

The smoke built to a stifling level and I coughed so hard I thought my ribs would snap. I motioned for Dario and Benedetta, who were also coughing, to follow me. "We have to get to the dining room!"

Of course this meant running through a wall of flame, but what choice did we have?

I ran through first, bolting out from the swinging door and throwing myself into a sideways dive roll to snuff out the flames that had caught on my clothes. Benedetta came through next, emerging screaming, her arms and hair on fire, the metal ladle still clutched in her hand. Dario leaped through, tackling her to the ground and forcing her to roll with him until she was no longer on fire.

The air was marginally less smoky here, but I knew

the respite wouldn't last long. I ran to the bar and grabbed the landline phone, putting the receiver to my ear. I was already dialing 911 when I realized there had been no dial tone. Tino must have cut the lines. *That bastard!* It dawned on me then that the smoke alarms weren't going off, either. Tino had probably disabled them and removed any backup batteries, maybe when he'd come over to the restaurant last Sunday morning.

"The phone's dead!" I shrieked at Dario and Benedetta, tossing the landline phone aside. "Do either of you have your cell phone?"

"No!" Benedetta cried. "Tino borrowed mine!"

"Mine, too!" Dario yelled, breaking down into a racking cough.

We were trapped here, in a burning building, with no fire extinguishers and no phone.

*Holy shit! We're going to die here!*

The only saving grace was that we'd probably succumb to smoke inhalation before we burned to death.

I gulped back an angry, terrified sob.

*We were trapped!*

*TRAPPED!*

My mind, which was spiraling like a piece of fusilli out of control, suddenly stopped and spat up an image of the fortune cookie I'd eaten not long ago and the strip of paper that had been inside.

*A trapped cat becomes a lion.*

I felt my inner lion rear its head and roar.

*I will not stand for this. Tino Fabrizio will not take my life.*

I looked around for another means of escape. We couldn't go out the front door or windows because they were blocked by the newly installed security gates. We certainly couldn't force our way through the brick side wall. None of us was the Hulk or the Kool-Aid Man. But

I remembered back to the first time I'd come with Agent Hohenwald to check out Cyber-Shield. I'd noticed the building had a triangular-shaped air vent at each end, just under the pinnacle of the roof.

I hopped up onto the refrigerated case and reached up to push a ceiling panel aside. The lights began to flicker now, the fire interfering with the electrical system. But I could see the triangular grate. It was just big enough that, if removed, a person could escape through the hole. Unfortunately, the case was not tall enough and we had no ladder to reach it.

I looked around and saw the solution.

"Quick!" I hollered. "We need to build a pyramid with the tables!"

Dario, Benedetta, and I moved like lightning, creating a base of four tables onto which we stacked three more, adding the final one at the top. When we finished, the makeshift steps reached nearly eight feet into the air. I grabbed the useless fire extinguisher from behind the bar, climbed the stack of tables, and stood precariously atop the pinnacle, my chest even with the bottom of the triangular grate. Using the metal canister like a battering ram, I slammed it over and over against the grate. The relatively flimsy aluminum buckled, bending more and more until the grate fell away, dropping to the asphalt outside with a clatter.

I put my hands on the ledge, sticking my head out and gulping the relatively fresh air as smoke billowed out next to me.

"Tara!" Nick ran up outside, his face frantic, Josh on his heels.

Though I wanted nothing more than to escape out the hole, I knew I had to get Benedetta and Dario out first.

I turned and hollered down to Benedetta, motioning with my arm. "You first! Come on!"

The ladle still clutched in her hand like an odd security blanket, Benedetta climbed the tables, stopping only when she was overcome by coughs. When she was standing on the table next to me, I intertwined my fingers to form a stirrup for leverage. "Hurry!"

She put her foot into my hand and I gave her a boost. Hanging on to the ledge, she pulled her legs through and then dropped from sight. It was twelve feet down to the parking lot. I hoped the fall wouldn't break her leg or ankle, or that she'd accidentally impale herself on her ladle.

Dario came up next. "Go on!" he cried, shooing me with both arms.

While I appreciated his chivalry, as a federal law enforcement officer I felt like a ship's captain. It was my duty to see that all innocent parties escaped safely before saving myself. If I couldn't do that, I'd go down with the ship. Or in this case, I'd melt with the cannoli.

"I'm an undercover cop!" I shouted. Not precisely the truth, but close enough to give him the message. Besides, *cop* was faster to say than *IRS special agent*.

His already wide eyes flashed with surprise, but he didn't waste time thinking things over. Being a cop meant I had last dibs on getting to live. Everyone knew that. He hoisted himself up and was out the triangular hole in a split second.

There was the sound of an explosion—*poom!*—as the flames engulfed something flammable, probably the cleaning supplies. Huge plumes of black smoke billowed up around me, blinding me. Eyes closed against the smoke, lungs racking with coughs, I reached out for the ledge I could no longer see. I pulled myself up and over it, hanging down the side of the building for a moment before letting go.

# chapter forty-three

## The Smoke Clears

Strong arms caught me and lowered me safely to the ground. Those strong arms, of course, belonged to Nick.

Benedetta was likewise uninjured, though she was crying hysterically on Josh's shoulder, thoroughly freaked out. Nick had even managed to help Dario land lightly on the asphalt, despite the fact that the chef outweighed Nick by a good forty pounds.

Nick grabbed me by the shoulders and looked into my watery eyes. Well, at least I assumed he did. I still couldn't see much with all the tears my ducts were producing to combat the smoke. There was just a wavering, Nick-like blur.

"Are you okay?" he cried.

"I'm okay," I said, punctuating my words with another rib-wrenching cough. "We all got out."

*WEE-OH-WEE-OH-WEE-OH!* A fire truck roared into the parking lot, its siren blaring and warning lights flashing. As the men hopped off the truck, I wriggled out of Nick's grasp and ran over to them. "It's an oil fire!"

The information would be critical to them in determining how best to battle the blaze. My earlier blunder with the sink sprayer told me that.

The men swarmed down from the truck in their yellow protective gear and set to work.

"Anyone injured?" one of the men asked.

I shook my head but coughed.

"Let's see about getting you some oxygen."

Nick, Josh, Dario, Benedetta, and I went over to Gallery Nico and waited inside while the firefighters attacked the flames, which had now spread to the roof. Clearly we'd gotten out just in time. While we waited, an EMT equipped the three of us who'd been in the bistro with oxygen masks.

Dario turned his eyes on me. "You're an undercover cop?" he said, his voice muffled by the mask.

Above her mask, Benedetta's eyes flashed in alarm and betrayal. "A cop?" she cried, her voice muffled, too. "Tori, is that true?"

I exchanged glances with Josh and Nick, who nodded.

"Yes," I said, taking a deep breath of the pure air. *Who knew oxygen could be so good?* "I'm a federal law enforcement officer." I gestured to Nick and Josh. "So are they."

Benedetta's expression was totally bewildered. "But why? Why would you be working at my bistro? And the art gallery?"

I took another hit of fresh, pure air. "We're investigating your husband."

"Tino?" She still looked confused. "Why? For what?"

I didn't want to tell her too much until I saw how things panned out, so I simply said, "A lot of things."

"You can add attempted murder to the list now," Nick said. "Tino started the fire."

"What are you saying?" Benedetta shrieked, her mask fogging with her warm breath as she looked from

Nick to me and back again. "That my husband tried to kill us?"

"It sure looks that way." Josh held up an odd-looking device that looked like a miniature model of the Starship *Enterprise*. "I caught him on my camera drone moving the catering truck to block the back door and tossing lit matches into the restaurant."

Presumably, Tino hoped his act of arson would be deemed an accidental grease fire.

Benedetta launched into a litany of denial, shaking her head so violently I feared it might pop right off her neck. "No. No! No, no, no. No-no-no-no-no!"

I wouldn't want to believe it, either, if the man I'd built a life with, the man who'd fathered my children, the man who was supposed to be with me till death do us part, had tried to make that time shorter than nature intended. Especially if it were for only half a million dollars in life insurance proceeds. Hell, a hedge fund manager earned that much each quarter.

As I watched Benedetta's face, saw her shock and disbelief, I realized one thing for sure. Whatever Tino Fabrizio had been up to, Benedetta knew nothing about it. Otherwise, the events of this evening would not have been such a surprise to her.

Nick turned to me. "I knew something was wrong when I saw Tino come out of the bistro with your pink phone in his hand. Just in case it was nothing, we didn't want to tip him off by following him around to the back of the restaurant. Josh had his bag of tricks with him and launched the drone from our back door. It took us a few minutes to fly the drone over the restaurant, collect the footage, and review it. Once we saw the video, we realized Tino had started a fire inside. There wasn't much smoke yet, so we wouldn't have known if not for the drone."

With no open doors or windows to escape through, the smoke had been trapped inside, like us.

Nick went on. "I was trying to break through the security doors when we heard the grate fall. That was smart thinking, Tara."

"Tara?" Benedetta said, wiping her eyes on her sleeve.

"I'm not Tori Holland," I told her. "I'm IRS Special Agent Tara Holloway."

Nick's phone rang then. He punched the button to accept the call and put the phone to his ear. "Yeah?" A smile spread across his lips. He looked from me to Josh and back again. "Our guys have Tino. They surrounded him in his driveway at home. As far as they know, he didn't have time to contact anyone."

Meaning he was apprehended before he could get in touch with Cole or Eric or any of his other goons and warn them off. *Good.*

"They're bringing him back here," Nick said. "I doubt he'll tell us anything, but they figured they'd let us see if we could get a confession out of him."

Benedetta spoke now, so softly we almost didn't hear her. "Can I see the video?" she asked Josh.

Josh looked to me. I nodded. Hard as it would be, Benedetta deserved to learn the truth.

As he pulled up the video on his laptop, I scooted my chair up next to Benedetta and took her hand in mine. She needed to know that, even if she had a lousy husband, she still had a friend in me.

She watched as, on the screen, Tino climbed into her catering truck behind the bistro and backed it up until it nearly touched the back door. She watched and sobbed as he rolled a large plastic barrel over to the door and inserted the hose in it. She watched, sobbed, and hiccupped as he opened the back door the inch or two it could open, sucked on the end of the hose to get the oil moving, and snaked the hose through the cracked door. And, finally, she watched, sobbed, hiccupped, and fisted her hands as he retrieved a matchbook from his pocket, struck a match, and set the entire book on fire, tossing it through the back door into her restaurant's kitchen.

"If I didn't see it with my own eyes," she said, shaking her head slowly, incredulously now, "I never would have believed it."

A black FBI cruiser pulled into the lot. Two agents sat in the front. Tino was buckled into the rear seat behind them. From the way he sat leaning forward it was clear his hands were cuffed behind him.

Benedetta followed me, Nick, and Josh outside. The FBI agents unrolled the back window of the cruiser and climbed out.

While Josh waited with Benedetta, Nick and I stepped over to the car and leaned down to look in the open window.

"Hello, again, Tino," I said. "I'm guessing by now you've been told that we're with the IRS."

His only reply was to cast an eat-stromboli-and-die look in our direction.

"Anything you want to say?" I asked him. "You might feel better if you come clean, maybe apologize to your wife."

"I've got nothing to say to anyone," he spat.

"All righty, then."

As Nick and I backed away, Benedetta stepped up, stroking the ladle as if it were a kitten. Probably some type of subconscious calming ritual. "Can I have a moment with Tino?"

I swept my palm toward the car. "Be my guest."

Benedetta stepped up to the car, stopping a foot away and staring through the open window at her husband. He looked straight ahead for a moment, but then cast a glance her way. There was no remorse in his expression, no regret. Obviously, his whole doting-husband routine had been nothing more than an act.

"You bastard!" Benedetta shrieked, pulling the ladle back and smacking him soundly across the face with it. *Smack!*

He grimaced and tried to duck his head as she pulled the ladle back for another hit.

"How dare you!" *Smack!* "You thought you'd kill me and collect the insurance money?" *Smack!* "Think again!" *Smack!*

As Tino tried in vain to evade her ladle lashes, we agents gathered together a few feet away.

"Should we stop her?" asked one of the FBI agents.

"Three more," I suggested. "Sound fair?"

The other agents murmured in agreement.

*Smack! Smack! Smack!*

I moved forward and grabbed the ladle as Benedetta lifted it for another strike. "As much as I'd love to let you beat your husband to death, I'm going to have to stop you now."

She turned and gave me that friendly smile of hers. "But I was just starting to have fun."

I put an arm around her shoulders and led her back into the gallery.

"Well," she said. "I married a real asshole, didn't I?"

We shared a mirthless laugh before she broke down in tears again. I held her, letting her get it all out.

When Benedetta was able to calm herself a few minutes later, Nick offered her his phone. "Would you like to call your daughters?"

She nodded feebly, her lip quivering, and took the phone from his hand. She turned to me. "How do I tell them what happened? How do I do this?"

I had no idea what to tell her. I couldn't even imagine

being a mother and having to break news like this to my own children, knowing how distraught and devastated they would be. But I knew it would all come out eventually. I decided I couldn't go wrong by suggesting she do what my mother, the best mother on earth, would do. "I guess you tell them that you love them," I said. "And then you tell them the truth."

# chapter forty-four

# *H*ey, Good-looking

Once Benedetta had spoken with her daughters and we'd given our reports to the fireman in charge of the scene, I offered to drive her home in her car. As devastated as she was, she was in no condition to drive. Nick agreed to follow us so he could give me a ride back to pick up my Hyundai.

The FBI agents nodded when we told them we were heading out. "We'll get some of our crime scene people out here to go over the bistro and Cyber-Shield," one of them said. They'd seize the server, computers, and monitors, and, with any luck, find evidence of doctored videos.

"We've got a team at Echols's house as we speak," said the other. "They'll be taking him in for questioning, too, and seizing any evidence at his place."

"Great."

It was nearly midnight when we pulled up to Benedetta's house. It was a nice two-story model with attractive landscaping, but a residence the couple could afford with their legitimate earnings. Tino must have hidden his dirty money from his wife. Perhaps he planned to spend it all on himself after she was gone, maybe live it up on a beach somewhere. Naples, perhaps, where he'd have access to all of the cannoli he could eat. It was doubtful he'd see much, if any, cannoli in prison, though. *Neener-neener.*

Tino's Alfa Romeo sat in the driveway at their house. It probably wouldn't be there for long. The sports car would be seized along with any of his other ill-gotten property and used to cover taxes on the unreported income he'd extorted or to pay restitution to his victims.

Benedetta's crying daughters came out of the house as we pulled up, tears streaming down their faces. Silently but swiftly, they ushered their mother into the house. Tino Fabrizio might be one sorry excuse for a human being, but he had somehow managed to produce three beautiful and caring daughters. It would be a long haul before their lives returned to any sense of normality, but I knew the four women would get through this together.

As we left Benedetta's house in Nick's car, a group text came in from Hana. *Kirchner's on his way to Looking Good.*

"Seriously?" I said. "That's happening tonight, too?"

I'd thought the fire at the bistro was the Thursday-night event Tino had referenced in the conversation recorded on the spy device. Apparently Tino had more in store. Kirchner obviously hadn't heard about Tino's arrest . . . *yet*. He was proceeding with whatever devious plan they'd concocted before Tino had been nabbed.

Nick drove like a bat out of hell and pulled into the lot of a fast-food chicken place a block down from the optical shop. We sat and anxiously waited for the signal for all hands on deck. I'd been exhausted only moments before, but the thought of catching Kirchner in the act gave me a second wind.

Nick reached over and fingered one of my singed

locks, a smile playing about his mouth. "Burning Embers seems to have been an appropriate color choice."

I cut a pointed look his way. "Don't even go there."

Josh pushed the button to unroll his window. "It smells smoky in here."

I scoffed. "Sheesh. Excuse me for stinking up the place." It's not like I'd wanted to smell like a campfire. The stench was drowning out my classic Chanel No. 5.

As Josh's window went down, a neon-green Cyber-Shield vehicle passed by, the number six noted on the back window.

"There's Kirchner now," Nick said. "Hope he's enjoying the drive because the next ride he takes will be with law enforcement."

Two minutes later, Hana sent another text to our phones. *If you want a piece of this action, you better get over here.*

Nick started the car and we drove to Looking Good, making our way slowly and with the lights off. We parked twenty yards away from the front door and climbed out of the car. Nick and Josh were armed with their Glocks, while I had my Cobra. Along with the others, we moved in, swiftly and silently, toward the shop's front door, stopping in the dark shadows that flanked the entrance.

Kirchner stepped out of the door, failing to notice us as he turned back to lock it. We agents swarmed him, guns at the ready.

"Hands up!" Hana yelled as she bolted toward Kirchner. "Federal law enforcement!"

He turned, saw the horde descending on him, and tried to run back into the optical shop. Stupid, really. The back door was covered by a group of agents, too. There'd be no way for him to escape. And there was no one at the store to take hostage, either, so he'd have no leverage, no bargaining chip. A canister of tear gas is all it would take to put a quick end to any standoff. But I supposed it was his fight-or-flight instinct kicking in. He couldn't fight such a large group of agents, and back through the door appeared to be the only place to flee to.

He wasn't fast enough, though. Before he could pull the door back open, Hana, Will, and Eddie were on him, slamming him against the glass and grabbing his arms to immobilize him. In five seconds flat he was cuffed and on the ground, the joint IRS/FBI team standing over him. As he squirmed on the ground, I frisked him and pulled a manila clasp envelope out of his jacket.

Everyone gathered around as I stood, opened the clasp, and pulled the envelope open. Josh shined his cell phone into it. Inside was a stack of twenty-dollar bills secured by a red rubber band.

I removed the bills and counted them. "Five hundred dollars," I announced when I'd finished.

Looked like the optician at Looking Good had decided to pay the protection fee, after all. He'd probably feared not only for his own life, but those of his wife and son. With any luck, now that Tino and his goons were in custody, the man would be willing to testify against the mobster.

I shoved the money back into the envelope and surveyed the group. "We did it! We took down Tino Fabrizio and his minions!"

The Operation Italian Takeout team exchanged smiles and high fives. *Slap! Slap! Slap!*

"Good job, guys!" I held out a hand and exchanged fist bumps with the FBI agents.

Once we'd finished celebrating, I knelt down and looked Cole Kirchner in the eye. "We got your boss tonight, too. Did you know he planned to set a fire at his wife's restaurant? With Benedetta, Dario, and me inside?"

He averted his eyes. *Yeah, he'd known.* That made taking him down all the more sweet. *Neener-neener.*

Relief flooded through me. It was finally over.

Nick took me back to the restaurant to round up my car, and I drove my Elantra back to my town house. With Fabrizio and his thugs now in custody, I could return to my home and my cats and my normal life. Not that my life could really be called normal . . .

Given the late hour, I tried to sneak quietly back into my place. So as not to alarm Alicia, though, I turned on the hall light so she'd be able to see that it was me in the house if she happened to wake up and peek her head out of the guest room upstairs.

Anne scurried up and mewed, rising onto her hind legs like a meerkat, desperate for me to pick her up and give her the loving she'd missed while I'd been gone. I proceeded to do just that, cuddling her in my arms and scratching the back of her neck with my fingers. "Mommy's home." I gave her a kiss on the head. "And she sure did miss you."

Anne responded by purring and rubbing her face against my shoulder.

Henry actually deigned to hop down from his perch atop the TV cabinet. While he wouldn't go so far as to come over to me, it was clear he would be willing to tolerate it if I happened to venture over to him and offer him a stroke or two under his chin.

Carrying Anne in my arms, I went over to Henry and knelt down. I set Anne aside for a moment, and gave Henry the strokes he'd never admit to wanting. *What an ego, huh?*

"Tara?" Alicia's raspy voice came from the top of the stairs. She looked down the staircase at me, her face breaking into a sleepy smile.

"I'm back." I put a hand on a chair to leverage myself to a stand. "We got Tino and his goons." Eric Echols was really more of a geek than a goon, but no sense belaboring the point.

"Way to go!" Alicia said as she descended the steps. "We should celebrate with a glass of wine."

A glass of wine sounded heavenly. I was still buzzing with adrenaline and would need something to calm me down if I had any chance of getting some sleep. We might have Tino Fabrizio behind bars, but we still had Adam Stratford to deal with in the morning. A woman's work is never done.

Alicia and I went to the kitchen, where she poured us each a glass of moscato. As she held out the glass, she leaned toward me and sniffed. "Why do you smell like smoke?"

I accepted the glass from her. "Tino Fabrizio locked me and his wife and one of the chefs inside the restaurant and set the place on fire."

Her mouth gaped. "Oh, my God!"

I shrugged. "All in a day's work."

She simply stared at me. "I will never understand what possesses you to do that job."

"It beats preparing tax returns."

Apparently, she begged to differ. "I'll take a depreciation schedule over a mobster any day."

I took a big glug of wine and eyed her. "Promise me that after you get married you won't forget about me."

"Forget about you?" She set her wine glass down and grabbed me by the shoulders. "How could I?" She shook her head as if the mere idea were preposterous. "I love Daniel, but I'll still need you. He's incapable of giving an opinion when I go shopping for clothes, and he refuses to go to high tea with me."

"I hate high tea, too."

"I know," she said, smiling as she released me. "But you're still willing to go with me because you know it makes me happy. That's a true friend and that's rare. If you think I'm going to give that up for some boy, you're crazy." She picked up her glass and raised it, as Benedetta had done the day I met her. "To true friends."

I gently tapped my glass against hers. *Clink.* "Hear, hear!"

## chapter forty-five

# $\mathcal{I}$ Need a Vacation

Just as Alicia had helped Nick with his undercover style as an art dealer, she got up early Friday morning to help me become my new alter ego, the octogenarian Melvina Cannoli.

*"Cannoli?"* Alicia said as she sprinkled talcum powder into my hair to make it look gray. "Couldn't you come up with something better than that?"

"It was short notice," I said. "Besides, I was hungry."

"Good thing you weren't horny or you'd have ended up Melvina *Orgasm*."

I shrugged. "I bet I would've been real popular in high school with a name like that."

Once my hair was properly powdered, she applied my makeup, using an old bottle of foundation. The color hadn't quite matched my skin tone and I'd stashed it in the back of a drawer, too lazy to throw it out. It had become thick and dry, the perfect consistency to spackle on my face to make me look older. She used a sharp black eyeliner to draw small lines around my eyes.

When my face was finished, we went to my closet to look for something for me to wear.

"Do you have anything that's outdated?" she said, sliding hangers back and forth as she looked over my wardrobe.

"I don't want to be one of those kind of old ladies," I said. "Not all mature women dress like Lu." Many of the women I'd seen at Whispering Pines were smartly dressed in clothes I recognized from the Chico's catalogue. They could teach my boss a thing or two about fashion.

We eventually settled on a pair of black pants and a red blouse, over which I draped a scarf in a black and gray houndstooth pattern. I looked like a grandma that had it going on.

Nick swung by to pick me up, laughing when I opened the door. "What's it say that even with gray hair I still want to bang you?"

It said a lot, actually. It said that, should Nick and I be lucky enough to live a long life together, he'd still find me attractive when the bloom was off my rose.

"You can bang me," I told him, "and afterward I'll pat you on the head, give you a nickel, and bake you some cookies."

"Freaky."

We drove over to the complex where Alicia and I had lived a few years ago, taking places in front of my former unit. Stratford wasn't due until ten, but the residents of Whispering Pines would be arriving shortly.

The first ones on the scene were Harold, Jeb, and Isaiah, who arrived with two ladies in a nice Buick. I directed them to a visitor's parking spot, waving my arms. "Over here, guys!"

Nick and I helped Isaiah into his wheelchair, and the gang joined us at the curb.

Lu and Carl were the next to arrive. Lu waited in the front seat while Carl walked around the car in his shiny white bucks to open the door for her. Such a sweet, old-fashioned gesture.

"I like your shoes!" Harold called to Carl, lifting his foot and wiggling it as if performing the hokeypokey. "See? I've got the same ones."

Carl stopped to admire them. "You and I share the same good taste."

Nick and I, on the other hand, shared a quiet chuckle.

Carl opened the door and helped Lu out of her seat. Her beehive stood proud atop her head, her extra-hold hairspray causing the pink mound to glisten in the morning sun.

Jeb, whose arm was linked through that of the woman who'd driven them over, gave Lu a wink and a nod. Looked like there were no hard feelings. *Good.* Life's too short.

The sixteen of us chatted excitedly among ourselves until Harold noticed the Ozarks Express van pull into the parking lot. He pointed to the entrance. "There he is!"

As the group murmured excitedly, Nick stepped away so it wouldn't look like he was with us.

The van pulled to a stop in front of us and out hopped Adam Stratford in his usual sunglasses and cowboy hat. He had a clipboard in his hand, a stack of preprinted receipt forms held in place under the clip. "Good morning, folks!" he called out in his spicy Cajun accent. "How's everyone doing today?"

I stepped forward. "We're just great." I held out my hand. "I'm Melvina Cannoli, the one you spoke with on the phone."

Stratford cocked his head, eyeing me closely. Could he tell that my face bore a quarter-inch coating of puttylike foundation?

He shook my hand, probably figuring my eyesight had gone so bad I didn't realize how awful my makeup looked.

I held up my purse. "We've all got our cash and traveler's checks."

Adam dipped his head and his eyes flashed with greed. "Wonderful. You all will have such a nice time on this trip. The last group I took up to Hot Springs has already scheduled another vacation with me."

*Sure they did.*

"You said we could take a look inside the van," I reminded him. "I'd love to get in there and pick my seat."

"Of course. You're welcome to take a look inside." He stepped over to the doors and opened them. "Climb on in, everybody. I think you'll find the seating very comfortable."

The group streamed toward the van. Though several of the people glanced his way, Stratford didn't seem to recognize any of them. That told me he'd ripped off quite a few senior citizens, too many for him to remember. I couldn't wait to see the look on his face when he realized this morning's look-see was a farce.

Jeb scraped his way toward the van. He'd removed the tennis balls from the feet of his walker. Removed the usual rubber tips, too. The ends were raw metal now. When he reached the door, he placed one of the tips on top of Stratford's loafer and bore down with all his weight.

Stratford grimaced. "You're on my foot, sir."

Jeb made no move to lift his walker. When Stratford attempted to pull his foot out from under the walker, Harold rolled Isaiah's wheelchair up onto Stratford's other foot.

Stratford buckled, putting a hand on the fender of the van to steady himself. "Careful, there. You're on my foot, too."

Harold looked up into the man's face, his eyes narrowing behind his thick lenses. "You don't remember us, do you?"

An uneasy look skittered across Stratford's face. "Should I?"

Nick stepped into place behind Stratford.

"Hell, yes, you should!" Jeb spat. "You took two hundred and fifty dollars from each of us over at Whispering Pines and never showed up on the day of our trip. I missed my sea salt scrub!"

"I have no idea what you're talking about." Stratford shoved the walker off his foot and forcefully pushed the wheelchair back. "There must be some mix-up."

"No, there's not!" Harold retorted. "I recognize your Cajun accent."

"You've got me confused with someone else, old man." Stratford stuck his head inside the vehicle. "Everyone out of the van. Now!"

"Hell, no!" Lu cried, thumbing her nose at Stratford from her place in the front row. "We won't go!"

The others joined in, and soon a loud chant of *Hell, no! We won't go!* had drawn a crowd of onlookers from their apartments.

"I'll wait you out," Stratford spat, crossing his arms over his chest. "Sooner or later you'll have to use the bathroom."

"Joke's on you!" called one of the men. "We're all wearing diapers!"

Stratford frowned. "I'll give you ten seconds to get out of my van and then I'm calling the police."

"Call 'em." Lu batted her false eyelashes in challenge. "Better yet, I'll call 'em for you." She pulled out her cell phone and began to dial.

Stratford stormed over and reached into the van to

grab her phone. But he was too late. Before he could get to Lu, Nick had grabbed his arms and yanked them behind him.

I whipped my handcuffs from my purse and stepped over to cuff him. "There's no mix-up, Mr. Stratford."

The crowd cheered, many of them applauding and several of them pumping their fists.

"What the hell is this?" Stratford cried, struggling.

Nick pushed him up against the van while I flashed my badge. "We're special agents with the IRS. You're under arrest for fraud and tax evasion."

The man's face turned purple with humiliation and rage as Nick dug through his pockets, pulling out his keys, wallet, cell phone, and loose change. "Get those people out of my van!"

"Not going to happen," I told him. "Your van is being seized as evidence."

Nick tossed me Stratford's keys and I snatched them out of the air.

The man's nostrils flared. "You can't just take people's property!"

I arched a brow at him. "You did."

He sputtered like the empty fire extinguishers at the bistro last night.

*Touché.* I tossed him a well-deserved look of disgust. "That's what I thought."

A U.S. Marshal pulled up and claimed our prisoner, escorting Stratford to the back seat of his vehicle.

"You haven't seen the last of me!" he hollered at the van.

"Who cares?" one of the women called, waving her hand dismissively. "By the time you get out of jail twenty years from now we'll all be dead."

Jeb, who was seated in the second row, stood up as

well as he could in the van, lowered the back of his elastic-waist athletic pants, and pressed his butt to the window facing Stratford. Who needs the old man in the moon when you can have an old man's moon?

I stuck my head into the van. "Everyone comfy and ready to go?"

Another round of cheers went up. Jeb held up a can of Ensure nutritional drink and a metal flask, proceeding to pour a healthy dose of what smelled like whiskey into the can. "Let's party!"

I climbed into the van and took the wheel. Nick hopped into the passenger seat. We planned to take turns driving. Luckily, a van this size required no special driver's license. Anyone with a regular Class C was qualified.

We headed out of the complex and made our way to Central Expressway, continuing north on U.S.75 all the way to Durant, Oklahoma, home of the Choctaw Casino. After everyone checked into their rooms for a two-night stay, we all headed for the casino floor. Well, all of us but Jeb. He'd scheduled that long-overdue full-body sea salt scrub in the spa.

This vacation was just what Nick and I needed after the intense pressure of the last couple of weeks. We played blackjack and roulette, switching to poker when the spinning wheel seemed determined to empty our wallets. A commotion in the center of the gaming floor caught our attention, and we wandered over to find Lu and Carl playing craps. While I'd attempted to play the game before, I'd never quite mastered all of the rules and nuances. Lu and Carl, on the other hand, played like pros. Their new friends from Whispering Pines cheered them on until they had stacks of chips in front of them so high they threatened to topple over and bury the green felt surface.

The two of them cashed in their chips and Carl held up a handful of bills. "Hey, everyone! Dinner's on me!"

We migrated en masse to the buffet, stuffing ourselves silly with Southern comfort foods like mashed potatoes, cornbread, and fried okra. Afterward, Lu, Carl, Nick, and I splintered off from the group to enjoy a glass of wine and the smooth styling of the pianist in the bar.

Lu raised her glass. "A toast," she said, looking from Nick to me, "to my two best agents."

We all clinked our glasses and took a sip of our wine.

I raised my glass next, looking meaningfully from Lu to Carl. "To finding your way back to the one you love."

We all clinked our glasses again.

Carl raised his glass this time, wagging his brows at Lu. "To makeup sex!"

Lu blushed and offered him a reproving head shake, but a moment later giggled and raised her glass along with the rest of us.

Though Nick and I had nothing to make up for, we weren't about to miss this prime opportunity for a roll in the hay, though the so-called hay was actually a very comfortable king-sized bed. Afterward, we lay spooned together, Nick rubbing his thumb slowly and softly up and down my arm.

He kissed my outer ear. "When I thought you might die inside that restaurant . . ." His voice became choked and he stopped speaking, finishing his sentence by leaning his face against my bare shoulder and giving my arm a tight squeeze.

I turned my head to look at him. "You think I'd let a punk like Tino Fabrizio get the best of me?"

Nick chuckled, his breath tickling my skin. "I have never been so glad that a case is over."

"Not me." I rolled over to face him straight on now. "I'm going to miss all that chocolate cannoli."

He gave me a smile. "When do I get my nickel and cookies?"

# chapter forty-six

## *C*iao, for Good

Though Tino Fabrizio had turned off the cameras at Cyber-Shield and Benedetta's Bistro prior to setting the fire, the video footage recorded by Josh's drone showing Tino climbing into the catering truck and pulling it over to block the back door would be more than enough to convict him of three counts of attempted murder. With direct access now to Cyber-Shield's computer systems and monitoring equipment, no doubt the FBI would come up with evidence to link him to at least some of his other violent crimes. He'd enjoyed his last cannoli. Finally, we federal agents would see that the man was served the heaping plate of justice he deserved.

Fabrizio was charged not only with murder, but also conspiracy to commit insurance fraud, extortion, and, of course, tax evasion. Given the strength of the evidence against him, and the number of crimes he was connected to, the judge had denied him bail. He'd rot in jail until his trial, and then he'd rot in prison for the rest of his life.

*Neener-neener.*

With Tino locked safely behind bars, the Cyber-Shield clients who'd been afraid to talk before came forward. Dozens of them provided evidence that he'd extorted money from them, giving us bank records showing regular, large withdrawals to cover the protection payments. By our best estimate, Tino had extorted over two million dollars from his clients.

Eric Echols had been arrested, too, and charged with aiding and abetting Tino in his crimes. While Tino had used some of the extorted cash to pay his henchmen, the majority of the extorted funds were found in small, fireproof cash boxes stashed inside outdated desktop computer equipment at Eric's apartment. Tino and his attorney tried to claim that Eric was the ringleader and that Tino hadn't been aware of his tech expert's extortion and violence, but nobody in law enforcement believed them. A jury wouldn't, either.

While negotiations were still in the works, it looked like prosecutors would work out a plea deal with Echols in return for his testimony. Though the guy admitted he had doctored video footage and thus helped Tino cover up his crimes, he, too, had been threatened by Tino, who'd said he'd off Echols's parents and siblings if he didn't cooperate. Prosecutors were likely to be a little more lenient given these extenuating circumstances.

It freaked me out to learn that the shifting camera Tino had mentioned on the recording wasn't one at Looking Good Optical as we'd originally thought, but rather was one of the cameras in front of the bistro. Tino had Eric working on footage that would make it appear as if Benedetta had been the one to pull down the security doors the night of the fire, not him. He'd also had Eric doctor a feed from their home to show Tino at the house when the fire started at the bistro. If not for Nick spotting my phone and Josh flying his camera drone over the building, Tino would have had a plausible alibi and our deaths would have been ruled an accident.

*Eek.*

Cole Kirchner was also being held without bond. When call records were obtained for a cell phone found hidden behind his refrigerator, an entry for Alex Harris's home number showed up, placed on the night his bar caught fire. He was likely the person who'd called for "Becky." He was suspected to have assisted Tino in the murder of the locksmith and the disappearances of the personal trainer and several other men with suspected ties to Tino Fabrizio. Copious amounts of cash were found in a safe deposit box he'd rented. Looked like he'd been saving up, too, but since he wouldn't talk we could only speculate what he'd planned to do with all that money. Given what he knew about Fabrizio, he was lucky to be alive. When we told him about his boss's history of killing off those who'd done his dirty work, Kirchner turned a little green, realizing he had likely come close to losing his life.

Given the developments in the case and the new evidence obtained by the joint task force, Alex Harris's insurance company finally paid the claim for the damage to his bar. The insurance proceeds would allow him to quit his job at the country club and rebuild his business. I was glad things worked out for him.

Benedetta was cleared of any wrongdoing. Footage taken from inside the bistro showed Tino entering and exiting before and after hours, but he took no cash in or out of her business during that time. All he did was fill his face with pasta, cannoli, and the occasional bombolone. The high liquor invoices proved to be valid, and no money laundering had taken place through the bistro. When I asked about her personal income tax returns, she said that it had been her accountant's suggestion that the couple file separately to avoid the marriage penalty at the higher income brackets. The reason for the separate returns was entirely benign.

With Cyber-Shield's reputation ruined and clients canceling contracts left and right, Benedetta sold off the company's patrol cars and equipment and took over the space to set up a bottling operation for her pasta sauces. She also changed the name of Tori's Mushroom Pasta to Tara's Mushroom Pasta on her new menus.

I had a chance to speak with her a final time at the restaurant as it was being rebuilt.

She had tears in her eyes and choked up when she talked about her soon-to-be ex-husband. "I knew his cousin in Chicago was up to no good," she said, "but I had no idea Tino had done the things he did up there or here in Dallas. He was always so loving with me and the girls, and the lies he told me made sense. A man who worked in the security business would likely have to make unexpected calls in the middle of the night to check on things. I never had any reason to doubt him." She dabbed her wet eyes with a napkin before steeling her resolve and standing up straight. "If I'd known what he was up to, I would have left him and turned him in to authorities long ago."

We never did figure out who the man was who'd come into the bistro and changed out the working fire extinguishers for the useless, empty ones. He appeared to be another random thug Tino had recruited to do his dirty work. We could only hope that with news outlets regaling viewers with tales of how Tino betrayed the men who worked for him, the guy realized he'd dodged a bullet and would take the straight and narrow path from here on out.

Sadiki was cleared of any wrongdoing in the Hookah Lounge robbery. Files on Cyber-Shield's server proved the video of him taking the funds from the safe was merely a spliced bit of footage from months before. Detective Booth was happy to give him the good news, and looked forward to the resolution of some of her cold-case files that involved men with links to Tino.

The government turned Gallery Nico over to a new artist's co-op formed by Mallory Sisko and Emily Raggio. The place not only gave both emerging and established artists a venue to show off their work, but the gallery was making money hand over fist and generating a nice amount of tax revenue for Uncle Sam, the state of Texas, and the city of Dallas. It was a win-win-win-win-win.

All in all, it was a good resolution to a trying case. Team Operation Italian Takeout had a lot to be proud of. A lot to hope for, too. With any luck, nailing Tino and his goon squad would result in a nice raise come time for our performance reviews. And speaking of performance reviews, I'd earned Tori Holland an A+ on her Cost Accounting final and an A- in Global Marketing. Unfortunately, I'd left her with an F in Linguistics. A little embarrassing, that one. But that's what happens when a student ditches the final exam for a road trip to an Oklahoma casino.

After all the hard work I'd put in, and all of the tips and extra income I'd earned working at Benedetta's, I decided I'd earned those ridiculously expensive Sarah Jessica Parker slingbacks. I was sitting with my feet propped on my desk and placing an order online when Lu walked into my office, her arms loaded with a fresh stack of files. *Sheesh*. I'd just come up for air, both figuratively and literally. Couldn't she let me slack off for a day or two?

*But no.*

Lu had high expectations of her agents.

She plunked the stack down on my desk.

"What's in there?" I asked, after hitting the button to place my order for the shoes.

"Couple of catfishing cases, for starters."

"Catfish?" I said. "That sounds more like something Nick would enjoy. He's the one with the bass boat."

Lu rolled her blue-lidded eyes. "It doesn't involve actual fish. Catfishing is where an unscrupulous person hooks someone online and promises them love in return for money."

I sat up and pulled the stack of files toward me. "I've heard of it. That's a sorry thing to do. Preying on someone's loneliness and gullibility."

Lu plucked the top file off the stack and waved it at me. "This is a good one, too."

I reached for the file and set it down on my desk. I opened the file to find a color picture cut from a newspaper. The woman depicted was fiftyish, with dark curly hair and a turned-up nose, on top of which rested stylish rectangular-framed glasses. She was wearing headphones and speaking into a microphone with the call letters KCSH. I was familiar with the local talk radio station, which was known as K-Cash to locals. The station was owned and operated by Florence "Flo" Cash, a media magnate who came from a long line of successful radio broadcasters and station owners.

KCSH's most popular show was the *Cash Flow Show,* hosted by Flo Cash herself. Flo Cash was radio's answer to Suze Orman. She doled out financial advice, recommended or advised against particular investments, and made predictions about the future of the economy. Viewers were invited to call in and she'd answer their financial questions on the air.

I held up the photograph. "Is this Flo Cash?"

Lu nodded. "Flo Cash might help people with their

money problems, but she's got a cash-flow problem of her own."

"How's that?"

"None of her cash has flowed to the U.S. Treasury."

Now Flo Cash had another problem. And its name was Tara Holloway.